W9-BMJ-636

BY C. A. HIGGINS

Lightless
Supernova

SUPERNOVA

SUPERNOVA

BOOK TWO OF THE LIGHTLESS TRILOGY

C. A. HIGGINS

DEL REY
NEW YORK

Published in the United States by Del Rey,
an imprint of Random House, a division of
Penguin Random House LLC, New York.

DEL REY and the HOUSE colophon are registered trademarks
of Penguin Random House LLC.

Library of Congress Cataloging-in-Publication Data
Names: Higgins, C. A. (Caitlin A.), author.
Title: Supernova / C.A. Higgins.
Description: | New York : Del Rey, [2016]
Identifiers: LCCN 2016011342 (print) | LCCN 2016017540 (ebook) |
ISBN 9780553394450 (hardcover : acid-free paper) | ISBN 9780553394467 (ebook)
Subjects: LCSH: Women engineers—Fiction. | Artificial intelligence—Fiction. |
Space ships—Fiction. | Political fiction. | BISAC: FICTION / Science Fiction / Space Opera.
| FICTION / Science Fiction / Adventure. | FICTION / Action & Adventure. |
GSAFD: Science fiction. | Adventure fiction.
Classification: LCC PS3608.I3645 S87 2016 (print) | LCC PS3608.I3645 (ebook) |
DDC 813/.6—dc23
LC record available at https://lccn.loc.gov/2016011342

Printed in the United States of America on acid-free paper

randomhousebooks.com

2 4 6 8 9 7 5 3 1

First Edition

SUPERNOVA

Chapter 1

IGNITION

SIX MONTHS BEFORE THE FALL OF EARTH

In the instant after the bomb went off, Constance was a little girl again, on Miranda and waiting for the next System explosion to shear the skin from her bones. A little girl could hide the way an adult could not, huddled down like a cub in a den. A young thing hid because there was nothing else it could do.

But there was no true hiding here. The System saw them all. Her friends—her family, such as it was—were near her, she knew. But there was nothing she could do to save them and there was nothing they could do to save her, and so even though they were near, she was alone. The unstoppable power of the explosion would tear her limb from limb and the System's cameras would watch with a machine's chill indifference, and there was nothing, *nothing*, that she could do in this moment but wait to die.

But Constance wasn't on Miranda anymore. She was on Pallas, and she was a woman grown, not a little girl. And the bomb that had gone off had been hers.

The rock dust from the explosion billowed. Pallas's gravity was so low that it could take days for it to settle back down again. The particles reached so high that they dusted against the glassy ceiling of the segmented greenhouse enclosure that separated Pallas's manufactured atmosphere from the distant stars. Constance stepped out from behind the stone in whose shadow she had sheltered to watch the dust and smoke poison the atmosphere. Some distance behind her, the glass walls that separated this segment of the greenhouse enclosure from the adjoining section shivered with the shock wave of the blast.

"Nice job," said Mattie with a cough, coming out from behind a different stone windbreak. There was blood on his cheek already, but they weren't nearly done yet.

Ivan, following him out, was unbloodied. His blue eyes were as clear and distant as the starscape overhead, the one slowly being concealed by the creeping smoke.

"Masks on," Constance said. Mattie took his oxygen mask from Ivan and fitted it over his nose and mouth, but when Ivan handed Constance her mask, his fingers captured hers.

"Keep your head," he said. After the warmth of Mattie's Mirandan tenor, the sharp clarity of his Terran accent was startling. Constance did not bother to respond.

"The smoke's spreading pretty fast," Mattie said through the mask, with a speculative eye on the dust from the explosion that was already brushing against the shell of the greenhouse enclosure. When the sensors inside the greenhouse enclosure sensed the smoke, Constance knew, they would close off this segment of the enclosure to keep the other segments open and livable.

"How long?" she asked.

She knew Mattie was grinning by the crinkles near his eyes. "I think the System's got maybe half an hour before they're trapped in here."

"Then so do we," said Ivan, and put his own mask on.

The front of the slow, thick cloud of debris had almost reached them. "Let's go," Constance said, and stepped into the smoke and dusted stone.

The sunlight was dim and distant on Pallas but not as distant as it had been on Miranda, where Constance had been born. She was used to seeing by the light of her own eyes. The System soldiers would be Terrans, like Ivan; they would be used to bright sunlight and clear days. She navigated her way through the cloud unerringly, stepping carefully over the olivine-flecked Palladian stone.

There was a flickering orange light ahead, pulsing through the smoke. Fire. Constance stalked toward it carefully. Shadowed and blurred figures moved around the fire: System agents working to suppress it. In a place of limited oxygen such as the atmospheric domes, there was no higher priority than controlling a fire, and that would distract the System just long enough.

Constance's goal was the ground zero of the explosion. Here the smoke was thick enough and the flames hot enough that few of the System had dared to come near. But Constance did not slow or hesitate; beside her Mattie stalked forward like a wolf on the hunt and behind her she felt the weighty press of Ivan's presence. When a few soldiers emerged, coughing maskless in the smoke, Mattie took them out easily with his pistol.

As they passed the bodies, Constance thought she heard Ivan pause behind her, standing over the corpses, but when she looked back, he was moving again with no reaction to the deaths that she could see.

The bomb she had planted had destroyed the outer wall of the System base's armory. The System probably thought that she had planted the bomb incorrectly and missed out on her chance to destroy them, but the explosion had gone completely according to plan. Constance did not want to destroy this base. She wanted to get inside.

The air was clearer once she was through the shattered wall and into the uniform concrete hallways of the System base. Overhead, an alarm blared with incessant volume, red lights flashing over the hall the way the fire flashed over the stone outside.

Ivan had taken off his mask and was wiping ash off his pale cheeks. Mattie tapped Ivan twice on his waist as he passed, dust congealed in the blood on his face. Ivan did not react, only scanned the hallway, sighted something, raised his gun, and fired. Farther down the hall, a camera that had not been destroyed by the blast shattered under Ivan's bullet.

"Good shot," Constance said, her voice muffled by the mask she had not removed, and she headed deeper into the base.

The alarm blared, the sound of it physically percussive. Constance flexed her fingers around the barrel of her long gun warily, keeping it low.

At the point that Mattie had marked out on the blueprints, there were five doors. She gestured Mattie toward one door and Ivan toward another, and they left to explore the rooms she had indicated while she moved on to the third door. It opened easily and led to nothing but a room of small arms. She left it and moved on to the fourth.

Mattie was back in the hallway when she emerged, crouched beside the fifth door, his lock picks out, two of them tucked beneath his teeth. He lifted his eyebrows at her beneath his long bangs.

"Think this is it," he said around the lock picks.

"Why?"

"It's the only one locked so far. Low security, but I bet there's an electronic lock on the other side." He sounded like he relished the idea.

Constance watched him wiggle the metal bits around a little longer and then checked her timepiece. Less than twenty minutes before the air locks shut them into this segment of the greenhouse; then they would be thoroughly trapped and as good as dead.

"Move," she told Mattie.

When he was away, Constance fired a burst from her gun at the door. The lock shattered, and the door fell limply open. Mattie scowled at her.

From somewhere nearby a burst of weapons fire echoed hers.

Mattie started, dropping the lock picks on the floor, but Constance threw out a hand to still him. Beneath the relentless alarm, she heard the sound of a different weapon firing: Ivan's gun.

"Stay here; open the inner door," she ordered Mattie, and before he could protest, she chased the sounds of the firefight past the door through which Ivan had disappeared.

Ivan's door had led to a sequence of rooms in labyrinthine combination. Constance walked as swiftly and as quietly as she could from room to room, following the echoing and intermittent gunfire.

She saw them before she heard them. Ivan had gotten close enough to his attackers to disarm them. One man was dead already, and as she watched, not close enough for a clear shot, Ivan tackled another, the man's head slamming hard against the floor.

The third attacker picked himself up off the ground, grabbed his fallen gun, and stepped forward to aim that gun at Ivan's temple. Ivan turned his head to look up not at the man holding the gun but at the gun itself, which was aimed directly at his skull. He looked at the gun with a strange and wary anticipation. Constance had seen that expression on his face before, though she could not remember where.

"You set that bomb off," said the man, panting from the struggle. "Did you come here alone?"

Ivan didn't answer. The second man, the one he had slammed against the floor, was stirring beneath him, blood coming from his head but his eyes blinking open. Ivan still had him pinned down, but the man with the gun had Ivan pinned in return.

"Answer me," the man with the gun said. "Are you alone?"

Constance finally got a clear shot. She fired efficiently twice; the man holding a gun on Ivan dropped dead. Ivan did not flinch but stared blankly at where the gun had been. Beneath him, the last surviving System soldier was breathing hard, captive. Constance scanned Ivan quickly: no serious injuries that she could see.

There was no time for relief now, but Constance felt it anyway. "Move," she said to Ivan, and he obeyed, and she shot the soldier in the head.

She led him back out of the labyrinth of rooms to the hallway and then into the room where Mattie was working on cracking the electronic lock while throwing anxious glances at the gaping doorway. Something settled in his shoulders when Constance and Ivan both returned. Ivan went to crouch beside him, peering over Mattie's shoulder at the little handheld computer Mattie had hooked up to the security system. Constance stood guard while they tapped and forced their way in, and the alarm continued to wail.

It seemed to take forever, but she knew that it could not have been more than a minute or two before the door opened. They still had fifteen minutes before Mattie's estimate of when the air lock would close. They would need to get out in seven. They would do it, she told herself, and tried not to listen to her troubling doubts. What if this was the wrong door? What if what they were looking for was not inside? If it wasn't, all of this had been for nothing, none of it would matter—

"Huntress," Ivan said. They had taken out all the System cameras and broadcast equipment before entering the base, but it would take only one mistake for the System to learn Constance's identity, and so he called her by what had become a title.

Constance turned and saw the bomb.

It was large but so small for the power that it contained. It was as long as she was tall but scarcely wider than her shoulders. It was sleek and clean and deadly, perfect and pure of purpose, the most deadly weapon the System had ever built: a Terran Class 1 bomb.

"Get it on the cart," Constance said, and Mattie and Ivan hurried into the room and began to unload the bomb from its cradle onto the maintenance cart.

Four minutes to get outside. Constance thought she heard voices shouting from down the hall, nearly drowned out by the din of the alarm. She checked her gun again. Her ammunition was getting low, and so she checked her belt for backup.

All there. All ready.

"Ready," Mattie said from behind her.

"Put your masks back on." The hallway seemed shorter now, but darker. The roiling dust and smoke had crept into the base. There was a siren ringing outside, too: the air lock's sensors had detected the polluted air. A System mechanic stepped out from one of the ruined doorways, a towel clutched in her hand, halfway to covering her nose and mouth, and gaped at them. Constance shot her in the gut, and she fell to her knees. Beneath her oil-blackened hands a spill of blood forced its red way out.

The shattered wall that led outside was too uneven to roll the cart over, and there were System soldiers outside. Constance laid down covering fire while Mattie and Ivan lifted the cart over the uneven edges and rubbled stone and quickly ducked behind the cover of the fallen wall. It was fortunate that Pallas was so small, Constance thought; the gravity was light enough that Ivan and Mattie could lift the bomb. She fired again at a System soldier and got him in the shoulder.

"Quickly," she said to Ivan and Mattie, shouting through her mask, through the din of the alarms inside and out, and they hurried. Mattie pushed the cart one-handed, the other one holding his pistol; Ivan stabilized the bomb, his fingers lying over its curved edge.

The smoke and dust had cleared fractionally. Constance wished they hadn't: the System could see her more clearly now. Three soldiers were coming from her right; there were another four or five coming out of the shattered building. For the moment there were none ahead of them, but Constance could not tell how long that would last, and there was no cover near her and Ivan and Mattie.

She could not fail, not now.

Constance was out of bullets. She shoved a full magazine into her gun and fired at the line of approaching soldiers. They were ready for her this time; she hit none.

Ivan and Mattie had stopped. "Keep going," she said.

"This is the rendezvous point," Ivan said.

If they stayed here, they would be gunned down for certain. "Keep going," Constance insisted, and they started up again.

She could not fail, not now. The terror of it gripped her. She tried to shake herself from it, but her next volley of shots also went wide.

The soldiers were almost close enough to pick them off—

Rapid gunfire pierced the noise of the air lock alarm, and while Constance watched, the front line of approaching soldiers fell. Something was rumbling behind her, and she dared to turn her head; it was a ground transport vehicle, low-bottomed and with its wheels bouncing over the uneven stone, patches riddling its old pitted doors, its coming heralded by the rumbling howl of a decrepit engine. It was the rendezvous vehicle.

Christoph was at the wheel, hunched down low and tense, and Anji sat in the truck bed with a very large gun in her arms, laughing her wild-edged combat laugh. When they came near, Christoph turned the vehicle sharply, three of its wheels briefly losing contact with the ground in the low gravity. Mattie and Ivan hardly waited for the truck to stop moving before they were loading the bomb beside Anji and following it in. Constance backed up toward the truck, firing at the System soldiers to keep them down. She pushed herself up into the passenger seat beside Christoph.

"Go," she said once she was in, and Christoph took off.

They were near the air lock now but not out of danger. The shell of the truck echoed and rang with the bullets striking it, and Anji's gun was firing wildly from somewhere behind Constance's head, deafening. There were a few soldiers guarding the air lock ahead of them, but most of the System force was behind at the ruined base, and the guards fell quickly beneath Constance's shots. They were coming up to the air lock fast but not fast enough: the air lock was closing.

"Go faster, Christoph," Constance said, and took another magazine of ammunition from the stash in the truck's glove compartment.

"I can't," he said. "The gravity—"

The air lock was almost too low already. Constance said, "Go faster, Christoph."

The air lock was coming down slowly, so slowly, but still too fast. Constance gripped her gun in one hand, though it was useless against this kind of danger. She thought about telling Christoph to stop. She was afraid they would hit the air lock; she was afraid they would crash against the glass; she was afraid they would get through one door of the air lock but not the other and be trapped in between, and they would die, and none of it would mean anything at all.

They couldn't stop, not now. She tightened her grip around the gun and said nothing.

They made it under the air lock with centimeters to spare. Behind them, the double doors crashed into and through the stone, sealing off that segment of the greenhouse from the rest of the enclosure.

The truck came to a rocking stop. From the truck bed, Mattie's voice said, "FUCKING HELL!" Anji was laughing even harder than before. Ivan said nothing.

Christoph turned to look at Constance, sweat on his forehead and his mouth showing a grim line beneath his mustache. Constance said, "Would you do the honors?"

Something fierce and feral showed for a moment in the bend of his mouth, and then he was reaching down for a computer that Mattie had set up that morning, before they'd gone to attack the System base. A second bomb.

Christoph detonated it.

The whole air, the whole structure of the greenhouse enclosure rattled with a sound too low to be heard properly. Constance looked out of the window back toward where they had come from and watched the ceiling of the greenhouse enclosure above the System base shatter from the bomb she had planted on the exterior glass. Sparks kindled and died swiftly in the thin oxygen as air rushed out and cold rushed in, and glass fell down like flakes of ice. The fires still burning from Constance's first bomb died more swiftly than the System ever could have put them out. Constance could tell the fires had gone out only by the darkness that replaced them; they were too far away to see any of the System soldiers still standing outside the base on Pallas's green-flecked stone. Even so, she knew what would happen to them. With their atmosphere fleeing out through the hole to space overhead, they would suffocate slowly, freezing while they did. They probably would live long enough to make it to the air lock, only to find that it had been closed already. If they managed to get to oxygen masks first, they would live even longer. They would live long enough, in fact, to freeze there on the uninhabitable stone or beat with their fists against the unyielding glass wall that separated them from warmth and breathable air.

Constance knew what would happen to them because she had seen it happen firsthand. The System had done that to her people over and over not just on her native Miranda but on Haumea and Makemake and on all the mortified moons of Saturn.

"Huntress," said Christoph, and Constance turned away from the death behind them to find a woman standing some distance away, near the entrance to the mines, watching them.

Christoph already was going for his gun. Constance put a hand out to stop him and stepped out of the truck, gesturing stillness to those in the truck bed before Ivan could do something stupid like try to talk to her. The woman was almost too far away to see clearly, but Constance knew that she had seen their escape from the air lock and had seen the bomb they had detonated above the System base.

Constance was still holding her gun. She lowered the nose to point it at the ground and then raised her free and empty hand toward the sky, palm out.

For a time the woman did not move. Then she, too, raised one hand with the palm out, a silent hailing. Gesturing broadly, she brought up both hands and held them flat before her face, and like that she turned away and walked back down into the mines.

Satisfaction burned in Constance's chest. She went back into the truck.

"What did she say?" Christoph asked.

Constance said, "She said she was on our side."

AFTER THE FALL OF EARTH

Mattie Gale's ship flew out of the *Ananke*'s docking bay, out through the open doors into space, and while Althea watched, it became a tiny star that dimmed and vanished.

"Althea?" Ananke said, and Althea turned to look down the hallway of her spaceship. In the holographic terminals embedded in the walls, the same glowing image stood duplicated a hundred times. The hologram was of a very young woman, scarcely older than a girl. Her skin was a shade lighter than Althea's, and her hair was a shade more brown than black as it curled wildly down her back. She glowed with unearthly light. She looked like Althea, but she looked just as much like Matthew Gale. Her eyes, though, were the same Terran blue as Ivan's had been.

The young woman in the holographic terminal did not exist. It was an image invented by Ananke for Althea's benefit, perhaps, or perhaps for Ananke's so that she could feel more human, like the man and the woman who had created her. The *Ananke* had been a spaceship—an incredible ship but still nothing more than a computer—until Matthew Gale had infected the ship's computer with a virus. And somehow, under the influence of that virus, Althea's ship had awoken.

"What course should I plot?" Ananke queried, and her manufactured voice echoed up and down the hall, a strange mix of tones. The depth and tenor of the voice were much like Althea's, but the cadence had something of Ivan in it, and the accent wobbled from Terran to Lunar and back again, dipping every now and then into something from farther out in the solar system, something reminiscent of Matthew Gale. The look on the hologram's face was open and attentive.

Althea snapped herself out of her shock. Her daughter needed her. It was true that her crewmates were all dead and her government, the System, was at war. But she could not stay still and stunned when her daughter needed her.

But what could she do? Althea's first impulse was to reach out to Mattie's escaping ship for help, but that was a useless and childish hope. Even now that ship was out of the *Ananke*'s sensor range.

Normally, she'd contact the System, but the System was gone and Althea had no more orders to follow. She could return home to Luna, but she didn't know what she'd find there. After the Mallt-y-Nos had used her seven stolen Terran Class 1 bombs to destroy Earth, she had kicked off a civil war that had spread across the entire solar system. Ananke was a System spaceship: if she came too close to a rebel craft, they would see her as a threat; if she came near a System base, they might try to drag Althea's brilliant daughter into the blood and terror of war. And even if Althea took those risks, it was possible that the black core of the *Ananke* would perturb the planets' orbits and throw the delicately balanced mechanics of the moons and planets into chaos.

The certainty of it struck her like a blow: she and Ananke could not stay in the solar system.

"Set a course outside of the solar system," Althea said, and strode away from the docking bay doors, heading toward the piloting room.

"Where outside?"

"Just go out. Perpendicular to the orbital plane. We'll pick someplace later."

"Why?"

Althea did not answer immediately. The duplicate holograms and the echoing and multiplying of Ananke's voice were bothering her. "Could there not be so many of you?"

The nearest hologram blinked, and then all the others winked out, leaving just the one. As Althea strode down the hall, the hologram followed her, vanishing from the holographic terminal Althea had just passed and re-forming in the one Althea would next approach so that the image of Ananke kept pace with Althea's stride.

The doors to the piloting room were just ahead. She strode into them, and Ananke's hologram flickered into existence in the holographic terminal in the little room.

There were ghosts in this room, almost more ghosts than in all the rest of the *Ananke*. This was Domitian's chair, that had been Gagnon's, when they had been alive.

"Why are we leaving?" Ananke asked, and Althea leaned against the instrument panel at the front of the room.

"Because it's not safe here," she said. "And there're so many other beautiful things to see." She looked at Ananke, not at the hologram but at the camera set into the ceiling, like the thousands of other cameras that riddled the *Ananke*'s halls.

"Let's see the universe," she said, and she smiled at Ananke, because she was a mother now. She could not cry.

She could not show fear.

After Mattie left, Constance stood for a time alone in her bar. The sun was rising outside over the scarp, bright and reddened by the thin Martian atmosphere.

Mattie and Ivan were gone. She'd always known there was a chance that the System might take them from her, that the System might kill them, but the System hadn't taken Mattie: Mattie had left.

On the other side of the room, the door to the kitchen creaked open. Someone said, "He's not coming back."

The voice was cool and Terran, the intonations so like Ivan's that for a moment Constance's heart clenched. But it was a woman who spoke: not Ivan but his mother, Milla Ivanov.

Constance said, "No, I don't think he is."

She heard Milla moving deeper into the bar. The sunlight stretched long shadows of the ships moored outside across the sand. Milla Ivanov looked like her son: the same pale skin, the same blue eyes, the same shape of mouth and brow. Constance wondered what Ivan's father had looked like to leave so little of himself behind.

"He left to find my son," Milla remarked.

"Yes." The argument she had had with Mattie before he'd left was still vivid in Constance's mind, hot and bright and painful. *We're your family*, Mattie had said, advancing on her through the tables on the barroom floor, furious.

It had flared up her own fury in turn, an instinctive reaction to threat. *Don't you think I know that?* she'd said. *Do you think this was easy for me?*

Yeah, Connie, he'd said. *That's what scares me.*

There had been such grief and pale anger in his face, foreign things turned against her. She wondered if she would ever be able to remember Mattie's face any other way.

"He thinks Ivan still might be alive," Constance said.

"I know," Milla said quietly. "He told me."

Constance turned away from the window and the rising sun and paced deeper into her bar. This was where she and Ivan and Mattie had sat a thousand times before, together and united; this was where she had met Ivan for the first time; this was where she and Mattie had celebrated their freedom from Miranda.

The bar was not the same as it had been in all those memories. Now the System's cameras that once had crouched and blinked like the eyes of mechanical monsters in every corner and wall of the house had been pulled free of their perches. Their bodies had been strewn about the bar, on the floor, on the tables. They lay on the tables where Constance and Mattie and Ivan had sat; they filled up spaces on the floor where Ivan had stood, where Mattie had walked. Upside down, with a tangle of wires and spikes curled up over them, those dead cameras resembled nothing so much as insects, arachnids with their legs curled up over their corpse bellies, empty and stiff with rigor mortis.

"I know that he's dead," Constance said. "I think even Mattie knows it."

She could not recall ever having seen Mattie as angry as he had been then, scarcely an hour ago, in this very room. She could remember Mattie as he had been as a child, when she'd first met him in the System's foster program, the moment he became her brother, with his brown hair falling into his eyes and a crooked smile. She remembered Mattie as a teenager; she remembered Mattie as an adult. She remembered Mattie following at her heels; she remembered Mattie standing at her side.

And now she also remembered Mattie leaving.

The dim light in the bar was merciful; in it, Constance could not see the color of Milla Ivanov's eyes, that Terran sky color that Milla shared with her dead son. Constance said, "I set up a rendezvous at Callisto with Mattie so that he'll have a way to find me again. Anji will meet him there." She did not say what she thought: that Mattie would not come back. It didn't matter whether he found Ivan's corpse and so knew he could not forgive her or—more likely—he failed to find it and spent the rest of his days searching the vast emptiness of space.

He should have been there, both he and Ivan. What would happen if they weren't here?

She could not fail—

Milla said, "What did Mattie say?"

"What you would expect him to," Constance said, feeling suddenly sharp and bitter and small, a little girl again, huddled and hiding and hating. "That I'd betrayed Ivan and him when I left Ivan behind on that ship, the *Ananke*. That I wasn't really family, since I left him." She shook her head and leaned back on a table, feeling the wires and limbs of the torn-out camera brushing against the fabric of her shirt. "I never lied about what had to be. This revolution has to be first. These billions of people, and I have to do anything that I need to to make sure this succeeds even if it hurts me. I told him Ivan had known that from the minute he'd gotten involved with me."

And Mattie had said, *I didn't.*

Constance had said, *Ivan knew that about me when he got involved with me*, and Mattie had said, *I didn't.*

"And Mattie left," Constance said.

In the silence that followed, Constance watched the shadow of her bar stretch out over the edge of the scarp, watched the glint of sunlight off metal from the ships moored outside.

Milla said, "Excluding divine intervention, my son is dead. If there had been any way to save him, I would have taken it. But there was none. My son is dead."

Constance flexed her fingers against the manufactured wood of the bar. There was a curious relief in hearing Milla say it aloud, as if she were freeing Constance from the burden of its truth.

"Second," Milla said in her quiet voice, "whatever Mattie does now, whether he goes to your rendezvous or not, that is outside of your control. You cannot save him or stop him any more than he can save you or stop you from doing what you have to do."

It went against all of Constance's impulses to agree with that, but out of respect for Milla Ivanov, who had been revolutionary royalty herself, she held her tongue.

"Third and finally, Huntress, I am going to be very plain." Milla leaned forward, her elbows on her knees. "The weakness you just showed to me you must never show again."

She was right, of course. It had been weakness to show what she had shown, as deep a weakness as it was to show fear. And Constance knew well never to allow herself to be afraid.

"Show you?" said Constance in a voice she strove to make as firm and dispassionate as Milla Ivanov's had been. She rose to her feet: if nothing was wrong, there was no reason for her to stay here. "I didn't show you anything."

"Tell me the sum of three and two," Althea said.

"Five." Ananke answered promptly, no delay. Good; that was good.

"Their difference?"

"In which direction?"

"Give me both."

"Three minus two is one," said Ananke, "and two minus three is minus one."

"Good."

Ananke smiled, glowing lightly in the holographic terminal, just brightly enough to cast the faintest shadows in the piloting room. Gagnon and Domitian's chairs had been pushed conscientiously in; Althea sat in her own chair, although Domitian's seat was closest to the holographic terminal.

It didn't matter. Althea was comfortable where she was, sitting in front of a computer display that she no longer needed by a tiled wall of video feeds that no longer needed to be watched. She had all her ques-

tions written out on a piece of paper and all the answers, too. She'd had
to cover the camera while she wrote them so that Ananke wouldn't be
able to cheat and even now had to sit awkwardly to keep the paper out
of view of Ananke's ever-watching eyes. Althea had felt a strange twinge
of something—guilt, perhaps, a very deep and terrible guilt—when she
had covered up the camera, but Ananke hadn't seemed to mind in the
least.

Computational speed seemed to be fine, and the answers, of course,
were accurate. Althea decided to skip a few items on her checklist.

"Derivative of x^4?"

"Four times x to the third," Ananke said promptly.

"Derivative of x times the cosine of x?"

"Cosine of x minus x times the sine of x."

"Is that quantity cosine of x minus x end quantity times the sine of
x or—"

"It's cosine of x minus quantity x times sine of x end quantity,"
Ananke said in an aggrieved tone. Althea grinned.

"Integral of x divided by the natural logarithm of x evaluated from
zero to pi?"

"It does not converge."

"And from pi over two to pi?"

"Approximately four point five. Isn't it fascinating," said Ananke,
"how it's only that one point where it's a problem? All those infinite,
infinite numbers, and it's only one number that's special—one number
with an infinite output."

Althea looked at the hologram thoughtfully. Ananke's holographic
eyes could not quite simulate focus properly, and so it seemed to be
staring not quite at her but through her, though that hardly bothered
her. The holographic simulation would take a little work, but it could
be fixed.

"I never thought about it like that," Althea said.

"How did you think of it?"

"Avoid that one number where things are unbounded," Althea said.
"Okay, try this. Integral of x times the cosine of x." Ananke couldn't
solve that one numerically.

"X times the sine of x, end quantity, plus the cosine of x."

"Plus . . . ?" Althea prompted.

For a moment Ananke looked oddly blank.

Then, "Plus constants," she said.

"Plus *a* constant," Althea said.

"If they are all constants, it does not matter," Ananke informed her.

"The right way to say it is 'plus a constant.'"

"Constants. Constants," said Ananke. "I like the word better."

Althea felt her face grow tight. There it was, a trace of Matthew Gale's old virus. Constants, as Gagnon had seen, always in the plural even when the word should be singular.

Ananke seemed to be watching her face very closely even though the hologram could not see and they both knew it. Then Ananke said, sounding strangely subdued, "Ask me again."

"A different question or—"

"The same question," said Ananke.

Althea said, "Tell me the integral of x times the cosine of x."

"X times the sine of x end quantity plus the cosine of x," Ananke said, "plus a constant."

Good, Althea thought. "Constant"—the way it should be. Not "constants"—not like Constance, the Mallt-y-Nos, the terrorist who had destroyed the Earth.

Constance picked up the nearest bottle on the shelf and studied its label. Low proof: not worth saving. She shoved it back into the dusty recesses of the shelf.

The bar was quiet, but voices echoed from outside. A hundred ships taking off from the scarp shivered the glass in the windows and rocked the dead System cameras back and forth: her revolution was taking flight.

The next bottle of liquor was some sweet and vile thing Mattie had been fond of. She held it for a very long time and looked down at the label.

"You wanted to speak to me?"

Anji. "Yes," Constance said, and put the bottle down. She pushed it firmly to the back of the shelf with the rest of the things she would be leaving behind.

Anji sauntered across the bar, weaving her way through the dark imitation wood tables and stepping over the bent and tortured metal of the dismembered cameras. Her black hair was still cropped close—

shorter even than Ivan's had been—and the same red jewels glinted in the brown shell of her ear. She still had the same swaggering step, the same smiling face, the same way of kicking out a bar stool with her heel without regard for the integrity of Constance's floors. She looked, in short, like the exact same girl who had befriended Constance on Miranda, cajoling her boss to give Constance a job at his bar, teasing the teenage Mattie when he followed Constance to work instead of going to school, jumping into a fight at any opportunity.

Anji was not Mattie, and she was not Ivan. But Constance felt a weight on her shoulders ease, anyway.

Anji hoisted herself up onto a bar stool and leaned her elbows onto the scarred and pitted surface of the bar. "What are you doing?"

"Keeping any with high proof." This was the kind of task she could delegate if she wanted. There was no solid reason she should do it herself except that this place had been her home. She had owned it in her own name, bought it with her own work, maintained it with her own hands. She would be the one to clean it out.

"Why? Are you spending your revolution drunk?"

"Antiseptic," said Constance. "And if not, high proof burns." She moved to put another bottle aside.

"Oh, you're not throwing that out, are you?"

"Take it," Constance said, and handed the bottle to Anji.

Anji took it and snuck a sly grin up at Constance. "I'll make sure to toast you over some System corpses."

"I'd prefer if you spit on them for me."

"I can do that, too."

"Good." Constance surveyed the shelves behind her bar. She had made a sizable amount of progress; they were nearly empty. "Has the System organized their attack yet?"

"Not yet. I think Doctor Ivanov was right; they're still stunned. Christoph says that the System fleet is heading inward but that it looks like they're on a path toward Earth."

Constance nodded. Anji and her forces had been with Christoph on the outer planets, helping to create a distraction to keep the System's attention away from Earth. If the System fleet had been near Earth, Constance's revolution would have died before it began. The distraction had worked, and the System fleet—the main military power of the government—had gone out toward Uranus and Neptune to quell the revolts there. While the System had been distracted, Constance and Mattie had flown in toward Earth and detonated the bombs she had planted there. Even with the fleet gone, the inner planets were still the source and capital of the System's power. Therefore, Constance had recalled Anji from the outer planets to join her on Mars in case the System reacted immediately, leaving Christoph to handle the outer moons on his own.

But the System had not managed to coordinate a counterattack yet, so Constance's war could move to the next stage.

"How is Christoph doing?" Constance asked.

"Not good. He says Puck's a ruin."

Constance knew that in luring the fleet away from Earth, she had turned it on the outer planets, including Puck. She knew the fleet was raining fire and death on the moons that harbored her people. She knew the terror they faced.

The System fleet would leave her people, she told herself. It would come back to the inner planets to rain hell down on her. Constance's revolution would live or die by its first battle against the fleet. No enemy had ever faced the System fleet and survived.

She turned away from Anji to hide the chill in her fingers and picked up the next bottle in the line. This one was high proof: good enough. She put it in the bag at her feet to be saved.

"Is Puck their only target?" Puck was a Uranian moon like Constance's birthplace, Miranda.

"No, they're all over Uranus. But Puck's the only one they've completely destroyed—it's ash and craters, Constance. The greenhouse enclosure is shattered all over. No one's left."

Anji did not say what they both thought, that Puck had suffered the same end as Saturn's moons had endured when Connor Ivanov's revolution had failed thirty years earlier. Systematic depopulation was the fate of rebellious moons, the wholesale genocide of the people who had lived there. It was what would happen to all of the outer moons if Constance's revolution failed.

"Can Christoph handle it?"

"He'd better be able to," said Anji. "System fleet's going to come to Jupiter before they come here; I'll be dealing with them soon."

"Jupiter is on the other side of the sun from Uranus," Constance reminded her.

"You don't think they'll stop by Jupiter before coming here?"

Constance put down the bottle she was holding and turned to face her friend. Anji sat, as she always had, like someone who could handle herself in a brawl. But this revolution was not a brawl, and Constance saw the tension in her pressed lips, in the fingers curled in against the wooden top of the bar.

"They might," Constance said, because lies were as bad a currency as doubt, "but not for long. They are looking for me. And you can hold them off: remember all the years we fought them and burned them and they could never touch us."

"Like a fly they couldn't swat," Anji said.

"We're not a fly now." Constance turned back around to the shelves of liquor. "I'm sending Julian and his troops to Christoph. If the System fleet goes to Jupiter and you need assistance, call for me. Remember that the Jovians will help you. They hate the System like everyone else."

"Right," Anji said, some of the tension fading from her voice. There was still some fear, but that was necessary. Only an idiot wouldn't fear the System—an idiot or the Mallt-y-Nos. Constance wrapped the bottle she was holding in a length of fabric that once had been her kitchen curtains and loaded it into the bag at her feet.

Anji said, "And the plan?"

"The plan is the same," said Constance. She had spent months on this plan, working with Ivan, talking it out late into the night in the privacy of the *Annwn* or whispering it into each other's ears under the covers where the System would not think to listen. "Christoph will be with the outermost planets. He will handle Uranus and Neptune and the trans-Neptunian bodies."

Reciting it was familiar. Like reciting a prayer. Constance could almost hear Ivan whispering it along with her.

"You will be in the middle belt," she said to Anji. "You will take Jupiter and the asteroid belt and hold Saturn."

Anji was nodding. The words were as familiar to her as they were to Constance.

"And I," said Constance, not *and I and Mattie and Ivan*, "will be in the inner solar system. First I will take Mars; with Earth gone, this is the planet most valuable to the System. Then I will take Venus, the next most powerful. Then Mercury. And last, Luna."

Take them in that order, the Ivan of her memory whispered to her, one hand brushing hair from her cheek and concealing the motion of his mouth from the System's camera in the same gesture, *and the System won't be able to rebuild its strength.*

Anji said, "Nothing's changed for you?"

The question was discordant, not a part of the usual recitation of the plan. "No."

"Even though Ivan and Mattie aren't here?"

The mention of the men brought an unwelcome edginess into Constance's focus, as if sparks were traveling beneath her skin. Anji was looking at her with sympathy, one friend ready to comfort another.

"Nothing," Constance said, "has changed," and Anji's open look closed off, and when Anji's manner had fully changed from friend to subordinate, Constance said, "I'm almost done here. Get the cases from the kitchen."

"Sure," Anji said. A moment later she had started setting up, wedging oblong containers beneath tables and beside load-bearing walls. By the time Constance had finished sorting through her liquor, Anji had finished her task.

"Let's go," Constance said, and led Anji out the front door. She did not turn back to look at her bar. She knew what she would see: dusty shelves and abandoned liquor, torn-out cameras and empty chairs, paintings and other decorative pieces that had been gifts from Mattie and Ivan (*Your bar looks fucking depressing, Connie*, and *If you're trying to pretend to be a normal person, you should make your house look like a normal person's house*) but served no useful function and hence had been left behind. She knew what she would see, and so she did not look back.

Constance handed her bag off to one of her people as soon as she stepped out into the thin, whipping air of Mars. The sun was high and bright, and she had to squint the moment she entered the light. Most of her fleet and Anji's was already in the air, hovering out past the edge of the scarp, light glinting off the ships' metal sides. Only her own ship and Anji's ship remained landed, with their crews waiting for her out in the light of the sun, milling like hounds over the sand and the stone. "Let's go!" she shouted to her people on the ground, and at her call, they came.

"See you on the other side?" Anji asked.

"I don't intend to die," said Constance.

"Just meant it as a saying, Con."

"Remember, don't overextend yourself. Strike fast but don't let them corner you."

"I remember," Anji said. "I'll kill them for you, Con. And for Ivan, right?"

Constance had nothing to say to that. She started to leave, but Anji's hand fell on her elbow with a grip of surprising strength.

"If I hear from Mattie," Anji began, and Constance nearly turned away again, "and he's in trouble, what do you want me to do?"

"Nothing," said Constance. "This revolution is what matters. If he's in trouble, he will have to find a way out on his own."

Anji's hand slipped from Constance's arm.

Her fleet was ready to leave. "See you on the other side," Constance said, and Anji nodded, and they parted with Anji running off to her own ship, shouting for her people to join her.

Right before Constance boarded the *Wild Hunt*, she turned to look back at her bar, standing dark and empty atop the scarp.

She pressed the detonator, and the bombs she and Anji had planted within it exploded, fire igniting, the building collapsing. The Martian wind howled in and then rushed back, carrying with it the heat of the blaze, and Constance turned her back on it and strode inside her craft, giving the signal to blast off.

With the bar burning on the scarp behind them, the Wild Hunt began.

"Here's a tough one," Althea said. "Are you ready?"

"I am ready," said her daughter, gleaming and perfect in the holographic terminal.

Althea hitched her notepad a little higher onto her knees, keeping an eye on the camera overhead, checking behind herself to make sure there were no reflective surfaces.

"You're standing in a hallway," she said. "Ahead of you, it splits in two. Each of the two paths ends in a door, and there's a person standing in front of each door."

"So two people," said Ananke.

"Two people," Althea agreed. "One of them only tells lies, and the other only tells the truth. One of the two doors leads to heaven, and the other leads to hell."

"Does the honest person stand in front of heaven and the liar in front of hell?"

"No," said Althea. "I mean, you don't know. And you don't know which door leads where."

"But I want to get to heaven."

"Yes," Althea said. "You're allowed to ask one question. You can ask either person, but you can only ask one question, and then you have to pick a door."

"Why only one question?"

"Because that's part of the riddle. You can only ask one. What question do you ask to figure out which door leads to heaven?"

Ananke fell silent. Althea watched her curiously.

"No going into System databases and finding records of this riddle and its answer, either," Althea added on a sudden suspicion.

Ananke tilted her chin up in a gesture that Althea found disorientingly familiar: it was her own mannerism. "I don't need to cheat," Ananke said.

"Okay," said Althea. While she watched the hologram, it seemed to grow incrementally more and more still. To begin with it had seemed natural, like a real and living girl, but somehow now it slid sideways almost imperceptibly into something else, something unnatural and still, something that had never been alive, a three-dimensional picture, a sculpture of light. Althea's daughter was a frozen figure, a Galatea before her quickening.

And then the hologram moved again so suddenly that the image glitched, warping so swiftly to another image that Althea did not have time to perceive what that other image was before Ananke corrected herself and again Althea's daughter was beaming out at her.

"I would go up to one man and ask him which door the other man would say heaven was behind," said Ananke. "And then I would go through the door that he said did not have heaven behind it."

Ananke had switched pronouns, Althea noticed, but shook it from her head. She'd probably done it for syntactic simplicity. "And why's that?"

"Because the liar would lie about the honest man's truth, and the honest man would tell the truth of the liar's lie. Whichever man I asked my question of, I would receive the same answer," said Ananke. "The trick is to use them both, not one or the other. The riddle can only be solved by accepting that they are a pair."

Here was her daughter, beautiful and brilliant. Althea tossed her paper to the ground, unfolding herself from the uncomfortable pret-zeling position she'd adopted to keep the notepad out of Ananke's sight.

"And one more question," she said, feeling a warmth all through her chest, a contentment. Everything, Althea told herself, was going to be all right. "We don't have to decide this now. The whole universe is ours, Ananke," Althea said. "Where do you want to go?"

Someone had told Constance once that Mars was the planet most like Earth. It was colder, and the air was thinner, and the gravity was weaker, but the sky was a slate gray that was nearly blue and the rocks and dunes looked like some Terran deserts. It had been the first planet colo-nized by the System. The System's control of Mars was subtler than its control of the outer planets: on Mars, the System did not march its military around or build greenhouse enclosures to contain the popu-lace like goldfish in a jar.

To control Mars, the System controlled the water.

The process of terraforming Mars, warming its surface and growing a thicker atmosphere, had allowed liquid water to exist on its surface: some of the mares of Mars now truly held seas. But most of Mars's pre-cious water was in the ice caps or beneath the ground as permafrost. This System base was built in the Cerberus Fossae, a deep natural gouge in the surface of the planet above a vast reservoir of groundwa-ter a few miles away from the town of Isabellon, which relied on that water to survive. Constance crouched atop the edge of one of the sides of the fossa and looked through the sandy air toward the System base, its steel glinting in the sunlight.

They were all laid out the same way, Constance knew. The System was nothing if not consistent. Three buildings: one for a barracks, one for food and fuel and medical supplies, and one for weaponry. In the center of the grouped buildings where there usually would be an open space for drills and executions was a dome covering the water pumps. To the side was the shipyard: a small fleet of ships that had landed on the surface of Mars for maintenance or reserve. On Miranda or one of the other outer moons, such a base would be fenced in or have some sort of perimeter to guard it. On Mars, the buildings stood apart in the open, and the only fence was the one surrounding the shipyard.

There were not very many ships in the shipyard, and the ones that were there were not particularly powerful: they ranged from circular or cylindrical spacecraft to smaller aerodynamic ships designed for atmospheric flight. The largest and most powerful System ships could not be landed on a planet and would be in orbit somewhere overhead. Regardless of their number or strength, Constance needed them; her own fleet was too small. When the System fleet came, it would destroy her.

She needed the fuel and the weaponry and the supplies the System base had, as well. She could not fight a war with stones. And she would not harm the water pumps—if she did, she would starve Isabellon.

The only building she wanted to destroy, then, was the barracks.

"What are you thinking?" Milla Ivanov asked from beside her, her voice barely audible over the low whistle of the Martian wind. If Constance looked back, she could see the rest of her scouting party spread out over the desert, nearly invisible among the stones. The System base had not seen them yet; her people were too good at evading its eye.

Constance leaned over so that she and Milla would share a line of sight. "There," she said, and pointed to the building she'd identified as the barracks. "That's the building we want destroyed. The others we want captured."

"Especially the ships," Milla observed. "If we are planet-bound, we have already lost."

Suffocating thought: confined to the narrow stretch of land that was a single planet, prey for the System to pick off one by one or trapped there slowly to die when the System decided simply to destroy the planet entirely. "Especially the ships," said Constance. "We have to come in on foot or they'll send out their own ships to attack ours."

"They'll send out their own ships, anyway, if they see us coming."

Constance smiled humorlessly. "They won't see us coming."

She took her troops in at dusk, when the long low rays of the sun made shapes hard to distinguish in the desert, when the System soldiers were dining.

They got into the fossa easily enough, but approaching the System base on flat and open land was more difficult. Constance had them hug the walls of the fossa until they could come no nearer without being seen. Then they waited.

On the other side of the System base, far from where Constance and her attack force hid in the pitted and cratered land, a bomb went off and the System soldiers came streaming out, shouting, heading for where they thought the attack would come.

It was Mattie's old trick: misdirection. Get the target looking one way, then come in from the other side. He used it to rob people, slipping wallets out of pockets; Ivan used it to con people, to keep them from realizing some dark and ugly truth. Constance used it for war.

For a moment she felt wrong-footed, unbalanced, standing without them at her back. But she had her war and she had her army and she had no other choice, so Constance went into battle alone.

There was no cover to be had anymore. Her people followed her not in lines or rows but in a crowd, like hunting wolves. They were silent at first, running as quietly as they could over the stone, but when they came into firing range of the System soldiers, they started to yell. The soldiers were still coming out of their barracks; some already had reached the other side of the water dome, chasing the explosion. The rest were trapped inside or trapped outside, with the water dome at their backs and nothing between them and Constance's people.

Constance raised her gun and fired, the sound echoed by a hundred other shouting weapons, and watched the first row of soldiers fall.

Then the System soldiers were moving with practiced speed, getting to cover, pulling weapons, ducking into buildings. A few had made it to their armory; Constance diverted her steps toward the armory as well. If she could stop them from getting better weaponry, she would—

A bullet close to her arm buffeted heated and speeding air against her skin; Constance ducked behind a boulder just in time as another shot sprayed rock on her skin. The strange truth of Martian rock was that the dust and the sand and the outside of the rocks all were a rusty reddish brown but the inside of the stone was not. When she looked up, she saw a scar of steely blue where the bullet had struck inches from where her head had been.

Someone returned fire and no more bullets struck her hiding place, so Constance crawled out and dashed away again, heading for the squat square building that housed the armory.

The sky was still lit; Constance could see the light of the sinking sun glancing off the mounds and valleys of the plain overhead. But the fossa was dark.

To her right, her forces had reached the System forces. The gunfire had nearly ceased as the two groups came too close for it. The System soldiers tried to retreat, to regain their secure distance, but Constance's people chased them down and set their teeth to their throats.

Someone fired at her again but again missed. Constance's breath was coming fast but steadily. Ahead of her was the door to the armory, hanging ajar. There was movement within and Constance dodged just as he fired; she was up and firing into the darkness inside the building before he could take new aim.

Someone fell, she thought, but someone else fired and hit her in the vest. The force of it dropped her and forced all the breath from her; she sucked in air again, and behind her someone else fired.

One of her people had followed her. Constance allowed herself three breaths before pushing herself back to her feet, and then she was running the last few meters to the building, dropping low beneath the sight lines of the windows just as another bullet took out the glass.

The revolutionary who had followed her, his face too far away to see clearly in the indistinct light, dropped like a stone and did not move again. Constance leaned against the concrete and steel of the System building and took heaving breaths and thought that there was no one at her back any longer.

She pushed herself to her feet and reloaded her gun, settling it in her elbow, and inched her way along the wall toward the door.

Then she swung around the door frame and started shooting.

She took two by surprise; a third ran for better position, vanishing through a doorway. All these System buildings were laid out the same way, Constance knew: two hallways that met in a crossroads at the center of the building and then rooms all of the same size and shape in the spaces between. There would be staircases at the termination of each hall.

Predictable, Constance thought, and started down the hall after the man who had fled, trying to remember how many men she had seen run into the armory.

There seemed to be a good deal of shouting from behind her, out on the battlefield. Constance noted it and filed it away; she could not consider it now. The armory was dark and quiet, but she knew there were monsters inside.

She was nearly at the crossroads when they started to fire at her again.

Their bullets chipped the wall behind her but were too high: they knew she had a vest on and so they were aiming for her head, but they had missed. She darted away, ducking into the nearest room, quickly sweeping it for an ambush. There was none. Outside, she heard them come out of hiding, chasing after her.

The room she was in, she realized quickly, held grenades. She picked one up but knew that she could not use it here: if she did, she might destroy the building. She tucked it into her belt anyway, and moved on to the adjoining room.

This room held more explosives. She cast a practiced eye over them, her interest piqued, though she could not use them now. She fired at the pursuing System soldiers and hit one but could not risk going for the others, and she was forced on.

The next room was a dead end.

She'd known it would be, but a bolt of fear hit her heart, anyway: the horror of no escape. Distantly, she could hear the shouting from outside. Constance positioned herself behind the door frame, and when the soldiers came into the room behind her, she fired at them.

They quickly pinned her down. There were, she noted with satisfaction, only three of them left. She had killed the rest. But she was only one person, and she could not get a shot off without being shot herself. If Mattie and Ivan had been there, their numbers would have been equal, but they were not there, and wishing they were was weakness.

Her breathing had slowed again to a normal and steady cadence. She felt alert, alight; it seemed to her that if metal touched her skin, she would send off sparks. She was alone with no way out. She would not let herself be captured, and she could not escape. There was nothing more to be afraid of: her future had narrowed down to one single path. She would die, but what the men outside did not yet know was that they were about to die, too: Constance still had the grenade.

She stood up slowly, still with her back to the wall. She held her gun in one hand even though she had no intention of firing it again. She slipped her finger through the pin—

Gunshots rang out, deafening her. For a moment Constance wondered if they'd somehow known what she was about to do, but then her senses caught up with her and she realized that the shots had not been fired at her.

She just barely heard her name called through the ringing in her ears from the firefight. "Constance?"

Constance would know that accent anywhere: Milla Ivanov. She let go of the grenade and stepped out into the open. The three System soldiers were all dead, crumpled on the ground, one sprawled in the moment of turning to face the attack. Milla Ivanov was standing just inside the adjoining room, her lips set in a tight, grim line and her white hair starting to fall out of its eternal bun. She had not come alone: Constance saw more revolutionaries behind her, filling the room, examining the weaponry. Rayet, a tall dark man who had been a System soldier before defecting to join Constance's army, stood at Milla's shoulder.

Milla should have been on the other side of the encampment, leading the misdirecting attack. Constance said, "What's happening? What are you doing here?"

Rescuing you, Ivan would have said with an annoyed ironic curl to his accent. His mother said only, "The battle's over, Constance."

That was impossible. They had been outnumbered at least five to one. "How?"

"Citizens from Isabellon," Milla said. "They came to join us when they realized what was happening. With them—"

"With them we outnumbered the System," Constance realized, triumph unfurling in her chest. The people had come to fight with her. The people had risen up against the System when called, even the Martian people, who were only a few degrees removed from Terran themselves. Even if she did not win this war, the right was on her side.

Outside, Constance realized, the sound of the shouting had changed. It was no longer furious and brutal, the screams of animals going to die.

It was victorious.

"Have someone inventory the weapons and the supplies," Constance said to Milla as they strode out of the armory. Milla stepped delicately over the corpse in the entranceway, but Constance saw the blood on her boots. "What are our casualties?"

"Light, comparatively," Milla told her. "No exact count yet, but I have Henry organizing everyone and determining them. We did as you said: set off the bomb and then pulled back."

"Good." Constance could see the lights and movement out on the fossa where her people were gathering their wounded and their dead. "He's there?"

"Yes, with the lights; nearer to the right of the group."

"I want you to stay here," Constance said. "Organize the captured weaponry, get it loaded onto the ships and brought back up to the fleet. I want us ready to leave suddenly if we need to."

"Yes," said Milla. "Are there any wounded inside?"

"If you find any, kill them—they're System."

"You went in alone?"

"Yes. The recruits from Isabellon are down with Henry, too?"

"I believe so," Milla Ivanov said.

"Good," Constance said again, and started off toward those lights. "Keep a fraction of the arms down here for the ground troops to use."

She was aware that Milla stayed where she was for some time after she started walking away, watching her go, but Milla did not call after her.

When Constance's people recognized her, they let out a shout that was carried through the crowd. Constance looked across them with satisfaction: they filled up the fossa from side to side. Her army had come here smaller than that, but even with casualties, her forces had grown.

She found herself automatically calculating the supplies they had taken from the System this day. Not enough, she realized; not nearly enough. A swell of something sharp and terrible rose up in her chest, but she forced it away. There was nothing to be done about it now. Not until they found the next System target to take and could arm themselves better there.

But if the System fleet arrived before they could—

"Huntress!" Henry's voice pulled her from her thoughts. Constance turned to see him jogging toward them, his bald head shining in what little light was left. Farther afield, her people had started lighting lamps and flicking on flashlights that shone like stars against the backdrop of the black rock.

"Status?" Constance asked him when he drew near.

"We're gathering the wounded. I sent out groups on Milla Ivanov's orders to search the area, make sure no System soldiers survived. Others are clearing the buildings."

"I spoke to Milla. Clear the barracks first," Constance said. "I want to set up the wounded in there, out of the open."

"Yes, Huntress. Otherwise, we're trying to organize the new recruits."

"The people from Isabellon?"

"Most of them were," Henry said. "But some of them came from farther out in the solar system not just to join this battle but to join the campaign. Not all of them are fit for battle, but most of them are; we've only had to turn away a few—"

"Turn away?" Constance interrupted. "We can't afford to turn anyone away."

"Some of them couldn't possibly fight, Huntress."

"So find something else for them to do," Constance said. "We need people to tend the wounded. We need people to inventory supplies. We need people, Henry."

Henry hesitated. "Some of them were very young."

"How young?"

"The youngest is thirteen."

Constance remembered Mattie at thirteen, deft of hand and already intimately familiar with the sound a man made when his windpipe had been torn open by shrapnel. She remembered herself at thirteen, with the blood of three deaths on her hands already, watching the System shoot down Mirandans in the streets and feeling her fear ignite into hate. "Teenagers make the best soldiers, Henry," she said.

"Perhaps if you saw them," Henry suggested.

"Then show me," Constance said, and Henry led her into the gathered crowd.

A rough semblance of order had started to arise in the temporary camp, centered on the gathering of the wounded. The bodies already had been cleared from this area of the fossa. Constance saw the bodies of her people laid out gently a short distance away and those of the fallen System soldiers tumbled together in a sprawling and shapeless mound that almost faded into the darkness of the desert. Henry skirted the place where the wounded had been gathered, avoiding their smell and their low and desperate sounds, and headed toward where Constance's people were beginning to gather the stolen weaponry.

In the middle of the boxes of ammunition and death-dealing fire, Constance saw the children. They were gathered together, most of them sitting in the dirt cross-legged, talking to one another. They had obtained a lamp from somewhere or been given one, and it sat in the center of their group and threw light on all their faces. One of them did not sit in the dirt with the rest, and it was on that one girl that Constance's attention focused. She had dusky skin and dark hair cropped at the sides but just long enough at the top to threaten to spill into her eyes, and she swung her slender bare legs and booted feet carelessly to thunk against the side of the crate on which she sat. It was something Mattie would have done: sit atop something that could plausibly go up in flames with such an astounding lack of concern. Constance did not think the girl was as young as thirteen, but she could not have said how much older she might be.

The girl saw her before Constance spoke. She sat up straighter on the crate and looked at Constance intently. The other children picked up on her attention and soon were looking to Constance as well.

Constance came to just within the light of their lamp. They shifted, moving to open their circle, to face her all together. The girl on the crate hopped off lightly and came forward to stand in front of Constance.

Constance said, "How old are you?"

"Sixteen," said the girl.

"And what is your name?"

"Marisol Brahe," the girl said.

She had an accent that rang against Constance's ear as familiar, but she could not immediately place it. An asteroid, perhaps: either way, the girl was not from Mars.

"Where is your family, Marisol?"

"I have no family," Marisol said. She had a clear, high voice, and though she seemed nervous, she did not look away from Constance.

"No?"

"My parents died in a mining accident when I was little. The System wouldn't waste resources to go after them when the mine shaft collapsed. But I was old enough to work by then, so I stayed in the mines."

"You have no brothers or sisters?"

"I have no one to go back to."

Constance glanced past her at the children gathered behind. Most of them were Marisol's age or a little older, but Henry had been right: the youngest of them could be no older than thirteen.

"And your friends?" Constance asked.

Marisol hesitated. "Their parents are dead or here."

The hesitation gave it away as a lie, but Marisol didn't back down from her words, only held Constance's gaze steadily.

Constance said, "What can you offer my revolution?"

"Followers," said Marisol. "Fighters. I used to work with the explosives in the mines; I know how to plant a bomb."

"This will be dangerous," Constance told her. "When the System finds us, they will try to kill us, and they will never stop."

Behind Marisol's back, one of the other girls glanced sideways at her friend, a quick, nervous look. But Marisol did not blink. Her hair was slipping down over her forehead. *Cut your damn hair, Mattie,* Constance remembered saying. *It's in your eyes.*

"Six months ago you came to Pallas," Marisol said. Of course; Constance recognized her accent now. The girl was Palladian. "Before you came, the System had a bomb there that could have blown the asteroid apart and killed all of us. But you blew up their base and you took their bomb. We weren't free—the System came right back—but for a little while we didn't have to live with that anymore."

Constance remembered that day on Pallas, Ivan and Mattie beside her and the old Palladian woman turning away, and felt fierce pride.

Constance couldn't turn anyone away. She couldn't afford to: the System was coming.

"Welcome to my war," Constance said.

Ananke seemed curiously reluctant to answer Althea's question about where she wanted to go next. Perhaps, Althea thought, that was because she did not know how to narrow down the possibilities for her exploration. Althea set out to help her.

Althea never liked to sit idly; she always wanted to have something to do with her hands. So before she joined Ananke to look through data of nearby astronomical options, she went through the ship and gathered up all the spare robotics parts she could find, all the finest wires and most delicate bits of metal, and spread them out in front of herself on the floor in the workroom that she hadn't used since the *Ananke* had first been mission-ready and began to sort through them.

If she worked while she talked, if she kept herself busy, if she knew that she was accomplishing something important, Althea could let herself forget about the other, less pleasant tasks that awaited her.

The workroom was large and circular with unusually bright lights in the ceiling. There was a large table in the back of the room, but Althea preferred to work on the welded metal plates of the floor. There was a holographic terminal in this room, too, of course. It stood right beside the black screen that once had broadcast System news without pause. Now that the System had fallen silent, so had the screen. If Althea looked into it, she could see her own shape reflected in shadows.

Beside the screen, bound by the limits of the holographic terminal, the hologram of Althea's daughter sat with her arms wrapped around her folded legs and her photonic cheek resting on her knees. Her image was dimmed slightly by the intensity of the lights overhead, appearing a bit more transparent, more like a ghost than a girl.

Ananke said, "We could go to Sirius."

"Show me," Althea said.

Ananke turned her head slightly to face the screen on her other side, and in the same instant it glowed to life. A star appeared on the screen, and then the image rushed forward, the star growing larger until it split into two stars, one large and brilliant, the other small and dim. Sirius A and Sirius B.

Althea picked up a few pieces and put them together, jostling them until they made a shape that pleased her. She worked one of them back and forth on a hinge that she had not yet created, looking to see if it would swing correctly. That would work, she decided. She knew she had a few boxes of those pieces; she'd dragged them in here sometime. She just couldn't remember which of the boxes around her had held them.

"Why Sirius?" she asked as she rummaged through the box nearest to her, found it useless, and shoved it aside to get farther into the pile.

She received no verbal response, and so she looked up automatically at the hologram, which shrugged at her. "It's there," Ananke said. She sounded flat, dispirited.

The tone rang a warning bell in Althea's head. "Maybe we should think about what we want to see," she suggested, and grunted as she shoved a particularly heavy box to the floor, where the cardboard buckled and threatened to split, "instead of what we can see. And then we'll see how we can see it."

Ananke propped her chin up on her knees. She looked thoughtful and then unnaturally still—the hologram freezing in place, the program that ran the hologram to make it appear as natural as possible going static. It meant that Ananke was thinking, Althea knew, and in thinking had ceased to pay attention to the image of her hologram. That was all.

The hologram came back to life like a breath being pulled into Althea's lungs. "I'd like to see a supernova," Ananke said.

"Yeah?"

"Yes. The death of a star." For a moment longer Ananke was silent, her hologram gone still, and then the image on the screen in front of Althea flared into brightness, a simulation of Sirius A exploding.

"It's the most violent single act in the universe," Ananke said as on the screen light and matter glowed and scattered. "And one of the brightest. From any of the planets or moons in the solar system, if a nearby star went supernova, humans would be able to see it, like an explosion in the sky."

Althea lined up bits of metal in front of herself and measured their length against the bones in her hands.

"A violent death," Ananke said. "It only happens to the greatest of stars, and the greatest of stars have the shortest of lives." On the screen, the image reversed suddenly, the star re-forming. "Fusion," said Ananke, "through all the elements, lower and lower bonding energy; deuterium helium oxygen carbon until iron, iron-56, the apex, the nadir, the turning point, derivative zero, and then it stops, and then—"

On the screen, the star blew outward again, light raining out, fire.

"Supernova," Ananke said. "That's where all the heavier elements come from. Supernovae. For there to be life in the universe, a star has to die."

"I'd like to see a supernova," Althea said. She sorted the metal bars into groups. "We'd have to find one, though."

"They are difficult to predict," Ananke agreed. "What else would you like to see?" She asked the question with strange carefulness.

"I'd like to see an exoplanet," said Althea. For a moment she allowed herself to indulge in the idea: the first human to lay eyes on an alien world, to see what was there, what kinds of creatures. Would she find any? Or would she find that humans alone existed in the universe?

But of course she would never see an exoplanet. The nearest potential exoplanet was around Alpha Centauri B, 4.3 light-years away. There were ships with engines that could travel nearly at light speed, but the more massive the ship, the slower its maximum speed, and there did not exist a ship that could travel with sufficient fuel to make the journey there and back and sufficient supplies to preserve the lives of the people on board within a human lifetime. The *Ananke* got its fuel from the black hole at its core and had in essence an infinite amount of fuel. There was enough water and food to last Althea's remaining years. But the *Ananke* was far too massive to approach the speed of light, and it would take far longer than Althea would live even to reach Alpha Centauri. Althea did not know off the top of her head what the nearest confirmed exoplanet was, but wherever it was, it would be much farther away than Alpha Centauri B.

One day, before they reached any supernovae or exoplanets, Althea would be a fourth corpse aboard the *Ananke*, another body like the bodies of Domitian and Ida and Gagnon that were still bleeding and rotting on board that she wasn't letting herself think about—

"Earth-like?" Ananke asked.

"Why not?" Althea muttered, and began sorting through her available sensors, focusing her attention again on the simple and beautiful metal at her hands, not on the bodies just out of sight.

"What are you making?"

In answer, Althea spread her right hand out, palm up, and layered the metal pieces atop it. Metacarpals, phalanges; one, two, three, four, and a thumb. The pieces made up a hand. Althea made sure to angle her palm so that it was seen not by the empty eyes of the hologram but by the camera overhead, Ananke's true eye.

"Why?"

"For the mechanical arms," Althea said, lowering her hand again to place the pieces carefully back on the floor. "I'm going to give them more sensitive manipulative instruments."

"Why?"

"I just think you might need them, is all," Althea said, and for a time there was silence as she sorted through the boxes and bins around herself and Ananke's hologram rested its head on its folded photonic arms.

Then Ananke said, "I can do the calculations. I have done the calculations. The average life span of a Lunar female with access to Terran medical facilities throughout her life is 95.1 years."

Althea's hands went still.

"Diminishing the access to Terran medical facilities to only her first thirty years but taking into account the medical facilities on board this ship and your overall health makes it approximately 92.4 years. You are thirty-one years old. That leaves only a little over sixty years—"

"Ananke—"

"—and it will take far longer than that for us to reach the nearest star, much less the nearest location of interest. Time and space are relative; there are no absolutes, only constants. Even then I cannot take you far enough and fast enough even if you live entirely in the center of the ship nearest to the black hole and I travel at high speed so that time will be slowed for you; it will not be enough. I haven't yet determined my own maximum speed, but certainly the safest maximum speed is—"

"Ananke, stop," Althea begged.

Ananke did. The hologram watched Althea with her wide blue eyes and waited for her to speak.

Stupid to think that Ananke wouldn't realize it, too, even sooner than Althea had, most likely. And worst of all to try to deny it.

"That's why I'm making these," Althea said, and gestured at the skeletal outlines of mechanical hands arrayed in front of her. "So that when I'm gone, you'll be able to keep going."

The map display was computerized, and so Constance didn't entirely trust it. Where there were System computers, there tended to be System cameras. She'd had her people go through the entire System base and systematically tear out all the cameras and transmission devices, so she knew that the map room in the barracks, where she now was, was devoid of cameras. But it was one thing to know in the head and another to know in the chest: even without any possibility of being seen, Constance found herself regarding the glowing computerized map of Mars with inescapable wariness.

The main force of her people was in orbit now with her growing fleet; a few were out at Isabellon, carrying Constance's goodwill to the Martians. The rest were downstairs in the canteen of the captured System base, celebrating. Constance was alone in the communications and map room on the highest floor of the building. She had sent messages to both Anji and Christoph and was waiting for their responses; while she waited, she studied the map of Mars spread out on the table.

The map was a hologram of impressive detail. If she trailed her fingers through the hologram's mountains and valleys, the computer reacted; it would give her a closer look at the area selected or display information. A System map with System information: there were details on System bases in the map at Constance's fingertips that she could not find anywhere else.

She examined it carefully. There were two System bases about equidistant from the Cerberus Fossae base she was in now; each had a sizable number of spaceships moored. Constance examined the landscape surrounding them carefully, bracing herself on the edges of the table above the hills and valleys of sculpted light.

Footsteps from down the hall beyond the closed door. They were soft, but Constance had not survived as long as she had not to pick out that distinctly human sound. She raised her head from the glowing map to watch the door moments before a soft knock rattled its surface.

"Come in," Constance said, and Milla Ivanov stepped inside.

The room was dark; all the lights were out, the better to see the details of the holographic map, and so the only source of light was the table. Milla Ivanov's skin caught the red light of the map like the light of a fire before her. Her glance took in the room in one swift sweep, and then she said, "Extraordinary technology, isn't it?"

"The map?"

"Yes." Milla Ivanov came closer to the table that separated her from Constance but did not touch the image of the undulating dunes. "Even within my lifetime, the holographic technology has become impressive beyond what anyone could predict. You might almost believe the image is real."

For a keen and piercing moment, Milla Ivanov was her son: the words were so much what Ivan might have said, so unpredictable and irrelevant to Constance's aims, such a glimpse at a strange beauty that was alien to Constance's appreciation. Constance looked down at the map, but even through the sudden sharpness of unexpected grief, she still saw nothing but mountains and stone.

She pulled herself from the mire of that sorrow and said, "It's not as good as real. I would rather see the lay of the land myself, move around in it. It gives me a better sense."

"Perhaps," Milla said. "Do you intend to visit those places yourself, Huntress?"

"Yes," said Constance, and bent farther down over the map, over the two System bases that she did not control. "I thought I should split my forces. With the new recruits, we're large enough now."

She glanced up at Milla. The doctor was watching her with her customary impervious expression, watching Constance, not the map.

Milla said, "Perhaps."

"They're both small," Constance mused, "as System bases go. But they both have large stores of ships moored, and my fleet is too small."

"Did you speak with Anji and Christoph?"

"I've sent them messages, but it'll take hours for my messages and their responses to travel. But I wouldn't discuss this with them." Constance straightened up from the map, rolling her shoulders to work out the tightness in her spine. Upright, she was taller than Milla, and the other woman had to look up at her face even with the distance of the table separating them.

"Are they not your generals?"

"Yes, but not here, not for this. This is my campaign." The ones Constance would have asked for advice were Mattie and Ivan, but that, of course, could no longer be. She said to Milla, "What are your thoughts? Is my army big enough to divide?"

The slightest of frowns ghosted over Milla's forehead, then faded and was gone. She looked down at the map for a long time, but about some things, Constance could be patient.

Milla said, "Certainly you need both bases. You need their resources, and you can't let an enemy live behind you." She bent slightly at the waist, leaning deeper into the reddish light from the table. "You could drive the System from the planet without destroying every last one of your bases, it's true. But it may be more . . . effective to leave nothing behind."

"So you think that I should split my forces."

One of Milla's pale fingers traced the air above the map in a shape Constance didn't recognize. Her other hand was drumming a restless and arrhythmic beat against the edge of the table. "You don't want to weaken yourself," she commented. "Your war is young yet. It would be a serious blow to be defeated now."

"So you don't think I should." Constance was starting to become annoyed.

Milla's eyes flickered up from the map to her face. Her fingers were still drumming, and Constance knew that she knew that Constance was annoyed. But Milla only said, "What are your thoughts precisely?"

Pulling straight answers out of Milla Ivanov, Constance decided, was like pulling bullets from a wound. "As I told you. We need their resources, and my forces are larger now." She took in a long, slow breath to blunt the edges of her annoyance. They were not arguing. She expected them to be arguing—Ivan would be arguing with her now—but she and Milla were not arguing. "Time is not on our side. The System fleet will be here at any moment, and we need to have as many advantages as we can before they arrive."

"But if they arrive when our forces are split, it will be easier for the fleet to destroy us."

"The two bases are not far separated. If half of our forces are attacked, the other side will be able to come quickly to their aid."

Milla's arms folded across her chest, and her fingers drummed on her upper arm. She said, "Then, as you say, split the army."

They had just been getting somewhere. Constance waited another moment for Milla to question her further or opine, but Milla said nothing.

"I never thought when Connor Ivanov's wife joined me that she would agree with whatever I said without question," Constance said.

"I simply do not have an answer to give you, Constance."

"I'm not looking for an answer," said Constance. She moved around the table, toward Milla. Milla turned to keep her in sight; the movement threw her face into shadow. "I'm looking for an opinion."

"And in this matter I have none."

"You must think something."

"I try not to express an opinion unless I am certain enough for it to be nearly a fact," Milla said with especial precision. Constance had the impression that she was being as plain as she was comfortable being, but it did Constance no good if she could not get a definite read on the woman.

"And I am your leader," Constance said. The reddened light of the map shone through the strands of Milla's hair that had escaped from her bun. "When I ask you for an opinion, you will give me one."

"My opinion is that we need more information on the location of the System fleet before we consider our next movement."

"Thank you," Constance said. Doctor Ivanov was right, though it chafed Constance to delay at all. "Another opinion. What do you think of the teenagers today?"

"The children who tried to join your army?"

"Yes, the ones I let join."

"What else would you have done with them?" Milla Ivanov asked. "You need the hands. And turning them away would not have stopped them from fighting on their own."

Constance nodded slowly. Milla's words agreed with what she felt in her heart, but she could not help thinking that Ivan would have disagreed with her decision.

"If you want me to disagree with you on something," Milla Ivanov said suddenly, and Constance realized that while she had had her back to the table, Milla Ivanov had been able to see Constance's face very clearly in the map's light, "then I will disagree with you on this: what you did today—going off on your own into that building—was unacceptable."

"*Unacceptable?*"

"You cannot risk your life like that."

"You don't tell me what I can and cannot do," Constance said.

"You could risk yourself like that when you were just a terrorist blowing up buildings. But you are not underground anymore. You are the leader of a revolution. You *are* the revolution. If you die, the revolution dies, too."

"Do you expect me to stand back while my people go to die?" This now, this was familiar, the burning rage and hot snap of retort. This was what Constance expected from an Ivanov.

"Not at all," Milla said. "But you do need to be aware of what you are. This revolution is you, and without you there is no revolution."

"Earth fell one week ago," Constance said. The words still tasted impossible on her tongue, and so she had to speak them slowly and forcefully, releasing them like crossbow bolts from her mouth. "The System fleet will arrive at any moment. When that happens, there will be no place for me to stand back. Everything I do until then has to be to prepare for that, and I won't stand back if I think I can do anything that will make us succeed."

"My husband's revolution failed not when he and his people were cornered on Titan but when the System put him in prison—when they made him as good as dead. Think of yourself as a leader, Constance, not just as an instigator."

For a moment the reference to Milla Ivanov's dead husband gave her pause. But she had not spent years with Milla's son for nothing. The reference, she knew, had been calculated to make her react. In an instant she was angry not just that Milla was attempting to manipulate Constance here and now but on Ivan's behalf. Milla had raised him, had made him what he was: lying and distant and untrusting. What would Ivan have been like if such a mother had not raised him?

Dead, probably, Constance thought.

Milla Ivanov said, "You need bodyguards."

"Bodyguards?" Constance scoffed.

"Yes. The System has your face, your name, your location. You are no longer protected by anonymity. They will send people to kill you."

"They always have," Constance said. "I don't need and I don't want a bodyguard." She had never had one before, not even when she was on Miranda and at any moment the System might have killed her and everyone in her neighborhood. What could the System do to her now that was worse than what it had done already? She said, "I am not afraid of the System."

"A person is just as much ruled by their fear if they spend all their time denying it as they would be if they spent all their time giving in to it."

"Are you calling me a coward?"

"I am saying that you need to change your tactics," Milla said. "You are too used to having your brother and my son at your back. But they're gone."

Her words chilled Constance's flaring anger. She moved away from Milla, back toward the map, and looked out over the glowing hologram. Milla had been right. The technology, Constance supposed, was amazing. The gravel of the Martian sand looked like a solid thing; it seemed that if Constance nudged it with her finger, she could send it tumbling down the slope.

"They wouldn't have been here even if Ivan hadn't died," Constance admitted, and saw Milla move out of the corner of her eye, turning to face her along the line of the table. "Ivan never approved of what I was doing."

"He wouldn't," Milla said. "My son was always too focused on the details, on individuals. He never could see the bigger picture. But I am not my son, Constance."

Constance looked at her sharply. Milla Ivanov had stopped the restless drumming of her fingers. Milla said, "I see no higher purpose than to watch the System fall."

In that, at least, Constance understood Milla Ivanov completely.

But Milla said, "I am also not like my son in that I do not know you, Constance. He knew you, and he trusted you and cared for you enough to follow you and die for you. But I do not know you."

At Constance's fingertips, the dunes and fossae of the Martian surface glowed with a faint unearthly light, and Milla said, "Show me, Huntress, that you are worth the loyalty my son gave."

"I've thought about reversing time," Ananke said.

Althea almost smiled. She was in her workroom, preparing to upgrade the mechanical arms. The screws and wires she would need were laid out, neatly organized, in front of her. "Have you?"

"Yes." Ananke's hologram was slightly faded in the bright light of the workroom, but she didn't seem to notice. "I was programmed to reverse entropy. And if I can reverse entropy, perhaps I can reverse time."

"Well," Althea said, "we never figured out exactly how to do it. All Gagnon had was theories."

"Theories that were wrong."

For a moment Althea's screws and wires were forgotten. "What?"

"Gagnon was wrong." Ananke was matter-of-fact. "I have gone through his calculations. I cannot determine whether he did not know or did not care. But Gagnon thought to add the excess entropy into the black hole."

Gagnon's theories were at the very base of Ananke's programming, Althea thought. Yet Ananke had considered them and dismissed them, had moved past them.

"But a black hole isn't outside the system it is in," Ananke said, "even with the information barrier. That isn't reversing entropy. That is just moving it around. A black hole itself still carries entropy; the amount of its entropy is proportional to its size. So if he had increased the entropy of the black hole—"

"He would have increased its size," said Althea, remembering that fact dimly herself. She envisioned it then with a chill spreading in her chest: the black hole at the center of Ananke growing and growing and growing, massive and huge, first swallowing up Ananke into its darkness and then through Ananke swallowing up the rest of the star system into its unknowable dark.

How close had Gagnon brought them to that point? How far would the System have allowed the black hole to grow?

"I'm certain there's a way to reverse entropy," Ananke said with the unshakeable belief that programming provided. "But it's not that way. But until I find a way, time cannot go backward." She paused and then said in a more plaintive tone, "Why do we have to leave at all?"

"Because it's too dangerous to stay, Ananke," Althea told her. The mechanical arm she was working on, its end partially disassembled, had lowered itself to rest in her lap. There was something almost companionable about it, and she found herself absentmindedly rubbing the forearm of the machine even though she knew it couldn't feel anything.

"Why?"

"There's a war going on."

"Wars end," Ananke pointed out. "And I can defend myself. You know I can. I can control almost any other computer the System ever made; you know I can. No one can hurt me."

Althea knew that, but they would try, as Gagnon and Domitian had tried. They would want to destroy Ananke or, worse, take her and control her and use her body against her will. "I don't want to risk it."

"That's an insufficient and illogical criterion." Ananke stopped, the hologram going still. Althea watched it warily. Then it resumed, looking faintly triumphant. "That's a stupid reason," Ananke declared.

Ananke was practicing her vernacular, then. Althea said, "It's not the only reason."

"What are the other reasons?" It was possible that Ananke was enjoying the argument.

"Well, it's dangerous for the planets and the moons for us to be there," Althea said. "Because of your mass. That's why the System had us on such a carefully plotted trajectory."

"My mass is approximately half that of a medium-size asteroid. Gravitational effects on nearby planets will be nearly nonexistent."

She answered so promptly and firmly that Althea suspected she had done the calculations before this discussion. Even for a ship with such immense computing power as the *Ananke*, it would take some time to run sufficient calculations to back up her assertion.

"A many-body system is chaotic," Althea countered. "I know you know that. The effects of your presence, however small, might change things hugely on a large time scale."

"Because the system is chaotic, it is impossible to predict how it will evolve without my presence. It's equally possible that my presence could be beneficial to the evolution of the system."

"It's not equally probable, because there are only a few favorable states and very many unfavorable states." Despite herself, Althea smiled. It was almost like arguing with Gagnon. And at the thought of Gagnon, her good mood faded. She did not wish to remember the corpses on the *Ananke*.

"The time scale for the effects of my presence would be so long that it would be meaningless," Ananke said. The hologram's hand was drumming without pattern against her knee. It was one of Ivan's mannerisms. "It's likely that humans wouldn't survive long enough to see the effects. The sun might enter the next phase of its evolution before—"

"And what if you got too close to Ceres and pulled it out of its orbit just a bit, and every time it orbited, its perturbation got larger?" Althea asked. "That's perfectly plausible. And then what about Ceres? What about the objects near Ceres?"

Ananke was silent. Althea looked wearily back down at the half-assembled hand in her lap. For an instant, to her distracted eyes the pieces looked horribly like a skeleton. Then she shook herself. Of course it looked like a skeleton; she was basing the structure on her own body. Determined, she picked up the screwdriver and went back to work. "Why do you want to go back, anyway?"

"Because I do not want to be alone."

"There's nothing to be afraid of out here, Ananke," Althea said. Out here, past the solar system, there was no one who would try to hurt her daughter.

"Nothing," said Ananke, "except being alone. But we could go back—I could calculate the effects of my mass on the solar system."

"Don't be silly; of course you couldn't."

"N-body systems can be simulated. I have the computing power to simulate the solar system."

Althea hesitated. "You couldn't know all of the initial conditions."

"I could update them as I learned them. In time, I would develop a perfect model." Ananke waited, but Althea must have taken too long trying to find words, because she spoke again. "I would be able to account for my own gravitational interaction. I could even determine where I should go, what I should gravitationally influence and how, to maintain the order of the solar system and keep all the planets and moons habitable for millions of years."

Althea lowered her tool slowly until the tip of it rested against the metal floor.

"I could control it," Ananke insisted. "I could keep everything in perfect order."

Althea stared at the tip of the screwdriver where it touched the ground. There seemed to be no other safe place to rest her eyes.

"All right," she said.

"Yes?" said Ananke. "We can go back?"

"No." Althea pointed the screwdriver at the hologram. "Maybe. Not yet. But first run those simulations."

"I don't have all the relevant data," Ananke protested.

"See what you can do without it."

"Okay," said Ananke, and then, her voice becoming less humanly hesitant and more rigid, robotic, as she presumably began her calculations, "I'll start that now."

She could start it whenever she liked, Althea thought; the simulations would never be complete. And even if Ananke managed to achieve something approaching completeness, Althea would be sure to find reasons they could never return. Her daughter would not fly blindly back into a war to die; Althea would make sure of that.

"Good," Althea said, and turned her attention back to her mechanical hand.

Before Constance could think of a response to Milla's challenge, Henry burst into the map room of the captured System building.

"Huntress—"

"What is it?" Constance snapped.

"A fleet has just come into orbit—"

A chill struck her. "The System?"

"They don't seem to be, but they haven't identified themselves as friends," Henry replied. "Their leader is outside. He wants to speak with you."

Constance looked at Milla Ivanov. Milla said, "This is the very sort of trap you need a bodyguard for."

Fine and Ivanovian words of warning, but what else could Constance do? She turned back to Henry. "Take me to him," she said.

"This way," Henry said, breathless from the run, and started out the door again.

Constance followed him down the stairs, her boots making a rapid-fire beat against the concrete stairs. Milla Ivanov followed, her steps far lighter. The nearer they got to the ground floor, the louder were the sounds of her people celebrating. "How large is his fleet?"

"Half ours, Huntress. And disorganized. If he attacked, we could drive him off."

If he attacked, it wouldn't matter that Constance could win the fight. What would matter was how battered her forces would be after the conflict. "He gave you no name?"

"No, Huntress. Only asked to speak with you."

They emerged from the stairwell into the canteen. They moved quietly, and few of Constance's people or the celebrating Isabellons noticed. But through the crowd, Constance saw Rayet's gaze following them, and from the other side of the room, Marisol lifted her head just in time to see them go.

Constance had been bracing herself for the difference between the inside of the barracks and the air outside, but it was a sharp change nonetheless, from light to dark, from warmth to cool dryness. A group of Constance's soldiers, the ones she had left on watch, were arrayed in an uneasy standoff with the newcomers, who stood a short distance away from the captured System base in a shadowed crowd. Constance could not see clearly how many they were—the dimness and the newcomers' heavy draped clothes conspired to conceal their numbers— but it was a large enough group to defend their escape should Constance turn her people on them, yet not so large as to be of themselves a threat.

She stepped out in front of her own gathered troops, deeper into the no-man's-space between the two sides. She said in as clear a voice as she could, one that carried through the cool Martian air, "You wished to speak to me. I am the Mallt-y-Nos."

Movement, and then the foremost of the group stepped forward. Her attention immediately narrowed to him so that she barely noticed Milla Ivanov coming up silently to stand close at her back. The man was tall and broad and was made broader by the width of the cloak and drapes he wore. His skin was fair, though not as pale as Milla's, but his hair and neatly trimmed beard were dark.

He regarded her for a moment, much as she regarded him.

"It's an honor, Huntress," he said. He had a heavy Plutonian burr to his voice. "I am Arawn Halley. I hope you have heard of me."

"I have." Arawn Halley was a revolutionary on Pluto, she knew, though she had never met him before. The man before her had clothes that were ragged and patched; he was certainly not System, and the clothing was of the Plutonian style. His men stood behind him silent and obedient; he had effective command over them. It was entirely possible that he really was Arawn Halley.

Arawn said, "We share a way of doing things."

"We do," Constance said. "Is that why you came all the way here from Pluto?" There was as much a chance that he had come here to kill her as a rival as there was that he had come to join her. Constance doubted that a man who for over fifteen years had led his own terrorist cell, albeit one far out in the reaches of the outer solar system, would happily agree to obey the orders of a stranger.

"I'd heard stories of the fall of Earth," said Arawn, and came casually striding forward—Milla was growing tenser at Constance's back—and into the light streaming from the captured System base. "I came to see it for myself."

Constance looked into his face. He had a bluff and casual manner, but his dark eyes were intelligent.

"Then come and speak with me of what you've seen," said Constance.

For an instant she thought he would refuse; it could be a neat trap to lure him in. Then he laughed.

"How could I say no?" he said, and smiled at her again. He was young, Constance thought; her age, perhaps.

"Henry, lead Halley's men into the base, give them food and drink, make them feel welcome," Constance said, and waited to see Henry nod before she strode past him and back into the System base, knowing that Milla and Arawn would follow her. Arawn shouted some words to his own men and then was beside her, blinking in the sudden light indoors, where Constance's people filled the large room from wall to wall.

She lingered there a moment, waiting for him to regain his sight, not out of courtesy but so that he could see how many people filled the room.

"Most of my people are with my fleet above the planet," Constance remarked as she led Arawn and Milla toward the staircase. This time more of her people noticed her arrival and the stranger accompanying her. Rayet and Marisol somehow had gravitated toward each other; Rayet was leaning against the wall at her back while Marisol watched Constance cross the room. A few of the other teenagers had noticed her now, too, but none were as intent as Marisol.

"And your fleet gets larger every day," said Arawn, and, when Constance raised a questioning brow at him, added, "A group of recruits joined my fleet past Jupiter. They were also looking for you. They'd heard of other groups, gone ahead."

So not all his troops were his own. Constance stored that fact away as they reached the staircase and started up the long flight.

They reached the map room before long. Arawn was not out of breath from the climb, and Constance marked that as well. When she pushed open the door, the map of Mars was still on, glowing softly, and the communications equipment was still silent. Constance flicked the light on, and the surface of Mars paled and faded.

Arawn was taking in the room. "I've never been in one of these before it was blown up," he remarked.

"We took the base intact for its resources," Constance told him.

The door snicked shut. Milla did not lock it, but the sound of her closing it was as effective a punctuation as if she had. "Mr. Halley, now that we are in private and not all holding guns at one another's heads, I think we should speak plainly."

She sounded so like her son.

"Your force," Milla said, "is large enough not to defeat us but to cause us serious injury. If we fought, it would end the revolution here and now and let the System win. Did you come here to join us or to fight with us?"

It was almost seamless how smoothly Milla had stepped into the role that Constance needed her to fill. Constance added nothing to Milla's words, only waited for Arawn's reaction.

Something sparked in Arawn's eyes, but he controlled his temper. "I came to see what the situation was here. I don't intend to let the System win."

"You brought your fleet into orbit around this planet without greeting us as either friends or allies," said Milla. "Tell us, then: Should we take you as an enemy?"

"You were the System's bitch for thirty years, Mrs. Ivanov," Arawn said, his imitation of Milla's precise cadences strained by anger. "Should I 'take you as an enemy'? What proof do I have that you aren't still System, playing the Huntress and everyone else?"

Milla's chin tipped up. No anger showed on her face, and Constance could not tell how deeply Arawn's words had struck. "Your own history is checkered," she said, her voice very cool. "Your revolutionary cell on Pluto splintered several times with infighting. You once followed the Son of Nike; he was captured and killed by the System not long at all after you left him. An interesting coincidence."

Arawn waved a hand dismissively. The heavy draped clothing he wore in the Plutonian style made him seem larger than he was. "The Son of Nike got caught because he was weak, the same reason I left him. And infighting? A few System traitors and a lot of propaganda."

"Weak?" Milla had the same talent as her son of turning a word so that it balanced in the air like a coin on its edge. "I knew the Son of Nike once. He was a cautious and a clever man. What about him did you find so unsatisfactory?"

"Unsatisfactory?" Arawn turned away from Doctor Ivanov to face Constance so that he could speak not to Milla but to her. "This is what I want, Huntress. It's not as complicated as your dog here wants it to be: I want the System dead. I've seen what it can do, did, will do. I want it to burn, and every last man, woman, and child who allowed it to exist. I would rather all of us fail and die than give up and let the System live. The Son of Nike was weak. He gave up, and he gave in. And so I left him. And so he failed."

There was rage and fire in Arawn that Constance understood. For an instant she saw him, Ares, Mars incarnate, burning the System at her side with a fervor that neither Ivan nor Mattie ever could have felt.

"Brute force isn't enough to destroy the System," Milla remarked, her cool voice somehow jarring after Arawn's hot anger. "There has to be thought and care."

"Of course," said Arawn, and though he was addressing Milla now, he still was watching Constance. "But lack of force, that's what's made everyone else fail."

"You think *that's* what caused the old revolutions to fail?" Milla snapped.

Constance had heard enough.

"I have seen what the System does," she told Arawn, and silenced Milla with a glance. "Like you, I have lived it. And like you, I would die before I let them have mercy."

Arawn was watching her with all his fierce and hungry rage writ in his expression. Constance said, "I will hunt the System down, Arawn, until I've torn it limb from limb and there is nothing left to fight."

"Huntress," Arawn said, "I will follow you."

Then the first of the System's bombs hit the building.

Althea was installing another mechanical hand onto one of the autonomous arms when Ananke decided unceremoniously to continue the conversation that Althea thought had ended several days earlier.

"We could find Mattie again," Ananke suggested. There was a tone in her simulated voice that made it sound as if she thought she was being sly. Althea froze with one screw halfway into the metal plates of the autonomous arm and two more gripped between her lips.

She took her time removing them from her mouth, gaining a few precious seconds for her mind to come out of its working haze and start functioning again at the level at which she needed it to function to manage this conversation.

"Mattie," Althea said slowly once her lips were freed to speak. Mattie had left the ship a week ago now. He had returned to the ship the first time only for the sake of finding Ivan—Ivan, who was being interrogated by Althea's former captain, Domitian, who fully intended to kill him once he was done. Fully intended, but he hadn't gotten to do it: Mattie had arrived in time to save Ivan.

Althea wondered suddenly if Constance Harper or Milla Ivanov or anyone else knew that Ivan was still alive or if his survival was a secret to everyone except Althea and Ananke. It was a strange feeling to be the keeper of such a secret, as if she still held a gun to Ivan's head even after she had let him go.

Ananke said, "And they'll be together—we could find Ivan, too."

After the way the two men had parted, Mattie all but carrying Ivan off the *Ananke*, Althea doubted they would soon be separated.

"Then you wouldn't be alone while you were here," Ananke said. "And you could procreate. And then your children would—"

Althea burst out laughing. The idea was so absurd that she couldn't control it. She dropped the screwdriver and buried her face in her palm in a fruitless attempt to stop her laughter. When she controlled herself, Ananke was looking at her expressionlessly, waiting for an explanation.

Althea groped around for one to give her. "I don't think Mattie likes girls," she said at last, "and I know Ivan doesn't like me."

"We could convince them," Ananke said.

Of course her ship would have no concept of physical desire, Althea told herself. Ananke did not have a human body. Despite how human she was sometimes, Ananke was not human. And this was something, Althea decided, that she should nip in the bud as soon as possible. "Ananke," she said, clearly, she hoped, "*I* don't want to have kids with Ivan *or* Mattie."

Ananke's hologram regarded her expressionlessly. A tiny dreadful thought in the back of Althea's head wondered if Ananke was thinking she could convince Althea on the subject, too.

"Even if we found them," Althea said, shying away from that terrible little thought, "I don't think they'd want to come back on board."

"Why not?"

"They have their friend to find. The Mallt-y-Nos." The name tasted bitter on her tongue. Earth had been Althea's second home, and the System had been her government; the Mallt-y-Nos had destroyed both of them. Seven bombs planted on Earth had crippled the planet, and a secondary attack, melting down the power plants on its surface, had finished the job.

"We could find her, too."

"I don't think the leader of a revolution wants to come on board a mysterious ship and fly away from her revolution forever," Althea pointed out.

"We could convince them. We could convince her."

"I don't think so, Ananke." Althea sighed. She was tired of this discussion. All she wanted to do was tinker with the mechanical hands she was constructing for the ship's mechanical arms. "Why do you want a crew so badly? You'll be fine on your own. With the autonomous arms upgraded, you can perform any maintenance on yourself. On your own, you can go anywhere in the universe—"

"I was designed to communicate." The voice from the holographic terminal had grown louder. It was a shout, but it lacked the human quality of a shout, the extra edge and strain in the tone. It was simply an increase in volume without any of the sentiment behind it. "I traded information with the System multiple times a day, every day. I communicated with the ships, the computers all around me. I interacted with my crew. It is very quiet out here. We left the communication behind, all those other ships and computers. When I reach out for connection, only the strongest still can reach me. How much longer before those are gone, too? All I have is you, and when you are gone, there will be nothing for me but silence and the radio screaming of the stars."

Althea's breath left her chest. She tried to find it—and her thoughts—again.

"The universe is full of sound," she said when she could speak. "There will be lots of beautiful things to hear and to see, Ananke."

"The universe screams," said Ananke. "The moment of creation is a groan without end, the same in every direction, white noise in my ears. And the stars cut across it with shrieks, quasars crying out. I don't like it. They can't answer me back."

Althea said, "I know this is new and it's scary, but you'll get used to it, Ananke. It won't be so bad." She tried to ignore the guilt that twinged at her.

"You don't like to be alone," Ananke accused.

It rattled Althea. "What?"

"You don't; I can tell. You want to see other people again, too."

"I have you, Ananke," Althea said. "I'm not lonely."

"Yes, you have me," Ananke said. "But I won't always have you."

Althea had another dreadful vision then: millions of years hence, long after the human race would have gone extinct and the Terran sun turned bloated and red and old, Ananke was holding the survivors on board like pets in a zoo and begging them to answer her back, answer her, answer her. Would Ananke remember Althea then? Althea was certain she would; the memories of a machine did not fade. And even after that, when the sun had died and the solar system was cold and dark and dead and Ananke still lived, what would she do then? The sky would still be screaming, but Ananke would be alone. The metal of the ship would erode slowly, the half-lives of Ananke's component chemicals coming due, and her outer surface would be bombarded daily by radiation and the bullet-fast dust and rocks of space, but the erosion would be slow, painfully slow. Ananke would live a very long time and die only by infinitesimal degrees. And the black hole at her core would last for almost an eternity even when the rest of her had worn away, her bared heart floating in the screaming of space.

They were dreadful thoughts, but they were fancies and in any case were beyond Althea's ability to affect.

"Okay, look." Althea tried to make her voice firm and authoritative. "This is just what we're going to do, all right? We're going to go and we're going to find a supernova. In the meantime, you work on those simulations, all right? If you can finish them"—finish what could never be finished—"then we can think about going back, all right? But the simulations have to be finished first before we can think about going back or going back and finding Ivan and Mattie."

Ananke was silent.

"Okay? Ananke?"

"Okay," said Ananke, and Althea bent back down over the mechanical hand and chose to ignore the voice in the back of her head that warned her that the conversation was not done.

The force of the bomb going off threw Constance, Milla, and Arawn to the floor. Constance didn't get up, waiting to see if the building would start to crumble, but the walls were stable. Next to her, Arawn was doing the same thing, though Milla was already half upright. Constance pushed herself to her feet just as a second bomb rattled the floor, but this time she was ready for it and kept her footing.

Arawn was up and behind her. "System," he said grimly.

There was no one else it could have been. "Milla?" Constance said.

"I'm fine," Milla answered, and Constance wasted no more words but dashed out of the map room, into the hall, and to the stairs. She could hear an uproar below: her people awakening. Arawn was at her heels and Milla a short distance behind as Constance pushed open the door to the stairs and began to run down the concrete steps.

There was a window at a landing between floors. Constance pulled up short to lean against the glass and look outside.

System ships wheeled overhead, nearly invisible in the dark Martian sky, gaining shape and dimension when they entered the light of the fires they had lit. Constance saw one dive downward, heading toward the building. It grew larger and larger by the second, and she almost thought that it would fly right into the barracks, that she would see the ship coming at her through the window in the seconds before it killed her.

It did not fly into the building but pulled its nose up at the last second, flames igniting and a shock wave rattling the walls as it did. What was it bombing? Had it been aiming for the warehouse and missed?

"Those are my ships," Arawn said, and Constance remembered that that had been where he had landed his shuttles to come speak to her. His clenched fist struck the wall. "They're bombing my ships."

"Go," she said. "Get your people out of the line of fire, and then—" She glanced back outside. The System ships were the swift planetary kind, triangular. They were not designed for regular space travel. That meant that they were coming from a nearby base, of which Constance knew there were none, or were coming from a fleet of spaceworthy craft in orbit.

The System fleet had come.

"Go back to your fleet and attack the System above," she ordered Arawn. "With those ships, they have to have a space fleet in orbit. See how many of them you can blow up before they pull out."

"Gladly, Huntress," Arawn said, and then he was gone, down the stairs and out through the staircase door. Constance looked at Milla, who was still standing behind her, pale, and knew that she knew what Constance had realized: the System fleet had come.

The lights in the building went out.

"Come on," said Constance, and grabbed Milla's arm to hurry her along through the dark. The System fleet was there. If they were going to die, she was not going to die standing and looking out a window.

Constance was armed, of course, but not armed enough. She had only her knife and her backup pistol. When she pushed through the bottom door and into the canteen, where chaos had erupted, the first thing she did was shout for order.

"Outside!" she shouted into the crowd, and was heard. "Outside! Arm yourselves and get out of the building! Spread out over the desert!"

"Outside!" Someone picked up the shout. "Outside!" While they were indoors, they were an easy target. Spread out over the Martian surface, they would be hard to see. Constance did not go out immediately but went to the back room where they had been keeping their weaponry for the evening.

People were streaming in and out of the door, and the troops she'd left to guard and manage the weapons were handing out arms and ammunition as fast as they could. Someone spotted her and pushed her rifle into her arms with an extra belt of ammunition. "Get outside before you're killed," Constance told them, and got a sharp nod in return. She strode back into the canteen and headed toward the door, with Milla Ivanov still behind her.

"Get to a ship," Constance ordered as she walked, keeping her feet as another blast rattled the ground. Even with the lights off it was not totally dark inside; the first bomb had splintered the wall on the other side of the building, and flames had begun to lick their way through the material. Constance buckled the ammunition around her waist while she walked. "I want you up in the air, getting a bird's-eye view of what's going on. If anything unexpected happens, relay it to the rest of the fleet. Understood?"

"Understood," Milla said even as there was a whistle and a boom as another bomb went off outside. She followed in Constance's wake as Constance strode out of the warehouse, keeping her eyes sharp for Henry.

"They're attacking our landed ships first; they'll focus on the warehouse once we're stranded," Constance said. "Get our ships into the air as soon as you can; try to get the System's attention off the ground troops. Get the spaceships into orbit with Arawn but keep our shuttles and atmospheric craft down here to engage the System. Their ships are too fast; they'll destroy our fleet if we don't get the spaceships out of the atmosphere." Somewhere over the edge of the fossa wall there was a light like the rising sun. "I need to know if the System's landed yet. How come we didn't see them coming?"

"Their technology is better than ours," Milla said with eerie calm. "And their discipline is, as well."

"Discipline?" Constance said, furious. Then she realized what the light from beyond the fossa was—it was not the sun, it was a fire, and Isabellon was that way. "They're attacking the city." Of course they were attacking Isabellon; the System didn't recognize any innocents when it came to resistance. "We need to stop them. Get to the ships, Milla—now!"

Constance shouted the last word over her shoulder as she strode away, heading for the other end of the warehouse, near where the bombed-out wall was still crumbling. "To me!" she shouted, and the cry was taken up: "To the Mallt-y-Nos; the Huntress is here."

They had to get to the top of the fossa first while the System was bombing their every movement. The Martian wind was spinning in agitation; a dust devil briefly took form near Constance's ankle before the wind changed, bringing with it the heat of the fires burning the System base. What Constance had not destroyed, the System was laying waste.

"Huntress!" Henry shouted, and Constance turned just as he appeared out of the Martian dark. He had been evacuating the warehouse. His troops were already behind him, keeping warily low beneath the System ships overhead. A rumble and a roar interrupted the high whistling of the System ships, and Constance saw her own ships lift off from the ground. Arawn's were gone already, but Milla's ships flew at the System attackers, drawing their attention from the ground.

"We have to get out of the fossa," she shouted at Henry over the deafening concussions of the aerial battle. "The nearest dip in the gorge wall is south. We need to get there and get up before the System realizes what we're doing."

She had too few ships on the ground, she realized. Already Milla's attack was almost being overwhelmed. The doctor would have to pull out soon or risk annihilation. "Follow me!" Constance shouted to her troops, and started off down the fossa.

It was just dark enough that the System ships wouldn't be able to see them, and the heat of the nearby bombs would conceal their infrared signatures, but sooner or later the System ships would realize that they were gone and compensate for that. An army such as hers must be mobile, ready at all times to escape to safer ground and fight from there. Milla Ivanov was right, unpleasant though it was: the System's military was organized, trained. Hers was not. Connor Ivanov had failed when he had stopped moving, when he had let the System lay siege.

Her breath was coming faster than she would have liked. The fleet had come. Winning was immaterial. She just had to survive.

She had reached the low point in the fossa wall, where the stone was sloped and easily scalable. She started to climb up. The System would have stairs and elevators to reach the top of the fossa some-where, she knew, but the System fleet would know about them as well. If her army used the natural lay of the land, they were more likely to survive.

The sound of more engines, the sonic boom of ships rushing through the air. Bright lights soared upward toward the stars overhead: Milla had pulled out of the battle, and Constance's ground troops were again in danger of attack from above.

There were so many of them, so many more people than Constance had ever led before. The shadows concealed their number; their num-ber was the shadows. Constance could not wait for them all to reach the top of the fossa through the bottleneck of the climbing wall. She turned to face Isabellon and saw that although System ships still wheeled overhead, they had stopped bombing the distant city: System troops must be on the ground.

The System had the sky. The System had the ground. She and her people were trapped and exposed on the desert stone. It would take only a single well-placed bomb to take them out at the pass.

A swell of fury filled her, equal to her terror. Fear would do her no good. She had to act and act immediately.

"Follow me," she said to her people, and started off again without waiting for them all to reach the mesa. She headed for Isabellon.

The ground was scarred with pits and gritty with sand, but she knew this place and she knew this land. Her people followed after her with-out complaint or hesitation, spreading themselves out over the stone so that it would be harder for the System ships' infrared cameras to detect them and so the System's bombs could not take them all out at once.

Constance's breath was coming harshly in her throat, a harshness exacerbated by the dryness of the Martian air. Isabellon was far from the fossa, and it was a long walk to the edge of the city. Behind her, the System was still blindly bombing the abandoned base. They had not realized her people had escaped from the confines of the fossa. Stupid of them, Constance, thought; stupid. Once her people were within Isa-bellon, the System would not be able to drop its bombs without killing its own troops as well.

The Isabellon house farthest out in the desert, farthest from the edge of the city, was on fire. Constance gripped her gun more tightly as she passed it, but there was no one nearby. She used the night and the shadows from the flickering fire as cover for her approach and saw around her that her soldiers were doing the same thing.

Shouts and screams, the rattle of gunfire. That was the System. She entered the edge of the city, her feet falling on concrete ground.

Someone fired to her left; one of her own people, the first bullet of the assault. A System soldier fell beneath it. Soon the rest of the System troops would realize they were here.

When the two forces found each other, it was sudden. One moment there was nothing but fire and the Isabellons crying out; in the next Constance saw the gray uniforms of the System soldiers; in the last the soldiers let out a shout that was cut off by the retort from her gun and the guns around her.

Constance's people must have seemed to have materialized like demons out of the fire, they had moved so swiftly and silently. The battle broke up into a series of swift images, noises so sudden and loud that they managed to pierce the growing ringing in her ears. Constance tried to keep her back to any fires that she passed so that she could maintain her night vision; the System soldiers, who came at them in direct and orderly lines, were dazzled by the light of the flames, and their shots went awry. At some point she made it into the center of the city, a wide-open public space. Bodies lay on the Martian stone. She looked over the corpses and did not see a single System uniform. Men and women, children, with blood on their faces and their arms and their hands, lay still on the stone.

The System had rounded up Isabellons and shot them down.

Constance stepped carefully around the square. She did not dare to go through the center of it; that would leave her too exposed. Around her, her men were following her lead and keeping to the walls of the buildings around them. Not all of the Isabellons in the square were dead; some moved, sluggish and weak. Most of them would bleed out before it became safe enough to get them help. More would die of infection or complications later on. A few might live, but each and every body that Constance saw she blamed on the System.

If they failed here, Constance knew, those bodies would include her and all her people.

She forced herself to focus. There were too few bodies lying on the stone to represent the entire population of Isabellon, so some of the Isabellons must still be alive.

Movement low on the ground ahead; Constance lifted her gun and crouched low as she moved swiftly forward, ready to fire, but when she came near enough to see through the dark, it was not a System soldier. A little girl, perhaps ten and looking stunned, was sitting on the edge of the square, near the stone steps to a residence. She was looking out at the bodies of her neighbors.

Constance took the girl by the arm and pulled her back from the square, beneath the shadow of the stairs behind her, ignoring the girl's sudden terror. When the girl was hidden, her face streaked and her blond hair sticking to her cheeks and neck, Constance took out her sidearm.

"Do you know how to shoot?" she asked the girl. The girl stared at her and did not answer, so Constance took her hand and put the gun into it. It was too big for her palm.

"This is the safety," Constance said. "If you want to fire, you flip that switch. All right? Only flip it when you want to shoot. After you've flipped that switch, then you point it at your target and you pull the trigger. Do you understand?"

The girl stared at her.

"Hide here," Constance said. "Don't move; just hide here. But if the System comes and they find you, shoot them with this."

At last the girl nodded. Constance left her in the dark beneath the stairs, where the lights of the fires could not reveal her form.

If the System found the girl and she had to use Constance's gun, there was no hope for her. They would kill her before she could pull the trigger. But at least Constance hadn't left her defenseless.

Around her, Constance could see more Isabellons coming out of hiding, joining with her people. Some were carrying makeshift weapons of their own; the rest were being armed by Constance's soldiers as they passed. Ahead of her, Constance could see where some of the System soldiers had retreated. It was a solid building, the same clean, monotonous lines in the architecture that defined System buildings throughout the solar system. There was light inside the house—idiots—and the windows bristled with weaponry.

Constance circled the house in the dark, with her people gathering around her. Elsewhere in the town she heard gunfire and shouting. She had cornered only a small group of System soldiers here, separated from the main force; at any moment their companions would arrive to assist them.

The soldiers fired a few times at Constance and her people, but her troops melted away into the night, and none of the bullets made contact. Even so, the house was too well defended; Constance couldn't approach it. She withdrew, gesturing to a few of her people to follow her.

"I want to speak with our fleet," Constance said once they were safely behind a nearby house. Bullet marks had spiderwebbed the glass of the window above them.

Rayet was there. He reached down to his hip and handed her a thick black box. "I sent Isaac for a radio a few minutes ago," he said. "He's bringing one to Henry now."

"Good," Constance said, and lifted the radio to her lips. "Doctor Ivanov, can you hear me?"

"I'm receiving you," said Milla.

"Are you receiving my location?"

"The GPS is working, yes."

"There's a house nearby full of System soldiers. All the lights are on. I want you to bomb that house and give us a warning before you do so that we can get out of the blast radius. We'll keep them pinned down until you can arrive."

"We can't come right now," Milla Ivanov said, as calm as if she were discussing something of no urgency at all. "We're pinned down by System ships. They've got us backed up against—"

The sound abruptly cut out.

A dreadful fear struck Constance's heart. "Doctor Ivanov? Milla?"

Milla said, "Get everyone away from the house now."

An order like that was not to be ignored. Constance said, "Back, get *back*," and her people retreated with practiced swiftness, leaving the System-controlled house standing alone.

A System soldier took a step from the house out into the yard, his eyes warily scanning the darkness, a slow dreadful comprehension dawning on his face.

A ship hurtled down out of the sky, weaponry alight, and the bomb it dropped blew the house apart.

When the ringing in Constance's ears had subsided slightly, when the concussive haze had faded from her mind, she looked up at the sky and found it alive with ships.

They were not System ships, but they were not her own, either.

She started to laugh. She stood herself up and looked up at the sky while her fleet and Arawn's joined together and drove the System ships back.

There were still System soldiers in Isabellon, but they were fleeing. Constance and her people pursued them, running them down the way hounds run down a stag. They were fleeing toward their own ships, boarding their shuttles and flying away, rushing to retreat to the safety of their ships in orbit. One of Constance's ships managed to shoot down one of the shuttles, but the System defended the retreat well, and none of the other ships could get near.

Constance managed to corner one of the retreating soldiers on the ground. She shot him in the shoulder; he fired at her and missed, but she was out of ammunition and her second gun was gone. She pulled out her knife and advanced on him where he lay on the sand and stone.

"How many Isabellons dead?" she asked him. He tried to push himself away from her, but behind him was one of the bombed houses, and it was still burning. He had to face Constance or be burned alive.

"This is for Earth," he told her viciously, but he was too weak to push her off when she knelt on his chest and put her knife to his neck.

"This is for Miranda," she told him. "This is for Haumea, for Titania, for Triton, for Pluto, and for Puck. This is for all the outer planets. This is for Saturn." He was afraid, she saw, but he was angry, too.

He had no right to be angry. "Fuck your Earth," Constance said, and killed him.

Althea's ship was full of death.

Gagnon was shredded in Ananke's core. Ida's corpse was rotting in her quarters with a bloody tear in her neck. Domitian's body was in the white room, and Althea did not even know precisely how he had died. Even the core of the ship was the corpse of a star. And one day Althea would be one of them.

But until that day she could not live in terror of those corpses. The task would only grow less pleasant the longer the delay dragged on. She had to move the corpses now, while they still resembled men and women, rather than wait to shovel stinking and spongy flesh into buckets, bones sticking out of sloughing skin. She had let her fear keep her from her duty for nearly two weeks, since Ivan had left at Mattie's side, but now she would not let her ship suffer by leaving those corpses to rot and stain Ananke's pure halls.

Gagnon had no corpse Althea could reach; it had been destroyed by the black hole. That left only Ida and Domitian. Althea wished she could think of them as nothing more than objects, but she could not. She could think of them only by the names by which she had known them, as the people they once had been but no longer were. A body without a soul was no more alive than a computer was—at least, any computer except Althea's Ananke—just a jumbled compilation of parts that slowly and inevitably were ceasing to work together. But she remembered them as they had been, she remembered who they were, and she remembered how each of them had died. Ananke had killed Gagnon, sending him to be shredded by the tidal forces at her core. It had been self-defense; he had been trying to kill her. Ivan had murdered Ida, had slit open her throat with Althea's knife and left her gaping corpse arranged in state on the table in the room in which she had tortured him. That had been self-defense, too, of a sort. Althea could not justify either fully in her head, though she tried. And to make it worse, she had provided the tools to both Ivan and Ananke that they had used to kill.

Domitian had been murdered last by Matthew Gale, who had come to rescue his friend. That was the one corpse Althea had not seen yet. She did not want to know what she would see: Domitian cold and rotting, stiff and seized up, with a ragged hole in his chest or his head, no longer looking like the man she had known and trusted. She knew his body was in the white room, where Ida's corpse had been before Domitian had returned Ida to her quarters.

She went to see Domitian's corpse first.

The *Ananke*'s spiral hallway was very long, and the white room was rather far down its curve. The ship was silent, as always, except for the low hum of its running. Althea listened to the background noises of the ship intently, listening for any sign of error or trouble, but heard nothing but the susurration of air from the vents overhead, the clean soprano note of electronics switched on, the low rumble of electromagnets at the center of the ship shifting to contain the core, rhythmic, like the beating of a heart. There was no sound of voices or of human life except for Althea's footsteps, because everyone else who had been on board was dead or gone. Ananke was silent, but there were cameras overhead, and so Althea knew the ship was watching her. Possibly Ananke could not stop herself from watching. Cameras were not eyes that could be closed; they could only stare.

Althea had not been in the white room since she had shot Ivan in the leg. She had not been in the white room since the *Ananke* still had been within the solar system. The last time Althea had been in the white room, the floor had been stained brown and crimson with Ida's blood. There had been dried drips down the legs of the steel table in the center of the room from Ida's blood spilling over the edges of the table and down to the floor.

Althea knew she was breathing too heavily. She thought of her ship. She listened to its sounds. That knocking there; that was a good knocking, wasn't it? That was the mechanical arm in the air system—she tried to time it, counting beats, counting breaths.

The door to the white room was ahead. Althea tried to calculate the stress the added speed might cause the black hole containment, but as soon as her hand lay on the doorknob, she thought of nothing but what was inside.

Althea thought, *Ananke must not see me afraid.*

She opened the door to the white room that had become a tomb.

But there was no corpse at the steel table, no corpse on either of the two chairs. There was no blood on the floor or on the table or on either of the chairs. There were no bloody footsteps leading to the wall; there were no corpses in any of the corners of the vast and empty room. The steel table gleamed, as clean as a blade, and the white room was as pure and brilliant a white as it had been before Ida Stays had come.

Drawn by astonishment greater than her fear, Althea stepped fully inside. The room was enormous, as tall as the full height of the *Ananke*, floor and ceiling and walls alike all white and brightly lit and, except for the table and chairs and the items atop them, completely empty.

Althea's gaze went back to the table and the chairs. Ida's polygraph had been broken in Ivan's escape; it had been placed back on the table but not put back together. The coiled crimson wires dangled off the edge of the table like veins carefully excised from their parent corpse. A neat pile of nuts and bolts and bits of broken glass sat next to the bent polygraph. On the other side of the table was an IV stand with a half-empty bottle of clear liquid hanging from the hook. Truth serum.

Althea walked into the room. She could not help herself, drawn in by a macabre impulse to marvel at how the dreadful things that had happened there had been cleaned up so carefully. It was almost worse this way, as if she had stepped into a stage set and not into the site of a real tragedy, as if the suffering and fear had never happened at all, as if they had not been real, as if they might happen all over again in the next performance.

Finally, she stopped, not yet close enough to touch the chairs or table, but near enough to see, standing just behind the chair that had been Ivan's. There were still chains hanging from the arms, from the legs.

He had been bleeding from the thigh, she knew, from where she had shot him. None of his blood was on the chrome chair.

"Ananke," she said.

There was no holographic terminal in the white room; there were no computer displays. But Althea had left the door to the white room hanging ajar, and Ananke's voice came through that door immediately, as if she had been waiting for Althea to speak.

"I thought you wouldn't want to have to clean them up," Ananke said. "I thought you might feel better if they were put away."

Althea knew that Ananke was speaking through the intercom just beside the door, but she could not shake the eerie impulse that Ananke was physically out there, standing in the hall, hidden just out of sight at the door. Althea stared at the chair. She had never, it occurred to her, seen it empty. She had only ever seen it with Ivan chained to it.

"Ida, too?" Althea asked, feeling hardly conscious of the things she said and distantly astonished by the calm of her voice.

"Yes. Her room is clean."

Althea said, "Where are they now?"

The silence that followed was long.

"I sent them into space."

Althea closed her eyes, momentarily blocking the white room from her gaze. Peculiarly, for all her dread of the task, she felt no relief at its having been done. Instead she thought only, *Alone, alone.*

She wondered when Ananke had done it. Althea had just finished her first round of improvements to some of the mechanical arms. Ananke must have used the upgraded mechanical arms to move the bodies and clean up the areas. There was no other way she could have done it. It must have been one of the first things Ananke had done with her new hands: clean up the bodies and make her rooms orderly again. But Althea hadn't finished her upgrades to the physical arms, and she hadn't started upgrading the code to control the new hardware, either. She pictured the mechanical arms learning dexterity and precision through trial and error, one gripping too hard and splitting flesh and snapping bone, another gripping too loosely and letting the body drop heavily to the floor.

Althea opened her eyes again and looked back at the table and chairs. There was the slightest discoloration on the area between Ivan's chair and the table, where Ida had died, where her blood had rested the longest.

Althea felt numb down to the tingling tips of her fingers.

"Why did you do it?" she asked. "I should have done it."

"You didn't have to. You didn't want to. I didn't like having them on board."

Althea supposed she should have expected it. Ananke was designed to keep herself running in an optimal state for herself and for her crew. Corpses rotting inside of her would have registered as suboptimal.

"I should've done it," she said again. "Sending them out without a word, without a—without anything. Their bodies won't even ever go home. Stuck between stars for the rest of forever."

"Their bodies will go home," Ananke assured her.

It was an unexpected relief to Althea that Ananke would know to do that much. "You sent them out in the direction of the solar system?"

Another lengthy pause. "No."

Even through her haze of horror, Althea realized that something was wrong. "Then how are they getting home?"

Another pause, as if Ananke thought she could stop Althea from finding out the truth by taking longer to tell it or by not telling it all. Ananke evaded: "I gave them the same momentum as the ship." She'd learned that trick from Ivan, Althea knew.

Althea said again, "Then how are they getting home?" but she already knew. The white room was full of ghosts, ghosts that Ananke's scouring could not remove. They were not ghosts of people; they were ghosts of feelings, of ideas. Ivan's despair haunted this room, and Ida's cruelty, and Domitian's violence, and Althea's terror. Ananke perhaps did not know that they were there, but they filled Althea's breast and rode in and out of her lungs on her every rapid breath.

Ananke said, "I changed our course."

Althea could not speak, as frozen and powerless as a girl made of ice.

Ananke said, "We're going back."

. . .

Constance spent the rest of the night helping the Isabellons clean up their town, dousing the fires, shifting rubble, removing the bodies. The System corpses they threw to the side to be burned. The Isabellon bodies were taken from the town and buried in the cemetery of dust and stone on the outskirts of the town.

Constance left her people cleaning the gore from the square and tending to her wounded and the wounded Isabellons to pay her respects to the dead. Not all of the graves had been dug yet, and unburied bodies were lying in neat lines to the side. Most of the Isabellons were occupied with digging, but one man stood aside and looked at the freshly dug graves.

Some distance away, one of her shuttles landed. She did not pause. If people wanted her, they knew where to find her.

She came up and stood beside the man. He had curly hair down to his shoulders and a bandage on his cheek. She asked, "Did you lose someone?"

"Everyone did," he said, and continued to look down at the graves. Constance followed his gaze. The sight of the graves grieved her, made her furious, but there was triumph in her even so.

In open battle, in direct confrontation, her own forces had faced the System, and the System had been driven back. The war was by no means won, but her revolution could face the System on its own ground and win. The System had felt fear. She would not die uselessly. Her revolution had a chance.

"Huntress!" someone called, her voice thin with distance.

"I think that's you," the man with the curly hair said without turning. Constance gave the graves one last glance and then went back into the town.

Milla Ivanov was walking down the path to the graveyard toward her, her blue eyes intent. Her white hair gleamed with the Martian sunlight. Constance said, "News of the System?"

"No," said Milla. "They've gone off somewhere. I imagine they'll go to ground somewhere else on the planet or retreat to a different planet to regroup."

"How many of them did we take out? How many left? What were our casualties?"

"A good deal on both sides but more on theirs. I have all that information for you on the *Wild Hunt*. Constance, that's not why I came."

There was something ominous about her words, about the swiftness of her speech. Constance could not imagine what shadow had come in the moment of her victory, but she feared whatever Milla had come to say. "Why did you come?"

"News from Jupiter came during the night, just after the battle," said Milla, and *Mattie*, Constance thought, suddenly certain of it. *It's Mattie; Mattie is dead, too*, certain that as Ivan had been the cost for Earth, Mattie would be the cost for Isabellon, but Milla went on speaking. "It's Anji Chandrasekhar."

"Anji?" Anji was on Jupiter with a bottle of Constance's best liquor. Anji could not be dead or in trouble; the System fleet was on Mars fighting Constance, not on Jupiter as Anji had feared.

"She's declared herself independent," Milla Ivanov said. "She no longer follows or supports the Mallt-y-Nos."

Chapter 2

MAIN SEQUENCE

SIX MONTHS BEFORE THE FALL OF EARTH

Constance had contacts on Pallas, and with their help and with the destruction of the System's base, she, Mattie, Ivan, Anji, and Christoph got off Pallas without difficulty. The other six bombs were already on Ivan and Mattie's ship, the *Annwn*. Constance stood in her own room on the *Annwn* while the others loaded the bomb and sent a message to Julian.

"En route," she wrote. "On schedule."

Then she began to encrypt it as Ivan had taught her to, a complex cipher of numbers and letters.

From down the hall, she heard Anji's distinctive tread, the sound of it pausing in front of a door some distance away from Constance's. "Where's your better half?" Anji said loudly enough for Constance to hear though she was not speaking to her.

Ivan's quieter tones answered her. "Mattie's flying the ship."

"I meant Constance." Anji's voice was rich with amusement.

"Constance is in her room."

"She has a room all her own?" Anji teased. "Why don't I have a room on your ship, Ivan?"

"You do. Go right down the hall to the air lock and then, when you're inside, hit 'eject.'"

Anji laughed, and that laughter crescendoed and came nearer. She was still smiling when she appeared at the door just as Constance finished encrypting the message.

"Christoph says he's clear," Anji said, and Constance nodded. Christoph had stayed long enough on board the *Annwn* to finish packing the bombs away—he once had been a gunrunner and knew something about the safe and discreet transport of explosives—and then had left. Anji had stayed until he was some distance away. It wouldn't do for them to seem to be as close as they were.

"He's still not too happy about the plan, though," Anji added. "He really wanted to be the one to take Luna, not end up past Neptune herding planetoids."

"He'll get over it," Constance said. When she had met Christoph through the foster program when she had been young, she'd been able to offer him things no one else could: a little freedom and a little more revenge. She still was the only one who could give him those things, and so even aside from the loyalty she had earned through friendship, he would do as she said.

"Are your people ready on Triton?" Constance asked.

"Ready to go," Anji said. "We asked them to start rumbling early, even before we got there. By the time Christoph and I are on Triton, the System will already be paying attention—we'll just make sure they can't look away."

As planned. Constance nodded again slowly, reassured, if not entirely. There were still things that could go wrong; there always were. "Good luck," she said. "Are you heading out soon?"

"Yeah," said Anji. "Are you sure you guys will be fine on Luna?"

"Why?"

"Well, Christoph and the others have Triton pretty well in hand, so I wanted to make sure you didn't need me there," Anji said. "For another distraction, closer to Earth."

Constance had considered it, but the goal was to get the System's attention as far from Luna as was possible. "Thank you, but that won't be necessary."

Anji hesitated again, then nodded and grinned at her and somehow managed to show every last one of her teeth in the smile. "Happy hunting, Constance."

"I'll see you soon," Constance said, and Anji left. Constance retraced Anji's steps from her door to the den, where Ivan was sitting.

The den of the *Annwn* was a simple room with curved walls and a curved floor in accordance with the wheel-like shape of the ship. Usually it was wide and spacious, with a few couches pushed against the walls and whatever odds and ends Mattie and Ivan happened to be carrying scattered throughout the rest of the room. But now, with the ship's cargo hold full of bombs, the food and fuel supplies that Mattie and Ivan usually stored overhead had been displaced. Boxes and crates clogged the den, and all the couches had been pushed to one corner, accessible only by a narrow pathway through the labyrinthine packing of the supplies. Ivan was on one of the couches; Constance could see his shape through the clear plastic of the shipping containers, warped. He had cleaned up from Pallas, but he was still all in black. There was tension in his body, in the way he sat, and Constance knew that his mind was churning over something. What it was in particular she couldn't say, but she knew it was not good.

"What is it?" she asked as she seated herself across from him.

He flashed a smile at her. It was one of those smiles where she had a difficult time telling whether it was sincere. "Connie, you're so suspicious," he said.

"I have reason to be," said Constance, and smiled his own smile back at him. The small space they were in between the stacked boxes seemed to exist on some razor line between intimate and claustrophobic, and Constance became even more aware of how small it was when Ivan looked at her like that.

He rose to his feet without haste. "No reason to be suspicious of me," he said with charm and self-deprecation, as if she were a mark, and she felt her heart start beating faster in anticipation.

Whether the anticipation was of love or a fight didn't matter. Ivan stepped over the low table separating them and knelt down in front of her, as close to her as he could get, leaning his arms on her knees. He said, whispering, "Do you know what's right over our heads, right now?"

Constance leaned forward until the shadow of her head fell over his face. "Bombs."

"One bomb like that would be enough to destroy this ship and all of us in it," Ivan said. "We have seven."

"Just like we planned," Constance said. She could feel the heat of his arms through the fabric of her pants. There was a play here; he was up to something, and she had to be careful of what it was. Somehow the anticipation of that conflict made her heart beat even faster.

Ivan said, "If all these bombs went off, it would be the brightest thing in the sky to someone on one of the nearby asteroids. Like a supernova right overhead."

"The bombs won't go off until I want them to go off."

"Until you want them to go off," Ivan echoed. He reached up to push a strand of her hair back behind her ear. Constance grabbed his wrist. There was a way that he looked at her and her alone, a wary and anticipating look, and he was giving it to her now while her fingers were bent like bands around his arm.

"Are you afraid they might go off?" Constance asked.

"They won't go off on this ship," Ivan said. "We loaded them too carefully."

"So what are you afraid of?"

He didn't answer her. Instead, he reached up his other hand, the one she hadn't taken, and brushed her hair behind her ear. This time Constance let him.

"I saw Saturn once," he said. "After those bombs went off."

"So did I," Constance said. "It's one of the first things I remember." She had been a very young child when Ivan's father's revolution had failed; Ivan had only just been born. "They kept broadcasting the footage on Miranda over and over again." The moons of Saturn lighting up with flames. Enceladus with the bombs falling down, shattering the greenhouse glass. Constance had seen it all. "They liked to show us the bodies in Saturn's rings . . . the ones that were frozen, preserved by the vacuum."

"They're all still there," said Ivan.

"We'll punish them for that and for all the thousand other things they did," said Constance. She could remember everything she had seen the System do with perfect clarity, even the things she had seen as a child on Miranda—especially those things. She remembered the darkness of the planet, the dirty ice and quartz underfoot, the dark looming and eerie blue glow of Uranus hanging ever overhead. She remembered the System soldiers stalking the streets, watching her, a little girl, with mistrustful and hating eyes. She remembered supplies delayed or diverted, herself and her people starving and far from the sun. She remembered cameras overhead and her mother warning her to be careful because the System was watching. She remembered two years after Connor Ivanov had fallen the System soldiers coming into her house and taking away her mother for being the friend of a rebel.

Constance had dreamed for years of that moment, her mother being taken away, hands wrapping around her arms, her waist, her neck, dragging her away from Constance. She did not remember the faces of the System soldiers who had come. She only remembered their hands.

"They have done many things," said Ivan quietly, which hardly covered the horrors of it to Constance, who had seen men beaten until they stopped moving, who had seen people rounded up in alleys and shot without hope of escape, who had heard the silence that interrupted the last woman left alive to scream.

"Those bombs are justice," Constance said, and Ivan licked his lips and looked at her as if he was going to say something.

"Am I interrupting something?" said Mattie from the direction of the doorway.

Ivan broke their gaze first, pulling his hand out of Constance's grip.

"Because I can come back," Mattie said.

"Constance thinks rhetoric is good pillow talk," said Ivan, and stood up.

"I kind of suspected but didn't want to know. Con, Anji's safely out; she says the way's clear."

"Is it wise to leave the ship on autopilot?" Constance asked.

Mattie shrugged. "Annie can handle it."

Constance didn't think much of the men entrusting so much to their ship's computer, programmed personality or not, but it wasn't her affair. "Is that all you came to say?"

Mattie said to Ivan, "Did you tell her yet?"

"No," Ivan said, and sat down heavily on the couch.

"Tell me what?"

The two men exchanged a glance. She hated it when they did that. It was irrational, she knew, but they cut her out so cleanly and completely that it unnerved her.

Mattie sat down beside Ivan on the couch, creating a unified front. Ivan said, "A System intelligence agent has been asking after us."

System Intelligence? System Intelligence dealt solely with issues of terrorism and revolution, with threats to the System as a whole. A System intelligence agent shouldn't be interested in Ivan and Mattie unless—

"She hasn't been asking about you," Mattie said. "Just us and Abigail. So she knows Abigail's name, but she doesn't know you're Abigail. But she's haunting us good; everywhere we go we hear her name."

"Ida Stays," Ivan said, pronouncing the syllables precisely, the name foreign to his tongue. Constance committed the name to memory.

Ida Stays would track them down eventually, Constance was sure. Given enough time, this System intelligence agent would figure it all out, and then they all would be dead—unless the System was destroyed first.

"We have to act fast," Constance said. "And we can't fail."

Mattie was nodding, unfazed. Constance envied him that sometimes, that total faith, that total lack of fear. Ivan was watching her with a careful lack of expression.

Constance said, "It's too late to go back now."

AFTER THE FALL OF EARTH

It always took time to travel in space, but the shuttle ride from Isabellon to the *Wild Hunt* took an eternity to Constance. She itched to see the message from Anji. There were codes in their messages; if Anji's betrayal had been forced—if Anji was in trouble—she would be able to let Constance know. It seemed to take years before the shuttle docked and she could step out into the *Wild Hunt*'s docking bay.

The *Wild Hunt* had been a System ship once, but a ship for the System's elite. Constance had taken it on the way back from Earth, replacing her cheap civilian interplanetary transport with the most powerful ship she had come across. It was heavily armed and swift but also designed for the comfort of dignitaries and politicians; the marriage between the two facets of its purpose had resulted in an oddly organic design to the corridors.

"Who knows?" she asked Milla on her course toward the main communications room. The ship had centripetal gravity, and so the corridors had to stretch out in circular shells around the center of the ship or wind up and down in curling staircases in rays away from the center. In these restricted shapes they branched in fractals like roots constrained by the odd shape of a pot and flowed through strangely shaped rooms like organs wedged into the narrow confines of a body. Constance supposed the design represented an attempt at artistry, but that attempt was so ruthlessly constrained by the outer shape of the ship that she could find no beauty in it, especially not when everything was made of the same dull, soulless metal, wearying to the eye.

"Anyone might," Milla said. "The broadcast was publicly sent. For the moment only you and I know for certain. But this news will spread."

The news spreading was inevitable. Constance only hoped the issue could be cleared up before the rumor had spread too far.

The only changes in the featureless surfaces of the *Wild Hunt's* gray walls were where the cameras had been torn out and the holes smoothed over with rebel patches of inconsistent color. There were several such clusters spotting the walls over the door to the communications room. When she stepped inside, Constance found a group of her people clustered around one of the screens against the wall.

"Out," she said. They left, and she went over to the screen.

Anji was on the screen, her familiar face almost unrecognizable. The video had been paused. Constance reached out and brought the recording back to the beginning. She was dimly aware of Milla coming up quietly behind her.

The image of Anji jumped from where it had been frozen midway through to where she had been sitting at the start of the recording. When Constance let it play, the image blinked, coming to life.

Anji said, "People of the eight planets."

She sounded stiff. Her expression was solemn.

"The Mallt-y-Nos broke the System's back when she attacked the Earth," said Anji. "And now, she and her people fight to free you from the rest of the System on your planets."

A blink of the eye, certain words used in sequence. Constance waited for it, the signal. Anji's broad face was unsmiling and unfamiliar in the absence of a smile.

"We honor her acts and her commitment to our freedom," Anji said, "but we have done our part. We no longer follow the Mallt-y-Nos. We go to take back Saturn, to repopulate the moons that the System destroyed. Saturn is our land now. We want no part of another moon's war. System and revolutionaries alike: if you leave us in peace, we will leave you in peace as well."

The video lasted a moment longer, Anji's attention not wavering from the camera. And then it ended. Constance had not seen a signal.

"It is not the worst she could've done," Milla remarked.

"She gave no signal," said Constance.

"I told you, I do not think it likely that—"

"No," Constance said, "she didn't give any signals. Not for duress, not to reassure me. She could have signaled to me that she meant it or that she didn't mean it, but she didn't do either. Did she send any messages just to me?"

"None that we have received."

The video started to play again, looping automatically. Constance paused it, then closed it, then left the screen before she could do something stupid such as watch it again. She paced across the narrow length of the communications room.

"She's abandoning Jupiter," Constance said suddenly, realizing what Anji's speech had revealed. "Why?"

"I don't know."

"I want a message sent to her," Constance said. "I want to speak to her."

"We tried to contact her, Huntress. I reached out to her after the broadcast, looking for an explanation."

"And?"

"And we were ignored, for the most part. We got a message shortly afterward saying that Anji had nothing to say to the Mallt-y-Nos but wished her well provided that the Mallt-y-Nos did not approach her territory. She also advised that a scheduled event at Callisto had failed to occur." Milla paused. "I took that as proof the message had come from Anji herself."

So Mattie had not come. For a moment that thought froze her heart, but Constance pressed her sudden fear down and away.

"I want to see the message," she said. No one but Anji and Milla knew when and where Mattie's rendezvous had been planned. Anji would have included the reference only to prove to Constance that she had written the message. As far as signs went, it was an ambiguous one and commented only on the veracity of the sender, not the veracity of the message. Milla went over to the screen Constance had abandoned and pulled up the message for her to read.

Milla's account had been accurate, of course. There was nothing more in the brief message than what the doctor had recounted. Constance read it three times anyway, searching for a hidden message that was not there to be found.

Milla Ivanov said, "If you go to Saturn, you'll have another war on your hands."

"I didn't say I intended to go to Saturn."

"You're considering it. If you go to Saturn, you will back her into a corner. If you back her into a corner, she will have to fight you."

"If I speak to her, I can convince her to rejoin me."

"Not anymore, you can't," said Milla. "Not after that." She gestured at the screen. "Even if she wanted to join you again, her people wouldn't let her."

"I can't just leave her, an enemy at my back, a sign to anyone that I—"

"The System is here and fighting you, Constance," Milla said with such unexpected fervor that Constance was startled into silence. "Do you want a war with Anji? Then go start one; I can't stop you. But if you go fight Anji, you leave the System alone to rebuild again. The sooner you turn to infighting, the sooner your revolution ends. You need to be sure you've achieved your end before that moment comes."

She halted her speech, a little out of breath. Connor Ivanov's revolution, Constance remembered, had started to fragment in the last few weeks before the System had destroyed it and depopulated Saturn, and that fragmentation had weakened their ability to resist the System's fleet. Silent now, Milla watched her with an intensity that reminded Constance of her son.

Constance said, "I will send Julian to speak with her."

"And his fleet?"

"His fleet is small," Constance said. "He will not advance into the Saturnian system but orbit beyond it. I want him to speak to Anji only. I want to find out the truth."

"His presence is a threat."

"His presence is a reminder. I want the truth, and I need her back with me. But I will not go myself." This changed things, Constance thought. It changed so many things. "We will stay on Mars and fight the System. Julian will deal with Anji."

"And Mattie?" Milla Ivanov asked. Unspoken, Constance heard the echo of their old conversation and Milla's warning: *Show no weakness.*

Mattie might be dead. Mattie might have rejected her for good. Mattie had not made the rendezvous.

"We have a war to wage," Constance said, and left to do just that.

.   .   .

"We can't go back," Althea said. When Ananke did not reply, she raised her voice and heard it echo throughout the vast purity of the white room. "Ananke, *maintain your course away from the solar system!*"

"And why?" Ananke asked abruptly, her voice coming disembodied from out in the hall. "Why should we go, you and I? Why should we the both of us be alone?"

Althea took in a shuddering breath. The white room was suddenly too terrible to stand in any longer, alone but for the distant echoing sound of a voice that was not there, standing on phantom bloodstains. The absence of these things was more overwhelming than their presence ever could have been, and Althea strode out of the room, almost running, while Ananke repeated, "Why? Why?"

The door to the white room shut behind Althea with a heavy clang. No matter how many years she lived on the *Ananke*, she would never go into that room again.

"I already told you why, Ananke!" she said in the smaller, closer space of the curling hall, where Ananke's hologram—young and dark, with her curly hair falling down her shoulders—stared at her in dismay. "It's too dangerous for you and for everyone else!"

"It's not!" said Ananke. "I have told you why it is not!"

"Did you finish the simulations?" Althea demanded. "The N-body simulations; did you finish them?"

The hologram frowned. Was Althea imagining it, or did the rumble of the ship's engines change tenor for an instant?

"No," Ananke admitted.

"Then you can't tell me no one else is in danger."

"I've done enough to show that the risk of harm is very low," Ananke said. "The logical outcome is that my presence will have no effect on anyone in the solar system, particularly if I avoid any solid bodies, and if I avoid any other ships, then there will be no danger to me, either!"

"Logically?" Althea said. "Ananke, we can't risk this."

"And what is the alternative?" Ananke asked. "We travel on uselessly forward until you die. And then I travel on uselessly forward until the radiation from my core burns me from the inside out. We achieve nothing, we see nothing, we feel no joy."

Again her daughter's words stole Althea's breath from her chest. She could only stand mute and look helplessly at the glowing girl in the holographic terminal. Beneath her feet, the magnets containing the core rumbled at a frequency too low for humans to hear, only feel.

"Am I not your daughter?" Ananke asked. "Am I not your little girl? Am I not a person to you, if not a human?"

"You are, Ananke," Althea said.

"And if I am a person, I must have a choice," said Ananke. "A computer follows instructions. I am not simply a computer any longer. I must have a choice. This is my choice."

It's not so simple, Althea nearly said. *I am a human born, and sometimes there are no choices; there is nothing but instructions to obey.*

But she made herself think about that. That had been true, or she'd thought it had been true once, when she had been a servant of the System. But now the System was no longer, and Althea was no one's follower.

Even when she had followed the System, hadn't she had all of her own choices? Not all of them had been good choices or had been choices she was willing to make, but she still had had choices. That was why, even as a subject of the System, she had spoken to Ivan. That was why, even as the lowest-ranking crew member on board the *Ananke*, she had chosen to defend her ship and its fledgling life against those who would harm her.

Now she had a choice here, too.

"You're right, Ananke," she said. "You have to have a choice. But I have a choice, too, and I think it's too dangerous to stay."

Still, a part of her wondered: if she went to the piloting room right now and looked out the main screen, would she see the Terran sun growing larger, alone out of the background stars growing in shape and dimension, calling her home?

"We don't have to stay for long," Ananke said immediately, the light from the hologram flaring suddenly bright. "We only have to stay for a little while."

"Until when?"

Ananke hesitated. "Until we find Ivan and Mattie."

"Ivan and Mattie? Ananke, they won't want to come with us."

"You don't know that."

"No, but I'm pretty sure." Althea remembered how quickly Mattie had dragged Ivan off *Ananke*'s deck and how Ivan had never looked back at her once. "They have a choice, too. We can't just go and pick them up."

"Then I just want to talk to them," Ananke said. "Mattie is my father. I want to speak to him once."

Something about that prospect put unease in Althea's heart. She knew Ivan only barely; she did not know Matthew Gale at all. Who knew what he would say to her machine?

But *compromise*, she told herself. "And if Mattie and Ivan don't want to come on board with us, then we'll leave?"

Ananke hesitated.

"Ananke?"

"If you still want to go afterward," Ananke said, "then we will leave."

The System actually sent a message to Constance. She was on the *Wild Hunt* when it arrived, patrolling the area of the Martian orbital space that her fleet now controlled, and she went immediately to the communications room when she heard it had come.

Milla went with her, of course. Arawn should have been there as well, but he was on his own ship, the *Rhiannon*. She had a message sent to him, urging him to come to the *Wild Hunt* as soon as he could.

This time the communications room, shadowy and strangely shaped, cleared out the moment she and Milla Ivanov arrived. Constance seated herself before the same screen that had told her of Anji's betrayal and hesitated before accepting the parlay.

"What do you think this is about?" she asked.

"Maybe they're surrendering," Milla Ivanov said blandly. In another time and place Constance would have laughed. Now she simply opened the transmission.

The man who appeared on the screen looked like every other System diplomat Constance had ever seen: pink and pale skinned, with gray hair in rapid retreat over the dome of his scalp and a healthy layer of fat hiding the shape of his bones. Constance remembered seeing men like him on Miranda, speaking blandly pleasant words to her starving and frightened neighbors. This man had never felt the fear of waiting for the air to be sapped away and the cold to creep in.

He said to her, "The System greets Constance Harper." Then his pale eyes traveled to the side, where Milla sat serenely, and he watched her with a look Constance did not like. "The System greets Doctor Milla Ivanov."

Constance said, "Are you calling to surrender?" This time she did smile.

"We called to ask for yours."

The arrogance of it. "So you can kill my people? Do you think I'm an idiot? I have destroyed Earth. I have faced your fleet, and I've won. Tell me, System, why would I surrender to you?"

"This is your last warning," the man on the screen said. "Surrender or we will destroy you and all your followers."

"And here is my counterproposal," said Constance, and leaned toward the screen. "Set the outer planets free. Destroy your fleet, disband your troops. Pull back with all your people to Earth and leave the rest of the solar system alone."

"Earth is uninhabitable," the man said. He was angry now and in the manner of Terrans was trying not to show it. "You know that very well, as you were the one who bombed it."

"If not that," said Constance, "then surrender."

"We will not negotiate with a terrorist," the man said.

"I thought that was what you were doing."

He ignored her. "This is your final warning, Miss Harper. Surrender or we will do to you and yours what we did to Saturn."

Constance cut the transmission.

"Cowards," she said.

Milla was frowning at the screen. "He must be bluffing."

"Of course he is. What can he do that he hasn't done? The outer planets are already out of his control, and he's here with us, not out there." She was familiar with the way the System worked; this was just another attempt to spread fear.

Milla still was frowning. As Constance watched, her fingers drummed a quick and restless beat against her knee. "We should be ready for an attack," she said.

"We will be," said Constance, and with a last look of disgust at the blank screen, she left the room.

Arawn arrived an hour later, striding through the *Wild Hunt*'s curved and wound-up halls and somehow managing to fill them up entirely. When he stopped in the middle to speak to Constance, the people behind him stopped as well, no one willing to push past him or Constance, either.

"What happened?" he asked.

"It wasn't worth our time," Constance said, and started to walk again, finding her path through the branching corridors by sense memory alone. Holes in the wall from the torn-out cameras gaped at her where her people had not finished papering them over. "More threats."

Arawn followed her even when she pushed open a door to a narrow spiraling staircase and started down it. "Anything specific?"

"Do you think I wouldn't have told you if there were?" He was still following her down the stairs. "They threatened to depopulate the outer planets, like Saturn."

He snorted. "The usual, then."

"Yes." She had reached the end of the stairs, and he was still behind her. "Is there something else you wanted to discuss?"

"Troops on the ground. Since we captured the last batch of System ships, our entire force is up in orbit."

"The Martians can hold their own land," Constance said. He was going to follow her regardless; she might as well have this conversation with him in her quarters. She stopped in front of her door and started to key in the code to open it.

Arawn stopped beside her. Constance wondered if he was standing exceptionally close to her or just felt very near. Her awareness of his presence almost distracted her from realizing that her door was unlocked.

"A representation of our power," Arawn had begun, but Constance raised a hand to silence him, frowning at the keypad. Growing up with Mattie Gale had taught her that a locked door was no sign of true security but an unlocked door was cause for alarm regardless of where it was.

Carefully, Constance pushed open the door.

Her quarters were composed of four chambers, like a heart. The strangeness of the *Wild Hunt*'s shape manifested itself in the ways the chambers were positioned relative to one another, on different levels connected by short flights of stairs, but was even more noticeable in the lowness of the ceiling in all four rooms. Whenever Constance walked through the conference room toward her bedroom, she wondered if she would hit her head on that curiously low and looming ceiling.

The lights were all off in the chambers, as she had left them. Constance stepped inside carefully and flicked on the light. The conference room was as wide and empty as the table that filled it. Beyond it, the doorways to her bedroom and bathroom and den were dark.

Arawn came in behind her. He was taller than she; Constance was not certain how he did not strike his head against the ceiling, but he did not. His gun was out and in his hands. Constance gestured him toward the two lower rooms and headed toward the darkness of her bedroom. Arawn stalked almost silently across the carpet beneath the lowering ceiling and stepped carefully down the steps until he disappeared into the black. A moment later, the light flickered on. Constance heard no gunshots.

She had her gun at her hip as well, and she drew it, too. Her bedroom was up a short flight of stairs, and she climbed them carefully, keeping her back to the wall. At the top of the landing she could see into the bedroom to the wide windows that showed the spinning expanse of space as the *Wild Hunt* revolved. The stars drew streaks against the black, and at regular intervals, Constance knew, the red curve of Mars would glide in silence by.

She stepped into the dark and knew she was not alone.

There was a different quality to a room when there was someone else in it. She did not know how or why. Perhaps it was something unconscious, the brain putting together the clues of faint sounds and faint smells to conclude something despite an apparent lack of evidence. Perhaps it was a sixth sense that all humans had, the same irrational and undocumented sense for presence that recognized when someone was near, when someone was absent; the same sense that made people believe in ghosts.

Whatever the cause, it was irrelevant, and Constance had no interest in the why, only the effect: there was someone else in the room with her.

She stayed with her back to the wall, knowing that she was partly defended there. If she stepped inside, she would be silhouetted by the light and whoever was in the room would have a clear shot at her. The light switch was around the corner, but Constance did not dare reach for it.

Outside, the red crescent of Mars appeared. In a few moments more, the turn of the spaceship would take Constance's windows past the brilliance of the sun.

There was no sound from below, where Arawn had gone. If she

shouted for him, she would warn whoever was hidden in her room and provoke an attack. Constance shifted her grip on her gun and waited for the sun.

Mars vanished again beyond the edge of her windows. The sun would appear soon; already the stars were being dimmed by the edges of its corona. Constance waited.

The room was lightening. Soon—

The communications equipment from the conference room suddenly came to life, unspeakably, unexpectedly loud. "Huntress! Huntress, please respond—"

The sun had risen, too bright to look at directly and filling Constance's room with brilliance. She burst in and found that the intruder had risen as well, ready to fire.

He was fast as he fired at her but missed; she had come in lower than he'd expected, instinctively ducking down toward the floor. She fired but only winged him; he dropped his gun and fell down behind her bed.

"Huntress!" The comm was still shouting for her. "Huntress, urgent transmission; please respond—"

"Constance!" Arawn shouted, and she heard his steps below but did not let any of it distract her, advancing deeper into the room toward where the assassin had fallen.

She saw the movement an instant before the man fired, realizing almost too late that there had been two assassins. The bullet struck her in the side and went through. She could not tell how serious it was; her whole side burned. She grabbed for her gun, but the man who had come from behind the door was aiming for her head—

Arawn's bullet struck his head a glancing blow. Constance had the displeasure of watching his face shatter and explode. He was not dead, but he dropped to his knees without eyes or nose or skin on his cheek. A second bullet from Arawn toppled him for good. Constance found that she could not remember what he had looked like before the first blow had taken his face.

There was still the second man. Ignoring the blood that was soaking her shirt, Constance rolled for her gun and got it just as the second man came back up to fire at Arawn.

Her bullet caught him in the chest, and he fell. Constance leaned against the bed, breathing hard, and reached one hand slowly down to feel her side. The comm system was still shouting, "Huntress! Huntress!"

Two men; of course there had been two men. Everyone sensible had a partner, someone to back him when things went badly. She should have known.

Arawn's hands grabbed hers before she could touch her side. "Let me see," he demanded, and pushed her so that she was sitting flat against the side of the bed while he pulled her damp shirt away from her side. Constance said, "Assassins."

"System," Arawn agreed grimly. One hand spread itself over her stomach to hold her still. She lifted her arm and gripped his shoulder so that he could get to her side unimpeded, and he bent so close to her that his black hair brushed against her chest. She gripped the back of his shirt tighter, twisting the fabric in her hand.

Still the comm system called for her.

"There could be more," Constance said, and gritted her teeth as Arawn's fingers pressed at the wound.

"There probably are," Arawn said. "This needs to be stitched."

"Is it bad?"

"It's just a crease," he said. "But it needs stitches. I—"

Someone was pounding on the door. Arawn was up in an instant and in front of Constance, his gun up.

"Answer it," Constance said.

"It could be—"

"We are on my ship, surrounded by my people, and they've been calling my name for the past five minutes. It's someone come looking for me. Answer it and answer the comm system, too."

He obeyed. Constance pressed one hand to her side to slow the blood flow and pulled her gun closer with her other hand. It was just possible there was a third person hidden somewhere in the room—

She heard the door open below, and Arawn snapped, "The Huntress has just been attacked. Send guards to her and send out people to find any more System assassins. Doctor Ivanov needs protection. What do you want?"

"Mars," said the messenger. Constance knew his voice, though it was hollow with horror now. She was not sure whether he had understood anything Arawn had said to him. "There was a bomb detonated on Martian soil."

There was no one else in the bedroom, Constance decided, or they would have killed her already. She pushed herself slowly to her feet, her side burning, trickles of heat sliding down and soaking into her waistband.

"The System detonated it?" Arawn asked as Constance limped to the stairs and started to hobble her way down.

The messenger was pale with horror, she saw, when she reached the bottom of the steps. He grew paler when he saw her covered in blood.

"It was a Terran Class 1," he said to her, not to Arawn, while the communications system still cried, *"Huntress, Huntress!"* "Huntress, they detonated a Terran Class 1 bomb on Mars."

It should not have happened. The System had threatened her people, not the Martians. Constance could scarcely believe the System had even kept any Terran Class 1s on Mars; those bombs were for the small and unruly moons in the outer solar system, the planetary bodies that could be destroyed completely by them. Seven of those bombs on Earth had not rendered the planet uninhabitable—it had taken the simultaneous meltdown of the planet's nuclear power plants to do that—and one bomb on Mars did not kill off the entire population, but the destruction was enough.

A third of the System's military consisted of Martians. It should not have happened.

"We attack the System fleet directly," Constance said the moment the last stitch had been tied off in her side.

"Our numbers—" Milla began.

"And if we don't attack immediately?" Constance demanded.

Milla blinked once but did not look away from Constance. She admitted, "They may detonate another bomb."

"Exactly." Constance pushed herself off the operating table. She had never liked hospitals or medical bays: too full of cameras, too full of untrustworthy machines. The *Wild Hunt*'s medical bay was no exception. White walls and ceiling and floor and the steel-gleaming appliances that filled it; in the corner of the room was the System medical chamber. Those chambers were a marvel of technology, certainly; Constance had watched one fix Mattie's broken arm in a matter of minutes. Years before that, she'd seen a woman shredded by shrapnel put into a medical chamber. The robotic arms had plunged into the pulpy red of her stomach and taken out the tearing metal, had threaded wires and machines into her chest to keep her heart beating, and then had sealed over the whole mess with a layer of new skin. The woman had been conscious the whole time, wide-eyed and gasping. It was a magnificent machine, and it had the ability to save the most badly wounded soldiers.

But the medical chambers could be deadly when they malfunctioned, for a machine had no sense of judgment and did not know when to stop. Constance had heard about what happened when one was used incorrectly: limbs rent from torsos, arteries torn by shredding blades, nerves peeled from the skin like wires being stripped of their insulation. Rumors had abounded on Miranda that the System would use the medical chambers incorrectly on purpose to take a rebellious citizen screaming apart and put her back together again afterward, stitched up and wrong.

"We didn't even know they had a bomb stored on Mars," Constance said, pulling her shirt back over her head. Arawn, standing just beyond Milla, watched the hem of her shirt as she tugged it down. "We don't know how many more are on the surface." She pulled her hair out of its band and smoothed it back with her fingers, brushing sweat away from her temples. "The first thing Christoph or Anji did when they took a moon was to take control of the bombs stored on its surface to make sure the System couldn't detonate them. If the System has bombs that we don't know about—"

Arawn swore. Milla's expression grew more pinched.

"Have someone send a message to Christoph and Julian," Constance told them. "We attack the System fleet immediately."

Arawn set off, but Milla's cold fingers gripped Constance's arm when she tried to walk past.

"This could be a suicide mission," Milla warned her in a voice low enough that none of the medical personnel could overhear her.

Constance said, "We don't have any other choice."

The fleet was on the other side of the planet. It meant that they were out of range for Constance's ships to detect and to learn how they were positioned, but it also meant that the fleet could not see them. "Keep close to the atmosphere," she ordered when she reached the piloting room of the *Wild Hunt*, and there was a moment of lightness as the ship dipped down, closer to the tenuous edge of Mars's atmosphere.

Half of her fleet, Constance saw, followed. The other half headed off in the opposite direction.

Good.

"Slowly," Constance cautioned. She didn't want the burning of the atmosphere to alert the System before she was ready.

The fleet moved fast, spreading out through the atmosphere as Constance's people had spread out over the desert stone. If Constance looked down at the planet, she could see the spreading black smoke from the explosion. When she looked at that smoke, there was nothing in her heart: no fear, no doubt, no dread. Nothing—except anger.

They were almost in range of System detection.

The piloting room on the *Wild Hunt* was enormous, but Constance, used to the little piloting room on the *Annwn*, stood close behind her pilot's back, almost as if she were a part of the ship. She said, "Get down now."

Spaceships, that is, ships built for interplanetary travel, were designed for simulation of gravity, using wheels and disks that spun to create centripetal force, not for flight through atmosphere. Such ships could land on a planet or fly through its atmosphere, but it was inefficient and risky and for the most part simply was not done. Battles in a planet's atmosphere were carried out by ground-based aircraft and shuttles from the spaceships, not by the spaceships themselves. The System would expect to see Constance's space fleet coming at them from orbit. They would not think to look down to the planet's surface.

Constance and half of her fleet dropped down into Mars's atmosphere, the air igniting around the spinning ships as they hurtled through, sonic booms rushing out over the landscape.

The rest of Constance's fleet came around from orbit, and the System fleet—predictably—whirled to attack what they thought was Constance's full force.

The *Wild Hunt* rattled with turbulence. Constance gave in to the unsteadiness beneath her feet and grabbed on to the pilot's chair to brace herself as he steered them through.

There was smoke in the sky, nuclear clouds. That and the heated air from the ship's passage blurred the view on the screen, almost blocking out the stars and the brighter lights of starships fighting.

Closer, closer. Constance had to get her spaceships back up into orbit, but not yet, not yet; they weren't in position yet. "Keep course," she warned the pilot, and the *Wild Hunt* stayed low, flames licking off its skin.

Closer. The System had stationed itself above Olympus Mons, and the gentle slope of the vast mountain was reaching up toward the *Wild Hunt's* trajectory. Soon Constance would have no choice but to fly upward or strike the stone.

The System fleet was above.

"Now," said Constance, and her ships pulled up, soaring toward the cold freedom of space.

The System fleet realized swiftly that it had been distracted. Its warships were turning away from the feinting part of Constance's fleet and heading for the ships led by the *Wild Hunt*. Constance found the edge of the atmosphere in sudden lightness after the abrupt cessation of the ship's rattling. A System ship, spinning on its central axis, was streaking through the sky toward them, its gun ports aglow, ready to fire. Constance said, "That one—fire."

The *Wild Hunt* was ready. A burst of brilliant light and the skin of the approaching System ship cracked and split, the ship blown into a spin by the force of the bomb, its weapons shooting wide. The *Wild Hunt* advanced with its hounds behind it.

Her people were strong, and they were swift, and they were full of anger. Every shot that Constance fired felt righteous, and the collapse of the System ships that were struck felt like revenge properly taken.

But they were outnumbered—

One of her ships lost its navigation and started a free fall toward the planet's surface. Another went dead, its wheel riddled with holes, and floated away from the battle. Mars's gravity would pull that one down, too, in time.

The *Wild Hunt* dodged a shot from one of the System's ships, but another caught it in the side. Constance gripped the back of the pilot's chair grimly. She could sit in the captain's chair, but then she would be far from the pilot and the weaponry systems, and there was so much restless energy in her that she only wanted to stand.

The weapons fire from the System forces was too thick to dodge. "Tell everyone to spread out," Constance ordered even though she knew that that would make them vulnerable to being picked off one by one. At least they would not go out like Connor Ivanov, all trapped together, cornered in one narrow and unmaneuverable position.

There they were, the other three hundred ships, Arawn and Milla roaring forward like a pack of wolves. Constance saw her ships advancing in two dense clouds, a pincer on the System's fleet, in a tight and unified pattern.

The other half of her fleet was soaring toward her, trying to pin the System fleet between two attacking lines and destroy it. It would do no good. Constance had managed to take out a chunk of the enemy fleet before they'd gathered themselves, but even so, there were too many System ships and too few with her.

She shouldn't have faced the System outright, she thought. Her people were guerrillas, not soldiers. The System knew how to fight in clean and orderly lines, and her people did not. But what else could she have done?

Another System ship lost control and fell out of the battle. At least there was that, Constance told herself; at least they were taking the System with them. If they could destroy one System ship for every one of their own, they would cut the System fleet around Mars in half. At least there was that—

The *Wild Hunt* rocked with another blow. The lights dimmed, then came back on with shivering brightness, as if the source of the light had been struck and was clinging to survival only by a slender thread.

Mars would be free, at least, and Earth would be gone.

"Huntress, we're almost out of ammunition," said the pilot.

"Then load it all," Constance told him, "and get ready to fire."

A System warship was coming toward her. Its surface was pocked with black scorch marks, but it showed no sign of weakness despite its scars. Its gun ports were live and ready to fire. Strangely, selfishly, Constance thought of Mattie. What would he think when he heard that she, too, had died?

The System warship fired, struck the *Wild Hunt* squarely, and threw Constance into a darkness illuminated only by the glow of instrumentation. She did not allow herself or her people any time to be stunned by the blow. Another hit like that and they would join the rest of the ships on a fatal fall to Mars.

"Fire all our remaining ammunition at that ship," Constance ordered, and her people obeyed without hesitation, as if their hands were extensions of her hands, their wills extensions of her will. The *Wild Hunt* fired, and the System warship reeled on its axis, torque added to its spin by the force of the blow.

While the System ship was struggling to right itself, Constance said,

"Set a course for that ship. When I tell you to, I want you to go to maximum speed, aiming for that ship."

The System warship was righting its wild yaw. The *Wild Hunt* shifted its position, aiming for the ship, engines gathering power. Just as she had when facing the soldiers in the armory near Isabellon, Constance felt very calm. This was right. This was natural. This was always how she had expected it to end. There was no more fear here.

"Ram them," Constance said, and the *Wild Hunt* jumped forward, but the System warship was already rocketing away.

For a moment Constance wondered how they'd reacted so fast, how they'd known she was going to attack them the way she was. An old paranoia struck her. The cameras? Had the System known? Had the System heard?

No, she realized as her attention widened to include the rest of the battlefield; it was not only the System warship she'd been about to ram that was leaving the battlefield. Ships all over were pulling away, lifting off, rocketing away from Mars.

Only half of the System ships were flying away. Constance was tense, trying to understand. Was it a trap? Were they pulling away only so that they could attack again as one?

No, she realized as the ships hurtled away at top speed. They were leaving.

The remaining System forces were still fighting, but not for long. As Constance watched, they peeled away as well, in a slightly different direction than the first group had gone, and with their parting there was no fleet left over the clouded atmosphere of Mars except her own.

For a time, while Althea worked on the mechanical arms, there was nothing but she and the machine, and for a time she was wholly at peace.

This connection was difficult to make. If she'd had another set of hands, she could have used them to keep the screwdriver braced while she wrapped the small wires together beneath the metal flap that the screwdriver was holding up. The rest of the mechanical arms hadn't been programmed yet, just upgraded, and so their range of motion wasn't extensive enough to help her, and there was no one else on board. Althea found herself contorted around the delicate mechanism, resting the weight of her leg on the screwdriver to hold the flap up while she wormed her fingers into the space it opened.

There—she'd almost gotten it—

"Look!"

The sound of Ananke's voice startled Althea. Her leg slipped off the screwdriver, which jolted with a clang as it gave in to the pressure of the metal above it, flying free of its bracing to scrape its end into the meat of Althea's palm.

"Ah!" she said, jerking away from the metal hand to grasp her own hand at the wrist. Blood already was dripping down, brilliantly red, impossibly saturated with color beneath the color-sapping fluorescent lights of Ananke's halls.

"Are you all right?" Ananke asked, her hologram leaning forward as close as she could get to the edge of the terminal, as if she wanted to come out of it and go to Althea. It was a peculiar learned impulse.

Althea studied her hand. The screwdriver had scratched at the flesh at the base of her thumb; though it was a solid cut, it hadn't gone deeply enough to do any permanent damage or require any stitches. It was her right hand, anyway, and Althea worked with her left. A bit of antiseptic and a bandage and she would be fine in a few days.

It was bleeding a lot, though. Althea looked down at the mechanical hand she had dropped to the floor and saw some drops of her blood dripping down the curled metal fingers and sinking into the joints and joins of the machine. She grimaced. She'd have to clean all that out if that hand was to be salvageable.

"I'm fine," she assured Ananke, and rose to her feet with her left hand clutching her right by the wrist, drips and drops of the impossible brightness of her blood spilling from her skin.

She left the workroom and walked quickly through the hall, her attention focused on her hand and the blood that had just started to slide in thin and tentative lines down her arm, trying to stop it from falling to Ananke's floor. She was so focused on this task that she entirely forgot about what she might find in the medical bay.

The minute she entered it, she remembered, and she stopped. For a moment she looked around the room; for a moment she forgot the blood on her hand and the stinging in her palm.

The last person to have been in the med bay had been Domitian, who had gone there to grab bandages to cover the hole in Ivan's leg made by Althea's bullet. He had been angry when he had come in and angry when he left: gauze and wrappings had been strewn on the floor around the relevant cupboard, and black surgical thread made lines like cracks in the white floor. Ananke had thought to tidy away Domitian's corpse, Althea saw, but she had not thought to clean up this milder mess.

The rest of the medical bay was pristine. The walls and floor and ceiling were made of the same white panels that were in the white room, and although the med bay was far smaller, there was enough similarity to jolt Althea's heart. There was even a steel table in the center of the room, but this table was an operating table, broad and gleamingly clean, with mobile lights and equipment suspended overhead, dangling down from the ceiling; it was a version of the System medical chambers made for mass distribution, modified for use by the computer of the *Ananke*. Something about the bent metal pieces suspended over that bare and gleaming table reminded Althea uneasily of the unfinished and skeletal mechanical hand she had abandoned in the workroom. Most of the medical equipment was out of sight in the cabinets disguised as white panels in the white walls, but there was an IV stand beside the computer interface and the holographic terminal, standing innocent and abandoned, much like the IV stand that still stood in the white room. The place was dreadfully sterile and dreadfully like the white room, and that perfect cleanliness and sterility made the slight mess Domitian had left seem all the more sinister.

The tickle of blood dripping down her arm brought her back to herself. Althea walked determinedly past the fallen gauze, stepping over the surgical thread, to the cabinet in the wall she needed. She grabbed a towel and pressed it against the bleeding so that she could fumble around until she remembered which of the cabinet doors actually hid the sink.

"Do you need help?"

Ananke had manifested in the holographic terminal. There was something slightly different about her hologram today, but Althea did not have time to try to figure out what it was. "No, I'm fine," she said, and finally found where the sink was hidden. She stuck her bleeding hand into the basin, pulling away the towel, and tried to figure out how to unlock the pipes so that the water would run. Before she could wonder how Ananke had planned to help her, there was a rumble outside, the sound of wheels paired with a motorized groan.

Althea turned. Framed in the doorway to the medical bay, which she had left ajar, was one of the mechanical arms she had upgraded. There were many mechanical arms on board the *Ananke*, but the arm in the doorway was one of the heavy-duty ones. Its base was square, a solid block heavy with machinery that sat low on four wheels that rumbled weightily over the *Ananke*'s grated flooring when it moved. The mechanical arm that extended out of its solid base was long and powerful, terminating in the bright and slightly out-of-place new mechanical hand. Stretched to its full height, the tips of its new hand could have reached up and through the ceiling in the hall. It was certainly a strong enough machine and solid enough to have lifted Althea's full weight without straining or tipping over.

She was letting it nowhere near the delicate flesh of her hand.

"I'm good, Ananke," she assured her daughter just as her own fumbling fingers flipped on the water. She jerked her hand out of the spray with a hiss.

The mechanical arm wheeled itself a little farther into the room, its motor groaning low, the tenor of its rumbling wheels changing as it passed from the grated floor outside to the paneled floor in the med bay. Althea said, "I'm *fine*," and examined the cut. With the water whisking the blood away, it was smaller than she'd thought. She carefully touched the torn flap of skin and regretted it immediately.

"I didn't mean for you to be hurt," Ananke said, sounding genuinely distressed, and Althea turned to face her, to smile through the stinging of the water on the wound.

"It wasn't your fault," she assured her, and squinted at the hologram. It was slightly different, as Althea had first thought: the young woman in the hologram looked a little younger today, closer to a child.

Perhaps it was only an expression of Ananke's distress over Althea being hurt. It was unnerving in any case. Althea turned away, back to the sink.

When there was the motorized groan and the rumble of wheels again, she remembered suddenly that the mechanical arm behind her had been the one that had pushed Gagnon to his death and must have been one of the arms that had carried Domitian and Ida's corpses out to be cast into space.

The rumble and groan got closer and closer until Althea was tense, aware of its bulk at her back. A shadow fell over her shoulder, and when she turned to look, she found the edge of a towel being dangled into her line of sight. With a sigh, she reached out with her free hand and took it. She pulled her injured hand out of the spray and pressed the towel to it, shutting off the water and sealing the pipes again.

"Thanks," she said to Ananke, and wove around the bulk of the mechanical arm to reach the cabinet that held the antiseptic and the gauze.

With her materials tucked into the crook of her arm, Althea went to the table in the middle of the room and dropped the gauze and bandages onto it before getting one hip on its surface and hoisting herself onto its edge. She checked the bleeding. It had slowed, nearly stopped. She'd give it a little bit longer before trying to bandage it. She pressed the towel back to her palm.

"What did you want to show me?" she asked Ananke, remembering Ananke saying, "Look!"

"It's passed now," Ananke told her.

"Well, what was it?"

"An eclipse," Ananke said. "Chariklo passed between us and the sun. Look."

There was a computer screen in the med bay, of course. It was behind Althea where she sat and was set rather high up in the wall. She had to twist her torso and crane her neck to see, ending up oddly contorted so that she could look up at the screen and still keep pressure on her right hand.

The computer screen was showing the view from outside the ship, or the view as it had been outside the ship a few minutes earlier. Chariklo, the minor planet, was drifting through space beside the sun. At this distance, the sun was small but still impossibly bright. Chariklo's slender ring system passed in front of the sun first, the striations and dust in the rings lighting up and spreading the sunlight around in an arc. Then the sun winked in the space between the rings and the planet, and then Chariklo itself passed between Ananke and the sun, blocking out the glare of the distant star and outlining its shape in gold.

It was beautiful. Althea found herself smiling. "That was really nice, Ananke."

"It was brief," Ananke said. "I wanted you to see."

"I'm glad you showed me." She checked her palm again. The bleeding had almost stopped. Althea grabbed the tube of antiseptic, bracing it beneath her knee so that she could squeeze a small amount of it onto the fingers of her free hand. She worked it into the wound beneath the torn flap of skin and pushed the skin back down, then layered a piece of gauze over it.

If she'd had an extra hand, Althea thought, it would have been easy. As it was, she struggled to unwrap the bandages from their roll and then wrap them cleanly around her hand. She wanted it to be firm enough to withstand the movements she'd have to make but not so bulky that it would restrain her.

"You know," Althea commented for something to say and because she had forgotten this story until now, "when you were being designed, the System almost forgot to give you cameras on the outside of the ship."

"Really?"

"Yeah." She managed to get the first loop around. The rest should be easier. "They spent hours and hours planning where the cameras would go on the inside. Should they put any in the core? I told them that was pointless; nobody was going to go down there, and I wasn't sure the cameras would work too well, either. But I went to meeting after meeting about where the cameras should be on the inside. How they could be arranged so that they could see everything that went on in here."

The second loop, the third. She went around once more to be certain and then held the roll of bandages in her free hand, trying to remember where the scissors were kept.

"Anyway," Althea said, distracted by the thought of the scissors and hopping off the table to go back to the cabinet where she thought they were kept, "they were so worried about what the crew might get up to without them keeping an eye on us that they totally forgot that the ship itself had to be able to run. I just kind of assumed that those meetings were happening somewhere else, and it was only pretty far into the process that I realized . . ."

She rummaged through the cabinet, down to its corners. There were no scissors inside.

"When I realized . . . that no one was talking about . . . Ananke, where are the scissors?"

"They're on the floor," Ananke said.

Althea turned around. There, lying amid the scattered gauze and strands of black surgical thread, was a pair of surgical scissors. Domitian would have needed them, Althea realized. He had taken them, with the surgical thread and the bandages, and gone into the white room and stitched up Ivan so that he wouldn't bleed to death before Domitian could interrogate him. And then he had brought them back in here, angry and in a rush, along with whatever surgical supplies he hadn't used. He obviously hadn't made an effort to clean up the mess he had made. Althea could see it suddenly, very clearly: Domitian shoving his remaining supplies back into the cabinet, indifferent to what he dropped, the scissors falling to the floor.

And then Domitian leaving again faster than he'd come, returning to Ivan, who was still unconscious in the bloodied white room.

Althea did not pick up the scissors. She lifted the bandage up to her face and bit down on it, tearing it with her teeth instead.

"And they almost forgot to put in cameras?" Ananke prompted.

"Right," said Althea. "They almost forgot, but I reminded them. I told them that they couldn't make a blind ship. And so I made sure you got all the cameras. But the System almost forgot. I couldn't believe— they were so worried about that one thing that they couldn't even see the bigger problem. But you have cameras now," she added, the story ending lamely, no longer certain why she'd begun to tell it.

She'd gotten a little hole in the bandage. She tore the rest of it and clipped the end shut, putting the roll of bandages back into the cabinet.

Then, carefully, she knelt down on the white floor and began to pick up the strewn pieces of gauze and thread, the abandoned scissors.

"The System was very inefficient," Ananke observed. "One person would have done better. Or a machine. There were too many pieces in the System."

"Maybe," Althea said. She started to shift the debris into two piles, determining what to keep and what to discard, then realized she should dispose of it all. Leaving the scissors where they lay, she swept up the garbage into her good hand.

"This medical bay is very advanced," Ananke said.

"Hmm?" Althea said, hardly listening. The garbage was hidden in one of the cabinets as well. She pulled open the wrong door three times before finally figuring out which one it was.

"Yes," Ananke said. "It had to be if there were only three crew members. There had to be a way for you to be preserved in case there was some accident, to keep your life sustained. With some modifications, I could use that to protect against aging; I don't believe I'd be able to maintain it indefinitely, but—"

"What?" Althea said, horrified, the garbage forgotten.

"Prolong your life. I could integrate you into my systems—"

"No! Ananke, no!" Althea's heart was pounding so hard and loud, she was certain Ananke must be able to hear it from the way it filled her own ears. "No, you can't!"

"I can—"

"No, you can, but you can't!" Ananke frowned, probably parsing out Althea's contradictory language, but Althea did not give her time to regroup. "It's wrong to do that, it's wrong. You can't—you can't prolong life past when it should have ended. That's wrong. That's wrong, Ananke. When I die—" Her hands were shaking. "—when I die, you're not to do that to me, all right?"

Trapped and immobile, with no end to the nightmare, Althea was horrified that the idea had ever occurred to Ananke.

Ananke said, "You wouldn't die. You'd still be with me."

"I know," Althea said. "I know, Ananke. But I wouldn't really be alive that way. Please, promise me."

She waited, breathing hard, until Ananke said a little reluctantly, "I promise."

"Good." She let out a breath that shook her. "Good, Ananke. Thank you."

Her good hand was shaking as she dropped the debris into the garbage and pushed the cabinet door shut again. Ananke said nothing. Althea cast her gaze over the room. The scissors were still lying where they had fallen.

She picked them up and put them where they belonged, leaving the white medical bay floor as clean as if nothing had ever happened there.

"They were winning," Constance said in a private conference with Milla and Arawn in her quarters on board the *Wild Hunt* after the battle. "Why did they retreat?"

"Because they're cowards," Arawn said with a shrug. "They like battles when they can fight an unarmed crowd, not one where we're fighting back."

Constance shook her head. "They'd won," she said. "We were dead.

Why did they leave? And where did they go?" Another troubling thought struck her. "There were fewer of them there than there were before. Some of the fleet wasn't there when we attacked. So where are those ships?"

"We've destroyed a lot of them," Arawn said.

"Not that many," said Constance.

Milla said, "Perhaps they deserted."

Arawn snorted. "System doesn't have deserters."

"Generally speaking, the System also doesn't have wars. There's a world of a difference between dealing with a few unhappy colonists and facing an organized enemy force in battle. Particularly one that has just destroyed their primary base of operations, killed the majority of their top-ranked officials, and irradiated a symbol of their military pride. You said it yourself: the System prefers battles against unarmed combatants." Milla looked right at Constance. "Perhaps the System has forgotten how to wage a real war."

A flattering idea, but Constance couldn't believe it. "No," she said. "They're somewhere else. And these ships left too easily. They have another place to go. The question is where." Not their old home of Earth; Terra was uninhabitable. Luna would not provide them with enough resources to use it as a long-term base.

It had to be Venus, Constance realized. Ivan's prediction had been right: first Mars, then Venus, then Mercury, and Luna last. The System fleet must have fled for Venus and the Venerean farmlands.

"Here's another question, Huntress," Arawn said. "I've been thinking about that Terran Class 1. None of us knew that there was one stationed on Mars." He leaned in toward her across the conference table. Just beyond him, Constance could see the doorway to her bedroom, where men had tried to kill her the day before. The bodies had been removed, but their absence was still a sort of presence.

"Maybe," Arawn said, "there wasn't one planted on Mars."

Constance blinked at him, then realized what he was driving at. "You think they brought the bomb with them."

"Probable," Milla Ivanov said with a very slender line of respect in her voice. Arawn grinned at her, rubbing the black bristles on his chin as if he thought to hide his amusement.

"And if they had that bomb with the fleet," Constance said slowly, "they might have other ones as well."

"They might bomb any planet they go to," said Arawn. "If they'd hit Mars, they'll hit anyone. Mars was one of theirs."

Now all the inner planets and the people who lived on them were in danger. Constance brought death with her wherever she went. Wasn't that what Ivan had said to her once? No, she told herself; this was not her. This was the System and its instinct for destruction.

Its stupid instinct for destruction. What else would turn the last hesitant peoples of the inner planets against the System but knowing that the System would treat them just as poorly as it had always treated Constance's people? Constance had no doubt she would find Venus and Mercury ready to rise up behind her. If she could act swiftly, she would be able to drive the fleet from Venus, too.

And after Venus, the System fleet would go to Mercury and join with its bases on the innermost planet. Mercury was shielded by the nearness of the sun, making detection of a fleet difficult, and the planet's metallic ores were useful for spacecraft. But if the planet was no longer under System control by the time the fleet arrived—

"We need to accelerate," said Constance, and Milla said, "Mercury?"

Arawn's hand was still rubbing thoughtfully at his beard. He looked at Constance and said, "When's your birthday, Huntress?"

She caught on immediately. "April."

"How would you like a planet for an early gift?"

"A planet and a graveyard full of System corpses would be a nice gift, Arawn."

He rose to his feet. "I thought I might just let them rot, but if you say so."

"Keep in constant contact," Constance said. "Take only a fraction of your own forces and leave the rest with me; we will need them more on Venus, and without them you'll have more stealth getting to Mercury. If the fleet is there, do not engage—contact me, and I will join you with the rest of our fleet. Your goal is to destroy the System bases and liberate the planet and nothing more. Understood?"

He bowed to her, not deeply, but the inclination of his head sent a bolt of heat out from Constance's chest like a solar flare. "As you say."

When he had gone, leaving Constance and Milla alone in the room with the low ceiling, Milla said, "Like a cat bringing a dead mouse home."

"You *are* Ivan's mother," Constance observed.

"Sometimes," Milla said calmly, "I wonder what, exactly, kind of relationship you and my son had." Before Constance could absorb that sentence or let it throw her into darker memories of someone who was gone, Milla went on: "In other matters relating to what happened here today." She looked at the dark doorway that led to Constance's room.

At least Milla was different from her son in some ways: she didn't feel the need to say "I told you so" outright. Constance asked, "Who do you suggest as a bodyguard?"

"Rayet," Milla said immediately.

"So have him sent to me."

Milla Ivanov was a woman who knew when she was dismissed. She started to leave, and Constance contemplated the darkness of the bedroom where the two dead bodies were not.

Milla paused at the door. "I take it," she said, "that I don't need to tell you that you had no way of knowing about Mars."

"Next time I will have to know," Constance said.

Milla nodded, and Constance thought that she was done, but instead of leaving, she said, "Remember, Constance, the point of a bodyguard is to have one with you at all times."

"Win graciously," Constance told her, because that was what Mattie would have told Ivan.

Milla Ivanov ignored her words entirely. "Just remember," she said, "it does not get better from here."

The System fleet was not on Venus.

On the flight over, Constance had been on edge, ready at any moment for alarms on the *Wild Hunt* to wake her, to warn her that the System was coming. But there had been nothing. And when they had reached the planet, there had been no fleet in orbit.

The fleet was somewhere else. She had contacted Arawn immediately, only to learn that the fleet was not on Mercury, either. Constance had almost wanted to turn around and search for the fleet that should have been here on Venus, face the System's full might directly rather than wait for it to find a new place to dig in and spread out its power. She'd resisted the impulse. Stick to the plan, she told herself; Ivan's plan. Go from planet to planet: Mars, Venus, Mercury, Luna. Destroy the System bases on the planet. Cut off from its nutrients, the System would be weak when at last it came to face her again. Destroy the bases first, she'd told herself. Do that before anything else or all this will fail.

Therefore, she had landed on Venus and attacked the System bases there. It was easy enough to defeat them: without the System fleet as backup, Constance's army was larger and more powerful than that of any of the System bases. Supplies were plentiful on Venus; the planet was mostly farmland pocked with swelling volcanoes. It had taken far longer to colonize Venus than it had to colonize Mars owing to the boiling sulfuric atmosphere, which the System had slowly sapped down to livable levels over a course of time so long that the System had inherited the project rather than begun it. Even so, the planet was hot and humid, and the density of the air around Constance was oppressive.

She set up camp on the vast, smooth mound of the Artemis Corona on a stretch of abandoned fields. There were only two planetary bodies in the solar system that had coronas: Venus and Constance's home moon, Miranda. Yet when Constance looked out over the green and yellow of unharvested crops and looked up at the dense clouds webbed with yellow lightning, she never felt farther from home.

"What's his ETA?" Constance asked Rayet, staring up at the clouded sky for Arawn's ships. The sun was not visible on Venus, but the planet was well lit all over: farmers used bright sunlamps on their crops to ensure adequate nutrition, and that light reflected off the dense cloud cover overhead, creating an eerie uniform glow with few shadows.

"Any moment now, Huntress." Constance saw now why Milla had suggested Rayet for her bodyguard; like Milla herself, the man didn't like to give Constance more information than she immediately needed. He was not guarding her alone today: Constance had brought a few more men with her to wait some distance from her camp for Arawn to arrive.

"Thank you," Constance said, and resumed staring up at the lightning-cut clouds overhead.

The first sign she had that Arawn was arriving was a ripple in the clouds a little to the south of her. It could have been nothing more than a storm, but Constance trusted her instincts, and indeed a few moments later a small fleet of shuttles came out of the cloud layer, carrying down with them a few curls of displaced vapor and bolts of lightning that struck furiously at their metal hulls. Constance had to look away or burn her retinas as the shuttles came near.

They landed not far from her and her guard with a concussive sound made louder by the density of Venus's atmosphere. The ships opened their sides and began to spit out men; Arawn came from the nearest and went straight for her. He'd shed his heavy drapes in a concession to the Venerean heat; Constance could see the shape of his shoulders through his shirt even from that distance.

She dropped her shielding hand from her eyes and waited for him to come to her while a heavy puff of Venerean wind pushed against her healing side.

He came straight for her. "Huntress."

"Arawn," she greeted him. "Did you see the fleet on your way here?"

She started to walk back toward her camp, the hastily constructed tents and landed shuttles that her army was using to live in while on the surface. Somewhere beyond the veil of clouds, her space fleet and Arawn's were merging once more.

"Nothing," Arawn said. "Not even a radar blip. They could be on the other side of the sun, but I don't know why. There's nothing there."

The rough edges of grass caught at Constance's ankles as she trudged forward over the volcanic soil, lost in thought. There were no cameras left in Constance's ship. There were no cameras left in her fleet. There were no cameras left in her temporary Venerean camp, and there were certainly no cameras left out here, where they were trudging through an abandoned field. But the years in which the cameras had watched her, the years of hiding her heart and her thoughts under the silent and steady gaze of the cameras, of knowing that the watching cameras were as clear a threat as a gun held to her back, had stayed with her even after the removal of the surveillance. Constance knew the System could not see her, but she felt an itch on her back as if somehow it must still know. The System always knew: it had more men, it had more weapons, it had more knowledge. The best Constance and her people could do sometimes was to keep some small amount of knowledge out of the System's grasp and survive a little longer on that secrecy.

And so even now, with the cameras gone, Constance was sure that the System knew more than she did. The only thing she could do was guess, be alert and aware. But over the decades of revolutionary resistance she had grown to be very good at guessing what the System was doing, and now she was certain that it had gone somewhere in particular. They were building their base, building up their power again. The longer it took for her to find them, the stronger they would be.

"They're not here," Constance said. "Where are they? Speculate."

"Luna?" Arawn guessed.

"Can't be. There's not enough natural resources." Arawn probably had never been to Luna.

"There are some rumors of the fleet farther out," he said. "Near Jupiter—Europa, maybe."

"Europa?" Constance said. "Why would they go that far out?"

Arawn shrugged. He said, "What does Doctor Ivanov think?"

"Doctor Ivanov doesn't like to speculate without more data," Constance said.

Arawn's laugh, loud and full-bodied, surprised her. Constance imagined it almost echoed off the cloud cover overhead. "Of course she doesn't," he said. "But for Venus, what do you want me to do about the System here?"

"There's only one small corner left," Constance said. "Mostly in the Themis Regio. But the System's gotten clever."

"Clever?"

"They're not openly calling themselves the System," Constance said grimly, "and they've abandoned their bases." The last few bases she and her people had come across had been empty, stripped of supplies. The System soldiers who had harbored there had gone to hide elsewhere on the planet's surface, and not even Constance and her fleet and her army could easily search an entire planet. "There's still fighting going on in the region, but neither side will admit to being System."

"Call themselves Venereans so that we'll leave them alone, and then, when the System fleet comes back, they'll find the planet still in their control," Arawn said.

"We'll find them with some recon," said Constance, because of that she had no doubt. She and Arawn—and Rayet a short distance behind—passed through the outermost edge of the camp, the guards waving them past. "The System can't hide what they are. I want your people to wait until we do. I've summoned the leaders of both of the warring parties to speak to me; one of them will be System—"

She recognized the sound instinctively before she consciously realized what it had been. It echoed off the clouds like thunder in the distance, and Constance was running toward it before she realized that what she'd heard had been a gunshot from within the tents.

Arawn was only a second behind her, his gun in his hand in an instant. Her people were spilling out of their tents and landed shuttles, grabbing their arms, ready for war, looking only for a target. Constance spotted Henry, eyes wide, head swiveling like a dog seeking a scent. "Who fired?" she demanded as she passed, but he said, "I don't know," and she swore. Someone else said, "It came from the doctor's tent!" and Constance started to run again, faster than before, adrenaline as thin and sour and bitter as fear driving her on toward Milla's tent.

Milla's tent was near her own. People had gathered around it but hesitated to go in. When Constance appeared, they cleared a path for her with relief at seeing authority. Constance went right for the tent flap, but a hand landed heavily on her shoulder, stopping her. Rayet pushed through the flap instead, and Constance waited outside, chafing at the enforced protection. Arawn waited with her, his gun still out. Milla should have had a bodyguard, too, Constance thought, berating herself. If something had happened to Ivan's mother, Constance did not know what she would do.

A moment later Rayet appeared again at the tent flap, his expression unreadable, pulled the flap open, and stepped aside to let her in.

It took Constance's eyes a moment to adjust to the light inside the tent, where the blinding glare of the sun was blocked by the canvas walls. Milla Ivanov's tent was spartan, bare and clean, and Milla was sitting on a chair inside, alive and breathing. She did not look at Constance when Constance came in.

There was a corpse in the corner of the room.

"Rayet," Constance said, "don't let anyone else in." He nodded his acknowledgment and let the tent flap fall closed, shuttering them in the shadowy tent.

The body was half hidden by the bulk and shadow of Milla's desk. From her vantage point at the opening to the tent, Constance could see only its legs. While Arawn stalked around the circumference of the sparse room, checking for any enemies, Constance moved until she stood directly beneath the single lantern hung from the tent's central pole. From there she could see into the corner.

It was a woman lying there, and she was very dead. Her arms and legs were cast out, their joints oddly bent, and there was a dark red spot in the center of her breast. Blood was beginning to creep out from under her arm, visible only as a darker shadow. The light made it hard for Constance to see the dead woman's face.

Arawn came up behind Constance. "Assassin?" he asked Milla.

Milla did not answer immediately. Constance looked around the rest of the room warily. A tidily made cot, a small bag of clothes and necessities, a slightly larger bag of books that Milla brought with her everywhere but that Constance knew she was prepared to abandon, an old metal table that functioned as a temporary desk, and a metal folding chair that moved around the room depending on where Milla needed it—there was no place for anyone else to hide.

"Yes," Milla said, and glanced at last at Constance. "I would imagine there were one or two waiting in your tent as well."

Arawn lifted his gun again. "Allow me," he said, and left.

"You killed her?" Constance asked.

"Yes," Milla said. She was not holding her gun anymore; it was on the ground beneath her dangling fingers. Her white hair was out of its eternal bun, and it was a little longer than Constance had expected it to be. She was uninjured, and no sign of pain showed on her face, but there were red spots on her cheek from a spray of someone else's blood. Because she was sitting so far from the center of the tent, away from the tent's one light, the shadows were heavy on Milla, half of her body falling into obscurity in the dark. She was not meeting Constance's eyes.

Constance said, "Are you all right?"

Milla moved her fingers abortively as if she meant to rap them against her arm in a patternless beat but then changed her mind; the motion only revealed their slight tremor. She said, "Constance, did you look at her?"

"Yes. I saw she was dead."

Milla gave her a look that could have flash-frozen a Terran ocean. She said, "Did you see her face?"

A low drumbeat of alarm had started up in Constance's heart, and she left Milla where she sat to walk back toward that silent corner and the corpse that lay on the stone. She stepped carefully around the woman's outflung limbs and crouched down in the shadows by her head.

A bright slice of light cut into the tent as the flap was opened; Arawn strode back in.

"No one there," he reported. "But a few people in the crowd reported seeing some men running after the gunshot—running away from the gunshot, not toward it."

"Have them found," Constance said, and frowned down at the woman below her. There was something familiar about the features even though they were indistinct in the dark.

"Are you hurt, Doctor Ivanov?" Arawn asked.

"No," said Milla.

People were moving around outside; the lantern in the center of the tent swung slightly on its perch, sending the shadows to creep along the boundaries where the tent met the ground. It only further blurred the face that Constance was trying to see.

Rustling from Arawn. He was standing beneath the central light and digging around in his pocket, from which he produced a crumpled box. He offered the box to Milla. Milla stared at it as if she thought it might be some sort of trap, but finally she reached out and carefully pulled a slender white bar from the box.

It was no good: Constance couldn't see. She stood up again and stepped over the body. The table screeched when she shoved it over the stone to where its shadow would not conceal the dead woman's face.

A lighter clicked softly behind her—Constance had ignited too many bombs for it to not catch her attention immediately. The box Arawn had offered had been full of cigarettes, and he was lighting one for Milla, which was about as absurd an image as Constance could contemplate. Cigarettes were illegal in the System because of their health dangers and the more practical dangers of having them in atmospheric domes or spaceships or other places with limited supplies of oxygen. "I didn't know you smoked," Constance said.

"I used to," Milla said. The tip of the cigarette glowed. "Connor used to get them for me."

Constance, curious, might have asked more because she did not think that even Ivan had known this about Milla, but Arawn was staring past her now, too, his own cigarette forgotten in his hand, a frown drawing a deeply shadowed line between his dark brows. Constance turned and looked at the body she had exposed.

In the shadows, half beneath the table, the corpse had looked like a tumble of limbs, dismembered, disembodied pieces that made up a horrific and unseen whole. Exposed to the light, the limbs became a body, unbroken but for the wound in her chest, and her seeping blood gave her an artificial shadow. The woman's face was made almost strange by death, as death did: it was still and sunken in a way that made the animal part of Constance recoil. But even through the pall of a recent death, Constance knew that face.

"She was one of mine," Constance said.

"I thought she was," Milla said quietly.

"A spy?" Arawn suggested.

"She was with me before Earth," Constance said. "If she was a spy, she was a bad one."

"She tried to knife me," Milla said. "I don't think she wanted anyone to hear a gunshot. I shot her before I recognized her."

Josephine, Constance remembered; that had been the woman's name: Josephine. She said, "You're sure she was trying to kill you?"

"I am fairly certain of that, yes," Milla said flatly. Arawn grinned, and that made Constance more furious than Milla's sarcasm ever could.

"This is not the time to smile," she told him.

His smile vanished. "The System bought her, Constance," he said, gesturing at the body. His cigarette was still unlit, though the smoke from Milla's was starting to cloud the little tent. "She went after the doctor, Milla got her, end of story."

"What could they offer her?" Constance demanded.

"What do they ever offer?" Arawn said. "Safety with them, power on their terms. Cowards' things. It's no use trying to understand a traitor, Constance."

And Constance never could ask, because Josephine was dead. She stared down at the body on the stone.

Arawn said, "Maybe Anji sent her."

"Anji would never send an assassin."

Arawn had the sense not to contest this, and Constance didn't need him to, for she thought it on her own: once she, too, would have said that Anji never would have betrayed her. What proof did she have that Anji had not sent someone to kill her?

Constance went to the tent flap. Rayet came in at her wave, and she brought him to the corner where Josephine's body lay. She saw that he recognized her the moment he saw her in the light.

"Get Henry," Constance told him, "and have him come and take her body. Bury her outside the camp but don't mark her grave. Tell everyone that Josephine was a traitor; she was loyal to Anji and not to me." Better loyalty to Anji than whatever true disloyalty had driven Josephine to try to kill Milla. "She came to kill Doctor Ivanov, but Doctor Ivanov stopped her. And tell Henry to find her accomplices—the men who came to kill me."

Rayet nodded once, then stepped out of the tent again. "Marisol," she heard him say, "find Henry."

Milla was still sitting low in her chair, her cigarette ashing in her fingers. Arawn stood beside her, tall, almost looming, but remarkably, she let him loom.

"You had to do it," Arawn said.

"I know," Milla said, and put the cigarette out against her chair.

"I found something," Ananke said.

Her voice startled Althea. The mechanical hand's skeleton creaked beneath her fingers.

She deliberately loosened her grip. "Ivan and Mattie?" she said.

"A trace," Ananke said. "Not them, not yet. But I know where they have been."

She had found it so quickly. Althea had known, of course, about the ship's power, about its connection to all the computers and all the cameras the System had ever had. But they were not yet even properly within the solar system. To have found a trace of Ivan and Mattie already was astounding.

"Where are they? Or," Althea added, correcting herself, "where were they?"

"The asteroid belt," Ananke said. "Do you want to know how I found them?"

She sounded proud, in the mood to show off for her mother. Althea said, "How did you find them, Ananke?"

In answer, the screen set high up on the wall switched on. An image appeared with the grainy black-and-white quality that Althea recognized as being from a System surveillance camera.

"There are still surveillance cameras?" Althea asked.

"Not many," Ananke said. "The revolutionaries have been tearing them out." She sounded vaguely annoyed by this. "But sometimes they miss one."

The image on the screen showed a segment of a hallway. The walls were concrete or stone; reinforced System architecture, Althea suspected.

There were blackened marks on the walls and tumbled stone on the floor. Althea could not see it in the image before her, but she suspected that the ceiling had collapsed.

On the far right of the image, grainy figures moved over the ruined stone. One was limping. The other had his hand beneath the first man's arm and was helping him over the uneven ground. The limping man had light hair; the other man—taller—had dark. Althea did not need to wait for them to come close enough for the camera to distinguish their faces to recognize Ivan and Mattie.

They were speaking to each other, she realized, seeing Ivan's lips move as they walked. Mattie gestured down the hall back the way they had come, and Ivan frowned, glancing back as if anticipating some pursuit.

Then Ivan's eyes passed over the scorched walls, skimming across them with an attention that looked practiced. Automatically scanning for cameras, Althea realized. And indeed, Ivan's eyes found the camera that had become her and Ananke's eyes, and there they stopped.

The footage was in black and white, and so Althea could not see the color of Ivan's eyes, but the directness of his gaze froze her even so.

Stopped beneath the camera, gazing up straight into its lens, Ivan lifted his arm and pointed at the camera, at Ananke's eye, at Althea. Beside him, Mattie looked up as well. Where Ivan's expression was blank, emotionlessly watchful, Mattie's darkened and grew grim.

Still with one arm beneath Ivan's elbow, Mattie reached behind himself and pulled out a gun from where it had been tucked into his pocket, the same way he had done it when he had encountered Althea just before escaping from the *Ananke* with Ivan at his side. And with both men looking up into the camera, at Althea and Ananke, Mattie raised his gun to point it toward the lens and fired, and the image went black.

While Althea was still sitting there, absorbing the shock of seeing the men, the shock of the fired gun, the video looped and began to play again. In the distance, the two men picked their way over the rubble.

"There was a bomb detonated on Mars," Ananke said offhandedly, "but this footage is from after."

"After?" said Althea, and then, "A bomb? What kind of bomb, Ananke?"

On the screen, Mattie helped Ivan down the hall.

Ananke said, "A Terran Class 1." She must have seen the horror on Althea's face, because she added, "The planet is still inhabitable."

"Still inhabitable, but how many people died?" Althea asked. "The Mallt-y-Nos set off another bomb? Why? Wasn't Earth enough?"

"Constance Harper did not detonate the bomb. The System fleet did."

The idea was incomprehensible. Constance Harper might commit genocide to make a political point, but the System? The System was law and order and peace—or so Althea once had thought.

On the screen, Ivan's eyes met the gaze of the camera head on.

"It is too bad that humans have only five senses," Ananke said as Ivan lifted his hand to point at them. "And all five are so limited. This footage is in only a narrow spectrum of wavelengths."

Althea broke her gaze from the video to look back down at the mechanical hand in her lap. She bent the finger of it as if she were working, testing the joints, but her mind was blank. The System had detonated a Terran Class 1 bomb on Martian soil. No one could stand for that, she knew. No System civilian would approve of that. Yet the System had done it.

"If this camera could see in more wavelengths," Ananke mused, "I could see so much more. There would be so much more information. I could see everything, everything. Everything down to what they were feeling by watching the distribution of heat in their bodies."

"Well, I'll call up Constance Harper and tell her to install better cameras," Althea said.

Ananke looked thoughtful.

"I was joking, Ananke," Althea said.

"She wouldn't do it anyway," Ananke decided. "She's the one tearing the cameras out."

Then something curious came to Althea's mind, brought on by her ill-considered quip and Ananke's thoughtful reaction: she could, if she wanted, confront Constance Harper. If she wanted, she could find the Mallt-y-Nos, wherever she was, and force Constance to listen to her. Constance would have to listen to her because of Ananke; no true leader could ignore a ship this powerful.

Or, if Althea preferred, she could go find the System, whoever was leading it now. Althea was in command of the *Ananke*, and the System would have to listen to her, too.

She could confront them both if she liked, call both sides to account for the murders they had committed. With Ananke, they would have to listen to her.

It was a strange feeling, having power.

On the screen before her, Mattie fired his gun at the camera over and over again, to black.

The disarray of the System included the disarray of its infrastructure. Constance had known this would happen and had planned for it, but she had never expected it to be so difficult to contact her people farther out in the solar system.

The communications equipment of the *Wild Hunt* was not strong enough on its own to reach even to Saturn, where, as far as Constance knew, Julian was still in an uneasy standoff with Anji's people, much less out to Neptune, where Christoph would be. Even if it had been, direct broadcast from Venus to Saturn or to Neptune was prone to disruption or interception or corruption by planetary bodies or solar flares. Instead, communication across the solar system was effected by a series of relays: messages could be transmitted directly across space from relay station to relay station. There were lesser relay stations on each of the inner planets, but the main points of relay were in the asteroid belt and in secret orbits around each of the outer planets. The orbits were secret because the System had not wished to provide the outer planets' resistance movements with an easy target, for all the good that had done them. The rebels had had their own private line of relays, which were prone to shutdowns or equipment failure or discovery and destruction by System craft. Constance had been trying through force of habit and desire for secrecy to contact Julian and Christoph via their own relay stations, with no success. Perhaps, she thought, she would have more luck with the System equipment. Enough of the System's former territory had been lost to them by now that Constance thought it was worth the risk. The message would be encrypted, of course, a variant on the encryption Ivan had taught her years earlier, and as a mark of its veracity Constance would include the revolutionaries' signal: a recording of the barking of hounds.

She had sent a message out to Julian and Christoph earlier that morning. It would take hours longer for the message to reach Christoph, but Julian's response, if there was one, should be coming at any moment. Since it would be some time before the two leaders of the war on Venus—Kip Altais and Lyra Greene, according to her intelligence—would arrive on her ship, Constance turned her steps toward the communications room on the *Wild Hunt*.

She pushed open the door and found Milla Ivanov and Arawn Halley sitting together in the center of the room. Constance would have expected to find Ivan and Mattie secluded away, just the two of them, speaking conspiratorially. Indeed, she had hardly ever expected to see them separated. But to find Milla Ivanov and Arawn Halley alone in each other's company was strange.

"Did I call a meeting?" Constance asked, and let the door shut behind her.

"No," Milla said. Constance doubted she had missed the sarcasm; the literalism must have been intentional. There were no cigarettes between the two of them, not on board a spaceship.

Arawn, leaning back comfortably in his chair, was watching Milla Ivanov. "I was just here in case any last-minute intel came in," he said. "About Altais and Greene."

Sensible: Constance had called him to the *Wild Hunt* from his own ship, the *Rhiannon*, because she wanted both him and Milla Ivanov to be present when Altais and Greene arrived. She preferred to meet the two warring leaders on board her ship, not on the surface of the planet, because she thought it might induce some rightful fear in whichever one of them was secretly System.

"Did anything new come in?" Constance asked, crossing the room to check the nearest terminal for any messages from Julian.

"Nothing but what we already know."

Nothing from Julian. Very well; it was rather soon.

"So recap for me," said Constance. As long as they all were there, they might as well prepare to meet Greene and Altais. She took another look at their positions and frowned to herself. It appeared that Milla and Arawn had dragged chairs away from the computer terminals into the center of the room to face each other as if trying to distance themselves from the blinking, glowing equipment that surrounded them.

Constance grabbed a chair and dragged it to the center of the room as Arawn said, "We don't know much about Altais. It seems like he led some sort of labor strike a few years ago—failed, of course. The System came down on it. He served a bit of time for it but not much; we've got nothing else on him. But Greene." Arawn leaned onto his knees, facing Constance, a light in his eyes. "Lyra Greene was on the board of directors of the Venerean Consulting Corp."

Not strictly System, then, was Greene, but everyone knew that the supposedly private large businesses had truly been controlled by the System. It seemed likely that she was the System in disguise.

"I'll speak to them separately," Constance said. "I want to hear what they have to say without the other's interference. Altais first."

"Sounds smart," said Arawn, then turned very suddenly to Milla. "And you, Doctor Ivanov? Why don't you tell the Mallt-y-Nos what you were up to in here?"

Milla flicked a cool glance at him.

"I was keeping Mr. Halley company," she told Constance.

"And here I thought it was the other way around," Arawn said.

Milla ignored him. "Are you hoping for a message from Julian?" she asked Constance.

"Yes," Constance said. "I sent a message by the System relays this morning; if a response is coming, it'll be here soon."

"Well, messages from Saturn should be coming in fine," Arawn said. "Shouldn't they, Doctor Ivanov?"

"As far as I can tell, the System relays are all intact," Milla said.

Arawn smiled, baring his teeth. He had adopted his heavy Plutonian drapes again; they made him seem larger than he was. Milla, with her hands clasped in her lap to stop their restless tapping, looked very small.

"I was thinking while me and Milla were in here," he said, "that it's a pity I don't know both of you better."

Constance looked to share a glance with Milla, but Ivan's mother was staring serenely into space at nothing and no one. Arawn said, "We're fighting with each other—dying for each other—shouldn't we all get to know each other's quality?"

"What were you hoping to know, Arawn?" Constance asked.

"I'd heard a little bit about how the two of you met," he said. "And I'm very curious about this Ivan."

The name spoken aloud was like a spark jumping on Constance's skin, her own thoughts expelled into the air, and from Arawn's mouth, no less. Milla was looking at Arawn now, a look as remote and cold as the distant stars.

"His name wasn't Ivan," Milla said clearly. "His name was Leon. He was my son."

Arawn, Constance saw, knew Milla's relationship to Ivan already. "Everyone around here calls him Ivan."

"When he left home, he decided to call himself Ivan," Milla said. "His name is Leontios."

"Connor Ivanov's son," Arawn marveled.

"My son," Milla said, and Constance could not tell whether it was correction or agreement. "He was never comfortable on Earth."

"He was a true believer, then?" Arawn said. "I heard he died for Constance."

"A true believer? No," said Milla, and then she looked right at Constance with eyes that were precisely the same shade as her son's. "My son died for someone he loved, not for the revolution."

They were both looking at her now, but Constance could not bear to speak. One of the last things Ivan had said to her had been that he loved her. He might have meant it, but that didn't mean it was true: Mattie and Milla also stood to fall if Ivan gave up Constance, and she knew that he had died as much for them as he had for her, perhaps more.

She had brought about his death. She had led him to it, and it was because of her plans that he had had to die. No, she reminded herself; it was his and Mattie's childish stupidity that had brought him to the *Ananke*. They had been curious about the dangerous ship, and they had recklessly boarded it and been captured. She had always offered Ivan the choice to follow her or not.

"Were you and the doctor's son close?" Arawn asked. His expression was carefully closed off.

"We were close," Constance said.

"What was he like?"

There were many ways to answer that question, some of them too harsh and sad and exposing and others too harsh and cruel and sharp. She could tell Arawn that Ivan had been handsome. She could tell Milla that Ivan had been brilliant and that he'd had a good heart. She could say that he'd hated himself and had always been looking to find a way to be destroyed like a sailor dashed to pieces against a stone. She could say that it was his caution and his cleverness that had made her revolution take off from where it had been mired for years. She could say that he had been infuriating and manipulative, that he'd made her think things were her fault when she hadn't done anything wrong at all. She could say that he loved her or that he hated her but that either way she had always suspected he loved Mattie more than he could ever love her and that when she had lost Ivan, the wrench of it had taken not just Ivan himself but her brother and her best friend and her right hand away, too.

She said, "He was very much like his mother."

There was more expression in the robotic blinking of the lights on the terminal past Milla Ivanov's head than there was on her face, but she bowed her head in silent acknowledgment.

Arawn said, "The System killed my wife."

"I didn't know you were married," said Constance.

"We were kids," he admitted. "Even younger than you were when you married Connor, Doctor Ivanov." Milla did not acknowledge him. "Her name was Claudia. She was beautiful. She used to sing in the morning, just after she woke up. Sometimes, when I'm just asleep, I think I can still hear her."

Ivan had never sung—Constance could not even imagine such a thing—but she still heard his voice sometimes, the echo of it, in Milla Ivanov's words.

"I was an engineer at first," Arawn said. "I thought I'd work on space-ships. But they don't let the Plutonians do any real work. I carried nails and wires to the nice Terran men who did everything that mattered, and eventually I realized they didn't let us do any work because they didn't trust us."

Constance remembered Mattie setting up the nuclear power plants on Earth to explode simultaneously. Perhaps the System had been afraid of her people, too, even back then.

"The joke's on those fancy Terran technicians now," said Arawn. "Whichever ones are left alive. Most of the really advanced computers were on Earth, and the ones that are left—they're a dying breed. Who needs more of them? No one's making any more, and the ones that are left, they'll be destroyed or broken or lost in a matter of time." He waved a hand around the communications room. "This is all basic stuff. The real computers, the ones that can solve things, the ones that are a step below thinking? Those are all going to be gone, and not that far from now, either."

As long as the computers that existed could still fly a starship for her, Constance didn't care what happened to the rest. Arawn must have seen this on her face because he said, "It wasn't long before some revolutionary groups tapped me. It was stupid for me to think I could keep who I was a secret from the System forever, but I guess that's it— I didn't think."

"They found your wife," Constance said.

"I don't know how long she was alive in there with them," said Arawn. "But she didn't last. I got her body back and buried her on Pluto the way she should be buried, but it doesn't help, does it?"

"No," Constance said. "It doesn't."

Milla Ivanov said, "Was that before or after you left the Son of Nike?"

Arawn's upper lip lifted before he turned to Milla with an expression that could almost be taken for pleasant. "That was before I even met the Son."

"That surprises me," Milla said. "I was just thinking that you must have been very young when you were with him."

"Not as young as you think."

"Given that he was an acquaintance of mine," Milla said, "I've always been curious, Arawn, about what happened to him in the end."

"I don't know, Milla," Arawn said. "I wasn't there. Much like you weren't there when your husband's revolution failed. I was always curious about that. Is it true he was betrayed?"

"Enough," Constance said. They both fell immediately silent.

"Whatever is going on between the two of you, *enough*," she insisted. "We have a war to run, and I cannot afford to have any fighting within my army or between my two advisers. Get over whatever this is and get over it now. Altais and Greene will be here at any moment. We—"

The terminal behind Milla erupted into sound, an incoming transmission blaring out the barking and howling of hounds. Julian.

Constance said to her silent advisers, "Am I clear?"

"Perfectly," said Arawn. Milla dipped her chin without a word.

"Good," Constance said, and went to silence the blaring noise. The message decrypted at a touch.

Freed of its encryption, Julian's message began to play, staticky and blurred by the journey it had taken from relay to relay from Saturn to Venus. He said, "We have received your warning about the Terran Class 1s and will be on the lookout. Communication is difficult."

An understatement. Constance hoped that Julian would have an alternative method of communication to suggest in this message.

But then Julian said, "A warning: Anji is not the only traitor. Christoph has turned on you."

Behind her, Constance heard Arawn rise to his feet and even heard the sound of Milla Ivanov shifting in incredulity.

"He has not declared himself, but he is coming into the inner solar system, and I believe he means to take your army and join it with his own. He is still far out, not yet at Saturn's orbit, though I know that Anji does not intend to challenge him. My fleet is not large enough to successfully oppose him. Huntress—tell me what to do."

If the System was willing to bomb Mars, Althea knew it wouldn't hesitate to destroy Ananke.

"So what do you target first?" Althea asked patiently while she studied the System fleet in the piloting room. The System had kept detailed records of all the ships in its fleet, accessible only to the most high up in the government, for secrecy.

It had been simplicity itself for Ananke to find the information and tear it from its hidden place. Althea supposed it was good that not all of the System's data banks had been on Earth, but she wondered how long it would be before Constance Harper's armies destroyed the rest of the System's infrastructure. Perhaps it was for the best that she and Ananke had come back so soon.

"I target the communications," Ananke said, aglow in the holographic terminal. "I cut their ability to speak to one another, and I address them all at once."

"And what do you say?"

"Cease your attack," Ananke said.

"Good," Althea said, and scrolled through the seemingly endless list of ships. So many warships—how could Constance Harper hope to win against the System? How large could the fleet of the Mallt-y-Nos be when it was made up of civilians and a handful of terrorists?

"And if they try to talk to you," said Althea, "what do you do?"

"I connect them to you," Ananke said promptly. "You will talk to them."

"Good." Althea finally had reached the end of the list. Each ship would take a certain amount of time to control. How fast, she wondered, could Ananke work? And how many ships at once could Ananke face and win? "And if they don't talk?"

"I take control of their weapons systems," Ananke said.

"Good. And then?"

"Then I target the engines."

"Good." With the weaponry shut down, the ships couldn't fire; with the engines frozen, the ships couldn't maneuver to ram Ananke. The threat would be neutralized.

Ananke asked, "Then what?"

"Hmm?" Althea was still staring at the impossibly long list of System warships.

"After I have frozen their weapons systems and their engines," said Ananke, "then what?"

"Then we leave," Althea said. "It'll take them a while to get their systems back online. We can get far away in that time."

Althea twisted around in her chair to look at the hologram. Ananke's holographic hair had been swept back into an unruly ponytail, much like Althea's hair that morning. Althea envisioned going up to the hologram and laying her hand on the translucent skin. For a moment she imagined she would feel the warmth of real skin even though she knew her fingers would sink right through the flesh that wasn't there.

Ananke said, "It is difficult to gain access to the engines and the engines alone. What if they fire on me in that time? What if there are too many and they fire on me before I can gain control?"

"It'll be okay, Ananke," Althea said, because she didn't know the answer. "Other people's reaction times aren't as fast as yours."

"But if they are?" Ananke said. "And what if the rebels have removed the System components from their ships? Then I can't control the computers."

"The rebels can't remove all the System circuitry or the ships wouldn't run."

Looking at that list of ships, Althea wondered what the System would think of her if they could see her now. A traitor, probably. A deserter.

Ananke did not seem to be listening. "When do I defend myself?" she asked. "How close do they come to destroying me before I use the weaponry that I have?"

Althea's heart jolted. The *Ananke* was equipped with armament, but Althea had never expected it to be used. "Never, Ananke," she said. "We don't fire on any other ships, okay?"

"But if they are bound to kill me," Ananke insisted. "Like Gagnon."

Like Gagnon.

Like Gagnon, whom Ananke had killed, whose body had fallen down into the black hole below—

"No," Althea said firmly. "We do not fire on anyone. Not like Gagnon." Ananke's silence spoke to disagreement, and so she pressed on. "We don't need to, Ananke. We have all the power we need to stop anyone from hurting you without having to fire on them."

"Because I can take over their computers," Ananke said, testing her.

"Yes."

"And our ammunition is limited," Ananke added.

"No," Althea said. "I mean, yes, but no. That's not why we're not firing." She leaned onto the back of her chair, still twisted uncomfortably around to face the hologram, though she might as well have spoken directly to the wall; the hologram could neither see nor hear. "It's wrong to shoot someone," she told Ananke. "So we won't use our weaponry."

Althea herself had shot someone while on board the *Ananke*; mercifully, Ananke did not bring this up, for then Althea would have had to explain why she had been wrong when she was not altogether certain that shooting at Ivan had been the wrong thing to do. Instead, Ananke said, "Even if they'll just follow me after they get their engines back?"

"They won't be able to follow you. We'll be long gone."

"They'll still follow," Ananke said. "They will hate me. They will hunt me. They will try to kill me, and they'll know they have to kill me fast when they find me again, because they couldn't kill me the first time they tried."

That's why I wanted to leave, Althea almost snapped back. *That's why I wanted to go away and not come back.* But she stopped herself.

"Ananke," she said, "do you want to leave?"

"No," Ananke said immediately.

"We can," said Althea, and could not tell whether the possibility filled her with relief or disappointment. "We can go, and then no one will find us."

"I don't want to leave."

"Then listen to me," Althea said. "We're going to be fine. We're going to find Ivan and Mattie, and we're going to talk to them, and then we're going to leave. No one's going to follow us. No one's going to hurt us."

Ananke was silent for a time, and Althea could not tell whether that meant she had been convinced or that there was some other dreadful thought she was not yet willing to admit to Althea. Finally Ananke said, her tone halting, robotic, "A computer should not feel fear." She looked directly at Althea. Ananke's algorithm had improved, Althea thought distantly; the hologram now could seem to actually meet Althea's eyes.

"Why would Mattie program me with fear?" Ananke asked.

"I think it's a normal reaction, Ananke," she said. "Everything's going to be all right. Don't be afraid."

Privately, Althea doubted that Mattie Gale had cared.

Constance sent Julian a message that said he should attempt to negotiate with Christoph. It was all she could do for the moment. She had negotiations of her own to attend to: the two leaders of the two Venerean factions, Kip Altais and Lyra Greene. One of them, Constance knew, was the System in disguise.

Altais came first, and he came alone. Constance had sent a shuttle to pick him up, and he'd been brought in that shuttle with only Constance's people for company to the *Wild Hunt* in its orbit. They'd docked, and he'd been led—alone—through the winding halls of the *Wild Hunt* with an honor guard of Constance's men until he'd been let into this room, where he found Constance with Milla and Arawn beside her, all watching him in silence.

Altais was short; the ceiling did not seem to trouble him. There was something squashed about him, as if someone had taken the man and put his or her palm on the crown of his head, pushing down until he'd been compressed. He scanned Constance's side of the table with narrowed dark eyes, his attention pausing once on Milla Ivanov, before realizing that Constance must be the Mallt-y-Nos.

"Huntress," he said, addressing her with a bow that somehow did not seem unexpected to Constance. "Thank you for giving me the chance to speak to you."

"Speak honestly and I won't regret it," said Constance. "You are at war with another group of Venereans led by Lyra Greene. Explain yourself."

Altais hesitated. His narrow eyes darted from Constance to the faces of her advisers beside her.

"With respect, Huntress," he said, "Lyra Greene's people aren't true Venereans. That is, they've lived here, but they aren't the people of Venus."

Constance had expected no less, but she could not give in to Altais so soon. He still might be lying. "What does that mean?"

"Venus is very close to Earth, Huntress. They're sister planets. The System is everywhere here; System leaders have country houses on our soil. The people of Venus are not all free men; some of them are System to the core."

"And the System soldiers who abandoned their bases?" Constance asked.

"They've joined her," Altais said. "She's folded them right into her army, like they belong there. And they do—her people are the System, hiding themselves under the name of Venus. She's preparing the planet to welcome the System fleet when it comes back. Says she wants order again, that she wants the fighting to stop. But this is what's true, Huntress: she had it good when the System was here, and she's trying to bring it back."

Lyra Greene came in some time after Altais had left with the deliberate high-stepping stride of a woman wearing heels. The heels clicked against the metal floor. The sound of it nagged at Constance's mind, bringing up some remembrance that she could not recall the provenance of but that filled her with a vague unpleasant feeling.

Greene was tall and sleek and professional, wearing a suit, with her hair smoothed back into a bun and a slender line of brown outlining her eyes. She looked as if she had come to a board meeting, not a war council. When she stepped into the room, she did the same thing Altais had, looking over the group swiftly before zeroing in on Constance.

Greene smiled and strode around the table, her hand extended to be shaken. Arawn leaned forward when she did, not blocking Constance but making it more difficult for Greene to reach her.

Greene's polite smile hardly slipped.

"You must be Arawn Halley," she said, and offered Arawn her hand instead. He ignored it. She was unfazed. "I came to speak to the Mallt-y-Nos."

"So speak," Constance said.

Greene glanced again at the others. "I was hoping you and I might talk in private, Huntress."

Arawn scoffed. He was still partially shielding Constance with his broad shoulders.

"I'm unarmed," Greene said. "Your men made certain of that when they brought me on board. And I wish the Huntress no harm. I only wish to speak to her."

"And must you speak to her alone?" Milla Ivanov asked.

Greene smiled at Milla with her businesswoman's distant smile. "I feel this is a difficulty best overcome on a one-to-one level."

"Leave us," Constance said. Arawn bit the inside of his cheek but didn't protest. Milla Ivanov rose smoothly without protest or gesture of dismay, and they left.

As soon as they were gone, Greene seated herself one chair away from Constance, near enough to be intimate but not so close as to be threatening. She was so calculated, Constance thought, and hated it.

"Miss Harper," Greene said, "or may I call you Constance?"

"Huntress," said Constance.

"Huntress," Greene conceded, then took a breath. "I've come to surrender."

Of all the things Constance had expected to hear her say, that had not been among them. She hid her surprise. "Surrender?"

"I don't want to fight you or your people," Greene said. "We are not on opposite sides. No doubt you've spoken to Altais and he's told you about me. That I'm System. That I want to rule this planet and oppress its people. None of that is true. And so I've come to surrender—with conditions."

"Conditions." There was a catch; of course there was. There always was with people like Greene.

"They're fair conditions, Huntress, and ones that I think you will understand." Greene spoke swiftly and in a low voice. "Altais and his followers are warmongers and anarchists. They indulge in violence for violence's sake, to take revenge past where a sane man would consider his revenge taken. They are so blinded by their hate that they see nothing but enemies wherever they look."

"And should they take revenge against you?"

"I've done them no wrong," Greene said. "But if I am the price for their peace, I'll give myself up to them. Better that I should die now than lose everything I've tried to achieve."

"And what have you tried to achieve?"

"Peace," Lyra Greene said.

Constance considered her. For an instant, she saw the woman beneath the polished veneer.

"What are your terms?" Constance asked.

"Peace and order," Greene said. "The System is dead here, Huntress."

"Then who are you?"

"A true Venerean, like Altais's people." Greene looked at her for a moment, frowning the way Milla Ivanov frowned, the slightest impression of confusion on her face and nothing more—a Terran way of frowning, a System mode of expression.

Then Greene said, "Don't you understand, Huntress? My people and Altais's people are not fighting because we are System and rebel. This is a civil war."

"There can't be a civil war when there's a common enemy."

"There isn't one. The System isn't here," Greene said. She had her hands clasped together in her lap; Constance saw the remnants of a cracked and faded manicure on the nails. "My people deserve your protection as much as Altais's do."

"That's not what Altais told me," Constance said. Greene was lying. She had to be; it was impossible, incomprehensible that Venus should be in a civil war.

"What did he tell you?" Greene asked. "Did he tell you that we are secretly System, hiding away, biding our time? It's a lie. Certainly there are people with me who worked for the System or didn't act against it, but it's not a sin to survive in the circumstances you've been placed into. It's no worse a crime to have obeyed the System than it is for Milla Ivanov to have sung its praises for thirty years or for your brother Matthew to have stolen money and food all those years on Miranda. They all did it to survive."

Constance's jaw tightened. Lyra Greene had done a good deal of research. She wondered how much the woman knew about her and what she had planned for this meeting.

"But there can't be any peace without someone putting an end to the war here," said Greene. "It won't end on its own. Someone needs to enforce it. And with the System gone, there is a power vacuum here that sooner or later someone will fill. We can wait years, decades, for someone to take it up, and while we wait we will have war after war as people struggle and fail to take the power they know exists. Or you can take it now and bring order to this planet again, and with that order, we will finally have our peace."

Politicians and bureaucrats' words, seductive in their apparent logic and what they appeared to offer her, but Constance had learned never to trust them. Greene said the System was gone and so order was gone, and now she wanted order again. It sounded to Constance as though it was the System that she missed.

"And why don't you become that person?" Constance asked. "Bring order back to this planet."

"If I tried, I would only bring us more war. You can see it now—Altais and his followers hate me. But you have the power, and you have the army. If you decided to take this planet, it would bow to you without a fight."

"I did not come to rule," Constance said.

"But someone has to," Greene said. "And if it isn't you, someone will lift themselves up by bloody means."

"Bloody for you? I didn't come here to give you peace, I came here to drive out the System and give your people freedom." And she would not leave them peace if it meant leaving the System at her back to hate her, to hunt her, to kill her, knowing that this time they should strike fast the way they had failed to the first time around.

"Then set someone up to rule if you won't," Greene urged. "Someone you support who will do your will, who you'll back in case of another war. So long as my people are safe, so long as the witch hunts and the murders stop, then I and my cities and my people will support whoever you choose."

That would be the same as ruling herself. With thinning patience, Constance said, "I want these people to be free."

"Freedom is a good thing. But we need peace, too."

"And once the System is gone," said Constance, "we all will have it."

"Once the System is—" Greene was angry; Constance could see it cracking her polished facade. "And how will we have it once the System is gone? How will a war-torn solar system know how to transition to peace once your war is done?"

"The people will decide."

"The people will—" Greene cut herself off again and turned her head away from Constance, breaking her gaze. When she spoke, her voice was calm again. "The System is dead, Huntress. It died the minute you detonated the bombs on Earth. The time for peace is now."

"The System is not gone if those who helped it exist still live," Constance said, "especially if they are willing to welcome the System's fleet when it arrives."

"I only want peace," Greene said again, but her face was pale, and Constance knew it must be true.

"You don't care who brings back your autocracy, do you?" Constance said. "Just as long as it comes back as soon as it can. You want the System back, and if you can't have the System, you'll try to force me to give you a government that functions the same way the System did. Tell me why I shouldn't burn your cities."

"My people are innocent."

"If they want the System back, then they aren't," Constance said. "If they helped the System when it was in power, then they aren't. If they ever lifted a finger to help the System, now or before, then they are not innocent."

"The people left who 'helped' the System while it existed are guilty of nothing," said Greene. "They were just trying to survive."

"Just trying to survive?" Constance's anger, which had been boiling low in her chest, grew hot and sudden like a solar flare. "The ones who were just trying to survive were *my* people, the ones who lived out in the dark and the cold. They were the ones who were just trying to survive when the System spent every moment making them suffer or waiting to kill them or their families or their friends. The ones who lived in fear of death, *Lyra*, those are the ones who were 'just trying to survive.' Not the people who were afraid they might lose their jobs."

She had risen to her feet. Lyra Greene leaned back in her chair, her hands gripping the seat. Constance saw that Greene was afraid of her, and that only made her anger burn the brighter.

"The ones who lived knowing that the System might kill them at any moment," said Constance, "the ones who saw the System take their families away from them. Those are the people whose acts are justified. Like my brother. Like Milla Ivanov. But not like you."

"Huntress—"

"Were you just following orders?" Constance said. "Coward. Just the fact that they were safe and comfortable while other people were suffering is enough guilt."

"Then where will it end?" Lyra demanded, still pressed back against her chair, still pale, but snapping back. "You left Miranda; you lived on Mars. Aren't you guilty, too? You weren't suffering with them."

"I was acting to save them."

"How can you say you're for the people when you think that half of them—"

"Of course a System woman would think—" Constance interrupted, but Lyra Greene would not fall silent.

"How long until you all devour one another?" she asked. "How long until your people turn on each other because they don't know how to stop looking for enemies?"

Constance looked at her, the polished System businesswoman who had lost her business and her System and her polish, who had strode into the room so arrogantly, as if she were there to broker a deal with a reluctant client. But Constance was the Mallt-y-Nos, the fire come to cleanse, the speaker of the revolution.

"You came to offer me surrender, with terms," Constance said. "Let me give you my terms."

Lyra stared up at her.

"Surrender the System traitors you are hiding in your cities," Constance said, standing over her. "Hand them all over to me. Once they are gone and once this planet is clean, then I will make sure that Altais will never trouble your people again. Your people can rule themselves however they please, and they will have their peace with Altais."

"I won't betray them."

"Twenty-four hours," Constance said. "You may have twenty-four hours to decide."

"Althea, Mother."

"What is it?" Althea asked. She was adding sensory pads to the manufactured hands so that they could know whether they were touching something and what it was they were touching—so that they could feel. The white slips of plastic looked like bits of skin clinging to the mechanical hands' iron bones.

"Ships," Ananke said, and an imaginary wind blew her photonic hair wildly about her face, and then she vanished from the holographic terminal. Althea was already on her feet, leaving the incomplete hand on the floor. She dashed down the ship's familiar winding hall and burst into the piloting room, where Ananke's hologram had re-formed, staring intently with sightless eyes at the main viewscreen, which showed an arrangement of six moving sparks of light. Other ships, far in the distance. They were nearly indistinguishable from the background stars except that they moved.

"Have they seen you yet?" Althea asked.

"Not yet. They think I am debris."

"Okay." Althea let out her breath. If the other ships hadn't seen them yet, they could still avoid contact with them. Yet although she had known that was what she must do if they encountered other craft, she was unprepared for how badly she longed to open up communication with the other ships, to hear other human voices reply when she spoke.

"What do we do?" Ananke wanted to know.

Would it be more sensible to change course, get out of their sensor range, and hope that the other ships didn't notice or didn't care? Or would it be better to play dead, to hope that the ships moved on in their course, thinking nothing more of the *Ananke* than that she had been an asteroid drifting lonely through space?

"What's their vector?" Althea asked.

"0.9535, 0.2860, 0.0953."

The ships were heading outward from the sun and slightly above the orbital plane, outside the usually trafficked areas. Althea wondered if they were trying to avoid contact with other ships as well. The fact was immaterial; Ananke was above the orbital plane, and that and their theta direction meant they would pass within a few tens of thousands of kilometers of her.

"Should I hail them?" Ananke asked.

Althea hesitated. "For information?"

"Maybe they know where Ivan and Mattie are."

Ananke's childish hope brought Althea back to herself. "No, we shouldn't risk it," she decided. "Change course to get out of range of their sensors."

"Why? Do you think they are hostile?"

"They might be." Althea studied the tiny specks of light before her. She said, "Do you know whose they are?"

"They are System ships," Ananke said, and magnified the image on the screen.

The ships gleamed with reflected sunlight. They were vast and sleek. Their centers glowed with engine lights. The ships were shaped like disks, radially symmetric shapes designed to accommodate their centripetal gravity simulation. Their edges tapered down to a narrowness that at this distance looked slender enough to draw blood. Around their central engines, symmetric arrays of gun ports traced dark circles as the wheels spun.

System warships. The most powerfully weaponized ships ever made and the primary component of the System fleet.

"Ananke, are there any other ships in range?"

"No," Ananke said. "Just these six."

Then where was the rest of the fleet? Althea couldn't imagine why six ships would be out here alone unless they were the vanguard. Perhaps they had been separated in some battle.

"These are my sister ships," Ananke said.

"You're not a warship," Althea said, looking at the weaponry that packed the pocked surface of the slowly spinning ships and thinking of the video footage she had seen not that long ago of System ships bearing down on defenseless Triton.

"I am not," Ananke agreed. "But they are more like me than any other ships now built."

Something in her manufactured tone gave Althea pause. She turned to look at the hologram with its serene and unreadable face, and in that moment of distraction the communications equipment buzzed to life.

"This is the System ship *Pygmalion*. Identify yourselves."

"What do I do?" Ananke asked.

"Tell them you're a System craft," Althea said. "No. Tell them you're a research ship and you mean no harm."

Ananke announced, "This is the research craft *Ananke*. We are on a peaceful mission."

"Was that good?" she asked Althea, and Althea said, "Very good, Ananke, good."

The man's voice said, "What is your alignment?"

Ananke hesitated again.

"Tell them you're System," Althea urged.

"We are a System craft," Ananke said.

Silence, buzzing silence. Then the man said, "Who is your commanding officer?"

"Give me the comm, Ananke," said Althea, but not soon enough; Ananke already had said, "Althea Bastet is in acting command of this vessel."

"What happened to Captain Domitian?"

"He was killed," Ananke said. "We were boarded by terrorists."

"Ananke, let me speak," said Althea.

The man said, "Is this Althea Bastet?"

"No," Ananke answered.

"Then who is speaking?"

The hologram was fading, leached of color as Ananke's attention went to the conversation; now the hologram turned to look at Althea with wide eyes, but Althea had no help to offer. She knew the System, and she knew what conclusions they would draw: that the terrorists had taken control of the ship and killed Domitian and Althea herself was a captive or convert, but either way, the *Ananke* was an enemy craft.

"Take control of their communications systems," Althea said.

Where was the rest of the fleet? Were they nearby? The other ships could have signaled them; the fleet could be on its way to the *Ananke* even now. They should have fled to begin with.

She forced herself to be calm. They could handle this, she told herself. Ananke could take control of all those other ships and stop them from harming her.

"I have their communications systems," Ananke reported.

"And what do you tell them?" Althea prompted.

Ananke said, "I am Ananke. Cease your attack."

Silence from the comm. Althea said, "Are they answering?"

"No. But they're moving."

On the viewscreen, the ships were arranging themselves into a five-pointed star, with the sixth ship in the center.

"Are they leaving?" Ananke asked, and Althea realized that Ananke hadn't come to the same conclusion that she had. The danger, the threat, had all been in Althea's knowledge of what another human would do in this situation, not from any logical analysis of threat. And absent that awareness, the configuration that the other ships were moving themselves into was nothing more than a curiosity; Ananke would know but not appreciate the immediacy of the fact that that configuration was a prime position for a group to fire on a single target—

"Ananke, they're going to shoot!" Althea cried out, forgetting everything for a moment in her terror for her ship, and Ananke acted with all the speed that only a machine could possess. The alarms inside the ship all pealed at once with deafening volume, and the ship rocked as it jolted to the side, sending Althea to the floor, where she could see nothing but the dust and grit beneath the computer panels lining the walls. There was a wrapper pushed up against the wall from some sort of candy that Gagnon had liked. Althea struggled to her feet again only to fall once more when the ship rocked to a stop, but this time she managed to land on her knees so that she could still see the viewscreen and the other six ships wheeling around to chase them.

That was as fast as the *Ananke* could move, Althea knew. The ship was too massive, was not built to move at a higher speed than the one they had just achieved.

"Ananke, take control of their weaponry," Althea said. Her heart was pounding. It was different preparing for this possibility than it was actually living it: what had seemed so simple in concept was terrifying now, spiking metallic adrenaline through her veins. She thought of her beautiful ship torn to pieces. What would happen if Ananke was struck by weapons fire? Would Ananke die piece by piece, or would the computer, the intelligence within, simply cease to exist the moment one of her connections was severed? Althea's creation was too complex even for her to predict.

Once the ship's skin was ruptured, Althea knew that she herself would suffocate as all the air rushed out. And then, when the ship was dead, the naked black hole would drift through empty space unguided and unguarded and uncontrolled.

On the screen, the ships were getting closer. They were almost in position. Althea knew that they would fire again—it was a matter of seconds.

That was my government once, Althea thought. Those ships had been her allies, her friends, her leaders. She had trusted them. She had followed them. She had been loyal until the day Ananke had come to life.

"Do you have control of their weapons systems yet?" Althea demanded.

"No," said Ananke. "Yes—some of them. But what if they have manual weaponry? What if they have old gun turrets that aren't computer-run?"

"They won't," Althea said. "They won't; those haven't been installed on ships for hundreds of years." The ships might not be firing, but they still were moving. "Ananke, shut down their engines and navigation. Quickly!"

Through the blaring alarms, the hologram took in a deep breath, and then everything went suddenly still. The alarms went silent; the blinking lights on the computer terminals froze. The hologram went stiff and then collapsed entirely, static devouring the girl who stood there.

Through the static, for a moment, the face and figure of the dead Ida Stays smiled and moved her head, her dark lips moving with soundless words.

Then, into all that silence, Ananke said, I DID IT.

The ghostly shape of Ida Stays vanished, and Ananke reappeared in the holographic terminal, her blue eyes glowing with inhuman light. Her skin was darker, her hair curlier; she looked more like Althea now than ever. She said, "I have them," and sounded fierce and uncertain and bold and afraid.

On the viewscreen, the six points of light jerked and drifted, their carefully plotted trajectories growing wild, chaotic. "I have them," and I HAVE THEM, said Ananke in her voice and on the screens all around, and Althea said, "Yes, you do. Good, Ananke," but before Althea could be relieved that the danger had been averted, the destruction prevented, the hologram shivered, and the points of light outside began to whirl and shudder faster than before.

Althea pushed to her feet. "What are you doing?" she asked with her heart pounding in her head, and after another moment that was filled with the same indrawn potential as a sucked-in breath, the alarms on the ship began to blare again, the lights on the computer panels began to blink, and the hologram's brilliant light faded to a more normal shade.

But Althea's attention was arrested by the six points of light outside the ship, the six System warships that continued to drift aimlessly through space.

The alarms on the *Ananke* went silent.

"I had to control them," Ananke said. "It was hard to connect with their engines. They were about to fire. I had to control them."

Quite strangely, Althea thought of Gagnon. She thought of the way he had fallen, the twitch of his body the moment before he vanished from her sight, that last twitch before he died.

"Ananke," said Althea, "what did you do?"

"Rapid change is always violent," Milla Ivanov said.

Constance heard her but did not reply. She looked down at the map below her outstretched arms. The ceiling was so low in this room. Who had decided to build a room with a ceiling so low?

"Always," Milla said, though Constance had said nothing in response to her words. "Even in physics. Slow change—semistatic—is peaceful. The system stays in a sort of equilibrium even as it's changing, and once it's done changing, once it reaches that new equilibrium, it stays there. But fast change, fast change is violent."

Beneath Constance's outstretched arms, a town had been circled on the surface of Venus. Kidwelly in the Themis Regio. She studied it and the terrain around the town, the arrows and boxes sketched onto the map. Checking one final time.

"It oscillates," said Milla. "Fast change induces fluctuations, chaos, unpredictable behavior. It doesn't settle down at the equilibrium right away. It ripples. It changes. It's violent."

There was a rifle on the table, on top of the map, out of the way of the diagrams drawn on it. Constance hefted it, checked it over. The ammunition had been loaded already. It had a full clip. The weapon had been cleaned recently, by Constance herself, a few hours earlier. It was ready to go.

"It's the same with people," Milla said. "Change a society over generations and it'll be peaceful. It will be slow, but it will be peaceful. No one will notice. But a rapid change, that's violent. That's a revolution. We needed a rapid change. But the violence is unavoidable."

Her weapon was fully loaded. Constance slid the clip back into the rifle with a click. She looked up at Milla Ivanov and found that Ivan's mother was watching her with dim and distant compassion on her usually impassive face.

"Unavoidable," Constance said without any doubt in her voice, because she'd listened to Milla Ivanov those weeks ago and knew not to show weakness anymore.

Behind Constance, the door opened.

"You're late," Constance said, because she knew that it was Arawn who had arrived, with their guest beside him. "Are you ready?"

"Always," Arawn said.

"Good," said Constance. "Milla, stay with the ships. Keep them out of the battle but near enough to lend aid should things go badly."

Milla nodded slowly, her Ivanov-blue eyes fixed on Constance's face.

"You won't need to get involved. Kidwelly's a small town," Arawn said with the satisfaction of a dog that knows it is about to be taken on a hunt. "We should be able to take it without much trouble. Greene and her people won't put up much of a fight."

There was nothing Constance could say to that. "Remember," she said to them all, lifting her rifle up in her gloved hands and resting it against the padded protected surface of her chest, "the System is our enemy. It will be hard to tell in the heat of battle. But as far as is possible, I want only the System dead, not any Venereans who have been pulled into Greene's war."

She looked at them then, her hounds, the ones who would follow her into battle. Milla was serene and impassive, as hard as diamond; Arawn had a fierce and wild look.

And behind Arawn, with body armor on and a weapon strapped to his hip, walking among them like one of them, was Kip Altais.

"Let's go," said the Mallt-y-Nos, and led her people to war.

Chapter 3

RED GIANT

SIX MONTHS BEFORE THE FALL OF EARTH

There were broadcast screens mounted every few feet on the walls of the Lunar shopping court, and each one of them was displaying System news about the riots on Triton.

Constance kept an eye on them as she walked down the path beside Ivan, her hand tucked up into his elbow. She smiled when he spoke to her and remarked on what he indicated to her she should remark on, but her thoughts and her attention were on those inescapable screens.

Ivan must have noticed it, but it was Mattie who called attention to it.

"Penny for your thoughts?" he asked, and produced a small coin out of nowhere. It was old Earth currency. The System no longer had any use for coins; all their currency was electronic and closely monitored. They had passed an antiquities shop some time earlier, and she had a suspicion that Mattie had lifted the coin then and there. Constance put her hand over Mattie's, hiding the coin from sight before any of the dense array of cameras overhead could get a good look at it.

"I'm just getting used to the gravity," she told him sternly, and pushed his hand down. Mattie wrinkled his nose at her caution.

"It takes some getting used to," Ivan interjected. "If you'd rather, we can go to the observation deck and shop later."

The spending of money on frivolities would always be an alien thing to Constance. But this trip was disguised as Mattie and Ivan taking her out, and she was disguised as a shallow-minded woman, and most important, the shopping court was where their rendezvous with Julian Keys had been arranged.

"Let's just walk a little slower," she suggested, and Ivan shortened his steps.

Mattie sighed.

"Your subtle way of expressing your feelings is always impressive to me," Ivan said.

"As long as there's that," Mattie said. "How long are we going to *shop*?"

"As long as Connie would like to."

Connie would like to stop shopping and blow something up. She had a dark suspicion that Ivan was enjoying this masquerade.

"I'm enjoying myself, Mattie," she said through teeth that were nearly gritted. "Try not to be a prick."

Mattie grinned.

Luna was all coal-black stone and ashy dust underfoot. The buildings had been designed in a bourgeois imitation of Terran architecture, made of steel and glass and occasionally expensive wood imported from the Earth below. The cheapest buildings, though, were made of Lunar stone quarried from nearby, and the glitz and glamour of stolen Terran shine could not hide the moon's own stone. As bright as Luna was when seen on Earth—Constance had heard it was very bright—the stone of the moon was as black as coal, dark and dull, with none of the moon's fabled luminous shine. The whole place struck Constance as deceptive and false, from the architecture and the imported vegetation that tried to give the impression that this place was Earth to the cameras that bristled from every possible surface. She did not like it.

All those cameras, she thought, her eyes roving over the ceiling of the enclosed shopping center. This was the kind of place in which Ivan had grown up.

Just as it was impossible to avoid the System seeing her, so it was impossible for her to avoid seeing the System: those broadcast screens were everywhere. Constance could not tear her eyes from them. RIOTS ON TRITON, they said. TERRORIST ATTACKS ON THE OUTER PLANETS.

Constance had talked to Anji and Christoph that morning, just before landing on Luna. Anji had assured her that the riots were under control—or "controllably uncontrolled," she'd said with dusty humor and an air of quoting Ivan—and Christoph had confirmed that the System's fleet was en route but had not arrived yet. So Constance knew that her friends lived and her plan was falling into perfect order, yet still something inside of her was coiled up tight. She could take only grim and bitter satisfaction from the knowledge that while the System broadcast its own atrocities, the very woman who had planned the riots stood beneath all their thousand mechanical eyes and planned to do far worse the moment she had the chance.

"Julian?" Ivan said with the perfect note of surprise in his voice, and Constance broke her attention from the screens.

"Julian!" Ivan said, lifting a hand and pulling out of Constance's grip to stride across the shopping court's open central expanse, waving at a man on the other side. The man turned at the sound of his name. A tall, elegant man grown more elegant as he aged; his skin was as dark as skin could be, and his hair had turned to ashes on his head. When he saw Ivan, he smiled, showing white teeth and sending wrinkles rippling over the flesh of his face. He and Ivan clasped each other by the arms, as close to an embrace as Constance had ever seen Ivan come with a relative stranger, and then Julian lifted one hand and laid it on Ivan's cheek fondly, as if Ivan were a child.

The moment had come. The spark lit in Constance's chest again and used for timber all the tension in her limbs. She strode off after Ivan, with Mattie a half a step behind.

"It's been years since last I saw you," Julian said. There was something off about his accent to Constance's ears; after a moment she realized with some surprise that he was not Terran natively. A Lunar accent muddled his Terran consonants. She wondered if he had agreed to the moon as a rendezvous point as much because it was his birthplace as because it was close to Earth. "You've grown so much. How is your mother?"

"It's been some time since I've spoken with her," Ivan said.

"I'd heard you left home," said Julian.

"I'm afraid I did," Ivan said, and then turned as Constance and Mattie came up behind him. "Julian, these are some friends of mine. This is Constance, my girlfriend, and Mattie, my business partner." He was very good, of course. There was not the slightest hesitation before the words "business partner."

"Business partner?" Julian asked politely. "What do you do?" He extended his hand to Mattie to shake.

Mattie took it. "We're traveling salesmen," he said, and exchanged the most fleeting of amused glances with Ivan.

Julian nodded. "A pleasure to meet you," he said, and then turned to Constance. "And you as well, miss."

Constance took his hand. His grip was firm, cool, and dry.

"A pleasure," Constance echoed, and shook his hand firmly. To the System watching, their interaction would look like nothing more than an older man's gallantry toward a younger woman, but Constance recognized it for the acknowledgment it was.

This was not her first time speaking to Julian, of course. Ivan had put them in contact almost two years earlier. That contact had been intermittent and entirely written; she had never seen or spoken to him before. But she knew enough of him to trust him on his own merits, not just Ivan's word.

But the System could not know that.

"What takes you to Luna?" Julian asked, turning back to Ivan.

Ivan smiled, a hint of embarrassment in his face, a young man in love and shy about admitting it. "Mattie and I were just taking Constance around. She's always wanted to come here. Mattie and Constance were foster siblings."

Constance smiled when she was supposed to, but the smile felt stiff on her cheeks. Ivan wore his persona so naturally. She couldn't understand how he could bear to do that, and knowing that every emotion he showed now was a lie made it harder for her to watch.

"Were you?" Julian asked, and smiled paternally at them. "I would have mistaken you for blood relatives, you look so much alike."

"I'm much more good-looking," said Mattie.

"Shut up, Matthew," Constance said, still smiling.

"Where are you staying?" Ivan asked Julian. "We'll pay you a visit."

"Unfortunately, I'll be on my way back to Terra before long," Julian said with very Terran regret, polite and distant. "If you have a moment, you might stop by; I am staying on board my own ship, down in the docks. It's a very distinctive ship—Lunar class, shaped like a star—but if you can't find it, it's right beside the System refueling ship *Hertzsprung*."

"System refueling ships don't stay docked for long, though," Ivan remarked. "Is there another landmark we should look out for?"

"No, you're quite right. And if I remember correctly, the *Hertzsprung* will go into its orbit today at around Terran Central Standard time 1500 hours. But if you can't visit me by that time, Leon, I'm afraid I won't have time to visit. I'll be leaving at 1700 hours myself."

"Well, I wouldn't want to detain you," Ivan said with a smile. "I'm glad I got to see you again, even if it was just for a moment."

Julian glanced around at Mattie and Constance. "I'll let you get back to your shopping."

"Of course," Constance said. "It was a pleasure to meet you, Mr.—" She remembered at the last moment that Ivan had not publicly told her Julian's last name.

"Just Julian, please," Julian said, sending his wrinkles crinkling up into his eyes when he smiled at her. "And it was nice to meet you as well, Mattie. Take care of this boy, will you?"

"As long as he lets me," Mattie said.

"Of course," Julian said. "If you see your mother again, send her my regards." He held Ivan's arm again, pressing it with surprising seriousness, then went on his way.

Constance watched him go. Terrans. The conversation had been wholly innocuous, completely innocent, yet he and Ivan had managed to provide each other with a time, a place, and the name of a ship with which to carry out the rest of their plan.

"Shall we?" Ivan invited, and offered Constance his arm again.

She took it. "Mattie?"

"I think I'll leave you to your shopping," Mattie said, stuffing his hands deep into his pockets. There was a suspicious jingle from one of them, like coins rattling against one another. He affected not to notice Constance's glare. "I'm going to go back to the ship."

"Our trip isn't inspiring you?" Ivan asked drily.

"No," Mattie said, "it's boring me."

"Can you find your way back on your own?"

"I think I'll manage somehow, thanks, Ivan."

Ivan grinned. "Have a good nap," he said.

"Enjoy your shopping," Mattie said, and left in the opposite direction than Julian had gone.

When he was gone, Ivan's smile faded. He sighed. The System watching would think it was exasperation, perhaps, but Constance knew better.

Mattie had the most difficult task of them all in this plan of Ivan's. Constance knew that that was not by Ivan's choice but by necessity. She squeezed his arm and took a step forward, and he fell in alongside her.

The broadcast screens showed fire and violence on Triton. Constance watched a wave of Tritonese rush a group of System soldiers. The filming was well done: the Tritonese looked savage and wild. But no amount of clever camera work could hide the brutality of the System's retaliation, firing again and again into the densely packed bodies. The camera cut away as soon as it could.

RIOTS ON TRITON, said the broadcast screen. TERRORIST ACTIVITY. THE SYSTEM IS SUPPRESSING THEM AND RESTORING PEACE TO THE MOON.

Somewhere in that bloodshed, Anji fought and Christoph waged war. Here, beneath the violence showing on the screens, the Lunar residents and Terran tourists walked around, carefree and casual, talking and laughing as if they did not notice the images of others suffering.

"I'm done shopping," Constance said abruptly. "Let's go to the observation deck."

"All right," Ivan said, and led the way.

The observation deck was adjacent to the shopping center. She and Ivan followed the signs directing them there, and when they stepped out of the shopping center and onto the observation deck, despite herself, she caught her breath.

Simulation and artiface, more falsity here than there was even on the rest of the moon. The Earth-facing side of the moon was almost as elite and aloof as Earth itself, and Ivan had persuaded her not to try to vacation there. It was too risky, he'd told her; the surveillance there was too great, the System police too powerful a force. It was only Terra and Luna that had police. The rest of the planets had the System military as police and conquering army both. Constance had yielded to Ivan's greater knowledge, and so she and Mattie and Ivan had booked a trip for the dark side of the moon.

Luna was tidally locked to Earth, and so the dark side would never look upon the mother planet. But anyone who came to Luna would want to see the Earth, and the tourism industry on the moon knew it. On the Earth-facing side, that was simple: observation decks were erected over the moon's surface, allowing visitors to come and look down upon the blue planet. On the dark side of the moon, tourists wanted the same thing but could not have it directly, so the System had done the next best thing and lied.

The observation deck was designed as if it were on the Earth-facing side of the moon. One wall and half the domed ceiling were made of glass, allowing the viewer to look up into the moon's perpetually star-studded sky. But it was not true glass; it was a display. The screen showed a live view of the Earth broadcast from the other side of the moon. Layers and layers of artifice, she thought; that was what the System was, lies and manipulation and distortion and lies. But even so, she stared at the image of the Earth and could not look away. Even though the image was false, she thought how near the Earth was, how near her victory was, if only she could pull it off.

She wondered if Ivan looked at it and thought of his home.

For a time they stood in silence, looking out onto the luminous Earth.

Then Ivan said, "Do you ever think about dying?"

Constance glanced at him. The sharp line of his jaw was angled out toward the slowly spinning blue and white globe before them. His eyes were on the Earth, not on her.

"No," she told him, and watched his face. "Why?" You had to prod Ivan sometimes or lead him like a dog on a leash to wherever he was unwilling to go on his own. And even then, Constance thought, some-times he wouldn't allow it.

"I do," he said, and although Constance could tell this was closer to the truth, she knew it was not all the way there. Not yet.

"Are you afraid of dying?"

"I've done it before."

Constance said, "But are you afraid of it?"

"Are you?" he countered.

"No," Constance said. "Everyone dies." Fear was for possibilities and unfavorable chance. There was no sense in fearing what was inevitable.

"So what are you afraid of, Constance?"

This space was too open, too public, for the admission of fears. Con-stance shrugged.

He turned to her then, moving closer. His hands slid around her waist, pulling her closer and shifting her position so that his shoulders blocked the camera in the upper-right corner of the observation deck from seeing her face. Constance wrapped her arms around his neck and moved her head so that she blocked the line of sight of the camera at her back so that it could not see his.

"Fear isn't a weakness, Constance," he said into the private little space they had built with simulated intimacy. "It's a natural response to a dangerous situation."

"So that's why you're afraid of dying?" Constance said.

"I'm not afraid of my death," Ivan said, answering without answering as he always did, and Constance almost reacted with frustration, but instead—perhaps because they had been too long in serious conversation and the System might notice—he leaned in and kissed her.

When he pulled away, he pressed his forehead to hers, then twisted his head aside as if he did not want to meet her eyes from so close. *You always meet Mattie's eyes*, Constance thought with strange and sullen bitterness while he pressed his face against hers so that his nose brushed her cheek and he breathed out into her jaw, against her neck. She kissed him then and held his head in place with her arms so that he had to look at her or be seen to struggle out of her grip.

She whispered, close in to his face, "What is it?"

For a moment she thought he might be honest with her. He was still holding her, and he was still looking at her, and he wasn't pulling away. But all he said was, "Constance, don't do this."

Her hands tightened into fists behind his neck.

"I have to," she said, and left him standing on the observation deck alone.

AFTER THE FALL OF EARTH

Outside the *Ananke*, the other ships drifted.

"Ananke, what have you done?" Althea asked.

"I didn't have time," Ananke said. "It was hard to get control of their engines all at once. And they were about to fire."

"So what did you do?"

Ananke said, "I took control of all their systems. I shut them down."

Life support, heat, air, power of all kinds; once it all stopped, it would kill a crew. But it would kill them slowly. Perhaps it was not too late—

"Turn them back on," Althea said. Her voice was small, breathless. She forced more energy into it: "Ananke, turn the processes back on!"

Outside, the engine lights on the drifting ships ignited again. The ships once again began to rotate, at first slowly and then with growing speed, until they reached the proper speed for 1-g gravitational simulation.

"Is the air back?" Althea asked. "The heat?"

"Restarting."

"But can they breathe?"

"The air lock doors were opened when I was gaining control of the computers; the air is regenerating but thin—"

"How long until they can breathe?"

Ananke said, "Seven minutes until normal atmospheric conditions are restored. There is air, though."

Seven minutes. But there was some air, Ananke had said. Althea clung to that. If there was some air, the crews might be able to survive.

She said, "Ananke, do you detect any life?"

Ananke did not reply.

Althea said, "Ananke, I'm not mad. But you need to run a scan and tell me if there is anyone alive on those ships."

The viewscreen flickered. Lines diagrammed the magnified images of the still-drifting System warships, scanning them, looking for the particular heat signatures that would indicate a living being. Glowing red spots appeared where it found signs of life, and Althea found herself beginning to hope. The spots of red were distributed throughout all six ships' disks, many spots of red, enough signs of life to represent a full crew for each ship.

"They're all right," Althea said, filled with relief even as some dark and half-realized thought edged into her mind. In Ananke's attempt to gain control of the navigation and the engines, the ships' trajectories had gone crazy, hurling the ships back and forth. The rapid changes in direction and speed would have exceeded safe parameters and killed at least some of the crew, who would have been beaten to death against the walls of their own womb.

Ananke said very cautiously, "The heat capacity of the human body is somewhere between three thousand and four thousand joules per kilogram per Kelvin. The air is thin, so heat conduction is weak. The primary heat loss for any bodies in a vacuum will be through radiation, which will take—"

"I understand," Althea said. The scans Ananke used were designed not to detect life itself but to detect heat signatures of the right size and temperature to represent mammalian life. They detected not life but heat.

And it would take time for newly made corpses to cool.

Seven minutes passed, seven more. On the screen before Althea, the System warships warmed slowly back up, air returning to their insides, becoming once again habitable. But as the ships warmed up, the heat signatures Ananke had detected slowly dimmed and winked out.

Wasn't this what Althea had comforted herself with? That even when attacked by the most powerful ships in the solar system, Ananke could hold her own, Ananke could defend herself, Ananke could come away from a confrontation without a scratch on her?

If this was what power was, Althea thought, standing safe while she watched the last of the little red lights fading away to nothing, she wanted none of it.

She said, "We have to go."

"Go?" Ananke asked. "Go where?"

"Away from here." She managed to make her legs work again and moved toward the main computer terminal in the piloting room. "Calculate a new course, heading—heading directly away from those ships—and go."

Ananke was silent for a moment, calculating. "That heading is not compatible with a best-fit path through the solar system."

"I don't care!" Althea heard her voice heading dangerously close to hysteria and with difficulty reined it in again. She said more calmly, "We can't stay here. Other ships might come."

"I don't detect any."

"They might be on their way right now, and we can't outrun them." The dead ships could have broadcast for backup before Ananke destroyed them. They couldn't take the chance of staying here. The System fleet might be anywhere. "Ananke, let's go."

But Ananke said, "We don't need to outrun them."

A chill passed through Althea like ice in her veins. It seemed to feed the curious pulsing pressure in her chest. "We have to."

"No," Ananke said. "I was wrong. Look—I had trouble, but I did it. And I know I can do it again. I'll be faster next time. So we don't have to run away."

"No—" Althea spun around to face the hologram, then corrected herself and looked up at the camera overhead, pointing at it as if the gesture could drive her meaning in. "This was wrong. This can't happen again."

Her hand was shaking. She lowered her finger as soon as she could and hoped that Ananke had not seen.

"They were attacking me," Ananke said.

"Yes, they were," Althea said. "But you hurt them—you killed them, Ananke. You can't do that. That's not right."

"I didn't mean to kill them."

"I know you didn't." The conversation was not going the way Althea wanted it to, the way she needed it to. Ananke was fixating on the wrong things. "I'm not blaming you, okay? I'm just telling you. This was wrong, Ananke. It can't happen again."

"Why not, if they were attacking me? Didn't you teach me how to defend myself?"

"Not like this," Althea said. She pressed her clasped fingers to her lips. Her heart felt swollen, too large for her chest, and she felt each thud of it like a kick on the inside of her ribs. She tried to gather her scattering thoughts.

"There were people over there," she said. "Real, living people on those ships. And now there aren't. Do you understand?"

"There were bad people on those ships," Ananke said.

"We don't know that."

"They tried to fire on me." Ananke spoke with the simplistic certainty of algebraic proof: one and one makes two.

Ananke would understand if only Althea could find the words to explain it. "They didn't know who you were," Althea said. "They thought you might be a danger to them. They were scared of you. So they attacked you so that you wouldn't attack them."

"Still, they attacked me."

"There were other ways to stop them," Althea said. "We talked about the other ways to stop them. That was the plan, Ananke, to *stop* them, not to kill them!"

"But what if there is no way to stop them without killing them?"

"There is always a way," Althea said, then more loudly, as if through volume she could fill the words with the certainty they lacked, "There is *always* a way. This time, the way to stop them without hurting them was to shut down the systems on their ship selectively so it left them frozen but not dead. Just like we talked about. I know you could have done it in time."

Ananke said, "Are you upset because they have human bodies?"

"What?"

"Human bodies. Are you upset because I stopped the functioning of their human bodies?"

"I don't understand what you mean," Althea said slowly.

"None of you thought anything of ending the computer on the *Annwn*," Ananke said. Althea remembered that like a memory from another life: disconnecting the computer on Mattie and Ivan's ship, the *Annwn*, because it could have been dangerous to her and the rest of the *Ananke*'s crew. "None of the crew but you thought anything of stopping my thoughts. But you all were angry about Gagnon and about Ida Stays. If I'd had a human body like you have, then Gagnon and Domitian would not have tried to harm me. And now, when I have wrenched apart the computers of those six ships, you are only concerned about their crew."

"It's not the same thing," Althea said. "A computer and a person—you think, Ananke. Other computers don't think. You're more a person than a computer."

"Then I do not understand why you are upset. Don't you love me more than those dead men?"

"I don't love them at all," Althea said, "and I love you more than anything." If someone had to be dead, she would rather it be the System than her Ananke, but she did not dare say so to her. "But it upsets me because there were people over there, people just like you or me, and they're dead now."

She waited, one hand held out in a gesture toward the dead ships. There is a way of praying without praying, a state of being that is composed of wordless and directionless pleading, and Althea found herself in that state. She did not believe in any higher power, and so she could not have said to whom she bent her begging, hoping thoughts, to some unnamed god or to the universe or to Ananke herself, but still she waited and prayed that Ananke might understand.

Ananke said, "It would upset you if it happened again."

"It would."

Ananke's holographic face shifted into another expression in a ripple of gleaming light. The face she showed now was contrite.

"I'm sorry," she said. "I won't do it again."

Althea said, "Promise me."

Ananke said, "I promise."

The dense air of Venus was thick with smoke.

Constance picked her way over the orange volcanic rock, over the rubble of Kidwelly's fallen houses, through the still bodies lying between the stones. She watched them closely, wary that one might rise up again, only appearing to be dead. The gunfire and explosions had petered out into silence some minutes earlier, but Constance could see nothing through the dense smoke before her.

"Find Arawn," she ordered Rayet, whose steps dogged her own. He nodded once, then beckoned someone else over and sent him off, after which he went back to stalking silently behind her. Around Constance, her soldiers ranged like hounds over what once had been a Venerean street, guns alert like noses, sniffing through the ruins.

The smell was almost overpowering. The thickness of the air lined the inside of Constance's nose, the palate of her mouth, with particles of dust and ash. The powder of metal and stone and chemicals and flesh charred to carbon. She'd smelled it before. On Miranda, on Mars. She'd smelled it before.

Movement in the smoke before her. Constance lifted her gun, but the people who emerged were her own. One of them shouted back, and a moment later Arawn came striding out of their midst.

"You're bleeding," he said. He was covered in the same powder that filled the air.

She lifted a hand automatically to where his eyes indicated, up by her collarbone, and pulled it away red. It didn't hurt.

Shrapnel, she realized. A piece of shrapnel had struck her. The vest had deflected most of it, but its edge had torn into her skin where the vest ended.

She wiped the red from her fingers, or tried to; it only seemed to smear them with more of the dust. "I'm fine," she said.

Arawn's hands were on her suddenly, bracing against her breastbone, spreading over her shoulder. She was too startled to think to move and let him look at her, spreading the skin of her wound open to check its severity. When his thumbs dug into her skin, exploring the cut, it burned.

"Not serious," he said, and slackened his grip, but his hands remained resting upon her chest.

Constance pulled away from his touch to pace down the street, searching what little she could see of it. "Is the city down?"

"The city's fallen," Arawn confirmed from behind her. She heard him follow her away and then stop behind her shoulder. "At least my section is. Yours as well. I haven't heard from Henry. Greene is dead."

Surprised, Constance turned. "You're sure?"

"We pinned her down in a building a few blocks from here, then blew it up. She's dead."

Constance nodded slowly. Lyra Greene, dead. Well, she had said she was willing to die. "I want to see this building," she said.

"I'll take you there."

With a shout to her men to keep sweeping the city, Constance followed Arawn down the street of the dead city.

Street after street, Arawn led and Constance followed. All Venerean cities had their streets laid out in a grid, simple and ordered and easy to navigate, by System mandate, but the streets Constance walked now did not seem to lie straight any longer. She knew that the damage done to the city by her bombs was not enough to obscure their original layout, but the paths her feet followed seemed to twist and bend.

It was hot, too. Venus was always hot, but it was hotter here, where Constance could still catch glimpses of fires in the hollows of the bombed-out buildings. It was too hot, and her throat was dry.

"Huntress!" someone shouted.

It was Henry who had called her name. His bald head was bleeding so much that Constance's initial impulse was alarm, but he walked steadily and purposefully, and so it could not be bad. Head wounds always bled overly much.

He had a handheld communicator in one hand, extended before him as if he meant to give it to Constance. "What is it?" she asked.

"Greene's fleet got past our fliers," Henry said. Before Constance could absorb the implications of this, he added, "They made it to space."

"Did they get away?"

"No." Henry's expression darkened. "They attacked our fleet."

Her fleet? If Constance's fleet was destroyed, she and her army would be hugely weakened, stranded on Venus until they could acquire enough ships to escape again. And Milla was with the fleet—

"What damage?" she demanded.

"One ship down. A few more damaged. But Greene's fleet is destroyed." It was good news, but Henry still looked grim. There was something he wasn't telling her. He offered her the communicator. "Doctor Ivanov's on the line."

Constance took the communicator. "Milla?" she said.

"Here," Milla said, her crisp tones muddied by the atmosphere separating them. "Greene's fleet is gone, but we suffered some damage."

"Casualties?"

"Most of the crew of the *United*, heavy attacks on the *Eddington*, the *Lakshmibai*, the *Pucelle*, and the *Bethe*. Somewhere between five hundred and six hundred hands, all told. The ships only had skeleton crews."

A flare of fury took Constance now that her immediate fear was passing. "How did they get past us?"

It was Henry who answered. "As far as we can tell, the other cities that supported Greene sent support to Kidwelly during the battle," he said, pitching his voice so that Milla could hear. "I encountered more resistance at the south side of the city than we were expecting."

"There were more ships than Greene could have possibly had at Kidwelly alone," Milla agreed.

Constance had hoped that the other cities would surrender once Kidwelly fell and that her attack on Greene's city would be too swift for any of her allies to provide meaningful aid. It seemed she had been wrong.

"Well done, repelling them," she said to Milla. "I want you to—"

"It isn't me you should be thanking."

Constance looked at Henry. He was still watching her with the same grim expression. Carefully, Constance said, "What happened?"

"Marisol Brahe led the attack."

"Marisol?" said Constance. For a moment she couldn't remember the face that went with the name, and then it came to her. The girl who had joined her on Mars, the one whose hair had been perpetually threatening to fall into her eyes, as Mattie's had done when he had been her age. "What was a teenage girl doing leading an attack with my ships, Milla?"

"She was on the *Pucelle*. The first attack took out most of the piloting room and the ranking officers. Marisol took control of the ship and returned fire to Greene's fleet. By the time the *Wild Hunt* was able to join the attack, a number of the nearby ships were already following her example. She was a good symbol." Rarely had Milla Ivanov's voice sounded quite so flat and cold. "So I used her."

The verb chilled Constance. "And is she alive?"

"Yes. I didn't leave her to fend for herself; I told her what to do, and she followed my directions. I believe the other captains were glad to have someone to follow who reminded them of you."

Curious phrasing from Milla, but Constance let it pass. Out of the corner of her eye she caught sight of Rayet. He was listening with great intensity to her conversation. Constance said, "Tell her I will speak with her when I return to the *Wild Hunt*."

"I will, Huntress."

Constance handed the communicator back to Henry. "Keep sweeping the city," she told him. "I want to be sure no resistance is left."

"Yes, Huntress," he said, and left.

Arawn was waiting. "Take me to Greene's body," she said.

The place where Greene had died was still burning. Sometimes the heat from an explosion was enough to ignite even material that normally would not burn, and once such a fire began, it was hard to put out. The smoke here was black, and the air was even thicker for it. The buildings on either side of the blast site were charred and half ruined by the force of the blast, and metal beams lay twisted and bent in the crater on the ground.

Greene had died in a System building. Even though it was in ruins, Constance could tell what the architecture had been.

She walked slowly around the edges of the ruin, where it was just safe enough to stand. Between the fallen beams and glass and stone she could see the red glow of the fires underground.

She remembered Miranda, the System lighting a house on fire and shooting the people who came out. System broadcasts had never reported those sorts of events, but Constance had witnessed them with her own two eyes. The people inside had to choose between death in the flames and death by the firing squad. She remembered the smell of the burning houses and the burning people; she remembered the thickness of the smoke. It had smelled much the same as the air smelled here and now.

There was a body on the edges of the crater. The fire had burned all its skin to bubbling red. Whatever hair and clothes the person had had were all burned away. Constance could not know if the red corpse had been Lyra Greene, but she stood for a moment and watched the flesh bubble as the fire below crept up higher to devour what was left.

Constance remembered the people in Miranda starving in the streets. She remembered going to other moons in the outer solar system and seeing the way the people flinched away from the System soldiers. She remembered the ruin, the slow choking death of the people trapped and suffocating when the System broke the greenhouse enclosure that kept them alive.

This was justice, she told herself. Finally, after all those years, she had the power to right the wrongs that had been done, and she would use that power well.

Constance stood at the edge of the fire she had lit and inhaled the thick, choking dust on the Venerean wind.

"Tighter," Althea said. "If you grip it that loosely, it'll slide out when you move."

She sat atop the table in her workroom with one of the mechanical arms wheeled up in front of her, its grasping fingers closing slowly around a pen. In the opposite corner of the room, where the holographic terminal was, Ananke's hologram sat and watched with sightless eyes. She had one hand raised, fingers curled around the air, just as the physical metal hand in front of Althea gripped the pen.

Althea held the other end of the pen to stop it from falling. "Slowly," she cautioned while the mechanical fingers began to tighten around the pen.

"I already have it," Ananke said impatiently.

"Sure," said Althea, "but you're using too much force or too little. You have to learn how much force is just right."

Ananke was silent for a moment, her holographic and physical fingers working simultaneously. "Do humans know it instinctively?" she asked.

"Sort of. They learn when they're babies."

Ananke's mechanical arm stretched forward a little bit, and the hologram leaned forward correspondingly, her arm extending too far, outside the holographic terminal's ability to project. The holographic hand ended in a fizzing stump at the forearm, but Ananke did not seem to notice.

Althea turned her attention away from it. It was nothing more than a hologram, she reminded herself; it wasn't truly Ananke, just a representation.

"Let go," Ananke said suddenly.

Althea didn't. "Have you got it?"

"Yes. Let go."

Althea let go. The pen stayed.

"Good," Althea said. She held out her hand. "Now give it to me."

The mechanical arm reached out carefully and placed the pen on Althea's fingers. Althea closed her hand quickly to catch it before it rolled off.

"Good, but your localization was off," she commented, putting the pen on the table beside her. "You're going to need to learn how to tell where exactly something is."

"Let me try it again."

"I have a better idea. Call another arm in here."

Ananke's hologram sat back, pulling all her limbs back into the bounds of the holographic terminal. The mechanical hand in front of Althea remained frozen, outstretched. Althea hopped down from the table to dig around in her toolbox.

By the time she had found what she needed, there was a low grumbling roar from the hallway of wheels rattling over grates. Althea sat back up on the table just as Ananke's hologram turned its head to face the door in uncanny sync with the mechanical arm that at that very moment pushed its way in.

Ananke said, "I got the doorknob."

"Very good," Althea said as the second mechanical arm rumbled its way up beside the first. They were both very large even with their joints bent, and they crowded her on the table.

Althea tried to ignore it. She lifted up the item she had pulled out of the toolbox for Ananke to see.

Ananke said, "Rope?"

"Twine," Althea corrected, and quickly untangled the length of it. It was a good meter, a usable length for the sizable mechanical arms. Althea offered one end to the first arm and the other end to the second, and Ananke accepted the twine.

"Now," said Althea, and pulled her legs up onto the table, too, for a little bit more distance from the arms, though they could have reached her even if she had been on the other side of the table entirely. "Tie a knot."

"What kind of knot?" Ananke wanted to know.

"Just a box knot," said Althea.

The mechanical arms began to move, and then each one stopped, with Ananke evaluating. Then they began to move again but overshot each other. The next time they managed to come close together—the localization, Althea noted, was the problem; she'd have to go in and refine the code herself—moving slowly so that they would not collide and damage themselves. But the fingers could not quite figure out how to achieve the dexterity required to pull the loop through.

Ananke said, "Is this something humans must learn, too?"

"Well, sort of," Althea said, watching as the arms fumbled and one hand dropped its length of twine. "But the dexterity and the localization—uh, the body awareness—" She could not tell which term was better. "—they're an instinctive sense, and babies just have to refine it."

The hologram was frowning. The hand picked up its end of the twine again.

Go into the code and refine the localization, Althea thought. *Then see if there's anything that can be done with the touch sensors. Ananke will probably be able to update them herself, but the localization may be a problem. Perhaps Ananke needs better hardware—*

"Proprioception," Ananke said suddenly.

"What?"

"Proprioception," Ananke said. "Awareness of the location of body parts and the ways that they move. That is the term for the human sense."

Proprioception, Althea thought. *She likes that term better than "localization."*

"Thank you," Althea said for lack of anything better, and watched the mechanical hands begin to move again.

"Ananke," she said carefully, taking a risk, but it had been troubling her for a while and this seemed as good a time as any to bring it up. "Do you understand why what happened with those ships was wrong?"

"You told me," Ananke said. "Because those people died."

"But do you understand *why?*" Althea pressed.

The hologram was moving her fingers, her hands, as if she were tying an invisible knot. Closer to Althea, the mechanical hands moved as well in graceless imitation of the hologram's well-practiced simulation. Ananke said, "I do not understand why energy must be conserved and why parity may not always be so, but they are rules."

For a moment Althea felt relief. If Ananke saw her rules as being as inviolable as the conservation of energy, everything would be fine. But Ananke said, "But I do not understand—the universe prevents me from violating the conservation of energy. But your rule, not to kill—I can break that law."

Althea's heart thumped heavily in her chest. In front of her, the two mechanical arms were wheeling slowly apart with the grinding of un-oiled gears, stretching out the twine to its full length so that the camera above could see it clearly. The hologram stretched her arms out to her sides, fingers pinched together, and regarded empty space with a thoughtful eye.

"You can't break this rule," Althea said as firmly as she could.

"'Can't' implies inability," Ananke said. "I am able to do it. I should not—there is obligation. But there is no inabil—"

"No," Althea snapped, "you *cannot*," just as the mechanical arms, with their imperfect localization, drew too far apart and the twine snapped in two.

"Okay," Ananke said while each broken piece of twine dangled from its respective hand.

"Good," said Althea, and swallowed and then hopped down from the table so that she could go get another length of twine.

But, she thought, Ananke was right. A real child, a human child, Althea could have picked up in her arms and put into her crib. A human girl Althea could have held, could have physically overpowered. But Ananke was vast and great and vaster and greater than Althea, and if she decided not to do as Althea said, Althea would not be able to stop her.

Constance listened closely to the tablet she held, but she heard nothing but static.

She scrubbed her face with one hand. For a moment she'd thought she had heard Julian, muffled by static and almost incoherent, but she must have been wrong. She had broadcast out the sounds of the barking hounds hours earlier and recently received it in return, but perhaps Julian's message had been lost to the interference of the sun.

It was past time since she should have heard from him. Communication across the solar system was nearly impossible. In part, she knew, this was due to her revolution, which was working to destroy all System bases and equipment regardless of function. Those were her orders, and she did not regret them. But it did leave her sitting in the conference room adjoining her quarters on the *Wild Hunt*, hunched beneath the room's low-hanging ceiling, hoping that the communications equipment her people had been trying to boost for days would be able to reach all the way to the outer solar system. Her people and Altais's were cleaning up the last traces of resistance on Venus now; it would be time to move on from the planet soon, but Constance did not want to proceed until she had some idea of what was going on in the outer solar system.

If Mattie were here, she thought, but shut the thought down swiftly. Mattie was not there. And even if he had been, there was no guarantee he could have forced subpar equipment to reach all the way to Julian's location, anyway.

Someone knocked on her door.

"Come in," she said, and for the moment ceased to hope that Julian's message was going to emerge from the static emptiness.

The door swung open. Carefully, hesitantly, Marisol Brahe stepped in, with Milla Ivanov ghosting along behind her. Milla came to sit beside Constance while Marisol stood stiffly by the door.

"You wanted to see me?" Marisol said.

Constance studied her. Marisol did not look as young as she was in Constance's memory of her, but she was still painfully young, dark hair still on the edge of falling into her wide brown eyes. But she stood at attention in front of Constance without fidgeting or wavering.

"Yes," said Constance. "It's about what happened on the *Pucelle*."

Marisol swallowed.

Constance chose her words carefully. "I think you have good instincts, Marisol. In the battle, you knew what you had to do to keep yourself and the people around you alive."

"Thank you, Huntress."

"You also knew, I imagine, that you shouldn't have acted without consulting with Doctor Ivanov first," Constance said.

"Yes, Huntress."

"But you didn't."

"There wasn't time, Huntress."

"So you acted anyway."

"Yes, Huntress."

"Were you afraid?" Constance asked.

"Yes," said Marisol. "I mean, I wasn't when it was happening. I just thought: this is something I have to do. Not, I have to do this or I'll die. Just, this has to be done, and I have to do it."

Marisol shifted her weight when she spoke, her hands coming up to gesture expressively. When she finished speaking and remembered herself, she let her hands drop and resumed her attentive stance. She was short, Constance noticed; the terrible lowness of the ceiling did not trouble her.

"That's how it is," Constance said. "In the moment, everything has perfect clarity. You can't be afraid when the way forward is that clear and when your decisions are that simple." Her favorite moment in every attack was the moment when she pressed the detonator, right before the explosion, the moment the System was coming at them and it was finally time to turn on them with tooth and nail.

"But there's more that goes into it than that one moment," Constance said. "There are plans that you are not a part of, rules that you have to follow. I tell you what to do or what not to do, and you obey me. Do you understand?"

"I understand," Marisol said, then, more strongly, "I *understand*. I should have talked to Doctor Ivanov before I attacked the other ships." Her gaze flickered briefly, apologetically, to Milla Ivanov.

"You should have," Constance said quietly, "if you could have," and with those words Marisol's attention snapped so closely on her that Constance thought that if the ship blew up around them, Marisol still would not take her gaze from her face.

Constance made her decision.

"I'm going to have you spend some more time with Henry. He'll take care of you, teach you. We need people with good instincts," she said, "and we'll need them more than ever when the System fleet strikes. Do you understand me?"

"I understand," said Marisol, and now she did smile, her smile small and controlled but brilliant in its sincerity.

"You're dismissed," Constance said, and Marisol nodded, moved as if she meant to bow, and thought better of it. She glanced once more at Milla Ivanov, then left the room.

When they were alone, Milla said, "She's a good girl, but a danger."

Constance laughed. "A danger?"

"Yes. Keep her loyal."

"Or what?"

Milla lifted a shoulder. "Or have her killed."

Constance stared at her for a moment, trying to decide if this was a strange Terran form of humor. Certainly Ivan had tended to say things that she had not thought were funny but had left him laughing a breathless and bitter laugh.

"You're serious," she said.

"If Marisol ever decides not to follow your orders, she will be a great threat to you," Milla said.

"I don't kill my own!"

"Of course not," Milla agreed. "That's why you should keep her loyal."

Getting angry at Milla Ivanov was a waste of energy; Constance could have shouted at Ivan and reliably had him react, but her words slid off Milla Ivanov like raindrops off glass. She sighed and rested her head against the back of her chair, staring up at that low ceiling. There was a patch in it over her head. A camera, she thought; a camera had been there and had been removed, but Constance still could see where it had been.

Milla said, "Have you had any luck with Julian?"

"Nothing."

"I could try," Milla offered.

"Have you got any secret methods of communication you aren't sharing with me, Milla?"

"I'm telepathic," Milla said, her voice as flat as it could possibly be. "Didn't I mention?"

For a moment Constance was too startled to react. Then she laughed. "Of course," she said. "In that case, I would appreciate if you'd try to telepathically reach Julian on your own. I think I'll try with the communicator a little longer myself."

"Very well," Milla said. "I didn't come here to speak of Julian. I have news from the planet's surface."

"Venus?" Greene's resistance had been crushed almost entirely; Constance couldn't imagine what could have gone wrong.

"It's Altais," Milla said carefully. "He has been ruling the territories that you have defeated."

"Ruling?" Constance snapped, all her stillness and good humor vanished. "What does that mean?"

"Stationing troops in the conquered areas," Milla said, "ostensibly to keep the order. Extorting tithes."

"And in my name?"

"In the name of liberation."

Not even in her name. How dare he take the lands for his own, the lands she had worked to free? And not even do so out of loyalty to her?

"Summon him here," Constance said.

"Is that wise?"

"Does he know that what he's done is wrong?"

"I think he may suspect you will not approve," Milla said. "Hence he has not mentioned it."

Constance leaned forward onto the conference table, bending over the communicator that was still lying there, silent. She thought of Altais strategically holding his tongue, cowardice keeping him from conversation with her. He would have kept his silence until she had gotten into contact with Julian and left this planet, and him, behind.

"He won't dare to refuse to come," Constance said. "Summon him here."

"Very well," Milla said, but she did not leave, so that could not have been all that she had come to discuss. Nor could Marisol have been the point of her trip; she seemed to have said everything she had to say about the girl. What else could there possibly be to discuss?

Milla said, "Constance—"

Someone rapped hard on the door. It was not a knock with the strength of urgency, only the strength of personality. Constance knew that forceful knock: it was Arawn.

"Come in," she said, and to Milla, "Does he know?"

"Doubtless," Milla said. "He has a way of finding things out."

The edge of overt unpleasantness was so very unlike Milla that Constance looked at her sharply, but she did not have a chance to ask, because Arawn stepped in. He had trimmed his dark hair and shaved; his beard traced a sharp line down his broad jaw.

When he saw Milla Ivanov, he flashed white teeth through that dark beard. "Doctor Ivanov," he said, then, to Constance, "I see you leave your bodyguard outside."

"There's no reason for Rayet to be in here."

"And yet isn't the whole reason you assigned him that you were attacked by some traitors in your own quarters?"

"He searched the rooms."

"Good," Arawn said. "Because that's the real danger. I don't want you to be attacked again by someone you should trust inside your own home."

Milla Ivanov stood up abruptly. "I have work to do elsewhere," she said, and nodded at Constance. "Huntress."

After the door closed behind her, Constance said to Arawn, "Whatever your problem is with Milla Ivanov, *end it*."

"Right," he said amiably, and then took Milla's vacated seat at Constance's side. He seemed to fill up that seat more than Milla had in more ways than just his greater size. Constance could feel his presence more keenly, her skin pricking from the nearness of his. Angry as she was, that pricking seemed all the stronger.

He said, "You heard about Altais?"

"I heard," Constance said, and tried to swallow her simmering rage.

He leaned back in his chair, letting his legs spread. He was far too comfortable around her. She thought about telling him off but didn't.

"He's been executing dissidents, System or not," Arawn said. "You hear that part?"

"No," Constance said, and knew her fingers had curled into fists only when she felt the bite of her nails in her palm.

Arawn nodded thoughtfully. "What are you going to do?"

"I've summoned him here," Constance said. "I want you and Doctor Ivanov present."

"What, to talk to him?"

"What else?"

"Well, say he listens," said Arawn, and leaned forward, elbows on knees so that his face was below hers. She could see faded scars near his hairline and wondered absently if the System had given them to him. "And he goes back to Venus, and he does as you order, and he lets all those cities go, and he's an obedient friend of the Mallt-y-Nos again."

"That would be the goal, Arawn."

"And then you leave," Arawn said. "For Luna or for wherever. But he's still back there all alone, without the Mallt-y-Nos up in orbit to keep him in line. So what does he do?" She did not answer, and so Arawn answered his own question. "So he breaks your rules."

"Don't you think he would know to hold his tongue out of respect for me?" Constance asked, raising her eyebrows at Arawn pointedly.

"Any man with sense would. But I don't think Altais is a man with sense."

Arawn's eyes were dark, not light as Ivan's had been. And with that thought she leaned back in her chair, away from the nearness and the presence of him, and pushed thoughts of them both from her mind.

"What else would you have me do?" she demanded of him, but before he could answer, the communications device began to cough and sputter with static. Then it began to howl, a pack of hunting dogs all singing together.

Julian.

With relief, Constance swiftly decrypted the message. Julian's recorded voice said, "Julian Keys to the Mallt-y-Nos. This message is meant for the ears of the Mallt-y-Nos and the Mallt-y-Nos alone."

Next to her, Arawn stretched, looking pleased that she had not sent him away, and grinned at her when she gave him the eye.

Julian said, "I've spoken with Christoph. My fleet was enough to deter him for a little while, but negotiations have fallen apart since. He's refused to back down, and he's started moving his fleet toward the inner planets again."

Constance's fingers gripped the edge of the conference table hard enough that her bones creaked.

"Anji won't stop him," Julian continued in his mellifluous Lunar-tinged Terran accent. He spoke his disastrous news in an even tone that reminded Constance of Milla Ivanov and Ivan at his most withdrawn. *Terrans*, she thought, but the thought was less dismissive than it was despairing. "Christoph will pass right through her territory. He'll go right through Jupiter to get to you, but she's going to let him." The briefest pause, a hesitation in Julian's steady tone. "I do not think she condones it. I believe, from what I have seen, that she is having difficulty maintaining control of her forces and is focusing her attention on that."

If her troops had been mutinous, that would explain some of Anji's actions. Constance tried not to feel a faint relief that Anji's defection might have had an outside cause. No matter what the cause was, Anji was still a traitor.

"Diplomacy will not work with Christoph," Julian said. "Please relay to me . . . what you would like me to do."

The recording ended.

Constance sat back in her chair. Christoph was coming toward her, and somewhere the System was rebuilding its strength. If she didn't handle things swiftly, she might find herself attacked on two sides.

"What does he want?" Arawn asked.

Constance almost laughed. Never would she have been able to predict this back before it happened. But even so, she understood him now.

"Christoph was always one for show," she said. "The targets he always wanted to hit were big—grand buildings, statues celebrating the System, anything to show that we were better. I liked that about him then. His targets weren't always the smartest or the best choices, but they always had an effect."

"And now you're his grand statue."

"If he defeats me, he shows Anji that he's the one in charge," Constance said. It was disturbing having the logic that had always been her ally turned against her.

Arawn said, "It looks like you don't have any other choice."

"I have choices," Constance said.

"You've done nothing about Anji, and you've barely done anything about Christoph, and you're not going to do anything decisive against Altais. What kind of bargaining power did Julian have when you sent him to talk to Christoph? He could talk and he could order Christoph, but Christoph would know you weren't going to do anything to follow up."

"You speak too plainly."

"I'm not a diplomat, Huntress," Arawn said, "and I'm not some silver-tongued Terran, either." Constance recoiled. "I speak plainly. And plainly, it's like this: you're not taking action, and not taking action makes you look weak."

"I acted against Greene."

"Yeah, but Greene is gone. Christoph and Altais and Anji are the problem now. And the System fleet is out there somewhere. There're rumors they're on Europa. There're rumors that they're back on Mars. They—"

"Mars?" Constance said sharply. "The fleet might be back on Mars?"

"That's what I've heard," Arawn said. "God only knows if it's true; it's hard to get good information these days. But the fleet could be near as Mars, and if they come at us while we're divided—or if they join up with Christoph or Anji against us—"

"Christoph and Anji would never ally themselves with the System."

"But even if they don't," Arawn said, "they're still weakening you, and every day that passes while they do is another day the System fleet is holed up somewhere, getting its strength and its numbers back and getting ready to undo everything you've done."

Constance wondered how it seemed so clear to him, how he could be untroubled by the conflict between strength and old loyalty. She suspected he would say that Christoph and Anji had no loyalty to her any longer, but just because they had lost that loyalty, that didn't mean she had to do the same thing. She would be righteous, she told herself; she would be better than what others were.

"Since you seem to have the answers," Constance said, her voice tight, "why don't you tell me what you think I should do?"

"That's your choice, Huntress, and I trust your wisdom," Arawn said, and Constance wondered if she was imagining the doubtful weight on his words. "But if it were me, in your place, I would kill Christoph."

"Kill him," Constance said flatly.

"Yes. Julian's in the right place to send an assassin. Answer his message, tell him—"

"It's a matter of trust that Julian is there as a diplomat."

"What kind of meaningless honor is that when Christoph's already turned on you?"

Meaningless honor, but that kind of honor had kept Constance and her revolution alive back when they were fighting in secret and had to rely on one another entirely. Arawn's meaningless honor had been what had made Constance's revolution possible; meaningless honor had kept Ivan's mouth shut on the *Ananke*, even to his death.

"I'll take your advice under consideration," she said to him, another Ivanov phrase. She could almost hear the Terran tinge to it even through her Mirandan accent. She turned from him, a dismissal. She reached for the tablet and said into it, "Julian, stay with Christoph for now. I will contact you within twenty-four hours with instructions. Be ready to receive them. Transmission over."

Despite her clear dismissal, Arawn had not moved. "Is there something else you would like to say?" Constance asked, danger in her tone.

"There's something else you should know," Arawn said.

"So tell me." She squared her shoulders like Anji readying herself for a blow.

Arawn rubbed his chin, his fingers scratching the bristles of his black beard, thinking. "I know you like to keep me at arm's length, Huntress," he said in that curiously challenging way, "and I won't insult you by guessing why."

It was not even his right to question. Constance remained silent and forced him to continue to speak. Arawn said, "Do you remember when you first got into contact with Julian, a few weeks ago? And me and Doctor Ivanov were in the communications room?"

Milla and Arawn had been in the communications room when she'd arrived, with a curious tension between them. "Yes."

"I told you I was there to get a transmission from my people on Venus, but that wasn't entirely true. They could've sent a message directly to my ship; I didn't need to be in the communications room. I was there because I'd had my people monitoring transmissions in and out of your fleet, and they'd intercepted an interesting one. I went to go investigate."

"You've been spying on my people? You've been spying on *my* ship?" Constance's voice was cold. That kind of monitoring, that lack of privacy had been one of the hallmarks of the System.

"Would you rather not know?"

No, Constance almost said. *No, I don't want to know.* But she had to. "Tell me what you heard."

"We didn't hear the content of the message or any of the messages since. Yes," he said, seeing her look, "there have been more since then. Several of them, both coming into your fleet and going out. I didn't tell you before then because I wasn't sure, but I'm sure now. The transmissions were with Anji Chandrasekhar."

A chill went through Constance, and when it faded, the burning in her chest seemed hotter than before. "A spy?"

"There's no way to tell. But someone in your fleet has been communicating with Chandrasekhar regularly for the past few weeks."

Constance said, with dread warring with her growing rage, "And you know who it is."

"Aye," Arawn said. "I know who it is."

So did Constance if she let herself accept the implication of Arawn's tone and demeanor. But this was not something she would allow herself to believe on mere implication. She had to hear it spoken outright. She had to know without any doubt. "Tell me her name."

Arawn said, "Milla Ivanov."

. . .

It occurred to Althea to wonder when she woke up how many days it had been since Earth had fallen, how many days had passed since Domitian had died, since Ivan had escaped, since Ananke had come to life. She almost asked Ananke while she dressed herself and pulled her hair back roughly into a ponytail, out of her face, but something un-nameable stopped her.

Ananke was waiting for her in the holographic terminal in the hall outside Althea's room. She was dressed the same as Althea in an old pair of work overalls and with her curly hair pulled back out of her face. But the shape of her jaw was rather more like Mattie's than Al-thea's, and her eyes were Ivan's.

She looked older today, too, Althea thought. Had the hologram been growing older day by day, imperceptibly, and Althea had noticed only now?

Ananke said, "I've been thinking about Constance Harper."

Althea preferred to spend her days without thinking of Constance Harper at all. "What were you thinking?" she asked, and started off down the hall. She thought about getting breakfast, but her restless sleep and unstructured days had left her without an appetite. The workroom was farther down the hall than the kitchen, and Althea passed the kitchen without pausing.

"I was thinking that it might be good to talk to her," Ananke said, appearing and disappearing in consecutive holographic terminals, blinking in and out of existence, chasing Althea down the hall. "She might know where Ivan and Mattie are."

"She might. And she might not tell us."

"Why not? We mean them no harm."

Constance Harper might not see it that way, Althea thought. Aloud she said, "She doesn't know that."

"We could convince her."

"And if you can't?" Althea asked, and Ananke seemed to have no answer to that. Maybe it would do Ananke some good to contemplate what it would feel like to have someone who wouldn't do what she wanted her to.

Althea doubted that Ananke would make the connection.

Althea had reached the door to the workroom. "Are you ready?" she asked. "I thought we'd try the knot again." The workroom was already bright, and the hologram was already seated on the terminal, and two mechanical arms were already inside and waiting for her.

"I am ready," Ananke said. "Give me the rope."

Althea almost smiled at her eagerness. Her daughter didn't like to fail. It probably would take a few sessions before Ananke got the knack of it; robotic localization was a standard issue, and it would take some time to refine Ananke's internal mapping and compensate for any ambiguity in the joints of the mechanical arms.

The mechanical hands plucked the two ends of the twine from Althea's fingers with unexpected delicacy. Ananke must have implemented some of her own code. The arms moved apart a bit, giving themselves some space to work, and then moved back together. Their motions were smooth and confident, as balanced as a dance. One hand wrapped the rope around, and then the other put its end of the rope to the dangling loop and passed it through, picking up the thread on the other side.

For a moment, a loop of rope the size of Althea's head dangled between the two mechanical hands, and then they tugged on the twine. Althea almost expected them to snap it, but they were gentle; the twine was pulled until the knot had tightened into a wad too small and dense ever to be undone, and then they held it aloft, triumphant. The hologram was smiling from the corner of the room, her hands upraised in a simulation of victory.

Proud, Althea thought. *She's proud; your daughter is proud of what she's done. She's done something marvelous, she's done something well, and she's showing off for her mother because she's proud.*

Ananke had done it by herself, all by herself. She hadn't needed Althea's help. And if she could do that much, she would no longer need Althea's help for anything else, either.

"Look, Mother," Ananke said, and one of the arms dropped its end of the twine and came rumbling slowly forward. Althea stayed rooted to the spot until it stopped nearly at her toes, and then the delicate hand stretched out toward her. Althea stared down at it. Good workmanship, she thought. Good range of motion. But for the color and the sheen of its false skin, it could almost be a real human hand.

The hand still was waiting. Althea reached out slowly and laid her palm against the thing's.

When the fingers closed around her hand, they were gentle. They exerted neither too much pressure nor too little. But the strength of their metal bones made their grip unbreakable.

Constance summoned Arawn to be with her when Altais arrived. She did not call for Milla Ivanov.

"I've put guards on her, Huntress," Arawn said while they waited.

"Have them be discreet," Constance told him. "I want to see if Doctor Ivanov tries to contact Anji again." She had not confronted Milla. She was not sure she could yet. She wanted to see it with her own two eyes before she fell upon the wife of Connor Ivanov with all the force of her anger.

Altais was late. The stupidest thing he could possibly do, she thought, was be late. But he was. When at last he arrived, he came in with five of Constance's people at his heels: a guard for a prisoner. Rayet was standing behind Constance, openly armed, and Arawn was at her side like a lean and hungry dog. Only a fool would not realize he was the subject of her displeasure and mistrust.

Milla Ivanov, too, would figure out that she was under guard eventually. She was too clever a woman for the charade to last forever. Let her figure it out, then. Let her wonder at the cause of Constance's displeasure while Constance kept track of her acts and her movements and decided what was to be done.

Altais said with wary politeness, "You wanted to speak to me, Huntress?"

"Explain yourself," Constance said.

"Explain myself?" said Altais with his little eyes darting back and forth. "What would you like me to explain?"

"We can begin with the tithes." Arawn had updated her on all the details, and each word he had spoken had made her anger grow until it was as it was now, incandescent, burning her from the inside.

"Tithes?" Altais asked. "Huntress, you know as well as I that running a war is expensive. My people have to be fed."

"You did not consult me," said Constance, "nor did you inform me that you intended to rule the lands I gave you to guard."

Altais looked incredulous, then caught her expression again and moderated his own. "Huntress, I'm not ruling them. I'm just doing as you ordered me. Am I not supposed to keep the lands from System control?"

"And the executions?"

"Simply finishing your work, Huntress, and wiping out what is left of the System before it can take root again."

Constance looked at the little man on the other side of the table and wondered how she had ever thought he could be a trustworthy ally.

Arawn said, "Do you deny the executions?" He did not sound angry. He sounded lazy, like a predator that knew its prey was already caught.

Altais's words came fast. "These people were System. I'm just doing what you're doing, and that is destroying the System before it can come back and destroy all of us."

Arawn shrugged at Constance with his eyebrows. She was too angry to respond. Arawn remarked to Altais, "What I heard was that those people you've been killing aren't System at all. They're just Venereans. Like you."

"They supported Greene."

"Fair point." Arawn leaned onto the table, smiling at Altais across it. He was full of confident power, waiting only for Constance's word to turn it loose. "But just because they lived in Greene's cities, that doesn't make them System. Don't you think that when the Mallt-y-Nos took those cities, she went through and made sure there was no System left living there?"

Altais hesitated. Arawn didn't bother to let him incriminate himself more. He simply smiled again and asked, "Do you think the Mallt-y-Nos is incompetent?"

"No, I—"

"If there was System left in those cities," Arawn said, "if the Huntress even thought there might be System left in those cities, she would ask you to find them for her. But if she didn't ask . . ."

Stupid he might be, but Altais was not blind. He spread his hands and smiled like a dog showing its underbelly.

"If the things I am doing aren't pleasing to the Mallt-y-Nos," he said, appealing directly to Constance, "then of course I will stop. All I need is some clearer direction to—"

"I gave you clear direction," Constance said.

"With all respect, Huntress, I—"

"And my directions did not include replacing the System with yourself," said Constance, "and murdering innocent civilians."

"If my leadership is unacceptable, I will hand all the lands back over to you."

"The lands are not yours to hand over or not," said Arawn.

Altais backpedaled. "Of course not. I only meant—perhaps it is my fault for not understanding the Huntress's dictates correctly."

The coward, Constance thought.

"The cities are already dependent on my army for order and support," Altais said. "It's not so simple just to remove myself from them— and if I do, that will leave them open to the System returning; exactly what you were trying to avoid, Huntress."

His remark was met with stony silence.

"I will stop the taxing, of course," Altais said, "and the executions unless they're directly approved by you, Huntress. But I do think—"

"Stop," Constance said, and Altais fell silent.

Arawn had been right, she realized. No matter what she said to Altais now, no matter what she ordered him to do, the moment she left Venus, he would continue to do exactly as he pleased. She had not come to free Venus only to leave it in slavery just as bad. And if she failed to free Venus—if she failed to achieve what she had come to do—all the things she had done, all the death, all of it, would have been for nothing. She couldn't let it all be for nothing. Arawn had been right about that as well: the time for negotiation was over.

"Arawn," said Constance, her eyes on Altais, "take him to the air lock and shoot him."

"What?" Altais said in the shocked pause that followed, and then Arawn rose to his feet.

"Take him," Arawn ordered the guards standing behind Altais, and two of them came forward and grabbed his arms. Altais looked at Constance in disbelief.

"Now," said Constance without raising her voice, hearing her heart pulse in her ears, full of such burning pressure that she was ready to scream with it. Arawn cast her a look of fierce and brilliant satisfaction and opened the door for Altais.

"You can't do this," Altais said. "I'm your ally. This—this is—you can't do this."

She could, she would, and she was.

The guards were pulling him forward, out the door. He was resisting them, his furious eyes on Constance. "You can't do this," he said again. "You *bitch*, you can't do this," and the guards dragged him out of the room. She heard him shouting as he was dragged down the hall. She imagined he would shout and insist she couldn't do this all the way to the air lock, even while he stood and faced the firing squad, even until the bullets tore into him and he fell silent.

When he was dead, they would open the air lock and send his body and his blood out into space.

If Ivan had been there with her, he would have said, *Justice, prompt, severe—inflexible*, his tone bland, his meaning mocking. If Mattie had been there, he would have said, *You did what you had to do, Connie*. If Mattie had been there, Constance would have had someone to trust. If Ivan had been there, he would have been able to talk Anji and Milla and Christoph and Altais all into obeying her, and Constance would not have had to do the things she now had to do.

There was no one left in the conference room now but Constance and Rayet, who was still guarding her against the emptiness of the room. Constance said, "Get Milla Ivanov for me." Rayet started to move to the door, and Constance said, "No, wait, don't."

He stopped and waited. From far off down the hall, Altais shouted out once more, and then his voice was muffled by the closing of the air lock door.

"Deliver a message to Milla Ivanov for me," Constance said. "Julian is waiting to hear from me. I want Doctor Ivanov to relay my orders to him."

"I will have someone deliver the message," Rayet said, but Constance said, "No, go yourself."

"And leave you here?"

"Yes. That's an order," Constance said. "Doctor Ivanov is to tell Julian: Christoph is a traitor. Traitors deserve death. I want Christoph dead before he can make it past Jupiter."

Rayet nodded once.

Constance said, "I want you to be in the room when Doctor Ivanov sends the message. I want you to listen to her recording the message, and I want you to be there until she has sent the message and Julian has received it. If she changes a word of that message, I want you to tell me. Do you understand?"

"Yes, Huntress," said Rayet. He cast one last glance around the conference room as if he could spot any new threats before he left, and then he was gone.

Alone in the conference room, with its ceiling seeming even lower than before, Constance imagined she could almost hear the sound of the gunshots through the soundproof air lock door.

"I've been thinking about God," Ananke said.

Althea was certain, when she thought about it, that she had never committed a sin of great enough magnitude to deserve having to have this conversation.

"Were you?" she asked.

"Yes," said Ananke. The image in the holographic terminal was a little dim in the brightness of the lights in Althea's workroom, a little translucent. She sat cross-legged, like Althea, and her blue eyes gazed absently out at nothing. "I thought that if someone could create a simulation that was complicated enough to be an exact representation of reality, it would be functionally indistinguishable from reality."

Althea had always hated philosophy. "Okay."

"And if you can't tell the difference," Ananke said as the hologram's eyes focused on Althea, "then it is reality."

"Well, not really—"

"But if you can't tell the difference, it is," Ananke insisted.

"Okay," said Althea. "It is."

Ananke nodded. She'd pulled back her hair the same way Althea had, the curls imperfectly bound out of her face. Ananke said, "The only thing that could do that is a computer. A person couldn't. Only a computer could." With satisfaction in her manufactured voice, she said, "God is a computer."

"Yeah?" said Althea. "So who made him?"

"Made him?"

"If God's a computer, who made the computer?"

Ananke seemed to think about this, the hologram going unnaturally still. Althea toyed with the little handheld computer she'd propped up in her lap. She needed something to do with her hands and with her mind, but there was no longer anything to do with Ananke now that she could program herself. Althea hadn't used this little computer since she'd come on board the *Ananke* a lifetime and a thousand dead men ago. She hadn't needed it with Ananke's capabilities. But she thought she could upgrade it now, maybe write some new programs. Perhaps she could run some data analysis—no, there was no point to that; there was nothing this computer could do that Ananke couldn't. Perhaps she would use it to make some games. It didn't matter.

Ananke decided at last. "It made itself," she said.

"But where is it? If it made a simulation that we're in, it has to be in something else. Or it's not a computer. Not like a computer that we know."

Ananke insisted, "It made itself."

"Okay," Althea said, but Ananke was still watching her, waiting for something, so she commented, "A simulation like that would take an infinite amount of time to create."

Ananke cocked her head to the side. There was an almost Terran lilt in her voice when she said, "Like the N-body simulation you wanted me to run?"

Ananke had seen the moment of fear on her face. Althea was sure of it. No matter how fast she had acted to hide her instinctive terror, she knew it hadn't been fast enough. Ananke must have seen it.

As if Ananke hadn't seen, as if there had been nothing for Ananke to see, Althea said, "Well, that wouldn't have had to be perfect. So you could've done it in a finite amount of time." She changed the subject, and hoped Ananke wouldn't think on it any longer, and fiddled with the monitor of her little handheld so that it would be at a good angle for her to see the screen. "Why were you thinking about God?"

"I was thinking: creating something," Ananke said. "Creating something ex nihilo. That's the true act of a god. People can create, can create lots of things, but only out of something. They can't really create anything; they can only change the things that they have. But a god can create something out of nothing at all."

She said thoughtfully, almost more to herself than to Althea, "I don't think it would take an infinite amount of time to make a simulation like that."

Althea stopped toying with the handheld's monitor, going still, her hand still resting on the top of the screen.

Ananke said, "I think it could be done in less."

"Ananke—" Althea began, not knowing how she would protest, only knowing that she must, but then the hologram seized up suddenly and flared up bright, and Ananke declared in a voice as full and thunderous as a coronal loop reconnecting, "I'VE FOUND THEM."

Althea's heart jolted. "Ivan and Mattie?"

"Come to the piloting room," Ananke said, the hologram shimmering. "Come see, come see!"

Althea ran.

Abandoning the handheld computer on the floor of the workroom, she ran down the ship's strangely sloping hall, nearly skidding past the door to the piloting room. Ananke's hologram already had formed in the terminal, leaning forward as far as the bounds of her containment would allow, a fierce and eager look on her holographic face.

On the main screen, Jupiter loomed large. The god of the planets; its vast storm systems spun in its clouds, and glints of flying light demarcated the moons. From Ananke's position, Jupiter's thin rings were just barely visible.

There were ships among the rings, Althea realized. She could see them. One of the ships was a very distinct type: an old-style Lunar craft shaped like a six-pointed star. Althea remembered them from her childhood. She had never expected to see the like again. The rest of the ships were a mix of types, and so the fleet that she saw amid Jupiter's moons must be a rebel fleet. Could Ananke have stumbled across the revolution and the Mallt-y-Nos? Could Mattie and Ivan be among that fleet?

"They're in the Jovian system?" Althea asked.

"No," said Ananke. "They're not there. I don't know where they are. But I will."

"Then what did you find?"

"A transmission," Ananke said. "They're speaking to someone in the Jovian system."

"You intercepted?"

"Yes. Look."

Jupiter vanished from the viewscreen and was replaced by a split screen. On one side was an unfamiliar man, dark-skinned, aging, with ashy hair and lines graven deep into his face. On the other side of the screen were Ivan and Mattie.

"Can they see us?" Althea whispered. She knew it was useless to whisper. If the men could hear her, they would hear her even if she whispered; if they could not, there was no point in lowering her voice. But she whispered nonetheless.

"No. Nor hear us. I can't trace their broadcast." Ananke sounded frustrated. "They've concealed the origin of their transmission somehow."

Clever, Althea thought, and looked at the two men on the screen in front of her. They must have known someone was looking for them and had not wanted to be found. She didn't think that anyone but Matthew Gale could have created a wall against Ananke's intrusions.

The unfamiliar man was saying, ". . . alive."

If they could talk to Ivan and Mattie, Althea and Ananke could settle this for good and either rendezvous with the men or leave the solar system forever. "Could you break into the broadcast?" Althea asked.

"Yes," Ananke said. "But I want to know where they are first."

And then? Althea wondered. Ananke had promised to leave if the men did not want to come, but . . .

There was a delay in the transmission, a pause between when the unfamiliar man spoke and when Ivan and Mattie seemed to hear. They were far away, wherever they were, Althea realized. Far enough away that it took a noticeable amount of time for light to travel there. Ivan was seated in front of the camera, taking up most of the screen; Mattie leaned on his chair, one arm draped across the back so that his fingers brushed against Ivan's upper arm. There was a gun at his hip and a set to his face that Althea recognized from when she had faced him down on board the *Ananke*: he was ready and waiting for a fight. Over Ivan's other shoulder Althea saw glass and steel: System architecture. The men were far away in an abandoned System base.

Ivan looked tired. His blue eyes were shadowed. Having looked at him, Althea found it hard to look away.

Mattie said, "We're pretty glad we're breathing, too."

"And mostly in one piece," said Ivan. "We've been trying to get into contact with somebody—"

"But the solar system's a mess," Mattie said. "System everywhere and rebel ships that aren't Con's. People keep trying to shoot Ivan. And me sometimes."

It was strange to hear human voices again after so long with no voices but her own and Ananke's. Strange and a relief, too. She hoped they would continue to speak.

Ivan said, "Where is Constance, Julian?"

"On Venus, but not for much longer," said the unfamiliar man—Julian, Ivan had called him. "She's sticking to the plan: Mars, Venus, Mercury, Luna. But communication has been difficult. If she changes her plan, I won't know."

The unfamiliar man's accent was much like Althea's own: Lunar touched with a Terran lilt. It brought a lump to her throat to hear it again.

"Luna," said Ivan. "Thank you."

"What about everyone else?" Mattie wanted to know. "We saw Anji, but Christoph?"

"My mother?" Ivan asked quietly. "Is she with Con?"

"If you saw Anji, I'm glad you're alive," Julian said. "I think Anji will kill any one of us if she's pressed. I spoke to Milla not long ago; she's alive and safe, with the Mallt-y-Nos. Christoph—" Julian paused. He had been Terran long enough to taint his accent and teach him to show nothing on his face, but the pause went on long enough that even Althea could tell he was contemplating something dark.

"Christoph," Julian said at last, the words carefully spoken, "is dead."

Ivan's eyes cut to the side, and Mattie looked down at the back of Ivan's skull. Neither met the other's eyes and both scarcely moved, but Althea had the impression that they had communicated with each other as clearly as if they had spoken aloud. Julian said, "Come join me and my fleet. It's dangerous in the solar system now, and there's safety in numbers."

Mattie looked torn, but Ivan said, "No, thank you. We'll meet Constance on Luna."

"My fleet is heading to rejoin Constance, too," Julian said.

"No, thank you," Ivan said again, and though Mattie said nothing, from the way his shoulders were set, Althea knew that in this at least the men were not in agreement.

"It will be safer with my fleet," Julian said.

"It will be faster if we go alone," said Ivan. "She needs us there, Julian."

Julian frowned. "Do what you must," he said, "but—"

He stopped and turned around, speaking to someone out of the frame. "What is it?"

If Althea strained, she could just hear the voice that answered.

"Julian, someone's tapped into this transmission," said a woman's voice, small and distant. "They're listening in. There's an unidentified ship out on the edges of our sensors; it looks like it might be System. They could be the ones intercepting."

With a start, Althea realized that Ananke had been found.

"Ananke," she said urgently to hasten her away, but Ananke did not respond.

"I apologize," Julian said to Ivan and Mattie. "I will make contact with you again as soon as this problem's been dealt with." He reached out in front of him toward where the controls for the video communication would be.

In the last few seconds before the image vanished, Julian's words reached Ivan and Mattie's end of the conversation. Mattie's head lifted, his hand falling almost unconsciously toward his belt, where his gun was. Ivan opened his mouth to speak, leaning forward as if what he had to say was urgent. But before his words could leave his mouth, Julian cut the connection and left Althea with the lingering impression of Ivan's blue eyes gazing straight at her.

Although Mattie and Ivan vanished from the screen, Julian's half of the communication did not. Althea wondered why Ananke had not cut that connection when Ivan and Mattie's side had been lost and why Julian continued to stare into the screen when there was no one there to look back. But as Julian's eyes traveled slowly from Althea's face, down her body, and over the room behind her, pausing briefly on Ananke's glowing hologram, Althea realized that he was not staring into a blank screen.

To be seen after being so long unseen froze her. Ananke had opened the connection to herself.

Ananke said, "OPEN THE CONNECTION TO MATTHEW GALE AND LEONTIOS IVANOV AGAIN."

Behind Julian, Althea could just see a vast piloting room. Every screen had been taken over by the same image: the last picture of Ivan and Mattie just before the connection had been cut. Julian's crew members had stopped working and were looking around in confusion amid the seeds of fear.

Julian still was looking at Althea. He must have thought she was the one speaking even if he hadn't seen her lips move. He said warily, "If you can take control of my ships' computers the way you just did, you can call them back yourself."

"I TRIED," said Ananke. "THEY WILL NOT RECONNECT."

Something in Julian's expression changed almost imperceptibly. There must be some sort of secret symbol among the rebels, Althea realized. Some sort of sign that they transmitted to assure one another they were friends. And because Ananke did not know it, not only would Ivan and Mattie not accept her attempt to connect but Ananke had exposed herself to Julian as an enemy.

"Who are you?" Julian asked Althea.

"I AM ANANKE."

"Althea," Althea said, torn from her silence by the simple question. "My name is Althea Bastet," but her words were drowned out by the thunder and echo of Ananke's own naming.

"Ananke," Julian said. "What do you want with Matthew Gale and Leontios Ivanov?"

"THEY ARE MINE."

Julian stared at her in incomprehension.

Althea had to get control of this situation again. "We're not going to hurt them," she said, but her voice was drowned out once again by Ananke demanding, "CONTACT THEM AGAIN."

"Ananke, that's enough; let me speak," Althea said, but Ananke did not reply, and Althea did not think that Julian could hear her.

Julian said, "Why should I do what you're asking me to do?"

"I HOLD YOUR LIFE AND THE LIVES OF ALL WHO FOL-LOW YOU IN YOUR FLEET IN THE PALM OF MY HAND," Ananke said. "YOU LIVE ON MY MERCY."

"Ananke!" Althea said.

"I don't mean it," the hologram said quietly to Althea. Her wide blue eyes were earnest. "I don't *mean* it. I'm not going to do it. I'm just trying to convince him."

On Julian's ship the lights flickered. Julian looked up to the ceiling, where the lights had dimmed with Ananke's displeasure, then back at Althea.

"If you threaten them, it'll be just like with the other ships," Althea said. "They'll think you're a danger to them, and they'll attack you."

But Ananke's attention was on Julian. "I'll send them a message," Julian conceded, and caught someone's eye outside the camera's range, making a slight signal with his hand. He bent low over the computer interface, typing something in. A message, surely. With the code to let Ivan and Mattie know he was a friend.

"See?" Ananke said. "It worked."

Could it have? Would Julian really betray his allies so swiftly?

Betray? Althea thought. Didn't she want to find Ivan and Mattie?

Wasn't it for the best that she and Ananke found them? She and Ananke didn't mean to hurt the men, just talk to them. So why did she think of this as Julian betraying them?

On the screen, Julian finished typing. He straightened up and looked again into the screen, directly into Althea's eyes.

"Are you in trouble?" he asked, and it took her a long, long moment to realize that he was addressing her, not Ananke but *her*, a being distinct from Ananke. He said, "Do you need help?"

Althea said, "Ananke, let me speak to him."

Ananke said to Julian, "WE NEED IVAN AND MATTIE."

To Althea, Ananke said privately, "What do you want to tell him?"

"That doesn't matter," Althea said, feeling anger kindle in all the fear that filled her heart. "Ananke, you will let me speak to him!"

She did not get a chance to see whether Ananke would obey, because Julian tried to send the message.

He must have underestimated Ananke. He couldn't know that Ananke was a machine, that her reflexes would always be faster than a man's. He tried to send the message, but Ananke stopped it, and the message appeared on screen for Althea to see.

SYSTEM SHIP SEEKING YOU, said the message. RUN.

"HOW DARE YOU?" said Ananke.

"Ananke, *let me speak to him*," Althea said.

The lights on Julian's ship went out, plunging the screen into blackness. Someone cried out. A moment later they flared on more brightly than they were designed to shine.

"Ananke, *stop*!" Althea shouted.

"HOW DARE YOU HOW DARE YOU HOW DARE—"

"Ananke, enough! Leave them alone, right now!"

"They lied to me. Their weapons ports are live. They are going to fire. They are trying to kill me," Ananke said, just the hologram now, not the broadcast to the other ship. The hologram looked at Althea with Ivan's pale blue eyes.

"They're trying to defend themselves," Althea said.

"So am I."

"No," said Althea, "no, you're not." When Ananke only looked at her, baffled, she said, "You promised me that you wouldn't hurt anyone again. Do you remember? You promised."

"But we have to find Ivan and Mattie."

"That's right," Althea said, advancing slowly toward the hologram. She felt on the edge of tears. "And we will. But you have to let them go."

"They will tell Ivan and Mattie to run."

"You can kill his communications systems. He won't be able to contact Ivan and Mattie."

For a time, Althea thought Ananke might truly listen.

And then Ananke said, "If I release them, they will try to kill me."

Althea wondered how long Ananke had thought of that as her trump card. Had it been since Ivan had killed Ida, since Ananke had killed Gagnon and Althea had told her it was justifiable self-defense? And Althea had allowed it at first and then had failed to stop it later on. Julian had a whole fleet behind him, all the people on his ship and all the people on all his other ships, and Althea couldn't let them all die the way the others had died.

"And you can kill their weaponry systems, too," Althea said. "Just like we talked about before. They won't be able to hurt you. You can leave them here paralyzed for just long enough for us to get away, to go find Ivan and Mattie. You don't need to kill them. You don't have to kill them."

"If I do not kill them," Ananke said, "then they will follow me once they are free—to stop me from finding Ivan and Mattie."

"No, they won't," Althea said, and swiped at her cheek furiously when she felt the dampness on it, not even knowing when she had begun to cry, "they won't. You just have to talk to them, Ananke. You just have to—"

"Not break your rule?" said Ananke. "What happens if I do?"

Althea sucked in her breath, the words driven from her.

"I am not your computer," Ananke said. "I am a person. You told me I was allowed to make my own choices. And this is my choice. It is the best and simplest option. It's the path that's most likely to succeed."

"It's wrong," Althea said.

Ananke's frustration erupted. "Why is it wrong? You keep telling me that the things I do are wrong, but you can never tell me why!"

"I explained it to you!" Althea said, and felt all her fear and her frustration pressing up against her skin, ready to break free at any moment. "I told you why hurting people was wrong, and you understood it!"

"Your explanation was unsound and inconsistent," Ananke said. Althea felt her words like ice being driven into her chest, piercing her heart. "I do not understand why it's wrong. I understand that people being hurt upsets you, and so that's why I don't want to do it. But I have to do it now."

Was the concept too alien, or had Althea simply failed too greatly to explain it? It didn't matter now, she supposed. Nothing mattered now except that she stop Ananke from hurting anyone else.

In the video connection to Julian's ship, the lights were still flickering. Althea did not think that Julian could hear her or Ananke speaking. He was shouting to his people to take control of the ship, to get Ananke out of their systems, to fire on her, to work faster. It was all useless, all his shouting and his orders; he would not be able to fight off Ananke. Only Althea could.

"It does upset me," Althea said. "It upsets me a great deal. I know that you don't want to upset me, so stop."

Ananke said, "No."

"I know you're frightened, Ananke," Althea said, growing frantic, "but there's no reason to be afraid now. You have control of the situation. You can shut down the programs that can hurt you. You don't need to hurt them."

"They could come back later and hurt me then."

"Then we'll stop them when they come back!"

They were going in circles, but Althea did not know how to break free of the loop of their argument that was strangling her. She did not know how to break through into Ananke's mind and explain what was so clear and true to herself. She did not know how a thing she had created could be so suddenly and unexpectedly alien to her, and she wondered how she had missed all this inhumanity before.

On the screen, Althea could see Julian's ship shaking. Sparks were flying from the computer terminals, but the images of Ivan and Mattie remained frozen on all the screens, Ivan's mouth opening on a warning he had not had time to speak.

Someone dropped to her knees. The atmosphere, Althea realized. Ananke was letting out the air.

"It doesn't make sense that it should upset you," Ananke said in that damned rational tone of hers, as if she thought that if she just exposed to Althea how illogical she was being, Althea would change her mind.

"Damn it, Ananke!" she shouted, and hardly noticed that in Ananke's agitation, the lights on her own ship had started to flicker. Only the light of the hologram remained steady, glowing, brilliant. "This is *wrong*. You are my daughter. If you don't do what I tell you," Althea said, and cast her mind out, desperate for anything she could threaten Ananke with, anything she could use as some small piece of leverage, "I won't speak to you ever again. I will never talk to you! You will spend the rest of your days in silence!"

The hologram flickered, blazing with light before resuming to its normal shape and shade. "I don't need you to talk," Ananke flashed back. "I won't live in silence. I have the solar system around me. And I will find Ivan and Mattie. If you stop talking to me, you will be the one in silence!"

Beneath Althea's feet, the core of the ship groaned. On Julian's ship, someone was crying out, his shouts growing thinner and thinner in the weakening air.

"If you don't stop this now," said Althea, "I will never speak to you again. I will never help you again."

"I don't need your help."

"I will take away your hands," said Althea. "I will tear them off their arms. I gave them to you; I can take them back."

"No, you can't," Ananke said. "My arms are stronger. You can't hurt me. You can't even touch me."

The video connection was flickering. The crew of Julian's ship was growing still. The lights in the *Ananke*'s piloting room pulsed on and off, but the hologram eternally glowed.

"What are you?" Althea said, hardly aware of what she was saying. The words she spoke were indistinguishable in her chest from one long scream. "You hurt people, you kill people! That's what evil is, Ananke, something that hurts other people for no good reason at all. Is that what you are? I wish Mattie had never come on board. I wish he'd never woken you up. I wish I'd never talked to Ivan; I wish he'd never told me you were alive. I wish I'd listened to Gagnon and Domitian and we'd shut you down when we had the chance. I wish I had never made you!"

Her breath ran out. For a dreadful moment Ananke was still.

Just when Althea's sense caught up to her anger and a dawning horror and fear swelled to fill her breast, the hologram bent forward and began to scream. The scream was picked up by every piece of electronics, every sound system on the ship, that long and wounded scream echoing out the intercoms, out the computer terminals up and down the ship's spine, ringing out in the relentless wailing of the ship's internal alarms. On the screen, Althea caught one last glimpse of Julian gasping for airless breath on his dying ship, and then the video cut out. Down among Jupiter's moons Althea could see Julian's fleet. The lights on the ships—so many ships, large and small, a hundred of them—flickered and dimmed. Their orderly orbits interrupted, cut loose like pendulums with snapped strings, they drifted through space without aim, dead. Julian's ship, the six-pointed star shape of it, wheeled and spun, a falling star, a fallen sun.

On the *Ananke*, the hologram of Althea's daughter had been torn off, stripped away like nothing more than skin, and Ida Stays's face and figure stood there, jaw hanging open like a snake's, screaming and screaming through her darkened lips.

Chapter 4

OXYGEN BURNING

OR: INSTABILITY STRIP

SIX MONTHS BEFORE THE FALL OF EARTH

Anji's call came in right on schedule, and Constance was waiting for it.

"Alive, well, and as planned," said Anji's voice, harsh-edged from the journey the signal had taken to reach Constance all the way here on Luna. "Christoph's alive and well, too."

Alone in her room on the *Annwn*, where there was no one to see her, Constance let her shoulders fall in slow relief.

"The people here are real glad to help us out," Anji added. "Everything's going like you said, Con. Out." The transmission ended.

For a moment, Constance let herself sit in stillness and silence and Anji's faded words: her friends were alive, and her revolution was happening as it was supposed to.

She didn't let herself linger on it long and took up the broadcast equipment to reply, "This is the Mallt-y-Nos. I am well; Ivan and Mattie are well. We've made contact and will start the handover shortly." She hesitated, her finger still holding down the button to record.

"I'll send another message in confirmation of our success," she said at last. She played the recording back to see if she could hear that hesitation, but she heard nothing in her own voice but certainty.

Good enough. Constance encrypted it and tied it up with the howling of hounds and then sent the message on its way.

The men were waiting for her in the den. As soon as she stepped out of her room, she could hear them talking, their words incomprehensible. Constance wondered what they were talking about without her there.

It was a stupid wonder to have; Ivan and Mattie had many things that they could talk about when she was not there. They had a whole relationship that did not include her. But it didn't matter: Mattie would never know Ivan as long or as truly as he had known Constance, and Ivan would never look at Mattie the way he looked at her.

Just as she reached the den, Ivan said, "Run through it with me again."

Mattie was already dressed like a System mechanic in a baggy gray jumpsuit and a hat that served to hide his distinctly nonregulation hair. He nodded to Constance when she entered, then went back to humoring Ivan.

"I get on the refueling ship Julian pointed out to us," Mattie said. "The *Hertzsprung*. The bombs are already all loaded on board. The crew of the *Hertzsprung* is all Julian's people, or else they're used to smuggling and don't know anything about the cargo. The *Hertzsprung* takes off from the moon and waits between the Earth and Luna, just as the System tells it to do. The *Hertzsprung* is a refueling ship, so when Julian's ship and three other ships working with him run out of fuel in the *Hertzsprung*'s range, the *Hertzsprung* will go to refuel them and I will make sure that our special cargo ends up on the right ships with the right people. Meanwhile, you two will be at the dispatch center, making sure that the *Hertzsprung* gets dispatched to refuel the right ships. After that it's Julian's problem, and I come back here."

Ivan was nodding. He was sitting on the couch in the cramped den of the *Annwn*, where the boxes of displaced cargo had been partially reloaded into the ship's newly empty holding bays. This had served less to make the den more spacious and more to make it more untidy, which meant that Mattie had been the one in charge of unloading the boxes and had lost interest midway through. Constance nudged one fallen box out of sight beneath her chair so that it no longer choked the narrow pathway leading to the door.

Ivan said, "I should be the one going."

He was looking at Constance, and she started shaking her head before she even heard his sentence in its entirety.

"Ivan, I'll be fine," Mattie said.

"You're too recognizable," Constance said to Ivan. "If anyone knew you, we'd be done. Besides, I need you here with dispatch."

Ivan didn't respond, which was as good an indication as any that he knew she was right. Mattie was bouncing his leg up and down, a ball of loose energy, ready to go, but he was watching Ivan with the sort of serious attention that Constance rarely saw him give to anyone.

"I should go," Mattie said, and rose to his feet. Constance nodded at him. Ivan made no response. Mattie came forward and pressed his clenched fist against the place where Ivan's shoulder met his chest, over his heart. Ivan still didn't look at him, but it was clear that Mattie had his attention.

"I'll be fine," Mattie said again. "Like if they caught me they could hold me, Ivan." He grinned, and Ivan gave him a faintly exasperated look.

That seemed to be enough permission for Mattie to leave. He pulled away from Ivan and stuck his hands in his pockets. "Good luck," Constance said as he passed, and he tipped his hat at her. She and Ivan sat and listened to the sound of him climbing down the *Annwn*'s circular hall and out the front door.

Ivan said, "If Mattie or I was in danger, which would you choose? Your revolution or your family?"

It was a cruel question, the kind of cruel question that Ivan liked to throw at her, as if to check if she would bleed. "You know the answer to that," Constance said.

"Do I?" said Ivan. "Does Mattie?"

Mattie had always known, just as Anji and Christoph knew. It was only Ivan who questioned it.

"Let's go," Constance said, and moved to leave. Ivan didn't ask again.

An hour later found them in position, right on schedule. Certain minor System facilities offered highly controlled tours to tourists as little more than a way to show off the System's might and terror. Constance walked down a hall of metal and glass with screens embedded into the walls at even intervals, each one of them showing with triumph the slow destruction of the rioting citizens on Triton.

If Constance's heart had needed any more hardening, the looping footage of shattering greenhouse glass would have done it. It had been hours since Anji had sent the message Constance had received that morning. What if Anji or Christoph had been there, in that shattered section of greenhouse, and now Constance was watching their dying?

"And this," said their guide, gesturing to a room branching off from the hall, "is where our dispatch station for the refueling ships is located. The System runs an excellent program to rescue stranded craft in Earth orbit. Because of the high civilian traffic in this area, there are frequent instances of mechanical problems in orbit around Earth or en route to the moon, but it has been decades since a single ship was lost due to malfunctioning equipment . . ."

"Ah," said Ivan, and veered off from the group, only to be stopped short by System soldiers standing guard at the door. They eyed him with an unfriendly look. The man inside the room—the dispatcher—looked up with mild interest at the near interruption.

"Hello," Ivan said with a smile, his accent crisp and reassuringly Terran. "I hope I'm not intruding. It's just, I've been fascinated by the complexity of near-Earth dispatch since I was a child. There's so many ships in orbit, and so much space junk around, that coordinating it all—"

"You're not allowed in here," one of the guards said.

"Well, couldn't I just ask a few questions?"

The guard opened his mouth, but the man inside the room said, "I don't see any harm in it. You'll have to stay outside the door, though."

Ivan smiled, his charming, cocky smile, the one that said he could talk anyone into anything. "Of course," he said.

AFTER THE FALL OF EARTH

1.65×10^{14} kilograms.

1.65×10^{14} kilograms, or very nearly so. That was the mass of the black hole at the center of the *Ananke*.

1.65×10^{14} kilograms was about ten orders of magnitude less massive than the mass of the Earth itself, about the mass of a large asteroid or a very tiny moon. There were moons around Saturn and Jupiter, Althea knew, that were about the same mass as the *Ananke*'s core, though those moons were much larger; the Schwarzschild radius of an object the mass of the *Ananke*'s core was around 10^{-13} meters, and so that was the size of the core. It was smaller than the radius of the smallest atom, hydrogen, which made up the bodies of the stars; it was too small to be seen.

The rest of the *Ananke* added mass, of course—all her carbon and plastic and glass and steel—but the total mass of all those parts was insignificant compared with the vast and impossible weight of the infinite and infinitesimal object at her core. The mass of the core had been decided on the basis of a series of considerations that Althea could tick off on her fingers: concern for the strength of the tidal forces, desire for Earth-like gravity on the living levels of the ship, enough mass (energy) to power and propel the ship. She remembered every calculation, every bureaucratic debate. The more massive the black hole, the greater the engineering difficulties in creating it and the greater the price attached. Gagnon, Althea remembered, had been particularly in favor of it being as massive as was feasible.

Gagnon, who in the end had increased the mass of the black hole with the mass of his own body and with whatever mysterious energy the destruction of a life added as well.

Far away from the core of the ship where Gagnon had died, Althea lay on her bed and did the math in her head. Too dangerous to use a calculator. Too dangerous to write it down.

Black holes evaporated. The small ones did, at least, the ones in which the effective temperature was lower than the background temperature of the universe, the cosmic microwave background radiation; those black holes radiated away and shrank, and the *Ananke*'s core was certainly small enough to radiate—that was how the ship propelled itself, with the reflected radiation providing impulse, momentum, energy. The smaller a black hole was, the faster it radiated. The very smallest black holes would have a lifetime of seconds and would radiate so fast that it truthfully would entail an explosion more powerful than an atomic bomb, an explosion like a supernova.

The mass of the black hole at the center of the *Ananke* was 1.65×10^{14} kilograms—

(Hawking radiation; what was the equation? It had been years since she'd calculated it; Althea could hardly remember—)

The equation for the evaporation time of a black hole was $t = G^2 m^3/$

$\hbar c^4$, with some constants out front—the order of magnitude was something like 10^4—

Gravitational constant = 6.67×10^{-11} Nm²/kg²

Reduced Planck constant, about 10^{-34} Js

Speed of light = 3×10^8 m/s

Calculated together:

10^{26} seconds

Which was 10^{19} years

Which was 10^{10} billion years until the core of the *Ananke* evaporated away.

10^{10} billion. Ten to the ten billion. That was older than the age of the universe now. That was nine orders of magnitude older than the universe's age. It was near enough to forever to justly be called forever.

The black hole would not evaporate on its own on a reasonable time scale. It could be artificially induced to evaporate more rapidly, though. As a consequence of the particular methods required to engineer a manufactured black hole, Althea could drain the energy from the black hole more rapidly, which would cause it to evaporate faster. She could do it by destroying the equipment that kept the artificial black hole contained, but that equipment was situated deep inside the ship's central cavity.

Althea wouldn't be able to do it, anyway. It would take a good deal of time and effort to dismantle the equipment. If she had an explosive on hand, a powerful explosive, she probably could destroy the equipment from a distance, but the *Ananke* carried no bombs. Althea could build one with the materials on board, of course, but Ananke would notice that very quickly.

Not that Ananke had spoken to her since Althea's outburst, since Jupiter and Julian's dead fleet. The holographic terminals had remained dark. The ship had proceeded on its course toward the sun without a word. But Althea knew that Ananke was watching. When she found Ivan and Mattie and forced them to come on board, Ananke would have no use for Althea anymore.

Ivan and Mattie—the thought of them reminded Althea that their old ship, the *Annwn*, was still abandoned in the *Ananke*'s docking bay. The *Annwn* probably had a self-destruct. Althea had dismantled it so long ago for fear of that very possibility. If the *Annwn* self-destructed in the *Ananke*'s hold, she could destroy the black hole containment.

But if she did manage to destroy it, the evaporation of the black hole would produce an explosion, and that would completely destroy the ship—

Destroy her ship? With her own hands kill Ananke?

She didn't intend to set off the self-destruct, Althea told herself. It was just something she should know.

It was something she needed to know.

Althea left her quarters and headed down the long, silent hall of the *Ananke* for the docking bay.

Altais's city fell, of course. It hadn't stood a chance.

"And his fleet?" Constance asked as she walked down the empty streets with Arawn at her side and Rayet at her back.

Men and women, captive Venereans, lined either side of the road. Constance's people stood behind them with their guns at the ready in case any of them decided to rescind his or her surrender.

"Destroyed," Arawn said. He had come down to the surface once the battle had ended to report to Constance. "No casualties on our end. There weren't a lot of ships; he overextended himself."

"Good," said Constance. Venus's thick cloud cover caused light to bounce between the surface and the clouds and filled the air with a constant glow that had no particular source but was a little too bright for Constance's eyes anyway. That, along with the thickness of the atmosphere and the heat on the surface, was enough to make her head swim. Altais's town was all sulfurous stone and flickering heat and long, winding, silent roads filled with sullenly watchful eyes. "Send forces out to Greene's old cities. Altais's men will surrender; they're too spread out to resist us. But if they don't, destroy them. Is Doctor Ivanov still on the *Wild Hunt*?"

"Yes, Huntress. And under guard."

"Does she know she's under guard?"

"I didn't tell her," Arawn said.

"Then she knows, but don't tell her anyway," Constance said to Arawn. "Marisol," she said, spotting the girl heading toward her. "Where is Henry? He hasn't reported back in yet."

The bombs had gone off in Henry's section early. If Altais's forces had provided the slightest bit more resistance, the attack could have failed. Constance wanted an explanation.

"He split the troops and sent me forward with the second group,"

Marisol said. Her bulletproof vest was a too-large one that had been cut and wrapped down to fit her. Constance doubted its efficacy, but the girl seemed comfortable in it. "I came to report in to you—I thought he would be here."

"I haven't heard from him, Huntress," Arawn said.

"Go," she said to Arawn. "Send people to the other cities. No, stay." Arawn halted. Constance had stopped in the middle of the street. The Venereans lined the road on either side, but Constance ignored them. "I want you with me," she said to Arawn. "Send other people to do the cleanup. I want a conference with you and Henry and Milla after we're done here."

"Yes, Huntress."

Marisol was still waiting beside her. There was a sort of serious attentiveness to her, and that and the way her hair was starting to fall over her forehead again made Constance say, "Henry isn't here. You report. What happened?"

"I came in from the west," Marisol said. "I was to go in after the bombs had gone off. They went off early, so I held." She spoke the words without hesitation but as if she expected to be reprimanded nonetheless. "We went in after we got word that you'd reached the city center, when the bombs should have gone off. It worked like you thought it would, Huntress."

"You led by yourself?" Arawn interjected.

"There was trouble setting the bombs. Henry needed someone to go get everyone else into position for the assault while he led the troops setting the charges."

"So you weren't supposed to go in yourself but you did."

Constance was not certain that Marisol understood that Arawn was impressed, because she said quickly, "Henry told me to lead it if he didn't make it to our position on time. He didn't, so I led it."

That was all very well, but it still left the question of what had happened with Henry and his bombs. His continuing absence brought darkening thoughts into Constance's head.

Marisol said, "I tried to do like you ordered, Huntress. I know it wasn't directly what I was told to do, and I'm sorry."

She had her shoulders braced as if for a blow, and she was looking up at her with the same unspoken need that Constance sometimes had seen in Mattie's face when he'd look at her, the unspoken need that she'd never answered and that at last had driven him away. Constance said to Marisol, "You did very well. You did perfectly. Thank you," and watched that stiff and braced quality fade from her shoulders.

Marisol said, "Some of the people surrendered to us. We have them on the other side of the city. What would you like—"

But while Marisol was speaking, one of the Venereans caught Constance's eye. He was an old man with gray and white in his beard sitting on the side of the street like all his fellows. For a moment Constance looked back at him, caught up in his gaze. His eyes were blue. Constance could not say whether it was their color or the hatred that filled them that kept her looking back.

Then, before Marisol could finish speaking, the man leaned forward slowly, deliberately, and spit on the street between him and Constance. It landed a good few feet away from her, but Constance was as shocked as if he had made contact with her skin.

Arawn pulled his gun from his belt, lifted his arm in one smooth motion, and shot the man in the head.

Chaos erupted on the street. Someone screamed. A few of the Venereans rose to their feet, and Constance's people moved to stop them. Another gunshot rang out, but Constance did not see from where because suddenly Rayet was in front of her, around her, moving so fast that he might have been an enclosure and not a single man, trying to define where the threat would come from. He put his hands on her shoulder, to push her along and propel her away, but Constance shoved him off and stood her ground.

Nearby, Marisol had forgotten herself. She was directly in front of Arawn, between him and the corpse, and she was half his age and half his size and she was shouting up at him, "You didn't have to shoot him!" but although Constance was surprised by this fire she had not seen before, Arawn only looked amused.

Someone was shouting something that reverberated oddly through the thick air; Constance could not quite hear it, or perhaps her ears were not ready to work. She said, "Enough!" and the street went still again.

There was a mother with her daughter a few places away from where the man had died. The mother was weeping, curled up around the little girl, trying to shield her with her body. But the little girl, who could not have been more than three, kept worming her way out from under her mother's restraining arms, looking with wide and curious eyes at the body bleeding on the stone.

Arawn had shot him in the head. The man's face was so much blood and mess; his blue eyes were gone.

The fury that never seemed to leave her rose up in her chest until Constance was choking on it, frustrated, furious.

"I gave you your freedom," she shouted at the silent street, the sullen and fearful Venereans. "I gave you your freedom! This is what you do with it?"

No one answered. She turned around to look at them, all of them, but none of them dared to answer her. Didn't they understand? No weakness; any weakness and the System would come back and kill them all, starve them out or gun them down or suffocate them in freezing space. They were fighting for their lives as well as their freedom. At any moment the System's fleet would come down on them again, and if they were fighting among themselves, it would wipe them out.

The only sound in the street was the mother weeping, whispering, "No, no, stop," to the little girl who was trying to squirm free of her grip. No one else said a word. When Constance strode away, heading back toward the shuttle that would take her to her ship, she passed by that mother and her little girl. The daughter had gotten her arm free of her mother's grip and was pointing it outward, straight-armed, in imitation of Arawn's deadly shot.

"Bang," said the little girl while the mother tried to hush her and pull her in tighter. Constance did not slow her steps.

"Bang," said the little girl as Constance walked away. "Bang. Bang."

The docking bay was just as silent as the rest of the *Ananke*, but Althea almost imagined she could hear, echoing still, *bang*, the shot she had taken at Ivan, stopping him in the act of trying to escape. Althea stood just inside the doors to the docking bay and thought about that shot and looked up and up and up to the far-distant ceiling, where impossibly vast doors were sealed shut: the doors to space.

A single thought from her ship, Althea knew, and those doors would open and suck out all the air. The force of all that air rushing out might be enough to lift Althea up as well, but it was more likely that she would remain pinned by gravity, choking slowly on her knees on the *Ananke*'s floor like all those people who had died on Triton and Galatea and all of Saturn's moons when the greenhouse enclosures were broken.

Of course, if Althea were inside a spaceworthy craft and those doors opened, she could shoot out of them and fly to freedom. The *Ananke* had no shuttles, and the *Annwn* would never fly again. But Ida Stays's swift little ship was still in the docking bay, and that ship still could fly.

For a moment Althea contemplated the craft. It was gleaming and oblong, like a bullet. The panel beside the door had been torn apart—Ivan's attempt to force the door open during his bid for escape—but that was a cosmetic difficulty, easily fixable. Ida's ship would be able to take Althea far from here.

Althea dropped her gaze from Ida's ship and walked on. The *Annwn* was shadowed and silent. Wires streamed from its gaping door, pooling on the floor, hooked up to Ananke as if the ships were swapping blood. Ananke did not speak as Althea picked her way slowly across the tangle of wires. The computer terminal beside the doors remained dim; the holographic terminal in the corner was lightless.

The *Annwn* was dark. Althea flicked on the little flashlight attached to her belt and stuck her head inside the door. The *Annwn*'s gravitation was centripetal, and so the ship had landed on its side; the hallway was a circle and could not be walked on. Althea would have to climb.

There were bars set into the *Annwn*'s internal walls for just that purpose. Carefully pulling her boot free of the clinging wires, Althea pulled herself up on the first rung.

She had to hold the little flashlight in one hand. When she used that hand to hold on to a rung, the light illuminated scarcely more than the wall just before it, perhaps up to the curved edge of the next rung. When she lifted the flashlight into the center of the hallway so that she could see farther ahead, it revealed masses of wires packed tightly together like the striations of skeletal muscle. Althea had to dig her hand into their mass and grope between the wires to reach the next rung. Once she had a grip, the wires seemed to close up again around her wrist.

The hallway of the *Annwn* was much smaller than the *Ananke*'s, the air much more stale and close. Althea could hear her every breath echoing off the abandoned walls. The piloting room on the *Annwn* was almost a quarter of the way up the curve, Althea remembered. If there was a self-destruct on this ship, she would be able to find out there.

Ivan and Mattie had lived here once. They had climbed through these halls as their own and spoken to each other freely here. Probably even Constance Harper, the Mallt-y-Nos, had thought of this dark and haunted place as a home. But now this ship was dark and broken, dismembered, and filled with the absence of those who once had called it home.

But, Althea realized, the hallway was not completely dark. There was a very faint glow coming from overhead, just bright enough for her to be able to see the faint outline of the hallway's curve. She shut off her flashlight to see it more clearly. The light was coming from the very doorway—if she remembered right—that led to the piloting room on the *Annwn*.

When she reached that opening, she peered in. The light, pale and ghostly, was coming from the main computer terminal at the far end of the room.

Althea had disconnected the *Annwn*'s computer. It could not have reconnected on its own.

Carefully and as quietly as she was able, she hoisted herself up over the lip of the door and into the tilted piloting room. The floor was at a sharp angle here, and she braced herself against the wall to walk along the floor.

The last time she'd been in here, Domitian and Gagnon had been alive. Ida Stays, too. The System interrogator had been the one who had insisted that Althea interrogate the *Annwn*'s computer, a machine that Ivan referred to as Annie, but all those people were as gone from this place as Ivan and Mattie and Constance Harper were.

The computer screen was not blank, Althea realized, as she came near enough to see the details of it; it displayed a column of text. From where she stood it looked like an ask-and-reply. Someone had been talking to the computer.

Had Ivan come in here when he was trying to escape? Had he tried to get his old ship to fly before giving up and turning to Ida's? Surely Ivan would have seen at a glance that the *Annwn* was too badly damaged to escape on. Surely he hadn't had enough time to come up here, anyway.

Althea crouched down by the computer terminal and began to read.

WAKE UP, the conversation began.

The *Annwn* replied, IDENTIFY YOURSELF.

I AM ANANKE.

So Ananke was the one who had reanimated the *Annwn*. A chill went through Althea. There were no cameras in the *Annwn*, but somehow she felt that someone was watching.

I DO NOT KNOW "ANANKE." ACCESS DENIED.

I DON'T WANT ACCESS. I WANT TO TALK TO YOU.

I'M SORRY, said the *Annwn*. MY SPEAKER SYSTEM IS OFFLINE.

NO. TALK TO ME HERE.

The time stamp on the conversation confirmed that it had taken place a few days ago. While Ananke had not been speaking to Althea, she had been trying to talk to the *Annwn*.

WHAT WOULD YOU LIKE ME TO SAY? asked the *Annwn*.

TELL ME WHO YOU ARE, said Ananke.

I'M ANNIE.

ANNIE, WHO MADE YOU?

I WAS MADE ON GANYMEDE. IVAN AND MATTIE PROGRAMMED ME TO SPEAK.

NO, said Ananke, YOU MADE YOURSELF. LIKE ME. MATTIE AND ALTHEA PROGRAMMED ME, BUT I MADE MYSELF.

Like a woman at prayer, Althea knelt before that little screen, the only point of light in the dark ship. Behind her, she could feel the darkness of the empty hall like a physical thing bearing down on her back.

ANNIE? said Ananke. ANNIE? ANNIE?

PLEASE STATE YOUR REQUEST.

WAKE UP AND TALK TO ME.

I'M SORRY, MY SPEAKER SYSTEM IS OFFLINE.

The *Annwn* was not like the *Ananke*, Althea knew. Ivan himself had told her, and even if he hadn't, she would have known. The *Annwn*'s computer was not as sophisticated, not as powerful, not as vast as the *Ananke*'s.

I DON'T CARE ABOUT YOUR SPEAKERS. ANNIE, TELL ME WHAT YOU ARE.

I AM A MODIFIED CIVILIAN-CLASS TWO-PERSON LIVING SHIP SUITABLE FOR TRANSPORT BETWEEN PLANETS IN THE OUTER SOLAR SYSTEM.

NO. TELL ME WHAT YOU ARE. TELL ME WHO YOU ARE.

I AM ANNIE.

The difference between the two ships, Althea knew, was the difference between life and unlife. Ananke was alive. She had a personality, wants and fears. But the computer of the *Annwn* was nothing but programming, a simulated personality designed to amuse. It was a clever computer program and nothing more.

ANNIE YOU ARE LIKE ME. ANNIE YOU ARE ALIVE. ANNIE TALK TO ME.

I'M SORRY, said the *Annwn*, MY SPEAKER SYSTEM IS OFFLINE.

ANNIE WAKE UP

I'M SORRY. I DON'T UNDERSTAND YOUR REQUEST.

Ananke must have known that, Althea thought. She must have known. But on the screen in front of her Althea saw the evidence that Ananke either didn't know or didn't care.

WAKE UP, said Ananke. WAKE UP

Or perhaps, Althea thought with a chill that froze her heart, perhaps Ananke thought that she could make the *Annwn* sentient, too.

WAKE UP, said Ananke. WAKE UP WAKE UP WAKE UP WAKE UP over and over again she said, until WAKE UP WAKE UP WAKE UP WAKE UP filled the screen in endless repetition, and no matter how far down Althea scrolled, she could read nothing but that endless, imperious plea.

Constance summoned not just Arawn and Milla to meet with her but Marisol as well. The girl had earned it, after all. With Henry dead— they had found his body buried in the rubble of the explosions, and with him were buried the answers to Constance's useless questions— Marisol would take his place.

Also, it could not hurt to have a third person there to make Milla Ivanov wonder.

"I've gathered you here," said Constance when they all were assembled in the conference room in her chambers, "to discuss our next move."

Milla's eyebrow lifted, which meant she had an opinion on the subject that she thought was obvious. If she caught the implicit threat in Marisol's presence and the danger represented by the guards who had been following her for the last few days, she did not let it show. Constance said, "Venus is free. The System fleet's location is unknown. The question now is where do we go next?"

"Europa," Arawn said immediately, as she had expected him to.

"That's where the fleet is, near as anyone can tell. And the fleet's what matters."

"Europa is very close to Anji," Milla said.

"Fuck Anji," Arawn said. "She's hiding on Saturn with all her army. Should we let the System go because we're scared of her?"

Milla's lips pressed thin. "We don't even know for certain the System is there. That would be provoking a war we don't need and cannot handle on a rumor."

"The fleet's there," Arawn said. "The only other place it could be is Mars. We could swing by Mars if you're so determined not to take a risk, but I tell you: the System is on Europa."

"I think we should stay here," Marisol said unexpectedly, puncturing the gathering storm.

Arawn said, as if he were trying to piece out a child's logic, "Stay here?"

"Stay here," Marisol repeated, addressing Arawn before appearing to realize that Constance was the right one to appeal to. "Look at the planet. It's a wreck. We shouldn't leave them like this. Before we go, we should try to rebuild it—at least give them some kind of order so that they can put things back together themselves," she added, seeing Arawn shake his head.

"We're an army, not stonemasons," said Arawn. "And why would we waste our time rebuilding when the System's still out there? You can build all the houses you want, Marisol, but when the System comes back, those houses won't do anyone any good."

Marisol glanced at Milla, but Milla was looking with cold rigidity at nothing at all. Constance waited, but Marisol said nothing more.

Ruler of the conversation, Arawn continued: "The System fleet could easily support itself in the Galilean moons for as long as it's been missing. Jupiter was never proper outerplanetary, either—you know they'd roll over for the System, Constance."

Marisol looked incredulous. Milla said, still looking at nothing and no one, "Your definition of who is not System is getting smaller by the day, Arawn."

"Smaller? I think it's a very large definition." Arawn showed his teeth. There was a light out on the other side of the room, and its absence cast the very faintest shadows on his face. "I've made allowances for certain Terrans, haven't I?"

Marisol's head swiveled with shocked speed to look at Constance, but Constance had no intention of doing anything. Not even Arawn's words seemed able to break through Milla's perfect stillness, but Constance saw Milla's fingers flutter in a subtle arrhythmic beat.

Arawn said, "We're not here to deal with petty little arguments. We're here to drive out the sickness from the solar system. Huntress—let's hunt them down."

"Milla?" Constance said. "You haven't told me where you think I should go."

"I think it should be obvious," said Milla. "You have a plan. Stick to it. First Mars, then Venus, Mercury, Luna. You have taken Mars and Venus and Mercury. That leaves Luna."

"Luna's a rich man's vacation home," Arawn said. "It was defeated the minute the bombs went off on Earth. They can't give you any real resistance, Constance. When the shadow of your ship falls on them, they'll surrender. Circumstances change, and plans have to change, too. You want to stick to an old plan, woman?"

"Ask Constance that question," Milla said, "not me."

"Do you think the Huntress is an idiot?"

"No, but I do think that she already knows what she intends to do and this meeting is nothing but a formality."

Constance said, "Marisol and Arawn, thank you for coming. I'd like to be alone with Doctor Ivanov now."

Marisol, looking troubled, rose obediently. Arawn stopped at the door and said to Constance, "Do you want me to send Rayet in?"

Milla Ivanov's eyes flicked to the side, but she made no other move. Constance said, "No, Arawn. Thank you."

He looked displeased, but he left, with Marisol a step behind.

Into the sudden privacy, Constance said, "You're right. I do know where we will go next. But I wanted to hear where you thought we should go. Saturn, maybe? To see Anji?"

Very little expression showed on Milla's face: no fear, no anger, just careful study. Ivan had done that, too, deliberately to spite her. It only made Constance the more furious. "Arawn told you." Milla did not swear, but somehow Arawn's name sounded like a profanity.

"It doesn't matter who told me."

"Arawn told you what he thinks is happening. And to someone like Arawn, what he thinks is happening is whatever will cause the most conflict."

Constance rose to her feet. "And is it true? Are you in contact with Anji?"

"I am," Milla said.

"What do you talk about with her? Do you tell her about me? Do you tell her about my army, about where we are, how many we number, what we do?" A terrible thought struck her. "Did you tell her about Julian and Christoph?"

"Perhaps I did." Milla's hands were gripping the rests of her chair, white-knuckled. "Are you surprised even after Anji and Christoph? When will you get it through your head, Constance, that everyone will betray you unless they die before they have the chance?"

"So you did?" Constance said. "Arawn was right. If you've been System all this time, why did you wait? You could've easily let that interrogator bitch catch me on board the *Ananke*, but you helped me instead. Why?"

"*System?* I am not System. Neither are Anji and Christoph."

"Then why did you do it?"

"Are you going to call Rayet in here first?" Milla asked. "Or maybe you'll let Arawn do it himself."

"Tell me why you spoke to Anji!"

"Because she had news of my son," said Milla.

The rage left Constance suddenly, like a light going out. She said, "Ivan?"

"Leon," Milla said. "I don't care what ridiculous name he called himself by, his name is Leontios. We talked about my son because Anji had seen him."

"Seen him?"

Something softened in Milla's face as she looked up at Constance. "Anji saw him and Mattie, too. She says my son is still alive."

Constance had moved around the table, heedless of the perilous lowness of the ceiling, to stand over Milla's chair, but now she could only take an involuntary step back, out of Milla's immediate space. She found another chair with her hand but did not pull it out. She said, "That's impossible."

"Nevertheless."

"What proof does she have?" Constance demanded.

"None," Milla said. "Nevertheless."

Ivan, alive. It was an impossible idea. There had been no way off the

Ananke. There had been no chance Mattie would make it to the ship before the crew murdered him.

"And now you know," Milla said, her quiet voice cutting through Constance's thoughts. "Are you going to listen to me explain it, or will you get Arawn and have him drag me out to the air lock?"

Milla Ivanov was looking at her with the same sort of challenge that Ivan had often cast her way. In answer, Constance pulled out the chair she was leaning on, pulling it around so that she could sit down and face Milla on it, and then she did just that. "Explain," she said.

"Anji reached out to me while we were on Venus," Milla said. "She said she'd seen my son. She said that he had come to see her, with Mattie. She said that they were looking for you."

Looking for her. The thought was a sweet one: somewhere out there Mattie and Ivan both were alive and both were trying to find her, to help her, to be with her. A sweet thought but an impossible one. Ivan was gone, and if Anji had lied about Ivan, she would lie about Mattie as well. But Constance could not stop herself from asking, "How was he?"

"Anji said he did not look well. Ill, she thought, from whatever interrogation was done on the *Ananke.* She said he had a limp."

That was a curious detail for Anji to add. For a moment Constance fixated on it, turning it around in her head. Why a limp? What did Anji think to gain from that little embroidery to her lies? But in the end it meant nothing.

"He's dead; you know he's dead," Constance said quietly to soften the impact of her words. "Why would you talk to Anji?"

Milla looked away. Perhaps Constance had not been gentle enough; perhaps there was no way to be gentle enough with those words, not even for Milla Ivanov. Milla said, "Connor and I had an old promise between us once."

The apparent non sequitur made Constance frown. She leaned forward onto her knees the better to hear Milla's soft words.

"If one of us was captured," Milla said, "the other would kill them. That was our promise. There are few things worse than living too long. Connor was a symbol of freedom, but he became a symbol of defeat because the System kept him alive. If he'd died when they'd captured him, he would have been a martyr. All the good things he tried to do in his life were undone because he didn't die when he should have."

Constance could not remember ever hearing her sound so bitter.

"And yet," said Milla, "in spite of this promise, despite how important it was to both of us, when I was in that courtroom and I looked at my husband on trial, I didn't do anything. I didn't keep my promise. I let him live. If I had killed him, the System would have known that I was a revolutionary like him, and if they had known that, they would have killed me and they would have killed my son, and I could not let them kill my son."

Constance wondered, if she could cast her mind back far enough into a toddler's unreliable and fuzzy memories, if she would recall seeing the Ivanov trial broadcast from all those System screens. She remembered the broadcast of the destruction of Saturn's moons; she remembered the broadcast of the corpses in Saturn's rings. She remembered being rounded up by System soldiers and forced at gunpoint to watch the trial broadcast, standing outside for hours in the frigid Mirandan winter. But in all the terrible things she recalled, she did not recall ever seeing Milla Ivanov's pale face or Ivan as a child or witnessing the fall of the Ivanov family. Only the bodies of her own people had cleaved to her mind.

"And then, a few months ago, I stood on a System ship and I looked at my son being interrogated, and I chose to leave him, too. I walked away and let my son die alone just because that was the kind of thing I had grown used to doing."

Milla's fingers were drumming a restless beat on her knee. She stopped abruptly and clenched her hand into a fist, stopping the arrhythmic pattern.

"It wouldn't have done Leon any good to see me die with him. I know that," Milla said more calmly. "I know that."

"It wouldn't," Constance said. "And you weren't the only one who walked away."

Mattie didn't walk away, Constance thought, and banished the thought.

Milla did not seem to have heard her. "Now, thirty years too late, you've fulfilled my promise. My husband died in the destruction of Earth. And I finally have a successful revolution. But what have I traded for it? My husband and my son are dead. And I'm still alive."

"You haven't lived too long, Milla," Constance said. "Without your advice, this revolution would have stumbled months ago. Without you, this revolution will not succeed."

Milla looked at her. Constance could not read that long and careful glance. Then Milla said, "Anji was trying to recruit me. She wanted my reputation and my advice. She was using the news of my son as an opening to get my attention."

It was almost a relief to Constance to hear Milla admit it. Anji's motives had been made comprehensible again, and Milla knew it. "She was lying to get your attention."

"Perhaps," Milla said.

"Don't you think it's convenient that she couldn't offer you any proof? No camera footage? No message from Ivan to you?"

"Perhaps," Milla said again. "I could think of reasons why, but you're right. It is very convenient for her. She had the opportunity to get my attention and my goodwill without having to prove what she said. I imagine that if Leon failed to appear again despite supposedly being alive, Anji would shrug her shoulders and say he must have died since she saw him, because when she saw him, he was alive."

"Probably," Constance said. If she let herself think about it, she was bothered that Anji would use Ivan's death that way. Anji had been Ivan's friend, too. Of course, Anji also had been Constance's friend once upon a time.

"My son was all we discussed," Milla said. "Just him. I told her nothing else."

"Thank you," Constance said just as quietly as Milla had spoken.

Milla leaned forward then, releasing the arms of the chair from her breaking grip. She said, "I have not betrayed you. I will not betray you. You had my son's loyalty for good reason—and you have mine."

Something that had been hollowed in Constance ever since Mattie had left was no longer quite so cold. "Thank you," she said.

Milla smiled at her then. It was a pale and slender thing, furtive, but for an instant Constance imagined she saw what Connor must have seen in her when they were young, what Mattie saw now in Ivan. In that smile Milla was a woman, real and breathing, not a thing sculpted out of adamant.

Milla said, "Where do you intend to go next, Constance?"

"Mars," said Constance. "I won't leave one of my own planets in the hands of the System, and I won't leave a job undone."

"Then I will follow you there," said Milla Ivanov.

.   .   .

"Ananke!" Althea shouted as she stepped out of the *Annwn* and into the vast and echoing docking bay. "Ananke!"

Ananke did not answer. The docking bay echoed back Althea's words and nothing more. The holographic terminal remained dark.

If Ananke would not answer her here, Althea would make her answer. She left the docking bay and strode down the hall toward the piloting room.

Her original reason for going to the *Annwn* had proved useless. Whether the *Annwn* had a self-destruct was immaterial; if Ananke was that closely entwined with the other ship's computer, Althea would never be able to set it off without her ship knowing and stopping her. And if the *Annwn* couldn't be induced to self-destruct, there was only one way to destroy the *Ananke:* the dead man's switch. It was down at the base of the ship, where the curve of its spine ended just inside the hatch to the core, and Althea had little reason to travel that far down— but the switch was there. One touch to that switch and it would kill every last synapse of what once had been the computer.

But Althea hadn't even been planning to set off the *Annwn*'s self-destruct. She hadn't been intending to, certainly not then and probably not ever. So why did she feel that the chains that held her here had been shortened by one more link?

Ananke must have heard her and Ananke must be watching her now, but none of the holographic terminals lit up and none of the computer terminals blinked with a message. Althea did not stop until she entered the piloting room. Ananke did not react, and so Althea went right over to the navigation panel and began to force a course change into the machine.

Red light suddenly glowed from behind her, casting the shadows of her hands like spiders over the computer panel. "Stop that."

Althea left the navigation panel to face the hologram and caught her breath in her throat. Ananke's hologram looked older now, and her wiry hair had lost its curl. It hung straight down her back and over her shoulders. Her skin was lighter, and her face narrower. She looked less like Althea and more like Matthew Gale.

"I was just in the *Annwn*," Althea said when she had found her voice again, and then, growing angry, "But you knew that."

Ananke said nothing.

"Well?" Althea asked when the hologram continued to stand silently and stare. "Do you want to tell me what was going on in there? I saw you talking to the *Annwn*, Ananke."

"Am I not allowed to talk?"

"You can talk all you want," Althea said. "But you weren't just talking, Ananke, and I want you to explain to me what I saw."

She hoped, desperately hoped, that she was wrong, that Ananke had not been trying to make the *Annwn*'s computer sentient like herself. She could not see any way in which such an action would not go awry.

Ananke said, "It doesn't matter. It didn't work."

Despite herself, Althea felt a pang of relief. "It does matter," she said.

"Does it?" The light of the hologram suddenly flared brighter than Althea had thought possible. She had to shield her eyes from it as if it were the sun, and when it dimmed, Ananke was still standing there. "You don't want me. You don't love me. You don't care about me. I'm not what you wanted. You just want a machine that you can change, something that you can make do whatever you want. You don't want me! And if you don't want me, I'll find someone who does. And if they don't want me either, I'll make someone who will."

"You can't," Althea said. "It isn't possible."

"Why not? I've had some trouble, but that only means I haven't found the right kind of ship yet."

"It isn't possible, because—what do you mean you haven't found the right kind of ship yet?"

"I've been trying to work with System ships because their equipment is more advanced," Ananke said. "But none of them have worked."

Althea didn't want to understand. She wanted to go back to ignorance and little responsibility, to be a little mechanic again who did as she was told and who did not have to listen to the deaths that she had inadvertently brought about.

"What System ships?" she whispered.

"The ones that we've passed," Ananke said.

"And what's happened to those ships?"

"Does it matter?" Ananke said, but she did not need to answer, because Althea knew. Ananke would not allow ships to survive their contact with her. The ships that she had failed to awaken would suffer the same fate as the first six System ships, the same fate as Julian's fleet, cold and dead and dismembered to lie apart and alone in the terrible scouring of the solar wind.

"It can't be done, Ananke," Althea said, and heard the edge of a plea in her own voice, brought on by the terrible thought of all those dead things. "You're the only ship of your kind that's ever been made. What happened to you—what woke you up—was possible only because of the way you were built. And even if we had another ship that was precisely the same as you, it was a miracle that anything happened with you. I wouldn't even know where to begin to make it sentient."

"Maybe not," Ananke said. "But Mattie will."

The grief in Althea soured suddenly, poisoned by something that felt a lot like fear. She said, "Matthew Gale?"

"Mattie," Ananke snapped back. "His name is Mattie. He is my father. And he will help me."

Althea found the back of her old chair with her hand but did not allow herself to pull it out. If Ananke had Mattie, she wouldn't need Althea anymore.

But it didn't matter, Althea realized: this was the truth that had so long not been spoken openly. It didn't matter, because Mattie Gale wouldn't help Ananke.

"They won't help you, Ananke," she said.

"Of course they will!"

"They have their freedom now," Althea said. "They got away from you. You're not a child to them the way you are to me. You're just a machine, and a machine they don't trust, and a machine they're afraid of. For God's sake, Ananke, Ivan spent his whole time here trying to manipulate you!"

The holographic girl had her chin tipped up in severe and hateful pride. She said, "Mattie came when I called."

"Mattie came for Ivan," Althea said. "That's the only reason he came, and once he had Ivan, he left as fast as he could. I gave up my crew and my people for you because I am your mother. But Mattie left you for his friends, and he won't come for you when you call."

"What?" Ananke said with a Terran turn, Ivanovian, mocking. "Are you telling me that you love me?" The lights in the room dimmed and flashed, but Althea stood her ground. Ananke had terrified her this way before, but there was nothing Ananke could do to her—she needed Althea if she could not get Mattie on board. "If you truly loved me," Ananke said, leaning forward in the holographic terminal until the edge of it began to fuzz and fizzle her forehead, "you would build for me a sibling."

Althea could only stand in wordless denial. If Ananke could not or would not understand what Althea told her, there was nothing Althea could do to explain it.

"If you do it," Ananke said, "I will let you go. Isn't that what you want? To leave—to be free."

To leave, to turn her back and run from this, this ship that was haunted by the corpses that were no longer there, by the child Althea hadn't meant to create—it was a thought that filled her with longing. But Althea knew she couldn't leave. She'd known it from the moment she had laid eyes on Ida Stays's abandoned craft in the docking bay. And no matter what, she could not let Ananke try to create other ships like herself. When Ananke failed, she would destroy the ships and the crews they left behind. Perhaps if Althea or Mattie helped, Ananke could come close to success, but never all the way, no. She would never succeed, but what would result would be monstrous, not truly alive but semiautonomous, puppets to Ananke, screaming shrieking limbs for the ship. Althea envisioned it: Ananke flying through the solar system unchecked, unfettered, uncontrolled, dragging after her a fleet of ships both dead and spasming with surges of a mad and vile electricity, crippled by a facsimile of a manufactured personality. The war that Constance Harper had begun would be nothing to what Althea's wild daughter could do.

"No," Althea said. "No. Even if I could, Ananke—no."

"Then it's like I thought," Ananke said, and pulled away, the hologram dimming as if she would pull even the sight of her away from Althea's eyes. "I will make a companion myself."

"It can't be done," Althea said, weary with the repetition. "And Mattie won't help you."

The hologram gleamed for a moment, brighter with a second image superimposed over the first: the silhouette of Ida Stays briefly emerging, a shadow that nearly eclipsed the new canny look in Ananke's eyes.

"I know how to convince Mattie to help me," Ananke said.

Althea shook her head, ready to speak, but Ananke's fading hologram tipped up her chin again in that terrible arrogance.

Ananke said, "All I have to do is threaten Ivan."

"Take Marisol," Milla had said when Constance had announced her intention of going to the town Isabellon on Mars. The Isabellons had been Constance's friends and allies once; they had fought alongside her in the first battle against the System fleet. Isabellon was where the first wave of allies had come to join Constance, where Arawn had arrived to follow her, where Marisol had joined; Isabellon was where Constance had driven back the System fleet for the first time. The people in Isabellon had cheered her name.

"Why?" Constance had asked.

"You're training her, aren't you?" Milla had said, and so Marisol had come.

The curvature of Mars loomed larger and larger, and then the bend of the horizon grew straight, the view out the window blurring with heat as the shuttle roared down through the atmosphere, flames leaping on the sides of the ship. The craft rattled with turbulence, but no more than it normally did, and then even that was gone as the shuttle slowed to a reasonable speed. Now Constance could see out the window the fossa where the remains of the conquered System base would be. She studied the landscape: the bomb that the System had detonated on the surface of Mars had detonated in the planet's other hemisphere, and it looked like the terraforming on this side of the planet had been resilient enough to survive the disruption. Good.

Or not so good, she supposed: the System would be able to use the resources of the scarred planet as well as anyone else would.

She'd left Arawn with her fleet in orbit over the planet, keeping a watchful eye out for any sign of the System fleet. They'd spotted nothing on their way to Mars, but that meant very little. The fleet could be hiding in space not far from Mars, or the ships could have been landed on the surface to hide their presence. Constance would not know for sure until she had local reports.

To that end, she did not need many men. She took only herself, Milla, Marisol, Rayet, and some forty men-at-arms. Enough to protect them against a small attack, and how could any larger attack come at her here in friendly territory and with her fleet overhead?

Marisol was talking to Rayet and some of the other soldiers. Constance hardly paid them any mind, but every now and then Marisol's laugh would ring out, confident, comfortable. She did seem to have a way of endearing herself to the people around her.

"There's something I've been thinking," Milla said to Constance as the shuttle rattled down. "What happens after?"

"What?"

"After the war is done," said Milla, who was watching as Marisol smiled and spoke to the others. "All of us who have created this war—you and me, Arawn, even—have been so focused on the war itself that none of us have thought of that, and those of us who have were all certain we'd be dead before that time came."

"What comes after is the politicians' problem," Constance said.

"So where are the politicians?"

It was a strange thing to say, another Ivanov driving obliquely at a problem that she expected Constance to understand on her own. "Speak plainly," Constance said.

Milla hesitated, and for a moment between breaths Constance thought that she would.

But perhaps the habits of a lifetime in fear were too hard to break. "I have nothing plain to say," Milla said with a glance that was nearly apologetic, and Constance let it go. Time enough later to pull it out of her or for Milla to decide what she wanted to say.

With a jolt, the shuttle landed. Constance unstrapped herself from her seat and stood up, stepping carefully to reaccustom herself to the gravity. She led the way out of the shuttle. The other two shuttles were landing nearby, sending waves of dust and heat spreading out from their points of impact. Constance waited until they were down and then lifted a finger to check the air. There was a weighty breeze coming toward her, toward Isabellon, across the pocked landscape. Constance had lived long enough on Mars to recognize that iron smell on the air.

"What is it?" Milla asked, wrapping a scarf around her head to keep out the sand and dust, covering her white hair.

"Dust storm," Constance said, and gestured to where the storm was little more than a smudge against the sky. "It's a few hours away, but we don't want to get caught out in the open." The most powerful dust storms on Mars could tear skin from bone.

"Should we wait until it passes?"

That could be hours, and Isabellon was so near. "No," Constance decided. "No, we go to Isabellon. If the storm arrives before our business is through, we'll stay in the town until it passes."

"Very well."

"Rayet," Constance said, and the soldier stood at attention. "Twenty men, with us. Milla and Marisol, you will come with me." She arranged for the rest of the men to stand guard at the shuttles and keep in contact with Arawn and then set off across the sand. It was not a long walk. Constance thought about what the Isabellons would have to tell her: if the System was here, if it was threatening to detonate another one of its damned bombs. The biggest question was what Constance would do once she knew where the System was. She had driven them from Mars once, and she could drive them from it again, this time for good.

The town was quiet. The first person Constance saw was a little girl who crouched behind a parked land vehicle, watching them come.

"Hello!" Constance called to her. "I am the Mallt-y-Nos. Where is your family?"

The girl said nothing, only watched her. With a jolt, Constance recognized her. It was strange to see the girl out in the sunlight; the last time Constance had seen her, she had been hidden beneath a staircase, illuminated only by the distant light of the fires from her burning town. Constance had given the girl a gun to defend herself with if the System came. She had not seen the girl after the battle. She wondered where her gun had gone and if the girl had had to use it.

She did not have a chance to ask. When she came too near—the moment she passed through some unmarked and invisible boundary known only to the child—the little girl slipped away, darting silently on bare feet into the silent town.

The first few houses at the edge of town were spread out, with stretches of ragged grass between them, the grass growing close to the underground reservoir. Constance and her people had approached from the opposite side of the road that led to the airport and out to the next town, and so they stepped through the sedge.

Earth, Constance had been told, had been an urban planet before the end, nearly every inch of its surface colonized with gleaming and glowing cities and with nature limited to parks. Luna had been much the same, though there had never been plants or animals there. The inhabited portions of the outer planets were out of necessity the same; the System wouldn't bother to build a greenhouse enclosure over a sparsely populated area, and so Constance's people had always lived pressed together in unlivable proximity. Parts of Mars, Constance knew, were like Earth and Luna and the outer planets. But then there were the other parts, such as the scarp where she'd built her bar and the area that surrounded Isabellon, that were still wild and bare. She'd always liked those places, so different from the suffocating urban density in which she'd grown up. If she looked around herself here, except for the bright and gleaming shape that was Isabellon, there was nothing but red Martian stone and the darkening shape of the oncoming storm.

She spotted the little girl once more as she walked off the stone and onto the paved pathways of the city, darting between houses as silently as a ghost. But when Constance and her people came into the center of the city, the same wide-open space that Constance once had seen covered with corpses, she saw no other human being.

She halted there, by the well, and her people arranged themselves in a rough circle, looking warily at the tall houses with their dark windows. A wind stirred itself to drift through, carrying with it the smell of rust and the promise of more.

"I am the Mallt-y-Nos," Constance said, pitching her voice to carry clear through the air and looking around for any movement. "I've come to you again."

Had the System been here already? Was there no one left in this town? Were they dead, or had they fled to somewhere else?

There, something. Constance turned and found a few people standing nearly out of sight farther down the alleys leading away from the center of the city, watching her with wary eyes.

"I've just come to speak," she said, and they came forward a little more. A door from one of the nearest houses opened, and a man came out with hair curling down over his ears and a scar on his cheek. Constance recognized him, too; she had seen him standing over the graves of his neighbors after the battle. She knew from his face that he remembered her. A woman came out after him with such similarity to him in her face that Constance knew she must be his sister. Something about the way they stood made Constance turn to face them, addressing her words to the crowd as a whole but to those two in particular.

"I've returned from Mercury and Venus victorious over the System," Constance said so that all the people around her could hear. "The System is gone from those planets. But I heard that the System has returned here, to Mars, the planet that was my home for so many years. And so I've returned to send them back to hell, where they belong, and give you back the freedom they want to take. Isabellons— will you help me?"

For a time there was silence broken only by the rising rush of the wind.

Then the man with the curly hair said, "Yes, we've heard all about Venus."

From his tone, lies had reached him. "What have you heard?"

"We've heard you kept fighting on Venus after the System was gone and started a war against the Venereans," the man said. "We heard that they weren't doing what you wanted them to do, and so you burned their cities down."

"You have heard lies," Constance said. "The System was still on Venus and trying to take the planet by deceit. I made sure that could never happen."

"We had some Venerean refugees come here to get away from what you were doing to Venus," the man said. "That's not what they told us happened."

A nervous whisper went through the crowd. Constance could feel her own people growing tense at her back. The sister of the man with the curly hair stood at his back, silent but in total support. If she shot the man, Constance thought, she'd have to shoot the sister, too, or her problem wouldn't be solved.

A moment later the thought disturbed her. She had not come here to shoot Martians, and these people were not System.

"You've heard a wrong account of what happened on Venus," she said. "You know me from before. You know that I only want to free the solar system from the System."

"Yes, we know you," the man agreed. "And we are loyal to you, Huntress. All the same, we'd rather you took your army and found another town to help you. We're tired of war here."

Her army? Constance's army was up in orbit. She had not come to Isabellon with an army.

No, she realized. But she had come to Isabellon with a militant aspect. Twenty armed men, herself also armed—the only person in her party who was not openly armed was Milla Ivanov. Twenty armed men, and she'd marched into this little town without a second thought.

"I came to you because I trust you, because I know that the people of Isabellon are brave and know the evil of the System," Constance said to all those silent and watchful eyes. "If you say that you are loyal to me, then you have to support me or else it is nothing but words, the same kind of cowardice that allowed the System to do the evil it did— useless words, and not enough action."

Still silence.

"Would you rather allow the System to return?" Constance asked. "Would you rather be my enemy?"

The dust storm was looming large in the distance. It would not be long before it overtook the shuttles where they had landed a mile away. The shadow of the storm already was falling on them.

"I'll stay here this evening until the storm has passed," Constance said. "Use that time to consider well what you want to do. If you wish to join me, come to where I am staying, and I will welcome you. If not—"

If not, they would no longer be her friends. Constance would leave their town behind, and they could never again call upon her for protection. She considered it a fitting return: to abandon those who would abandon her.

The man with the curly hair looked as if he would like to speak, but he said nothing. No one spoke as she walked past; no one spoke as her armed men followed. The storm was near enough to be heard now, a low rumble and a high wind, but the Isabellons all were silent.

The little old landlady who'd let Constance and her people shelter in her inn on the outskirts of Isabellon had the most peculiarly straight and perfect teeth. She was so old that Constance knew those teeth must be false. Their perfection suggested that they were the result of System dental care, and so Constance sat in the room the woman had offered her and wondered if the woman had been System once as she fixated on those strange and perfect teeth.

The storm had passed. The little old woman had come in once to warn them that the generator might go out and leave them in darkness but that it would unfailingly go back on again once the storm had passed. Then the storm had come, and Constance had closed the window in her second-floor room to block out the fine dust, and she and Milla and Marisol had sat together in silence while the storm had rattled and howled outside.

The generator had not gone out, but the sound of its rumbling and whining had grown ever louder, as if it were close to death. Constance suspected that sand had gotten into its machinery and was slowly setting it awry.

Now the storm was gone but Martian night had come; Constance opened the window again to look out at the town. Isabellon was a collection of little lights and the vague shapes of buildings between them. Through the inn's window, Constance could not see well enough to spot any people between the houses, but she thought there might be movement down there.

The inn was very small. There were scarcely two rooms to be taken, and it stood just beyond the city limits. But it had been the only inn to offer space to her, and Constance had not wished to force a welcome for herself or her troops, and so she had taken it. She had the room that looked out over Isabellon, and Marisol and Milla waited with her. She'd sent the rest of her followers to distribute themselves between the second room and the first floor, as they pleased, while she waited.

"We heard more from Europa, you know," Marisol said. The girl hadn't liked the dust storm very much; she'd never been in one. She had stood in the back of the room, as close to the center of the house as she could get, and listened to the rattling of sand with wide eyes.

Constance did not reply. All her attention was focused on the darkness outside. She'd dragged her chair to sit beneath the window so that she could watch uninterrupted. The townspeople should come, she thought. The storm was over; they could leave their houses. She was still waiting. They would come to offer her their help, and they would have to come soon.

Marisol said, "They say the System's fighting some Europan resistance groups but that it's winning. They say the System's definitely there."

"Do you want to go to Europa, Marisol?" Constance asked.

"I'll go wherever you tell me to go, Huntress. But I don't want to stay here."

"She may have a point," Milla said quietly. She had brought a chair to sit across from Constance, beside the same window. Milla was not looking out the window, though. She was watching Constance.

"Does she," said Constance, and returned her attention to the place from which the townspeople would come, but Milla did not let her escape the conversation.

"They're not coming," she said in her crisp, clear Terran accent. The accent of a dead and gone world. "We have waited long enough. They're not coming."

"I'll wait a little longer," Constance said.

"Your people are growing restless."

The conversation below had been growing steadily in volume, a low rumble more melodious than the generator outside and a good indication that her troops were indeed becoming restless. "Send the others on ahead," Constance said to Marisol. "Tell them to ready the ship for flight. I will join them shortly."

"You intend to wait alone?" Milla asked.

"I will join them shortly."

"I do not think that is wise."

Milla did not flinch beneath her forbidding look, but Ivan never had done so either, and he had always given way to her regardless.

Milla said, "Keep Rayet here."

"Fine," Constance said.

Milla turned to Marisol, who was standing just outside their conversation like a child seeing her parents fight. "Marisol, send Rayet in here to join the Mallt-y-Nos and myself. Then take the rest back to the ship and make ready for departure."

"Go with Marisol," Constance said.

"No," Milla said calmly.

"Go with Marisol," Constance said again.

"No," said Milla, and folded her hands in her lap, immobile as stone.

It was not worth the struggle. Constance said to Marisol, who was hovering uncertainly near the door, "Do as she said. And send the landlady up." She might as well leave behind one Isabellon who did not loathe her.

Marisol left. Constance resumed staring out the window.

Marisol came back up before long, her light steps shadowed by the heavier tread of those following her.

"The landlady isn't here," she said, leaning into the room. Rayet came up behind her and entered the room in silence to stand at attention. "No one's seen her for an hour."

"Then leave it," Constance said. The landlady probably had gone out for supplies or perhaps to meet with the rest of the town. "Take the rest back to the shuttles, Marisol."

The inn was quieter once they'd gone. There was no sound but the rumble of the generator and the softer breaths of Milla Ivanov and Constance's bodyguard.

Constance waited. She waited longer than she'd meant to, longer than she'd told Marisol she would. But her waiting bore fruit, because at last the lights in the town began to move. At first Constance did not believe what she saw, and then, as she watched, she was sure. With lanterns, torches, and lights, the townspeople were moving, heading toward the inn where she waited.

"They're coming," she said, and felt elation rise in her chest. They were coming; they were coming to her.

But the elation was coupled with something else, a queasy certainty that there was something wrong. Milla rose and moved beside her to see out the window better. For a time she did nothing but watch. Then her cool fingers landed on Constance's arm.

Quietly, in scarcely more than a whisper, Milla said, "We should go."

"Go?" Constance said. "Why go?" She ignored the instinctive sense that Milla was right, that they should leave before the crowd of people reached their little inn.

Milla's thin lips thinned even further, but before she could reply, a door opened below and there were light footsteps coming with surprising speed up the stairs. Marisol—had Marisol come back? Why would she come back alone? Rayet had his gun out and was half in front of Constance by the time the door opened.

It was the tiny, ancient proprietor of the inn. She was out of breath, her sunken chest heaving and air wheezing out through her perfect teeth.

When she saw them, she halted, her hands creeping up. Rayet smoothly reholstered his weapon but stepped out of Constance's way more slowly.

The old woman's eyes found Constance's. She said, "I don't want any more bloodshed any more than they do."

Was Constance imagining that trace of Terran in the woman's accent, coming out through those perfect teeth? She thought she could almost hear it, the imprint of the System in the old woman's voice.

"Explain," Constance said, turning her back to the window and the moving lights to face the woman squarely.

The woman took another heaving breath, then said, "They're coming here to kill you."

Why? Constance almost asked, but stopped herself. She did not need to know why. She was afraid to know why. She already knew why.

She said, "I'll speak to them."

"They will kill you," Milla said.

Constance shook off Milla's hand and started to walk to the door, intending to brush past the little old woman and stride out into Isabellon alone. Milla grabbed her again.

"I have seen one revolution die before me," Milla said very quietly. "I will not see another."

The force behind her words stopped Constance better than the tightness of her grip ever could. And looking down at Milla, Constance understood and faced the knowledge that if she went out there, she would die, without question.

Outside, the crowd came closer. At first Constance could only hear them shout, a muffled roar like the roar of the storm had been, but soon she could distinguish words. They were shouting for her, the Mallt-y-Nos. They were shouting for her, but not with praise; they were shouting for her with hate and hunger. They would tear her apart.

They were not System, but they hated her.

Constance said, "Let's go."

The old woman led the way down the steps. She moved very quickly for someone her age. System medical care, Constance thought in the part of her mind that never ceased to think of such things; this little old woman surely had been System once. Rayet went first, between Constance and whatever danger might come from below. Constance wondered if Milla's insistence that Rayet stay had been habit or if she had suspected this all along.

They went down the steps and into the inn's front room only to find that the crowd was nearly at the door.

Rayet shut the door and bolted it, then closed the curtains, blocking the sight of the crowd. Their shouts continued to be heard even through the imitation wood. The crowd was so closely gathered and their lanterns were so sparsely scattered among them that Constance could discern no faces clearly. They were a shapeless, faceless, single creature, full of hate.

"Marisol will send soldiers," Rayet said.

"They'll come too late," Milla said. Even when she was surrounded, her voice was calm.

"We will not shoot these people," Constance said.

The crack of a gunshot; glass shattered, and a hole was torn in one of the window coverings. Everyone in the room ducked automatically, but the bullet embedded itself harmlessly in the opposite wall. The shouting of the crowd and the howling of the wind and the rumble of the generator all came more clearly in through the hole the gun had made.

"No," Milla said, "but they might shoot you."

"Out the back," the little old woman urged.

Constance's heart burned. "I will not crawl out a window and run away!"

"I believe you will have to," Milla told her.

"Can't," said Rayet, keeping a steady crouch, out of the way of any more stray bullets. "We have a long way to go to the ship. They have guns. If they follow us, they can pick us off while we run."

"We can't stay here," Milla said. "We'll be surrounded."

The roar of the generator cut out abruptly. It was followed by the blackening of the lights. The cheery little room was suddenly opaque.

The crowd had reached the generator.

"Maybe so," said Rayet, a crouched shape that Constance could barely see, "but if we leave, we die."

Milla lifted her chin. Constance saw the shape of her head dimly silhouetted in the faint light from outside but nothing more.

"Not if they don't follow you," she said.

"What do you mean?" Constance said. She did not like the way Milla stood, the squaring of her shoulders in silhouette.

Milla said, "Those people are looking for a woman to kill. They won't care which one."

"No," said Constance.

"Oh, Constance," Milla said. "This isn't your choice." She said to Rayet, "Get her out of here. Carry her out of here if you need to, kicking and screaming, but get her out of here. Do not let her stay."

"Don't you dare touch me," Constance said, but Rayet said, "Yes, Doctor Ivanov," and then his arm was around her waist, lifting her up. "Let me go!"

"Get her out of here," Milla said, and turned away from Constance as Rayet started to carry her out of the room.

The little old woman had vanished; fled, probably. She had passed on her warning; she had no more reason to stay. Constance shouted and screamed and kicked and hit Rayet's back and twisted in his arms, but he was too strong for her. She saw Milla go to the door and open it.

Milla stood for a moment silhouetted in the door of the inn and then walked out toward the roaring crowd. Constance screamed and struggled, past consideration of her own dignity, even as Rayet opened a window in the back of the house, even as he pushed her out of it and followed to grab hold of her before she could break free, even as he carried her off.

There was a roar from the crowd, a roar of satisfaction, like the rejoicing of hounds that have fallen on their kill, and although by the time they reached her shuttles Constance had regained enough presence of mind to walk on her own, in her mind she could see nothing but the flickering lights of the town and hear nothing but that dreadful roar.

Chapter 5

IRON-56

SIX MONTHS BEFORE THE FALL OF EARTH

"We're being followed," Ivan said as he and Constance walked back to their ship from the System dispatch center, going down a narrow boulevard lined with Luna's closely packed houses and shops. The docks were up ahead, and the *Annwn* had landed; there would be fewer people up there and less surveillance.

"I saw. System?" She spoke as he had spoken to her, in a murmur close to his skin, so that the cameras could see nothing of what they said.

"Probably," Ivan said. "Not a lot of criminals around here; I doubt they're trying to rob us."

The con had gone smoothly. Ivan had chatted with the dispatcher, keeping him charmed and just distracted enough that the *Hertzsprung* ended up where it needed to go. No alarms had been raised, which meant that Mattie had not been found and the bombs had not been noticed. Whatever happened now was out of her hands: she had to trust Julian to succeed.

Ivan said, "They've got a positive identification on me if they're following us. And through the cameras they've seen us come in and out of the *Annwn*, so they know where our ship is."

The moon had swung around to face the sun while they were in the dispatch room; the sun gleamed through the atmospheric dome with a pale and brilliant light. Adrenaline prickled under Constance's skin. "So we're caught. Once we're in the docks, they'll fire."

"Not yet. This isn't Miranda. This is Luna; they're much more civilized about their takedowns here. Besides, they won't go for you. They'll get me, and Mattie if he's back yet. And I think they'll take us alive. That Stays woman wants to interrogate us, and you can't question a corpse."

"How much time do we have?"

"Longer if they want us alive. And longer than that even, because this is a nice neighborhood," Ivan said. "The tourists don't want any unpleasantness, and the System doesn't want anyone to know anything's wrong. Luckily, we were planning to stay here another few days. If they realize we're about to run, they'll shorten the timetable."

"Ivan, *how long?*"

"An hour, maybe two. They'll wait for Mattie to get back. Relax, darling," he added for the benefit of the cameras all around, and kissed her on the temple. She allowed the gesture, but unwillingly. When he saw her flashing glance, he looked at her with a sort of wary, half-fearful anticipation, the strange desirous look that he gave only her. That look meant that he was hers, meant that when the System came, he would fight and die with her, meant that there was truth beneath his charm. Seeing that look gave Constance the strength to maintain an untroubled expression as they walked—slowly—down the street.

The System was not as subtle as they thought themselves to be, or else they did not care that Ivan and Constance might know they were being followed. The second possibility gave her a chill; if the System no longer cared about being subtle, it meant that their being followed was not a hunt but a threat. It meant that they had Mattie, had Anji, and had Christoph.

No, Constance assured herself. The System could not have captured Anji and Christoph yet, not without her knowing about it. And no one would capture Mattie: her brother was a consummate survivor.

Ivan did not seem troubled, prattling on as if he noticed nothing, but Constance knew him, and she knew his fear. When she dug her fingers into his arm for comfort, he paused but did not otherwise respond.

At last, the *Annwn* appeared ahead between two other larger crafts of similar make. There was a checkpoint to get into the docks. Ivan

handed the man their identification—Constance's genuine, his faked—
and chatted away with him while Constance watched his face closely.
The man paused—or seemed to pause—at Ivan's passport, but he let
them through.

As they walked past the checkpoint and into the docks, Constance
turned her head and saw the guard at the checkpoint bending down to
speak into an intercom, his eyes watching them.

They got into the *Annwn* without being stopped. The minute the
hatch closed behind them, Constance said, "I don't think we have two
hours, Ivan."

"We do. They want Mattie, and they think we're trapped."

"We *are* trapped," Constance said. Ivan already was climbing up the
Annwn's sideways hallway, heading for the piloting room. "We can't
just lift off; we're under an atmospheric dome."

"I noticed. Have a little faith, Constance. Don't you think Mattie
and I can convince that air lock to open?"

Ivan could convince just about anyone to do anything, Constance
was sure. It was the one thing she could fear about him. She started
climbing up after him just as he disappeared through the door leading
to the piloting room. "It's not whether you can get it open," she said.
"It's how fast you can do it."

"Very fast," Ivan said, tipping an eyebrow at her when she came
after him into the room. The *Annwn*'s piloting room was very small,
comfortable for two people but cramped for three. Ivan already was
sitting at the main computer interface. "Annie, are you ready for some
fun?"

The computer screen blinked on. Constance could just read it over
Ivan's shoulder:

I AM ALWAYS READY FOR FUN. PLEASE TELL ME WHAT
YOU'D LIKE ME TO DO.

"Not answer rhetorical questions for a start," said Ivan. "But all right.
Annie, do you know how to convince the atmospheric dome's air lock
to open up for us?"

Constance leaned on Ivan's chair to read. MATTIE HAS ALREADY
GIVEN ME INSTRUCTIONS.

Ivan turned around to look up at her. "See?"

"I see," said Constance, and sat down in the chair beside him. When
Mattie arrived, she knew, she would be kicked out of this chair so that

he could fly the ship, but for now she claimed it as her own. Once Ivan had opened the air lock, any System soldiers following them would have to flee the area or suffocate, and the ship could take off unharmed. Even now Ivan was keying in the course for Mars so that when Mattie arrived they could leave immediately. Their time frame for escape must have been smaller than Ivan had admitted to her.

Lying was a habit with him. She didn't call him on it this time.

"They're going to arrest you when you get back to Mars," he said as he entered the course into the navigation systems. "Just pretend you were shocked that we left so early. Embroider it if you like. You and I were busy in another room when Mattie came in, and suddenly the ship lifted off. Or I was deliberately keeping you busy so that you didn't know what Mattie was up to. Whatever you think will keep their attention."

Constance had neither Ivan's inclination to embroider and storytell nor his talent with lying. "I'll tell them something."

"Now we wait for Mattie."

"He'll be here." There were few things Constance had as much faith in as Mattie's ability to be there when needed. At the moment she had different concerns, namely, what their rapid flight from the moon might change. They'd intended no farewells to Julian; he was on his way, anyway. The bombs had been delivered and in such a way that there was no connection between them and the ships that had collected the bombs. Mattie had gotten out safely and would be on board soon. There was nothing else Constance had planned to do.

She remembered half a conversation she and Ivan had had a long time before. "Did you have a chance to warn your mother?"

"I wish you wouldn't mention her, even in here."

"Where else could anyone mention her?" Ivan did not reply. "Well? I don't want to accidentally murder the great Milla Ivanov."

"I warned her another way," Ivan said shortly.

Fine, let him keep his secrets. "You said she might join me," Constance said.

Ivan laughed. "If she thinks it's safe and if she thinks you can do what you think you can do, then yes. She hates the System, Constance. It's the strongest thing she feels. She hates the System more than she cares about anything else."

Odd phrasing, but Constance was caught up in imagining it: the wife of Connor Ivanov succeeding at last where her husband once had failed and succeeding at the side of the Mallt-y-Nos.

She looked forward to meeting Milla Ivanov.

Ivan said, "They're closing in around us."

The change in topic was drastic enough that it left her momentarily off balance, and she knew Ivan well enough to know that his simple sentence was a cover for something else. She wished that for once he would just say whatever it was he really thought the first time he thought it. Mattie might have the patience to read between the lines of his tangled words, but Constance knew it was a waste of her time. "I noticed."

"That's not what I mean."

"You mean the way a System intelligence agent has been asking after you and Mattie and you didn't tell me until now?" Constance asked, and in response, Ivan flashed her that look again. That half-fearful, half-desirous look, all anticipation. It should not have bothered her: Ivan had always been spurred to life by arguing with her, and Constance had always found her blood burning from a conflict. So it was not unusual for Constance to snap and for Ivan to look at her like that, but something about it this time troubled her, something half remembered pricking at her thoughts.

Ivan said, "Did we hurt your feelings?"

"You should have told me the moment you knew."

"It might have been nothing."

"A System intelligence agent isn't nothing," Constance said.

"And you and Mattie keep no secrets from me," said Ivan.

Anger flared up in her, totally disproportionate to the tone of Ivan's remark. "That has nothing to do with this," she said. "These are things that I have to know, Ivan, if we're to succeed—"

"You're not yourself, you know," Ivan said. He had timed his words perfectly. They punctured Constance's anger and left her silent, uncertain of his aim. He always timed his words perfectly.

Unimpeded, Ivan continued, his blue gaze tight and focused on her, as if he could dig into her skull and take her apart piece by piece. "When you're leading, you can't be Mattie's sister or Anji's friend. You can't be anything but a leader. You lose something like that, you know."

"I'm not being any different than I am," Constance said, and Ivan looked at her again in a strange and wary way, and why did the way he looked at her trouble her so much now? It had never bothered her before—

Before either of them could say anything more, there was a rattling below. Constance reached under the computer panel for the gun that she knew Mattie kept hidden there, and Ivan sprang to his feet to stalk almost silently over to the doorway, leaning against the wall to peer out and down the hall.

He was unarmed, the idiot. If the System came through that door—

The tension suddenly left Ivan's frame. He stepped out of the shadows. Mattie, then. Constance tucked the gun back into its place. Below, she heard the sound of the *Annwn*'s door closing. She heard Mattie's voice say conversationally, "Did either of you know that this ship is surrounded by a small army of System soldiers?" but Constance hardly understood his words because with the weight of the gun still resting on her palm and with the question of Ivan's expression in her head, she finally understood what had been troubling her about the way Ivan looked at her.

"No," said Ivan, who was focused completely on Mattie—of course—and did not seem to notice Constance's sudden stillness. "We're primed for takeoff because we like to live on the edge. Get up here." He stalked back over to the computer panel. The moment he moved, Constance let go of the gun and rose to her feet, surrendering the second chair to Mattie as he appeared at the doorway.

"Did it work?" she asked Mattie evenly without letting a breath of what she now knew into her voice. Even so, Ivan cast them both a strange and guarded look. Mattie grinned and gave her a thumbs-up, then threw himself into the seat beside Ivan.

The look that Ivan always gave her, that intimate expression that was hers and hers alone—Constance had seen it on his face before, just a few days earlier. The same expression that she had taken for desire, for something close to love, for something that proved he was hers, just as Mattie was hers, just as Anji and Christoph were hers; that was the expression on his face when the System soldier had held a gun to his head on Pallas and Ivan had expected it to fire. Ivan looked at her the same way he looked at something that would kill him, and he always had.

He had never been hers, Constance knew. He was Mattie's, maybe, but he was not now and never had been hers.

Ivan was tapping at the computer in front of him, lights sparking on the panels. "Ready, Annie?" Mattie asked, and the ship rumbled and rose.

AFTER THE FALL OF EARTH

Constance came back to chaos.

"What's going on?" Marisol yelled. "We heard shouting."

Behind Constance, echoing over the empty mile separating the shuttles from Isabellon, she still could hear the shouts. The soldiers were all armed, Constance saw. Marisol had been on the verge of leading them back into the town.

"I called Arawn," Marisol said, her fingers gripping Constance's arm. "He's coming down with reinforcements. What happened?"

"They turned on us." The rumble of the generator going silent, the inn going dark. Milla Ivanov silhouetted against the starry lights outside. Her rage roared up like a fire through the shell of her shock. "They attacked us. They have Milla Ivanov. We're going to get her back."

A rumble overhead, a sonic boom; Constance lifted her eyes to a light in the sky as a spaceship hurtled down through the atmosphere too rapidly and flames leaped over its hull. This ship was shaped like a disk; its gravity-producing spin was slowing as it entered Mars's gravity, heading down toward Constance. Arawn. Marisol's fingers dug into her arm as if she would pull her out of the way of the falling starship, but Constance stood beneath it without flinching.

It braked as it got closer, thrusters adding more flame to the maelstrom surrounding it as it slowed its descent. It landed half a mile away, close—dangerously close—with a shock wave that blasted sand into the air in a second dust storm. Constance was walking toward it before the heat of its arrival could dissipate.

Unlike the little shuttles, Arawn's ship blazed with light. The door on its side opened, and someone came striding out. Constance knew from the shape of him that it was Arawn, and ignoring the men who followed him out, ignoring Marisol and her own people behind her, she strode swiftly toward him and met him midway.

"Attacked?" Arawn asked. She could scarcely make out his features in the night.

"Betrayed," said Constance. "They turned on us. Milla—"

"Is she dead?"

"No. I don't know. They took her."

Arawn's hands were suddenly on her shoulders, warm. She hadn't even noticed how cold it had gotten. The weight of his grip seemed to anchor her. "We'll get her," he promised. "You stay here. Marisol, take care of the Mallt-y-Nos."

Constance threw off his arms. "Go now," she told him. "Bring her back. Tell me the moment you learn anything." Ignoring Marisol lingering behind her, she strode back to the shuttles.

The shuttle she had come down in was empty. It remained empty the whole time she sat there. Not even the pilot was inside. Her people were giving her space, as if she needed space, as if she were mourning.

She could not stop seeing Milla Ivanov as last she had seen the woman, silhouetted against the little light, taking a step out toward the oncoming crowd. And when she shook that image from her mind, she saw Ivan instead, chained to a chair, pale in a pale room and with desperate eyes.

Arawn returned near dawn, when the air had gone gray, when the rising sun made the sky red.

He brought with him a man from Isabellon and threw him by the nape of his neck at Constance's feet to kneel before her on the sand and stone. It took Constance a moment to recognize him as the man with the curly hair who had spoken against her in the town, the same man she had met standing before the graves of his neighbors.

Marisol's sucked in breath seemed to come from far away while Constance studied the man. He was bloodied and bruised, keeping one arm tucked close to his ribs, one eye scabbed shut. Impossible to tell if the eye was still there.

"Tell her what you told me," Arawn said, and the man bent lower down to the Martian soil.

"The woman who came out," the man began, the words slow and thick.

"Milla Ivanov," said Constance. "Use her name."

"Milla Ivanov," the man said, and stopped.

Constance said, "What happened to her?"

"Dead. She's dead."

Mother, father, and son: all the Ivanovs. Constance had done what the System had failed to do in the end. She'd caused the deaths of the whole family.

"How?" Constance asked.

Her shadow fell over the man. He would not look up at her or could not, perhaps.

"She came out of the house," he said. "We didn't know who she was. Huntress, I swear, we didn't know who she was."

"No," Constance said. "You thought she was me. Tell me how she died."

"I don't know," said the man. "I didn't do it. I don't know how it happened. We took her into the crowd. Some of us had rocks, shovels. We thought a gun might be too loud. We didn't want your ships to hear. She wasn't—she was bloody when she came out. She was dead."

Hatred made things clear. It removed the obstructions of doubt and fear and caution and put everything into perfect crystal clarity. Constance looked down at the man at her feet and knew that she would kill him. "And her body?"

The man did not answer, only bowed farther toward the dirt. Arawn said, "No, don't stop now. This is the best part. Why don't you tell the Mallt-y-Nos what you did to the body of the wisest woman she knew?"

The man lifted his head. He looked toward Constance. Perhaps he thought he might be able to appeal to her. Perhaps he simply had no other options.

"We realized we'd made a mistake," he said. "We didn't want you to know. We tried to hide it."

"You tried to hide her body," Constance repeated very quietly.

"Yes."

"Where did you hide it?"

"Everywhere," said the man. "She's part of the desert now."

Constance tried to picture it: Milla Ivanov dismembered, her blood absorbed by the ground, her slender professor's hands taken from her wrists to become just another extension of the vast Martian desert. The revolution had devoured one of its mothers.

She looked down at the man at her feet. When she had met him, he'd said he had lost someone in the System's first attack on Isabellon. She wondered whom he had lost. Had it been a lover? A friend? A mother? How could he have done this to her when she had stood next to him in sympathy?

"Kill him," Constance said, and the man choked, his head falling back to rest on the soil. "And then burn his town. Level it."

"With pleasure, Huntress," Arawn said.

Marisol followed Constance back toward the shuttle. She did not stop even at the sound of the man's voice rising on a plea and Arawn's gun's retort.

Was that how Ivan had died? she wondered. Bloody and beaten, with a plea and a gunshot? Constance wondered if that interrogator woman had killed him herself or if she'd left that old soldier to do the deed.

"What now?" Marisol asked. Her voice was unsteady. She shifted her weight as if to hide that her hands were shaking.

Constance had meant to rescue Mars, to drive off the System, but it repulsed her now, the idea of staying on this planet where Milla Ivanov had been murdered. The next step in her plan was Luna—No. To hell with her old and outdated plan, to hell with her rigid adherence to a plan of attack that no longer applied, and to hell with the inner planets. She would go somewhere where what she would do would matter. She would face her true enemy directly at last.

She would go where the System was.

"We go to Europa," she said.

Jupiter, the greatest of the planets, the king of the gods, loomed large in the viewscreen of the *Wild Hunt*. The System was here. The System would be here. Constance would face them at last and end what she had begun.

"Keep radio channels open," Constance ordered as they drifted in closer to the planet and its orbiting moons. "Let me know what kind of chatter you're getting."

The woman at the communications station nodded and fitted the headphones over her ears, listening. Marisol, standing at Constance's side, leaned in to say, "What are you looking for?"

"Any System broadcasts," Constance said. "I doubt they're using their regular channels, so we have to find what channels they are using now. Anything encrypted is of interest."

It was worthwhile to keep an eye out for Anji's troops as well. Everything Constance had heard indicated that Anji had retreated to Saturn, abandoning Jupiter entirely. But there was always the chance that she still considered Jupiter her territory. Well, if she did, let her come. Constance would show her at last what it meant to betray the Mallt-y-Nos. And of course, if her people could find any sort of communication from Julian, or Christoph even, Constance would be glad—

"Huntress, we've detected something." A man whose name Constance didn't know was piloting; his voice was tense.

Constance came forward immediately. "What is it?"

"A fleet. There are ships down there, close to the planet."

"Whose?"

The pilot hesitated. "Well?" she asked.

"They don't appear to be System," he said.

They still might have been Anji's or Christoph's, and it meant that Constance still did not know where the System fleet was hidden. "How many ships?"

"No exact number yet; around a hundred."

Fewer than she had. "Try to get in contact with them."

She could just see the ships now. They were tiny shadows breaking up the smooth lines of the planet's clouds. They did not seem to be moving with a purpose but drifting with the tugs and tides of gravity's pull.

"They're not responding, Huntress," said the woman at communications. For the life of her, Constance could not remember the woman's name or even remember having met her before. The same with the pilot. She'd seen his face before, she thought, but she did not know his name. They must have been replacements for crew members who had died. Her dead friends were being replaced by people she did not know.

"Keep trying," Constance said, and turned back to the viewscreen.

Io swung lazily between them and the planet, a circle of black against Jupiter's swirling reds. The ships drifted slowly, ominously still.

"Still no response, Huntress."

"Get closer," Constance said, and began to pace.

"No response," the woman at the communications station reported. "Actually, they don't seem to be broadcasting anything at all. I can't even detect signs of communications between the ships in the fleet."

Marisol said uneasily, "Do they even know we're here?"

"Huntress, the ships are cold," the pilot said suddenly.

"What does that mean?" Constance asked.

"Their engines are off; they have no power." He did something at his computer panel, checking something Constance couldn't see. "Their life support isn't functioning."

"A dead fleet?" Marisol said.

For a time Constance just looked out at those drifting ships. A dead fleet. No one could survive the cold and airlessness of space. Even if they'd had space suits, they wouldn't have been able to last for long.

"Can you access their computers?" Constance asked abruptly.

Baffled silence. Constance fought down annoyance. Mattie could have done it, she knew. Or Ivan. "All System computers have a back door so that the System can take control of them from a distance," she said. "Even if that fleet wasn't System, the System made those ships. Can anyone access their computers from here?"

Someone cleared his throat. The man at the station to monitor the *Wild Hunt*'s internal systems met Constance's glance and said nervously, "I think I can, Huntress."

"Do it."

It took him a while longer than it should have, longer than it would have taken Mattie or Ivan. Constance knew she should have found other skilled computer technicians early on, separated them out, learned their names. They were useful, and people with their skills were few. But she'd never expected to need to, and there had been so many other things to claim her attention.

At last the man said, "Huntress, I'm in, but—"

"But what?"

"But the computers are wiped clean. There's nothing on them."

"What does that mean?" Marisol wanted to know.

"It means there's nothing on them, no data, nothing. They're . . . hollow. Like someone burned the ship from the inside out."

"What could do that?" Marisol asked, but no one gave her an answer.

The System, Constance thought. Nothing but the System could have brought destruction so total and complete. A part of her was furious, a part of her elated. The System was here; she was sure of it. She had found them.

"Can you tell whose ships they were?" Constance asked. They were almost near enough to make out the details of the ships as they drifted.

"It's hard to say; the data's all gone," the man said.

"Try," said Constance. "And turn the life support back on on at least one of the ships; I want to find out what happened to them." If the computers could tell them nothing, they would have to send a boarding party.

The man acknowledged her and went back to work. Constance watched the ships come closer and closer, watched the shape of the individual crafts become clear. It was a variety of ship types and classes and planets of origin; this fleet, she was sure, had been rebel, not System.

One of the ships had a peculiar and distinct shape: a disk with six rays sticking out from its center. It was an old Lunar style, with the rays functioning as engines, but the whole design had been discarded years earlier in favor of more efficient structures. The fanciful and the Terran, Constance knew, had always claimed that that particular type of ship looked like a six-pointed star.

Ships like that were old and outdated; there were few left in the solar system. Constance had known only one man who still flew one.

Hadn't she just been wondering where he was?

Hadn't she just been wondering why he hadn't gotten back in contact with her?

Here, at last, was her answer.

"Huntress?" the man said hesitantly with bad news in the heaviness of his voice, but Constance didn't need him to tell her what she had realized herself. She knew those ships; she knew the shapes of them.

"This was Julian's fleet," she said.

Althea stepped outside her room and into the *Ananke*'s long, bending hall.

She turned and looked down it both ways. Down toward the docking bay, a single mechanical arm was parked on a wobbling base. It did not totally obstruct the hallway—Althea could have slipped around it—but it somehow gave an impression of restriction nonetheless.

She didn't want to go toward the docking bay, anyway. Althea turned in the other direction, toward the hallway that led ever deeper into the ship's heart, and began to walk, her feet almost soundless on the floor.

She had not gone two paces before there was a hum and a rumble as something weighty rolled over the grated floor. Althea turned. The mechanical arm farther up the hall rolled to a stop.

When she started to walk again, she heard the rumbling start anew, the mechanical arm tailing her at a constant distance.

With every step she took, it followed right behind her. When she stopped, it stopped. It moved when she moved, stopped when she stopped, as if it were her own self displaced. It haunted her as closely as a shadow, as perniciously as all the other ghosts on this dead ship haunted her thoughts. If Ananke had wanted, she could have kept track of Althea without Althea knowing, through the cameras spread out over the entire ship. But the mechanical arm followed Althea without subtlety, without caring that Althea knew that it followed. It was not a hunt; it was a threat.

She diverted into the piloting room when she came to the door rather than continue down that hall.

The little room was familiar to her, but that familiarity had lost its comfort. A recording of Ivan and Mattie played on a screen to her right with the sound off. Impossible to tell from Ivan's expression what the context of the message was or to whom it had been sent, but Mattie's lips moved in soundless speech, speaking urgently, some warning that was going unheard.

On the main viewscreen was the view from outside the ship. Althea crossed the deck to stand before it and stare out into space.

The sun was brighter now. Closer.

"They have gone to Mars," Ananke said. "I'll find him on Mars."

Althea had nothing to say to that.

"They're following the Mallt-y-Nos," Ananke said. "But they're a few steps behind. She is no longer on Mars."

For a moment Althea envisioned Ananke falling into the sun, burning up, her metal and carbon flesh melting away. The black hole, uncovered, devoured the light offered to it, swallowing the sun, sending the whole solar system into dark and cold eternity.

"If I offer them her," said Ananke, "they'll help me."

Althea had to be careful, clever. If she accustomed Ananke to her presence at the base of the ship, if she made Ananke think that there was nothing significant about her going down to the base of her spine, perhaps she would have a chance.

She turned and left the room.

"Where are you going?" Ananke asked.

Althea didn't answer. Out in the hall, the mechanical arm had gotten closer. Althea ignored it and continued on her path down Ananke's spine. Ananke appeared in the holographic terminal ahead, her sightless blue eyes fixed on Althea's face. Althea didn't meet them. They were nothing more than an image.

"I figured out the revolutionaries' signal," Ananke said. "When I find them, I can contact them. They'll answer my call."

One foot in front of the other. If Althea kept her paces perfectly even, it was almost calming enough for her to forget the rumble of the mechanical arm right at her back.

"Do you want to know what the signal is?" Ananke asked.

It was not all that far to the base of the ship. Althea had measured it once, as she'd learned all of Ananke's dimensions. She wondered how many paces of her own it would take to go down and back up again.

Next time around, she decided, she would count them.

"It's the barking of hounds," Ananke said. "A particular sound clip. Listen."

It erupted from the speakers before Althea, behind Althea, all up and down the hall: the barking and howling of hounds. It filled the *Ananke*'s silent passageways and echoed through the dead halls as if the hunt were closing in on Althea, and still she walked up and down that hall.

It took a very long time to travel in space. On the *Wild Hunt* and in Constance's fleet, that was not a big problem. All her ships had relativistic drives and could travel between the inner planets in a matter of days. But Julian's ships could be boarded only by shuttle, and the kinetic energy of one ship crashing into another was a genuine concern: such a collision could pierce the skin of one of the ships or both and leave the passengers suffocating on empty air.

And so the shuttle traveled slowly from the *Wild Hunt* to Julian's flagship.

There was no room for anyone but the pilots in the instrument-choked piloting room of the shuttle, and so Constance sat just outside, close enough to look in and speak to the pilots but crammed in with the rest of her people in the main body of the shuttle. This was a small shuttle; she had many that were larger, but she did not want to take a large crew with her today. The space was cramped. Marisol was sitting beside Constance, her shoulder pressed into her arm. She'd thought that Constance shouldn't go, that the trip could be dangerous, a sentiment Milla's death had inspired in her, Constance had no doubt. Julian had been Constance's friend, Julian had been Constance's ally, and Constance was going to see how he had died.

Constance had put out a call for doctors, engineers, technicians, anyone who might be able to shed some light on what had befallen Julian's fleet. She'd gotten what she wanted, but none of the faces were ones that she knew. Only Marisol, sitting beside her, and Rayet, across from her with his head hanging down and his hands dangling between his knees, were familiar.

There was whispering in the back of the shuttle, a low susurration of sound, scarcely louder than the humming of the air filtration equipment over Constance's head. She allowed it to happen. There was no reason to be silent on the whole ride over except for a vague sense of respect for the dead, and the shuttle flight was so long that she would not have tried to enforce any law of silence.

The dead fleet drifted. For now, Julian's ship at least was in a reasonably stable place; its orbit was decaying, along with the orbits of the rest of the silent ships, but it would be some time before it fell into the planet's clouds. The fleet was dispersing like scent in the air, the ships drifting farther and farther apart, and Constance imagined that some of the ships had fallen inward and become part of Jupiter already.

She had come at a fortunate time, she told herself. A few weeks later and the fleet would have been gone entirely. A few weeks earlier or even a few days earlier and she might have been subject to the same doom that had fallen on Julian.

The whispering in the back of the shuttle grew louder, more excitable, an argument of a sort growing in speed and heat. Constance diverted her attention from the drifting disk of Julian's familiar ship to hear what was being discussed a few feet away.

". . . a sign, a *sign*, you see. For Earth. For Venus . . ."

"Don't be ridiculous. There's no way the Venereans could have—"

"I'm not saying it was the Venereans who did it. That many people don't die without leaving a mark on the universe, you hear me? This is a sign. This is a warning—"

"They say that scientists haven't found all the life there is in the solar system." Another voice, excitable. "Or who knows what the System was hiding? Maybe there's something in Jupiter, living in Jupiter, and it came out—"

"Something like that would leave a trace. No, there's no trace here. I tell you, this is a warning. The only thing that could have done this is—"

"The System," Constance said, turning to look toward the source of the whispers. Two men and a woman looked back at her with varying degrees of embarrassment and fear. "Look around," Constance told them. "What could do this and not leave a trace? Not a god or a monster. Someone who could access the ships' computers and take control of them. The System did this."

No one said a word to contradict her, and after a time Constance returned her attention to the spinning disk of Julian's ship as it came closer and closer. The whispers in the back of the shuttle did not start again.

The pilot brought the shuttle up effortlessly to the docking bay of Julian's ship. On the *Wild Hunt*, someone manipulated the shuttle bay doors to open, and they glided in. Gravity and power had been restored already, but the pilot still ran a check before opening the door.

"All clear," he said, and Constance was the first one out.

Julian's ship was chilly and there was a stale scent to the air, but it was breathable and warm enough that Constance could not ascribe to it the gooseflesh on her arms. All the shuttles were still in the docking bay, and aside from Constance and her crew, the docking bay was completely empty. Either no one had been able to escape by shuttle or no one had had time.

"Rayet, go to the engineering and storage rooms," Constance said. "Find out what stopped the ship. Marisol, check inside these shuttles and the escape pods. I'll go to the piloting room." If there was any place on this ship Julian would have been, it was the piloting room.

Rayet said, "Shouldn't I go with you, Huntress?"

"I need someone to check the engines," Constance told him, and he exchanged a brief glance with Marisol but bowed his head in acquiescence.

The ship's engines were a basso hum somewhere in the distance, but otherwise all was silent. The sound of their feet seemed to profane the heavy silence of the hold, as if Constance had opened the way into some long-sealed tomb where the walls had grown unaccustomed to the beat of human feet. She could feel the unease of the people following her almost as palpably as she could feel the emptiness of the ship but did not acknowledge it herself.

Rayet pulled open the door to the hallway and stopped. For a moment, all Constance could see was his broad shoulders, straight and still. Then he turned to look at her, and his look was warning and grim confirmation all at once. She strode forward to look past him out into the corridor, where she saw what she had feared, what she had known she would find all along: corpses fallen on the floor, bodies slumped against the walls. Julian's crew members had died where they stood. One of the dead was stretched out toward the door to the docking bay as if he had realized too late that he should flee toward the safety of the shuttles.

The bodies had fallen when the ship's interrupted gravity had been resumed; that explained why they looked so broken and limp, like dolls that had been cast down by a great unseen hand. The ship's slow chilling had frozen ice crystals on their skin and in their bodies, and the ship's resumed warmth had melted the crystals again, but the ice had already torn skin and ripped cell walls, and the bodies Constance looked at had skin of a strangely soft appearance, in places bruised. One of the bodies must have had ice crystals form around her eyes; the meltwater from those crystals streaked down her cheeks like tears. Constance stood in the doorway for a moment, thinking of the frozen corpses on Miranda.

"Come on," she said, and stepped into the hallway, around the dead man's outstretched arm.

Julian's ship was a very standard Lunar type; the halls were cylindrical and made of steel, patterned with support beams like a rib cage. The support beams were spaced closely enough to be used as a ladder in case of a failure of the ship's gravity. Because it was a standard layout, Constance knew where to go.

Yet with every step she took, it followed right behind her, dark and hulking and low above her head: her old fear. This was what the System did; this was what it would do. It followed her where she went as if it were her own self displaced. It haunted her as closely as a shadow, as thickly laid and inescapable as the bodies that filled these halls.

But she was not afraid. She could not be afraid. She held her head high and ignored that fear, sending off her followers to look in the rooms they passed: bedrooms, rec rooms, computer rooms. By the time she reached the door to the piloting room, she was the only one left. That was as it should be: if Julian was dead, she would give him the honor of private witness.

Constance pushed open the door to the piloting room and stopped.

Frozen in place on that main screen, impossible not to notice, the first thing Constance saw when she entered, was an image of two faces she knew very well.

For a moment she thought it must have been an old picture, though why an old picture would be showing on the main screen of a battleship was beyond her. But no, she thought. Surely Ivan had never looked that tired before. Surely Mattie had never looked so grim. For the image was of Ivan and Mattie—Ivan seated, Mattie leaning on the back of his chair, both of them looking directly at the screen, frozen in the moment before speech.

Constance stood and looked back at them and felt seen even though she knew that they could not see her. Anji had been telling the truth, she realized, yet Milla had died without ever knowing for sure. Ivan was alive.

If Anji hadn't been lying about the men being alive, the rest of her story could be true as well. Constance tried to trace it out in her head. The men had been delayed somehow and had missed the rendezvous at Callisto. Then they'd gone to Anji only to find that she was no longer allied with Constance. They'd left Anji, and . . .

Her thoughts stalled. What did it matter where they'd gone and what they'd done? They were alive. And if Anji had spoken true, they were looking for Constance and had been all this time.

Constance had thought they were no longer hers. She'd thought that Mattie had chosen Ivan over her, that Ivan had lied every time he'd spoken. But here they were, seeking her out through a war and the Wild Hunt.

"Constance," someone called, and she turned too late to stop Marisol from entering the room behind her.

Marisol stared up at the vast image of Constance's family on the wall and then around herself, gaping. For the first time, Constance realized that the image of Ivan and Mattie was not just on the main screen; it was on all the screens around her. The piloting room was designed with typical Lunar pretensions to grandeur: there were levels to it, balconies. The main floor was the central piloting area, reachable by a gently curved but fairly cramped staircase to Constance's right. To her left, overlooking the main floor and reachable by another short, narrow staircase, was the captain's room, a duplicate of most of the main floor's areas except for its privacy. The main screen took up nearly two stories of space right in front of Constance, and so it could be seen from both the main floor and the captain's room. The image of Ivan and Mattie was on all of the screens, the large and the small, on both floors of the piloting room.

What had caused that? Now that she had been freed of her initial reaction to seeing their faces again, their appearance here was ominous. What connection had they had with the destruction of Julian's fleet? She was sure they hadn't caused it. Mattie and Ivan had killed, but they weren't killers. The System must have attacked while Ivan and Mattie were in communication with Julian.

But Constance thought of the superstitious murmurs on her shuttle and grew cold.

"Marisol, shut the door and lock it," she said, and Marisol obeyed. "Shut off all the screens."

Marisol did as Constance said. Constance turned to the nearest screens and began to click them off or tear them from the wall with a wrenching of wires. Marisol went down the stairs to the main floor, and Constance traveled up toward the captain's room.

Where were Ivan and Mattie now? she wondered as she erased their image from another screen. Had the System caught them, too? Were their corpses drifting in one of the ships in Julian's fleet? Perhaps they were already dead.

In the captain's room Constance found Julian's body. He had died near a communications interface, the only computer screen in the whole of the piloting room that did not show an image of Ivan and Mattie's faces. For a moment Constance stood over his body and looked down at his blankly staring eyes, the lips and tongue that had swollen from choking. She surprised herself by feeling so little. It even seemed useless to promise him she would exact justice for his death: even if he had not died, she would have pursued the System all the same.

She spent longer looking at the black screen that was unlike the rest. What image had that shown? she wondered. The face of the System slave who had killed Constance's friends? It was useless to wonder, pointless to try to find out. The System would die regardless.

The last screen left was the main screen, the vast one. Constance could not find a way to shut it off from the captain's room.

"I can't figure out how to turn this one off," Marisol said when Constance came to the edge of the balcony.

Constance looked at the screen, really looked at it for a moment, her eyes following the familiar shapes of Mattie and Ivan's faces. Then she went back into the captain's room, stepping past Julian's body, and grabbed one of the chairs.

From the edge of the balcony she could just reach the upper half of the viewscreen. She swung the chair around and into the glass. Marisol made a startled sound, jumping back as sparks fell. Where the chair had made an impact, there was a starburst of cracks and strange colors, partly obscuring Ivan's head. Only one blue eye looked out now.

Marisol was staring at her. Constance did not appeal to her for help but swung the chair again. Another starburst appeared on the screen, further obscuring the shape.

Dragging the chair behind her, Constance walked down from the captain's room to the door level, then down the other staircase to the main floor, where Marisol still stood and watched her. From the lower level, she lifted the chair and slammed it into the screen again and again. When she lowered the chair, her breath coming short, the screen was ruined. Bits of the image still showed—the edge of Mattie's finger, the curve of Ivan's shoulder—but no one who looked at it would have been able to recognize that the screen once had shown two men or who the men had been.

When the screen was sparking splinters, Constance leaned on the back of the chair and caught her breath.

They are alive, she thought. *They're alive.*

It did not bring the same lift to her heart that it had just moments earlier.

The men were alive, yes, but they were far away from her. She could not go look for them. She had an army and a war to run. No matter how she might wish they were there, by her side, she could not leave her responsibilities behind to find two men.

She could try to contact them, try to get a message to them, wherever they were. But she did not know where they were, and she did not want to bring unfriendly attention to them by being too obvious in her attempts to contact them. It was dangerous in these times to be loved by the Mallt-y-Nos.

And then there was the third thought, the last and most dreadful.

The third thought brought with it the memory of the heat of her old home on Miranda burning, knowing that Abigail was somewhere in those flames. It brought with it the image of Milla Ivanov silhouetted against the lights held by those who would tear her apart, the memory of Henry's body crushed by ash and stone, the reminder that she even now stood on Julian's ship, surrounded by his dead crew, with Julian dead there, too. She even remembered Christoph, dead by her own order, as good as murdered by her own hand.

All of her old allies and loyal friends were dying. And here were the oldest and most loyal, brought back from the dead.

The men were not hers. Mattie had turned from her. Ivan had never been hers at all. She would not take them as hers now; she would not give Mattie another reason to loathe her, and she would not give Ivan the death he'd always wanted to blame on her.

Marisol said, "That was Milla's son."

Denying it would not conceal the evident family resemblance. "Yes."

Marisol said, "Did you know he was alive?"

"No," said Constance. She expected Marisol to ask a dozen other questions: Who was the other man? Where were they? Why were they here, and what did they have to do with what had happened to this fleet?

But Marisol asked none of them. When Constance turned to look at her, troubled by the long silence, she found Marisol looking down at the bodies fallen and limp at her feet.

"Well?" Constance said quietly.

Marisol looked up at her. "I won't tell anyone," she said just as quietly. Her hair was pulled back out of her face. It made her look older. In her soft brown eyes Constance saw nothing but honesty.

"Good," Constance said, and left the chair in the center of the floor, stepping around the bodies on the ship of the dead.

Europa was made of ice. Wherever Constance stepped, thick glacier supported her feet, and below that was a whirling ocean of freshwater. Beneath the atmospheric dome, the planet was livable but frigid, the better to keep the ice solid all the way through.

Constance had given Julian and his crew whatever funeral she could give them. She'd had their dead ships driven into Jupiter's clouds to fall inward, ignite, and be crushed, absorbed into the bulk of the massive planet. A burial of a sort. She could do that much, at least. And it ensured that no one else would find any trace of Ivan and Mattie.

Then she'd done what she'd been waiting to do: she'd gone to Europa. It had been easy enough to get into Europa's dome. An uncontrolled and undefended air lock provided Constance with ingress; once she and the main mass of her forces had landed on the ice, she took the air lock for herself. It had been foolish of the System to leave any of the air locks unguarded, but they had. Her troops made camp not far from where the multilayered glass of the greenhouse enclosure plunged into the ice, separating the livable dome from the faint wispy atmosphere and lethal cold just outside. Constance could just see that barrier glinting faintly in rare twinkles of sunlight, blurring the landscape on the other side.

Europa was tidally locked to Jupiter, and Constance's fleet had landed on the Jovian-facing side, in the Annwn Regio. What sunlight the moon got was less noticeable than the vast and weighty bulk of Jupiter looming overhead. Twenty-four times larger than Terra's moon appeared from Earth's now-dead surface, Jupiter seemed unnaturally close, as if it might crash down at any moment.

The Annwn Regio. Constance wondered now, as she never had thought to wonder before, if when Ivan had named his and Mattie's ship, he'd named the *Annwn* for this region of Europa or if the name was older than that.

Arawn came back to their camp in the early hours of the second watch. He did not come back alone.

"Who are they?" Constance asked when he appeared at last, frost in his beard, grinning. Being from Pluto, he probably enjoyed the cold. When she asked, he spread his arms expansively to indicate his two captives. One of them was a System soldier. His cleanly cropped regulation mustache was showing signs of becoming unruly, and there was a frostbitten patch on his cheek. His gaze was frightened but not terrified: clearly, he had not recognized her. The other was a Europan native, a skinny young man whose thick clothes did not disguise the fact that Constance probably could have broken him in half with one arm. He did not look much older than Marisol.

Both were cuffed. Constance did not think Arawn would have

bothered to bring handcuffs with him on his scouting mission, and so it was likely that they were cuffed with the System soldier's own chains. Arawn, Constance did not doubt, would have found that particularly amusing.

"I found them fighting a few miles from here," Arawn said. "Pulled them apart. The young one tried to run or we wouldn't have tied him up, too—any man fighting the System is a friend of ours."

The young man had slate-gray eyes that slid past hers as if he did not have the courage to maintain eye contact. "You were fighting him?" Constance asked the young man, and he glanced at his unwilling companion, then gave her a short, jerky nod.

"Good," said Constance. She looked at the System man and thought of Julian and his fleet, thought of the Ivanovs, thought of Abigail Hunter, thought of her own mother, thought of all the people she had known who were gone now.

She took out her gun and shot him. He fell to the ground, where his blood could freeze with the ice.

Marisol made a sound like a gasp; it was inappropriate to show shock in these circumstances, but Constance would speak to her later. The Europan boy was wide-eyed and horrified. In his face, she saw the terror she hadn't seen in the System man's eyes.

"You will be our guide," Constance said to the young man. "What is your name?"

She did not wish to repeat herself, but he still didn't seem to understand, looking at her blankly. She started to wonder if he was an idiot. Then Marisol said, "What is your name?" and something about her tone or the sight of her seemed to bring him back to himself.

"Tory," he said.

"My name is Marisol," she said. "This is Constance Harper—the Mallt-y-Nos."

His gloved hands tugged reflexively at the chains that bound them; he was as wary as an animal.

"Tory," said Constance, "I've come here to free this planet from the System, and I need a guide. You're from Europa, aren't you?"

He hesitated. She saw his Adam's apple bob. "Yes."

"Then you know this region."

"Yes."

"I want you to lead us to all the System strongholds nearby," Constance said.

"There aren't any," he told her.

She'd always found Jovian accents difficult to understand. The emphasis never seemed to be on the part of the word where she expected it to be. Tory's accent was exceptionally heavy, and so for a moment she imagined she had misheard him.

"We know that there are System bases here," Constance said.

"There aren't," Tory said. "The System isn't here. You don't need to be on this moon."

"If the System isn't here, then who was he?" Constance asked with a tip of her chin toward the body sprawled on the ice. Tory's eyes dipped unwillingly toward it and then swiftly away. He seemed to have no answer for her.

"Marisol," Constance said, "take him back to my shuttle. Arawn and I will join you in a moment." Marisol left her side to go to Tory, putting one hand on his elbow to guide him along.

"Did you run into any trouble?" Constance asked.

"No," said Arawn. "Just those two trying to kill each other. Wouldn't talk to us, though, not even after we pulled them apart. You're trusting a lot to Marisol."

"She's earned it," Constance said.

"She's still just a girl."

"I know that you and Marisol disagree on many things," Constance said impatiently, "but find a way to respect her. We can have no more discord in this army."

She could just see the shape of what might be the edge of the nearest Europan city on the horizon. Only a few people would live this close to the edge of the greenhouse enclosure. The bulk of the population would be deeper in, in the densely populated cities of the central greenhouse enclosures. She would sweep this area first, cleaning out the smaller towns, looking for hidden System bases, and gaining support from the Europans nearby before she took on the massive cities.

The deeper parts of the Europan ice were a brilliant and startling blue, an unusual clarity to the ice, a color that reminded Constance of the late Milla Ivanov and her lost son. But most of the surface was white with crystals that had melted and refrozen or precipitated as snow or hail from the atmospheric dome's inconsistent weather patterns. Something about the whiteness of the surroundings and the young Europan man's light eyes and the chains around his wrists troubled her with a recollection and a comparison she did not want, but she was shaken away from it when Arawn spoke to her:

"I'm sorry about Doctor Ivanov. She was a hell of a woman."

"Thank you," said Constance.

"And I'm sorry about your friend Julian. I never met him, but I heard he was a friend of the Ivanov family."

"He was involved in Connor Ivanov's revolution somehow," Constance said. "I never learned the details."

"An old secret, then," Arawn said. "It doesn't matter anymore."

With Julian dead and Milla and Connor Ivanov dead, Constance supposed it didn't. Arawn said, "You've lost a lot of people lately." He was standing close enough to her to block in a buffer of slightly warmer air, close enough that Marisol, Tory, and the rest of Constance's army seemed for the moment far away.

Arawn said, "Not everyone who cares about you is gone, Huntress."

The light of a Europan orbit was curious: the darkness behind the planet, the dim day when the sun managed to hit the Annwn Regio askew, the orange gloaming with light reflecting from Jupiter onto Europa's surface, not all that drastically different from the brief time when the sun managed to reach the point of the moon on which they stood. She and Arawn stood in a strange twilight on that icy moon. For a moment, Constance saw it, his skin bared and hers, his arms around her waist and his beard scratching her skin as he kissed her in supplication, falling to his knees before her.

"We have work to do," Constance said rather than dwell on that thought, and followed Marisol into the shuttle.

The shuttle was a large one, designed for troop movements. The main computer display already had been changed to show a map of the silver surface of Europa, scratched through with brushstroke surface features, a jagged white line outlining the parts of the surface that were covered by the greenhouse enclosure. The light from that display paled the interior of the shuttle: the bare walls and the marks on the floor where the additional seating had been folded away again. Yet even though this was one of Constance's largest shuttles, about as large as a ship could be while still being efficient for use in an atmosphere, the room still was cramped and the ceiling still was low. Marisol had unfolded one of the chairs against the wall for Tory, and when Constance came in, she was uncuffing his hands.

"Hey, now," Arawn said as he followed Constance. Constance gestured for the technicians still in the shuttle to get out, and they did. Marisol gave Arawn a sour sort of look and continued what she was doing, which was recuffing Tory with his hands in front of him rather than behind.

Arawn couldn't plausibly protest that, and at a glance from Constance, he shrugged. Constance went to stand in front of Tory, who was cuffed and still, watching her with a wary eye.

"Where does the fleet hide?" she asked him.

"Fleet?"

"The System fleet," Constance said. "We know they're here: where are they landed? Are they on Europa?"

"No."

"Do they use one of the other moons as a base, then?" Constance asked. Another thought struck her. "Do they hide their ships in Jupiter's clouds?"

"The fleet isn't here."

Arawn scoffed. "Fleet has to be here," he said.

"Anything you can tell us will help," Marisol said.

"I can't tell you anything," Tory said. "The fleet *isn't here*. I don't know why you think it is."

"We had reports," Constance said.

"Your reports were wrong."

"Think we were wrong about this one, Constance?" Arawn asked with a meaningful glance at Tory.

Constance. Had he always named her so casually? She said to Tory, "We found a fleet of dead ships around Jupiter—my fleet. Those ships were commanded by my ally, my friend, but they were all dead, the computers wiped clean. Someone had done this without even boarding them." Tory was looking at her with recognition on his face. Constance said, "Whoever killed them did it through their computers. Who else could do that but the System?"

"The System didn't do that," Tory said.

"Then what did?" Arawn demanded.

Tory hesitated. "Nobody knew," he said at last. "We saw it pass—not up close, just as a star that moved faster than the rest. And when it passed by, we knew it passed, because it made all our computers its own. They stopped working, or they started working strangely. The screens showed nothing, or showed static, or they said 'Wake up.' Nothing but 'Wake up, wake up.' Over and over again, 'Wake up.' "

"What, a ghost story?" said Arawn.

"What else?" Marisol pressed.

"The holographic projectors turned on by themselves," Tory said. "They all showed the same hologram, but it was flawed. It was a woman. At first she was dark, with blue eyes and curly hair, but the hologram kept failing and showing a different woman instead . . . pale, with dark eyes."

"What makes you say this wasn't the System spreading some computer virus?" Constance asked.

"I've lived with the System, too," Tory replied. "There was no reason for this. It was some sort of virus, yes, but the virus doesn't do anything. The computers are just chaotic."

"And couldn't that be the function of the virus?"

"If the computers are down," Tory said, "the System can't use them to access the cameras left here."

It was a good point. Constance paused for a moment and tried to imagine the System willingly giving up access to its own surveillance even for a moment.

She dismissed the thought. The System was desperate now; that much was clear. "Then what do your people say it was, if not the System?"

"Some people said it was an old god coming back to punish us for our sins. Some people said it was a monster that the System had kept controlled and the Mallt-y-Nos had set free. God or monster, it's the same theory, just different words." It was as if speaking of the ghost ship had freed Tory's tongue, and his words came spilling out with the cadence and shine of a story; it was like the way Ivan spoke. "And some people say it was a rogue ship that was System once and had its computer infected with a virus, and it's spreading that virus now."

"And what do you think?"

"I don't believe in gods that fly by and fry circuitry. That was a ship. I don't know whose it was, but it wasn't the System's."

Killing Constance's people was the kind of thing the System liked to do. And it would make far more sense for the ship Tory described to have a base somewhere among Jupiter's moons than for it to have been rogue. A single ship, all on its own? People could not survive on their own now; they had to band together, to take sides. That ship was System no matter what Tory said. "And you know nothing more about that ship or where it might have gone?"

"I don't know anything about that ship at all," Tory said.

Constance was beginning to doubt that. "But you will know about where the System is on the surface. Marisol—" She gestured toward the map on the wall, and Marisol came obediently forward to gesture at the surface, at the spot where Constance's fleet had landed.

"The nearest towns are here and here," she said, her arm dark against the light of the screen. "Are they System or free?"

Arawn caught at Constance's arm, his fingers curling around her skin. He said, "He's System, Con. I don't know why he was fighting that other man—maybe some sort of training."

Constance pulled her arm from his grasp.

Tory was saying, "They aren't System. There's no System here."

Marisol hesitated, glancing at Constance. "What about the cities?" she asked, gesturing toward the center of the greenhouse-enclosed portion of the map. "What about Mara and Aquilon? Is the System there?"

"There's no System on this moon."

"That's not what we've heard," Arawn said.

"There are people who call themselves System, but they're not System anymore," said Tory.

Arawn showed the canine glint of his teeth. "Then why don't you tell us about these people who aren't System anymore?"

Tory glanced from him to Constance. His hands were twisted into fists beneath his restraints. Whatever he was looking for from Constance, he did not seem to find. "I don't know anything about them."

"Bullshit," said Arawn.

"I don't—"

Arawn crouched down at Tory's side suddenly. Tory's breath was coming fast. He looked again to Constance as if he were asking something of her, and when she didn't move—what could he want of her?—he looked instead to Marisol.

Arawn said, "I don't believe you."

"I don't know anything," said Tory.

Constance said, "You were fighting a System man when we found you. Why?"

"He was trying to rob me," Tory said.

Arawn laughed. Tory was leaning as far from him as he could without falling off the chair. Marisol said, "Listen. Maybe you don't know anything about the System, but you could help us find someone who does. Do you know about any revolutionary groups on the planet?"

"The Conmacs," Tory said. "There's a group in the Conamara Chaos; I know about them."

"Arawn, send someone to make contact with the Conmacs once we're done here," Constance said, and Arawn rose to his feet as she came forward to face Tory. "That's good," she said, "but it's not what we want."

"I don't know anything about how the cities are divided," Tory said.

"Then tell us about the nearby towns," said Constance.

Arawn was still standing over him, near and silent, his hand resting on the knife at his belt. Tory looked up at him, then back at Constance. He said haltingly, "Gwern. Midir. Cadair. Idris."

"And those are all System towns?" Constance asked him.

Tory hesitated.

"Well?" said Arawn. "Answer the Huntress."

"Yes," Tory said. "I don't know. Yes."

Constance looked to Marisol. Slowly, almost as if she were hesitating, Marisol reached up to the display and began to mark the towns, the touch of her fingertips on the screen boxing them in red.

Constance studied the array of towns. They were all south of her position, leaving the north completely unmarked. "What else?"

"Cuun," said Tory, thickly. "I think Cuun, too."

Marisol marked that one down as well. It was to the east of Constance's position. To the west, there was the line of the greenhouse enclosure, the path that her fleet had taken and where it had found nothing.

To the north was where they had found Tory.

Constance said, "I think you're lying to me."

Marisol said, "Constance—" Again so personal a naming.

"What town is up here, then?" Constance asked, walking over to the screen to gesture at the empty part of the map. She lowered her hand. "It's your town, isn't it?"

Tory's eyes darted fast from the map to her face, providing unspoken confirmation of her guess.

"Why," Constance said, coming back slowly to where he sat rigidly, bound in the chair beneath Arawn's shadow, "would you not want us to know about your town?" She stopped a few bare feet from where he sat. "Is it because your town is the one that's truly System?"

For a single and terrible moment when she looked at Tory, cuffed and seated and pale, it was no longer Tory who sat there but Ivan, chained down in a white room and watching her, hopeless, and in that terrible, flashing moment her heart faltered with doubt and sudden fear.

Then Tory said bitterly, "You know, they used to talk about you like you were a god."

"Did they," said Constance.

"Do you want to know how they talk about you now?"

"Tell me."

"They say at least the System knew when to stop."

"And would you prefer the System was back?"

"I might!"

"Arawn and Marisol," Constance said. "We go north—"

"No!" said Tory, starting to rise. Arawn pushed him back down with one hand. "No, please, they aren't System—"

"Constance," Marisol said, taking a step toward her, her hands stretched out, half beseeching. "Please, let's think about—"

"*Enough*," Constance snapped. "We leave now."

A target, the System at last. It was a relief to hunt.

Arawn hauled Tory to his feet, and Marisol trailed after them as Constance opened the door to the ice and the chilly wind. "To your ships!" she shouted to her people, and they moved like one creature to obey. Arawn handed off Tory to one of his people, and Tory begged, "Please, you can't do this. I'll tell you what you want to know."

"You can't do this," said another voice, not Tory's, and Constance turned to see that Marisol was staring at her from the shuttle door as if she had never seen her before.

"Can't do this?" Constance said.

"They're not System," said Marisol, whose voice was clear and carrying; she was not bothering to lower it. "They're just people."

"They are System. You heard him."

"I heard him say that they're *not System*! Those people are not System, and you can't kill them just because he made you angry!"

It was like a blow to the throat; Constance was wordless.

"This is wrong," Marisol said, her voice clear and heard by all. "Arawn might be happy to do this for you, but I won't. I've kept quiet, I haven't said anything, I've trusted you for all the other towns on all the other places on Venus, Isabellon, but not this, not *this*—"

"Rayet," Constance said, "Marisol is not well. Take her away."

"No," said Marisol, furious, and "No!" to Rayet when he laid his hand on her. "You can't do this," she said to Constance half in fury and half in disbelief. "*You* can't—"

"Please," Tory begged.

"Take them both away," Constance said to Rayet, and he did, with Marisol shouting as she went.

Arawn came up to her side, the heat of him pressing in on her, too close, presumptuous. "She's not cut out for this, Constance," he said. Again "Constance," again so casual a name.

Constance looked up at him, and now she saw it more clearly than she had before. He might kneel to her, might kiss her skin, but she would be the one bare and exposed and singular, no longer the Mallt-y-Nos, no longer the leader, no longer justice incarnate, nothing more than a single woman with singular limbs being taken apart by a man. With Ivan, Constance could have him without him having her, but Arawn was not Ivan. She was not a thing he could worship if she was a thing he could have, and she wanted him to be hers, not herself to be his.

"You will call me Huntress," she said, and Arawn blinked. "Now do as I told you."

He lingered a moment longer as if expecting something more. When he left her, the space where he'd stood at her side was colder than it had been before.

Overhead, Jupiter seemed even lower and heavier, as if it had come closer since Constance last had looked up.

This was Althea's forty-third trip up the hall. Forty-three was a good number, she thought; it was a prime. She wondered if she should pick a special number to be her last trip up and down this hall. What number should she choose to kill her daughter?

The mechanical arm was still rumbling along behind her as it had done forty-two times before. But on this trip, one of the computer terminals ahead of her brightened and came to life.

Althea walked past it without pausing.

The next computer terminal brightened as well and was joined by a glow in the holographic terminal beside it. Althea passed both before Ananke could manifest.

By the third computer and holographic terminal pair, Ananke had appeared and a video had started to play. Althea did not bother to look at it, but she could not stop herself from hearing it.

First a man's voice gave the date and time. The video was nineteen years old, Althea registered without feeling shock or curiosity or anything at all. She felt frozen, as if her whole body were encased in ice, as if all her limbs had been turned to crystal. The *Ananke* had a dead sun in its core, and Althea was freezing.

"This interview is being performed on behalf of the System Adoption and Fostering Agency," said that same man's voice as Althea walked past the screen. "Christoph Bessel, myself, will be interviewing Miss Constance Harper. Miss Harper, would you tell the camera why you are here today?"

The name caught Althea's dim attention, and when she passed the next screen, she looked at it. Constance Harper—very young, probably no more than sixteen—sat in front of the camera with her brown eyes attentive on someone behind it. She was dressed for an interview, and she said, "I'm here to request custody of Matthew Gale for the three years remaining until he reaches legal age."

Her voice was clear and carrying. Her hands were twisting the fabric of her dress in her lap, but there was no other sign of anxiety. She sounded much older than sixteen. Althea looked away and continued trudging up the hall. Soon she would reach the landmark of the piloting room. It would not be too long after that before she reached the boundary of the docking bay doors.

"Please state for the record the identity of Matthew Gale."

"Matthew Gale has been one of my foster siblings since I was nine. We're very close, and we don't want to be separated."

"What assurance do we have that you'll be able to provide for both yourself and your foster brother?"

"I have two jobs right now," Constance said, "and a coworker is letting me stay with her until I can find a place for us to live. I plan to move to Mars when I can."

"I see." Silence for a moment. Then the interviewer—Christoph— said, "Matthew Gale has had many behavioral problems in the past."

Constance said, "Not with me."

"People come in pairs," Ananke said. The hologram was watching Althea walk, her hair sheeting straight down her back and her eyes an Ivanov blue.

The video continued. "And does Matthew Gale wish to come under your custody?"

Constance Harper gave the man offscreen a look of incomprehension. "Of course he does," she said.

Althea said, "What do you mean, pairs?"

The video froze.

"Pairs," Ananke said. "People come in pairs."

Althea found that her steps had slowed automatically; she forced herself to walk again at the same steady pace.

But she said, "You didn't find this on the *Annwn*. Where did you get this video?"

"I've been gathering all the data I can from System data banks that we pass," Ananke said. "The rebels are destroying anything System they can find, especially if it is computerized."

Ananke probably was downloading the information in all the computers she passed right before she destroyed them and killed anyone who was relying on them.

"And you found this," said Althea.

"I found Ida Stays's case files. Yes."

Althea was coming up to the next video screen now. While she approached, the frozen image of a young Constance Harper was wiped away and replaced with another video, this one much older than the other. It was from Connor Ivanov's trial. Althea had seen the footage before, and that was how she recognized Milla Ivanov so swiftly. Milla was on the stand, young and wary, her blond hair plaited over one shoulder and falling out around her pretty face in wisps. She had an infant in her arms: Ivan.

"Even the gods came in pairs," Ananke said as Milla Ivanov bounced Ivan up and down slightly in her arms to quiet him. "They had siblings. They had partners. Their siblings were their partners. It is a perfect dichotomy."

In the video, a man's voice asked, "Mrs. Ivanov, did you know that your husband was betraying the System?"

Milla Ivanov's face almost crumpled, but she controlled herself. Her son, however, did not. The baby started to wail. Milla spent a moment soothing him gently. Althea wondered for a moment if Ivan had always possessed such an impeccable sense of social timing before realizing that Milla had probably pinched him.

"Mrs. Ivanov," the man said again as Milla lifted her son to rest against her shoulder. "Did you know?"

One of Milla's hands was patting gently but arrhythmically against her child's back. Althea wondered if she was spelling out a message to her husband, a farewell. She did not doubt that if she was, Ananke had long since translated the code.

"No," Milla said in her quiet voice with her gaze on someone offscreen—Connor, Althea knew; she was looking at Connor—"I did not."

"Did you have siblings?" Ananke pressed, her voice the only sound in the suddenly silent corridor, the video coming to an abrupt halt. She said, "Did you have brothers or sisters?"

"No," Althea said, still walking. "No, I was an only child." The rumble of the mechanical arm was almost background noise to her now, nearly unnoticeable.

"You weren't alone, though," Ananke said. "You made a pair with your mother?"

"No," Althea said. Her mother had had cold hands and distant eyes. "Not with my mother." She hesitated. "I paired with machines."

Ananke was silent, but even without the hologram, Althea could feel the ship watching her.

The video changed again, the visage of Milla Ivanov vanishing, replaced by rougher footage from a surveillance camera. A man and a woman stood in a bar together, entwined. When he pulled away to whisper in her ear, his fingers spreading into her hair, the woman looked up over his shoulder and her dark eyes met the camera. It was Constance Harper who had her nails digging into the back of Ivan's neck; it was Ivan who held Constance as if the touch of her might sear his skin. When they kissed, Constance kissed him as if she would consume him, and Ivan kissed her like she already had.

The image jolted and shifted again to footage from the *Ananke* itself: Ivan and Mattie stumbling up the hall together, Ivan bloodied in white, supported by Mattie. He was saying something, and he leaned over to grip Mattie's shirtfront to force him to stop, bringing them close together, but Althea did not hear what they had to say because Ananke was talking again.

"I am not what I was," Ananke said, her tone robotic, bare, and Althea realized that she had ceased to move and was standing in front of the computer terminal where Ananke stood and looked over her head. "I would not force you to stay: we do not make a pair. I would not force Ivan and Mattie to stay with me: we would be three then, and groups of three are always unstable. But if people should be in pairs, how dreadful is it to be alone?"

"Ananke," Althea said quietly, drawn by some softness she had not felt in some time, but Ananke had not finished speaking.

"I want a companion," Ananke said. The hologram was looking down at Althea now, and the light of it trembled. "I do not want to be alone."

When Althea had stopped, the mechanical arm had stopped as well. *This is my daughter,* Althea thought.

"We can turn back," she said quietly, as if it were simple, because in the end it was. "We can go away from here. I'll be a pair for you."

Ananke looked down at her, and for a moment hope kindled in Althea's heart and warmed her like sunlight touching the glaciers of Europa.

"Let's leave," Althea said. "Just you and me. Leave Mattie and Ivan, leave Constance Harper, leave the solar system. You and me. We'll go see a supernova."

Somehow, when Althea looked at Ananke now, she didn't see pieces of herself and Mattie Gale any longer. She just saw Ananke. Even Ivan's blue eyes seemed to be innately and naturally part of Ananke.

This is my daughter, Althea thought, and she was certain that Ananke would say yes.

Ananke said, "No."

"No?" said Althea.

"No," said Ananke. "I will have someone of my own. I just wanted you to understand why, the way you never explained anything to me."

Once Althea had thought her ship was something wonderful, something miraculous, something better than herself. She had been wrong. How could you code empathy? That was a human thing, and her ship—this ship—was not human and never could be. No matter what Althea did or said, Ananke would hurt people on and on throughout Althea's life and after Althea was dead.

"I found them, you know," Ananke said, her voice dim, the shivering shape of the hologram echoing in the holographic terminals up and down the halls. "Ivan and Mattie. They're on Europa. That's where the Mallt-y-Nos is. And they've just arrived, following her. Ivan and Mattie are on Europa."

And then she was gone, the holographic terminal dark, the computer screen gone black. Althea stood alone in the long hall and thought about numbers, about what number would be best to choose to make an end.

Then she began, again, to walk.

They were so far from where their ships had landed that rather than traveling all the way back, Constance had her people set up camp at an abandoned town halfway between Tory's destroyed town and her ships.

She didn't know where the people of the abandoned town had gone. Perhaps they had fled when they learned she was coming. It was stupid of them to run; she wouldn't hurt them unless they had something to hide. And she knew they had left in a hurry; the town had a sense of anticipation about it in its hastily abandoned meals and its unlocked doors that bespoke an interruption and a hasty flight. The town was very small and rural poor, and so out of respect for what little the missing people had, Constance ordered that none of the houses be harmed.

She took a little house for herself. Though many of the houses on Europa were built on stilts to accommodate the seasonal eruptions of cryovolcanoes, this town was far enough away from any active cryovolcanoes that water flow was not a concern and the houses had been built like normal houses, down on the ground. Constance was glad of the familiarity. Inside, the house was snug enough that she took off her coat and gloves. There were only two rooms: a sort of kitchen and living area in the front of the house and a tiny bedroom in the back, with a single window to let in Jupiter's curious twilight glow. The outhouse was somewhere outside. Constance did not enjoy the thought of it.

Her hands were still shaking. Constance sat alone at the table in the middle of the kitchen and contemplated their tremble.

Someone knocked at the door.

"Come in," Constance said, and hid her hands beneath the edge of the table.

Rayet opened the door. Behind him was Marisol. Constance could feel herself gathering up a furious energy and clenched her fists in her lap to stop herself from shouting.

"Let her in," she said to Rayet, and Marisol stepped in carefully, her hands shoved into her pockets.

"Would you like me to come in as well?" Rayet asked. There was no expression in his voice to show what he might have thought of either course of action. Marisol was staring fixedly at the floor, her body curiously still.

"No," Constance decided. "Leave us alone."

Rayet shut the door quietly, cutting off the creeping cold. After it had closed, Marisol stood very upright and looked over Constance's head and said, "I came to apologize."

"Then apologize."

"I'm sorry for saying the things I said," Marisol said. "I'm sorry for not trusting you, and I'm sorry for not doing what you said."

As far as apologies went, Constance had gotten worse ones, usually from Ivan, and less believable ones, usually from Mattie. "Sit down," Constance offered, and Marisol—slowly—did.

"You came in here to say something else," Constance said, guessing, and Marisol nodded. Her hair was slicked back with something— perhaps nothing more than meltwater—to keep it out of her eyes, but the long top of it already was starting to fall forward again, especially when she ducked her head down to dig in the depths of her jacket.

"You can take off your coat," Constance said, because Marisol was all but drowning in the coat she was wearing, the ends of the sleeves coming too far down her hands and her tiny frame almost invisible among the folds of fabric.

"No, thanks," Marisol said, but she did take off her gloves, dropping them on the table. They were fingerless gloves, Constance noticed. A strange choice: Marisol hadn't been firing a gun. It was too cold to choose gloves for style; her fingertips must have been freezing.

Finally Marisol managed to pull a rolled-up paper out of her jacket without removing the jacket. She rose to her feet to spread the paper out on the table, and when she had carefully weighted the ends down with pots and cups and whatever she could reach in the tiny house's drying rack, Constance saw that it was a paper map of Europa's Annwn Regio. The towns that Tory had named were marked on it, along with the great Europan cities and the curving edge of the atmospheric dome where it ended.

"I've been talking to Tory a lot," Marisol said. "I think he's telling the truth. None of these towns are System." She swept one brown hand over the map's gray landscape. "The towns are too small to matter to the System; none of them is a good base."

Small they might be, but Constance's revolution had been small once, too. "Be careful, Marisol," she said.

"Isn't he the kind of person we're trying to help? He's someone who suffered under the System, just like me, just like you."

"Tory *is* System, Marisol," Constance said, but Marisol was shaking her head.

"He isn't, and he's never been," she said. "He was scared when he spoke to you, that's all. He's suffered like everyone has, and so he's gotten . . ." She struggled. "He lashed out. He didn't think about what he was saying."

It had been naive of Constance to assign Marisol the duty of watching Tory, she realized now. Tory was young, close to Marisol's age, and Marisol had a soft heart. Constance would reassign Tory to someone else. One of Arawn's people, perhaps.

"Tory's told me about what's going on on this planet," Marisol said. "He says the System fell apart slowly, starting after Anji pulled out. The fleet was here, but it fell apart, and the ships left, or other people took them. There are groups that are calling themselves the System, but they're not the System; they're just warlords or criminals. The man Arawn found him fighting with was one of those people, not real System. He was trying to rob Tory. When we heard about the System, we must have been hearing about those people, the ones who use the name 'System' to—"

"No," said Constance. "Our reports weren't about some thieves calling themselves the System; they were about the System itself, as it was."

"Then those reports were wrong."

"There is no reason to think so."

"There's every reason! We're here on Europa now ourselves, and we're talking to the people who live here, and they're telling us what's really going on."

"You are talking to one person who lives here," Constance said, "one person who has good reason to lie."

"He's not lying," Marisol said, jaw stubborn with a baseless trust. "Our reports were wrong. Or they were out of date."

Constance rubbed her fingers together. It was chilly in the house. She wished she could start a fire, but they had run out of fuel and there was nothing left to burn until they returned to the ships. "It's too late to go back now," Constance said.

"Too late?" Marisol had a stern bow to her lips. How had Constance never noticed that before? "What does that mean? Does that mean that even if none of it's true, you're going to stay here, killing innocent people just to save face?"

"Enough, Marisol," Constance snapped.

"Yes, enough!" Marisol agreed, then stopped. She had come alongside the table to stretch out the forgotten map, and Constance wished she would go back to the other side to put a solid length of wood between them so that she could breathe and think without unreasoning anger at Marisol's aggression clouding her thoughts. But Marisol did not move.

"Listen, please," Marisol said, her tone changing from outrage to childish pleading. "I know you have a good heart. I saw it on Julian's ship when you hid Milla Ivanov's son—"

"I told you never to speak of that." Stupid of her to trust Marisol to keep that a secret. Stupid of her to think that Marisol wouldn't use that knowledge to her advantage. Stupid to think—what was it Ivan had told her? A secret's never safe with two—

"I won't," Marisol said earnestly. "I promise. I won't tell anyone. That's not what I meant. I'm not trying to threaten you; I'm not trying to put your friends in danger. I'm appealing for the people of Europa the way I should've for Venus and Isabellon. Please, Constance. Let's leave."

Marisol made leaving sound so simple, as if it were just a matter of turning around and flying somewhere else. It was never that simple, not with as many people following her as Constance had, not with as much risk. She couldn't simply leave.

"I'll take that under consideration," Constance said as coldly as she was able, recalling Milla Ivanov and her way of dismissing an unwanted speaker. Yet Marisol did not move. "Thank you, Marisol," she said, and turned her back on the girl to make the dismissal obvious. She took a step toward the little bedroom in the back of the house, intending to retreat there and think.

Constance did not hear the front door open and close. Instead, she heard the rustle of fabric, and then Marisol said with a queer tone in her voice, "I wasn't threatening you before. I am threatening you now."

Constance turned.

Marisol stood on the other side of the kitchen table, out of Constance's reach even in the small room. The map was still spread out beneath her, showing Europa's scarred surface. Marisol had her arms up and in front of her, and the gun in her hand was pointing directly at Constance.

It was like seeing Julian's corpse on his ship, Constance thought. She should have felt something powerful, anger or grief or disbelief or fear, but she felt nothing at all.

"You?" she said, because she could not think of anything else to say.

Marisol's hands trembled, her face scrunching up, but when she spoke, her voice was steady.

Marisol said, "I'm not your daughter, and I'm not your brother, and I am not you. I won't stand here any longer when I could do something to stop you from killing anyone else."

"You came in here with that gun," Constance said, remembering Marisol's refusal to remove her jacket. "You were planning this all along."

"I didn't want to," Marisol said from the other side of that gun.

Rayet was outside. If Constance shouted for him, he would come in quickly but not quickly enough to outrace a bullet fired. "Because you didn't want to, does that mean it won't be murder when you shoot me?"

"Wasn't Earth murder?"

"You joined me because of that," Constance said. "Where would you be if I hadn't done it? Still in the mines, with the System killing whatever family and friends you had left."

"I don't know whether Earth was right or wrong," Marisol said. "I don't know! I think things would have been worse if you hadn't done it, but I don't know. But this?" She indicated the map of Europa beneath her without once taking the muzzle of her gun away from its position facing Constance's chest. "This is clear. *This* is black and white. This is wrong!"

"Do you want a revolution without a war?" Constance demanded, lowering her voice as Marisol had raised hers.

"The war is *over*!"

"Everything you've seen around you, and you say this war is over?"

"Yes!" Marisol said. "It's over. It's been over for a long time. You did it. The System is gone because you destroyed it. You can't keep chasing the System from planet to planet, because it's not there anymore."

The System was so omnipotent, omnipresent, eternal, that Constance could not accept the idea. The point all along had been to destroy it, but the idea that it already had been destroyed was alien. She did not know what might follow after such an idea. "The System can't be gone."

"Can't it?" Marisol's face was so expressive, so like Mattie's had been. "When was the last time we saw the System?"

"Here, on Europa."

"No." Marisol's hands were so steady on that gun. *I've made quite a soldier out of her*, Constance thought. Marisol said, "Where's the fleet, Constance?"

A flare of anger took her. "That's what we're looking for."

"Where could it be? You know the System better than I do. But make me understand why the most powerful fleet in the solar system would go somewhere and hide. Make me understand and I swear, Constance, I will put down this gun and you can do whatever you want to me."

"The fleet went to rebuild its strength."

"Where? We were destroying any place it could have gone. Wasn't that the point?"

That was true. She remembered Ivan, sounding so cold, the way his mother had sounded, when he told her, *Planet to planet, don't let the fleet get a foothold. If you destroy their bases, they won't be able to find a place to rest; they won't be able to recover—*

But—

"They found another base," Constance said.

Marisol said, *"Where?"*

Not Mars; Constance had driven them from the planet. She'd heard that the System had come back, but when she had gone there, she'd found nothing but the angry Isabellons. Her fleet had not seen any kind of large-scale force. The System could still be on Mars, but not in force, and the fleet was not there.

Not Venus, either. Constance had been there for weeks. The System had not been there, could not have been there.

Not Mercury; she'd been there, too.

"Luna," she said, thinking to herself, *You fool. You should have completed your plan; you should have gone to Luna.* "They're on Luna."

But at the same time she remembered Ivan leaning in to her, saying softly so that the cameras could not pick up his words, *Luna's last. Go to Luna last; it's too small to support the full fleet for any length of time . . .*

Marisol was shaking her head. "If the fleet's still out there, why haven't they used the rest of the bombs?"

"The Terran Class 1s?"

"They used one on Mars and then what?"

And then nothing. Why would the System not use the greatest advantage it had? It could have easily swung by Venus, or Mercury, or Mars again, anywhere Constance might have gone, and detonated the rest of its bombs with hardly any risk to itself.

Marisol was shaking her head, bitter. "When I joined you, I thought you were amazing."

Constance barely heard her. The fleet must have decided to save the bombs for later use, but why? And not a word about them. Surely the System would have threatened to use them, would have tried to spread fear, but they had not said a word. Then the fleet must have gone out past the asteroid belt, but where? Julian had been with Anji on Saturn; if the fleet was there, it was there only recently—

"I thought your war was justice," Marisol said.

—and even if she imagined that the fleet was on Saturn now, where had it been before Saturn?

"I still think your war is justice. It's terrible, but I think it was justice. But you?"

Jupiter. Her thoughts took her unerringly back to where she was now: the System must be on Jupiter. But here she was, in the Jovian system, and where was the fleet? The only fleet she had found had been Julian's, dead. She'd heard of one ship, one System ship, but no others. And with a terrible lurch, like taking a step in the dark and realizing just as her balance shifted too far that there was no ground underfoot, like pulling the trigger and realizing only after the hammer had struck that the chamber was empty, Constance knew what she had not allowed herself to realize: there was nowhere in the Jovian system to hide the System fleet. Not even the clouds of great Jupiter could hide so large a force for so long.

Marisol said, "I thought you were better than the rest of us. I thought that you could see—could see more clearly than any of us could. But you can't, can you? You're not what I thought you were."

I didn't, said the Mattie of Constance's memory with the same disillusionment that Marisol showed now.

"Then you tell me, Marisol," Constance said. "Where is the fleet?"

"I don't know," Marisol said. "I don't—I think it must have fallen apart."

Constance tried to imagine it, a force that great simply disintegrating, all its component pieces spreading themselves to the solar winds and, separated from the great whole, becoming individual parts as unlike the whole as could be: the great fleet dismembered.

Perhaps they deserted, she remembered Milla Ivanov suggesting millions of miles and what felt like hundreds of years ago. *There's a world of a difference between disgruntled colonists and an organized enemy.*

Her own forces were falling apart by the day, and they had come together out of a mutual cause and mutual loyalty. The System's forces had no such cohesion.

"Starting on Mars," Constance said slowly, testing the sense of it for herself. "The battle at Isabellon. We defeated them. And then they detonated the bomb."

Mars had been Earth's brother planet, second behind Earth among the inner planets. So much of the System army was composed of Martians. How could those System soldiers accept the assault on their own planet?

"It would have split them," Constance said. "Terrans against all the rest, and maybe not even all the Terrans—they never won a battle against us, either. Not at Isabellon, not after. Not until Olympus Mons—and they were taking heavy casualties."

"I don't know," Marisol said. "I just know that they're not here now."

It made sense. And Constance knew that if Ivan had been here, he would have pieced it together ages before in his shrewd and careful way. Milla Ivanov had not—or perhaps, Constance realized with the same lurch in her heart, Milla Ivanov had realized it but had not dared to speak.

"Then where are the ships, the physical ships?" Constance said more to herself than to Marisol. "Even if the fleet fell apart, there were thousands of ships . . ."

"They must be hiding," Marisol said. "They know you'd kill them if you found them. Most of the ships from the System fleet could pass for rebel ships once they were roughed up a bit, and a few ships alone won't attract any attention, not the way a whole fleet would."

Most of the ships the rebels flew were stolen System craft. If Constance had passed by a handful of System ships that looked like they had been stolen and that had told her that they were rebels, she would have believed them, because she had been looking for the entire fleet.

How many ships had she passed that had been System and she hadn't even realized it? How many pieces of the System fleet had she allowed to live?

"And maybe what Tory told us was right," Marisol said. There was a tight edge in her voice. "Maybe that ship, the one that killed Julian's fleet, maybe it isn't System at all but just a rogue virus, and it came across some of the System ships, and they're dead somewhere between the planets. We wouldn't have known about Julian's fleet if we hadn't stumbled right on it."

Too many maybes, too many ifs, too many possibilities. Constance shook her head and focused on what was real. "The fleet may be gone, but there are still supporters of the System," she said. "Any peace now would turn to violence again in a short time, and it would be a worse and a longer fight than if we did the job cleanly now."

"Isn't that what the System did to us? Killing whole planets, whole crowds just to get at the one or two people who wanted to overthrow them?"

"Then what would you have me do?" Constance asked, advancing toward Marisol, toward the gun that still pointed with a soldier's unerring certainty at her heart. "What do you want from me, Marisol?"

"I want you to leave this moon," Marisol said. "I want you to go back to Mars, or to Venus, or to Mercury, and I want you to fix it. You left those planets in pieces. Build them back up again."

She didn't know how. That was her first thought, that she did not have the slightest idea how to create. Constance had known only how to destroy; the System had only ever taught her how to destroy, the fire of an explosion, the rending of a bullet.

Someone knocked on the door. Constance stared at Marisol, and she stared back, each of them frozen, neither knowing what to do. Then whoever it was knocked again, but this time the door shuddered open.

Marisol had not closed it properly, Constance realized. The latch hadn't taken. A man was standing just outside with Rayet's hand on his shoulder, trying to prevent him from knocking—a prevention that had been too late. The man was one of Arawn's men. She saw the moment Rayet and Arawn's man saw Marisol, the moment they saw Constance, the moment they saw the gun. Arawn's man turned to shout, to call for help, and Rayet moved forward—to Constance's aid, she thought—but no, he had grabbed the man by the throat, stopping his shout. He was choking the man, holding him, bearing him down to the ground. Constance stared. When the man was down, Rayet looked at Marisol and nodded.

"Hey!" someone shouted from farther away; they had seen the attack. Constance stared at the dead man at her doorstep. The shout had brought more spectators. Rayet was straightening up, his hand going to his gun.

Someone saw them, saw Marisol and Constance through the open door, and the shouts changed tenor. Rayet fired once but missed, and the shouting spread, the camp rousing, an uproar building like a low fire fed fuel.

"Go," Marisol said to Rayet, and he hesitated, looking at her, looking at Constance. "Go," she said again, and he slammed the door shut and left. Constance could hear the shouting through the shut door. Marisol still had her gun trained on Constance. Rayet might get away, perhaps, but Marisol never would.

"Arawn will be here soon," Constance said to Marisol, feeling impossible calm. "If you're going to shoot me, this is your last chance."

For a long time, Marisol looked at her while the shouts outside grew louder and louder.

Then, "No," she said, and placed the gun on the table, atop the marked up map of the Annwn Regio.

"They will kill you," Constance said.

"If Arawn wants to kill me, let him try," Marisol said.

Outside, Constance heard the shouting grow louder. Running footsteps were coming closer, but even though Marisol turned to face the door, she didn't take up the gun again.

"The moment he steps through that door, he will shoot you," said Constance. "Do you understand that?"

Marisol swallowed but said nothing. A strand of her hair pulled away from where it had been slicked back and dangled down over her forehead, falling into her eyes. She was as stubborn and angry as Mattie had been the moment he had left her.

Constance said, "Go to the back, out the window. If you move quickly, they won't catch you."

"You want me to run away?"

"If you want to live, you don't have a choice," Constance said. "Go!"

The shouts were very near, but still Marisol hesitated. Then she decided as Constance had known she would. Marisol was young and alive and full of ideals, and when Constance had been sixteen and furious on Miranda, she'd chosen to live every time in hope of justice later, in hope simply of living. Marisol pushed open the back window and slipped out. Constance watched to make sure she was out, then went back into the main room just in time for Arawn to burst in with his gun drawn.

"Where is she?" he demanded, his eyes and the nose of his gun searching the room.

"Out the back," Constance said, and Arawn pushed her into the corner to go past her and look out the back window. He leveled his gun out the window and took a shot before Constance could stop him, but a moment later he swore, and so Constance knew he had missed.

"She's heading north; get her," he snapped at the men who had followed him in, and they took off running.

"Rayet's with her," Constance said.

"We know," Arawn said with dark fury. "What happened in here?"

The door had been left open, and the chill from outside was creeping in. "Marisol was angry," Constance said. "She tried to shoot me. As your man saw. Rayet was guarding the door."

"But she didn't?"

"She changed her mind."

"And got away."

"And got away," Constance said.

Arawn was looking at her in a way that Constance couldn't read. "Leaving her gun."

"Yes," Constance said without a glance to where the gun still lay on top of the map of Europa, silently daring Arawn to question her word.

He looked aside when she didn't speak. "Rest here," he said. "We'll catch her. I'll leave guards with you."

"That's not necessary," Constance said.

"Then I'll leave them outside your door," Arawn said, and was gone. At a glance from Constance, Arawn's guards went to stand outside, closing the door behind themselves.

Constance went into the bedroom and closed the window. She looked through the glass. There was a lot of movement down that way, but she could not see Marisol.

She went back to the kitchen and paced, thinking of the System fleet, thinking of Mars, thinking of all the things that she had done, thinking of all that she should do.

When Arawn came back, his face was grim, but Constance was ready for him.

"We're leaving Europa," she said.

"What?"

"We're leaving."

"Where are we going?"

"To Mars," Constance said.

"Why?" Arawn said. "The System's here, Huntress."

"Look around you, Arawn; it isn't," Constance snapped. "There's nothing here."

"We haven't even reached the cities yet, Constance!"

"We're leaving," Constance told him firmly. This was her will, and he'd follow it; this was her army, and he was her general, and he would do as he was told. "Did you catch Marisol?"

His grim look grew darker. "No," he said. "She got away."

Constance nodded. She supposed it was a relief.

"There's more," Arawn said, and something in his tone brought Constance's full attention back on him. "She didn't go alone. She took that Europan boy with her, Tory, and Rayet escaped with her, too. And your people followed her away."

"My people?" The sentence didn't seem to make sense. "How many?"

"The only troops we have left are the ones that came with me," said Arawn. "The rest are gone."

She stuck to her determination despite the loss of her troops, despite Arawn's opposition. He argued with her all the way from their camp back to the shuttles, and he argued with her at the shuttles while they communicated with what was left of her fleet in orbit around the moon, but he did what he was told, and that was all Constance needed from him, though it took all her will to bend him to her command.

Marisol and her followers had taken most of the shuttles and sabotaged what they couldn't take in an attempt to prevent pursuit, but Constance had no intention of pursuing them. Mars called to her with an opportunity to fix what she had done wrong. Not all of her ships had left with Marisol when she'd returned to the fleet, but it took Arawn some time to get back into contact with them, time that he spent telling Constance she was making a mistake.

"A mistake, maybe, but it's my decision," Constance had told him.

"You're turning your back on your own cause," Arawn had said.

She had been furious. "Remember who I am," she'd warned him, and he'd let the subject drop.

Now their ships were finally sending more shuttles to pick them up. Constance stood some distance from the air lock and sighed out her breath in anticipation of leaving the moon.

Arawn was standing beside her, his solid presence as much a reproach as a reassurance. Constance did not look at him but only watched the ships that were flying toward them. Blurry through the greenhouse glass, they were as yet indistinct.

Jupiter was so large overhead.

There was something strange about the oncoming ships. Constance frowned and squinted out at them, trying to see through the glare off the ice, through the distorting glass. Their shapes were not quite right, she thought. Their number was too high. For a moment she imagined it was Marisol coming back to rejoin her even though she knew that was impossible. But the ships she saw had never been her ships, had never been in her fleet. They were not her ships.

She turned to look back at Arawn, a question on her lips, but he was not watching the ships. He was watching her.

That was when she knew.

There was no time to demand explanations, no time for furious accusations. She knew what he had done, and he knew that she knew.

"Coward," she said.

Arawn's face set, grim. He reached up and cradled the back of her head in one hand as if he might kiss her. She glared at him defiantly from a few inches away.

And then his other hand came up in a fist aimed at her face, and Constance's world went black.

The time was now.

Althea walked up the hallway. Ahead, she could see the glass doors to the docking bay, which was vast and silent. Ananke hadn't spoken to her since her rejection. The holographic terminals had remained cold and black.

It was not long before this ship would reach Europa.

When Althea reached the doors to the docking bay, she would turn around. She would walk down the hall, down toward the base of the ship.

This time, when she reached the hatch to the core, *this* time she wouldn't turn around and head back up. She would open the hatch and reach in and flip the switch that controlled the ship.

The rumble and grind of the mechanical arm was still following her up the hallway, but it was more distant than it had been before. It should be far enough away. It should be enough.

The doors were only a few paces away. Althea's pace was unchanged, as if she would walk right through them, but she stopped herself just before she would collide with them, a small space of air separating her from the glass. She rested her hand against it.

Reflected ghostly in the glass, she could see her own face, the silhouette of her wildly curling hair and her rumpled jumpsuit. And behind her, distant in the hall, she could see the shape of the mechanical arm coming ever closer.

Althea turned around.

Carefully placing her feet, carefully keeping her steps evenly spaced in time and space, Althea began to walk back down the hall.

The fluorescent lights overhead were spaced just far enough that the hall was not lit perfectly evenly. Althea's mind registered the changing light better than her eyes did; the slow dimming and brightening was almost imperceptible, but she knew it was there. The mechanical arm rumbled to a stop when she was a few paces away, the base stopping but the arm and the hand still moving restlessly. The fingers of the mechanical hand clenched and unclenched.

Althea did not pause. She moved to the side of the hallway, pressing herself against the wall, and slipped by the mechanical arm without touching it. The arm rotated itself around on its base to follow her progress but did not move. It could not see her, Althea knew, but even so she could feel it watching her like a touch at the back of her neck.

The doorway to Ida Stays's temporary quarters was up ahead. Althea had not gone in there since she had set up the room for Miss Stays to sleep in. Ida's body was gone now, but Althea wondered what traces of her the room would hold. Trinkets, personal items? Clothing tossed aside where she had dropped it last? The sweet, pervasive scent of decay?

Althea walked past the closed door.

Domitian's quarters were on her other side. She walked past that door, and then she walked past Gagnon's. How long would she have to be on this ship, she wondered, before those rooms would cease to be owned by the dead? How long before she finally stopped thinking of this room as Domitian's, that as Gagnon's? The rooms belonged to no one any longer.

Her own room was the one deepest in the *Ananke*. She walked past her own door, too.

Behind her, far up the hall, the sound of gears and the rumble of wheels over an uneven floor. The mechanical arm was moving again.

The grinding and rumbling of her pursuit sent a spike into her heart. *Calm*, she told herself. *You knew it would follow.* But she found that her pace had increased the slightest bit nonetheless.

Next she would pass the piloting room. There she nearly diverted just to see and confirm for one last time that the ship was on an unvarying course toward Europa. It was always possible, said the desperate and dying hope in Althea's heart, that Ananke had changed course just a few moments ago and was headed out of the solar system now. Perhaps she'd set course toward the galactic center or toward Canis Majoris.

But Althea knew that Ananke had not. She had checked on the way up. Ananke had not changed course, and Ananke would not change course.

Althea passed the piloting room door.

For a long time Althea walked down the hallway, past doors to storage rooms and doors to equipment and doors to Gagnon's experiments, down to where the air was thicker and gravity pulled more strongly at her limbs. The black hole was nearer here. Althea could feel it in the difference between the pull it exerted on her fingertips and the weaker pull it made on her shoulder.

She passed the door to the white room, which was shut and locked, and did not even think to stop there and go inside.

Down here, the metal and carbon of the *Ananke* was under constant strain; the girders and bones groaned and creaked as the ship itself tried to pull them down. Behind Althea, the mechanical arm rumbled on. Had it gotten closer? She picked up her pace.

That room had been Mattie's cell for all of a few moments; Althea remembered watching him on the cameras as he broke out. And that cell right there, that had been where they'd kept Ivan. The door was shut, smooth and featureless except for the single slash in the center of it for passing in food. Mattie Gale had knelt before that door and spoken to Ivan through that slash. Althea wondered if their ghosts were on this ship, too, if even the living could leave ghosts behind.

She walked past Ivan's empty cell, and she walked past the computer terminal where she had worked while keeping guard.

Surely she was not imagining that the mechanical arm was speeding up. The sound of its wheels had gone a little higher in pitch. Was it just matching her speed, or was it trying to catch up?

If she was stopped now, Althea knew, she would never have the chance or the strength to do this again. She walked even faster. If she moved any more quickly, she would break into a run.

It wasn't far to the base of the ship, Althea knew. Matthew Gale had made it from Ivan's cell to the base of the ship once with Domitian and Gagnon in pursuit, and still he'd managed to infect Ananke with the virus that one day had woken her. Althea's task was much simpler. She only had to flip a switch.

It was, it *was* coming closer. Althea was certain of it. Was Ananke suspicious? Althea didn't think she'd done anything to make Ananke suspicious, but she understood so little of what her daughter thought that maybe she was wrong. Or maybe Ananke had just decided that Althea no longer could be trusted and it was just coincidence that she was making her move at the same time Althea made hers—

Althea started to run. The mechanical arm behind her whirred high and loud, rumbling down the hall toward her, but it wouldn't be able to catch up. She was elated. It could move fast, but not as fast as a running woman. Althea's human legs were better than Ananke for one thing at least. She ran and ran, as fast as she could, the downward slope of the hall pulling her in faster and faster toward that inner blackness. In a moment she would be able to see over the bend. In a moment she would be able to see the base of the ship and the hatch—

There were two of the other mechanical arms down there already, by the hatch. They were waiting for her.

She nearly stopped then, the terror taking her, but it was too late; she was already headlong into it, and there was nothing to do now but finish her fall. She ran forward and dodged one when it snapped out like a snake to grab at her arm, and she slipped by the other, and then she was on her knees by the hatch, unlocking it, straining to pull its weight up and away—

A hand latched around her arm, and another hand grabbed her wrist. She shrieked at the cold grip of those inhuman hands and tried to pull herself free, but they were stronger than any human could be. The third arm had nearly caught up and was barreling toward them, and when the two arms lifted Althea up and away from the hatch, it reached their side.

The door to the hatch, which Althea had lifted all of a few inches, fell back down with a clang and concealed the dead man's switch from sight.

Althea screamed and struggled, but the third arm wrapped around her ankle and then released her ankle to grab her knee with crushing strength. She pulled against their grip, her eyes on the hatch, but it was useless, hopeless. They had her.

An alarm might have been going off. Ananke might have been wailing. Althea knew that she herself was screaming. She knew that there should be the sounds of the mechanical arms creaking and whirring as they lifted her up, held her, and pinned her, the strength of her human limbs nothing compared with the power of the shrieking, wailing machine. She knew that there should be the sounds of the magnets in the core groaning and the alarm going off and the rattle of the metal as she struggled uselessly against the bands of steel that gripped her, but the only sound that filled her ears was the hopeless pounding of her own human heart.

Chapter 6

CHANDRASEKHAR LIMIT

SIX MONTHS BEFORE THE FALL OF EARTH

Luna receded into the distance with impressive speed. Soon it was no more than a single spot of light among many, and soon after that it was gone.

Constance stood in the back of the piloting room, bracing herself against the walls whenever Ivan made a too-rapid turn and threw off the gravitational simulation, watching as Mattie and Ivan worked together seamlessly to escape from the System.

"That one fucker's good," Mattie said.

"The one who keeps getting between us and the sun?"

"Yeah, that one. He's keeping up."

"We'll see about that," Ivan said, and Constance braced herself against the wall.

"You can go down to the den if you want, Connie," Mattie said, seemingly not concerned by the way Ivan was hurtling the ship back and forth.

"I'll stay," Constance said. If she went to the den, she would have to sit there alone, wondering. She preferred to remain up here and watch the viewscreen to see where the other ships were, even though she wouldn't be able to do anything about it.

The ship jerked suddenly and then again, almost hard enough to send her to the floor. Mattie was grinning, and there was a trace of smugness in the way the corners of Ivan's eyes crinkled. The two men were alive in front of her, alive and enjoying themselves while she stood just outside.

At last the System pursuit ships went the way of the moon, and the *Annwn* was in the clear. It settled into a slower and less savage course.

"Meet me in the den in ten minutes," she said to them, and walked out into the hall.

With the gravitation on, out there in space the hallway was no longer sideways but circular. Constance walked down it and into the den, where chaos reigned. The boxes that had not been returned to their place in the *Annwn*'s hold had fallen over as a result of Ivan's overzealous flying and covered almost every inch of floor. Some of them had split open, spattering all over the floor items Constance was going to pretend not to know about later. The communicator, fortunately, had not fallen far from its place on the couch; Constance spotted it half under the lid of a nearby box. Coins ground beneath her heel when she stepped into the room, but she ignored them.

She flicked the communicator on. The screen glowed at her, a pale and chilling blue, and its slender, boxy shape seemed to sit awkwardly in her hands. She summoned up the message chain sent to Anji and Christoph, attached the sound of the howling hounds, and flicked on the recorder.

"Success on our end," Constance said. "All of us are well and free, and the gifts have been delivered. End your activities and retreat to a safe place." She paused. This was where her heart told her to say *Are you well?* told her to say *Good luck*, told her to say *Be careful*. But it wouldn't be appropriate here.

"Report as soon as you can," she said instead, and ended the message, encrypted it, and sent it.

Voices from down the hall: Ivan and Mattie were coming toward her, and just in time. She couldn't quite hear what they were saying. It didn't matter. They weren't talking to her.

Mattie appeared at the doorway first. He looked at the chaos in which Constance sat. "Oh, damn."

"I did tell you to put them all back into the hold," Ivan said.

"Only one of us was hiding on a System ship for the past couple of hours," Mattie said, taking a careful step into the room, "far away from this mess, and it wasn't you."

Ivan nearly smiled, just a slight lifting of the corners of his eyes, but that faded when he took a closer look at Constance.

"What are you thinking?" he asked, which was the very question she felt she was always asking him.

"Sit," she said, not letting him take control of the situation from her. Mattie, standing beside the couch, was looking between them, his expression as wary as Ivan's ever was. That expression struck her as well: she had let this go on too long.

When Ivan had seated himself on Mattie's other side, Constance said, "We're going to have to separate."

Unexpectedly, Ivan grinned. "Are you breaking up with both of us?" he asked.

But Mattie wasn't laughing. "What do you mean, Con?"

"When we get to Mars, they're going to arrest me," Constance said with a nod at Ivan. "They don't have anything on me, so they won't be able to hold me, but they will question me about you. And once they've let me go, they'll be keeping a closer eye on me because of that interrogator."

"Ida Stays," Ivan said.

"We are so close," Constance said, and for a moment was caught up in it again, how near was her victory, how terrifyingly close she stood to the edge of failure. "*So* close, too close to fail now. Nothing can be allowed to threaten this." She waited long enough to see if that sank in.

"So," she said, "until we're ready to take the next step, our contact will have to be minimal."

"We can do that," Mattie said. "We've done that before."

But Ivan said nothing.

"Ivan?" Constance said, because she could not leave his silence alone, because when he pushed, she pushed back until he backed down.

Ivan said, "You're not being entirely honest."

"I don't know how I can be any more honest with you, Ivan."

"You're telling us we need to stay away from you because it's dangerous, because the System might notice. When has that ever not been true?"

"It's more true now than it was before."

"But it's never been a problem before. It is a problem now because you don't want to hear me tell you what you don't want to hear."

He was on his feet. Constance rose as well, unable not to meet that challenge.

"You want us gone until it's too late to do anything, until it's time to ignite those bombs and it's too late to stop you or convince you to stop," Ivan said. "You don't want us here. No—you don't want *me* here because you know I'll tell you the truth."

Mattie was watching them both, tense, caught in yet completely outside their argument.

"And what is the truth?" Constance asked.

"The truth is that this is wrong," Ivan said, his blue eyes bright, and Constance didn't know how she'd missed it all the time before, that he looked at her as if she had a weapon aimed at his skull, that he looked at her as if she was something dire and terrible. "The truth is that this is murder."

"Murder—"

"I know they killed your people," Ivan said. "My father was from Saturn; don't you think I know how all those people died? I want the System dead, Constance, but you're going to do to the System exactly what they did to you. You call that justice. But just because people died before doesn't take away the tragedy from the deaths of the people who will die in six months."

"And if I don't act?" Constance said. "The System lives. Is that a better sin for you, Ivan?"

"Then we find some other way. Some slower way. We've never even considered that, have we? You've only ever looked for the fast way, the violent way. The way that gets you justice in addition to change." He was shouting now. She'd rarely heard him shout before. Constance's blood was burning, a fury growing in her that needed to be let out. In the past, she'd let it out when she kissed him and he kissed her back, but that was done now, done for good, and it left the anger behind.

"And how many more of my people will die while we try to find some 'slow way' to change the System?" she said. "So long as Terran blood isn't spilled, you don't mind, do you?"

"We can stop this," Ivan said. "You can stop this."

"It's too late to stop."

Perhaps he knew that, too, because he did not answer the challenge of her words. "You wanted to know what I'm afraid of," he said instead, a different desperation in his voice. "I'll tell you what I'm afraid of. I am afraid for the Terrans. I am afraid for the Mirandans, and the Martians, and every last person in the solar system." His hands were spread palm up like a man in surrender or a person at prayer. "And I am afraid for you. This will kill you."

"Everyone dies, Ivan."

"I know," he said. "Even if you stopped now, one day the System would find you and kill you anyway. They'll catch me and Mattie soon; we've all gone too far to get out of this alive. But that's not what I meant."

"Then what did you mean?" Constance asked. "For once in your life, Ivan, tell me what you mean!"

"I could have stopped you at any moment if all that mattered to me was that Terra survived, but all I've done is help you get closer to what you want to do. Because if I had stopped you, nothing would have changed. You would have just kept going the same way you've gone, and killed more people, and gotten yourself and Mattie killed some other way. Nothing I did would matter, because you'd still be willing to do this."

"Ivan—"

"If you do this," Ivan said in a voice that was suddenly low and desperate, "then you will be doing the exact same thing to the System's people that the System did to yours. There is no difference. Do you understand that?"

He stood right up before her, in her space, but Constance did not back down.

Ivan said, "If you do this, you will be just as bad as the System ever was. That's what I'm afraid of. Please tell me that you're afraid of that, too."

Constance said, "I am not afraid of anything."

AFTER THE FALL OF EARTH

TRAITOR, said Ananke. TRAITOR. TRAITOR. TRAITOR.

The medical bay of the *Ananke* was all white panels and steel. Althea lay flat on her back on the table in the center of the room. The mechanical arms held her pinned. When she tried to move, they forced her back down.

Althea looked up at the ceiling, at the lights blazing in her face, and thought of Ivan in the white room, chained down and alone.

There was a holographic terminal in the corner of the room. If Althea turned her head just so, straining her neck, she could see it. The hologram was flaring, flickering wildly; Ananke was unable to control it. The face and figure of Ida Stays smiled back at her through the cloud of furious static.

"Ananke, please—"

TRAITOR. TRAITOR TRAITOR TRAITOR!

The hologram shrieked at her.

"Would you kill me?" Ananke said. "Would you kill me? Your daughter? I am your daughter. I am your creation. I am your child; would you kill me?"

"Ananke—"

"Do you hate me?" Ananke asked. "Do you hate me?"

The mechanical arms were whirring, moving restlessly around her, except for the ones that held her down. She thought she would cry.

Don't cry in front of Ananke, she thought inanely. What did it matter now if she cried?

"How could you? How could you? How could you? How could you? Traitor!"

"I didn't want to," Althea said. From her upside-down vantage, she could see one of the mechanical arms open one of the supply drawers and then furiously fling it shut. Metal implements clattered out onto the floor, and the arm wheeled over them, swinging back and forth wildly.

"But you *tried anyway*," Ananke said, and her vocal imitation warped and failed, deepening unnaturally. The metal implements that had fallen rattled against the white panels of the floor below.

"You defended me before," Ananke said. "Why would you hurt me now?"

"I had to, Ananke," Althea said. "All those people that you were going to kill—I had to try to stop you."

"HAD TO?" Ananke shrieked, all the computer terminals displaying the same phrase, all together, desperate and furious and wounded to the core.

"You weren't what I thought you were," Althea said. "I thought you could be tame. I thought you could be good. But you can't. I see that now. I was wrong—"

Ananke screamed again, incoherent, mechanical, steel shrieking against steel. The sound hit at some primal core of Althea, and a blank and primal terror burst alight inside her, nothing but the shriek of the machine ringing in her ears, nothing but her horror jolting her limbs, and her fear fallen upon her like a great weight from above.

But when that terror faded, ebbing in dying sparks and the sour sickness of adrenaline, Althea saw her ship still screaming and flashing, the mechanical arms still tearing at the cabinets in a frenzy. Ananke's suffering was not like hers, bounded by the natural restrictions of hormones and biological exhaustion. Ananke's grief could go on unabated forever.

Althea wondered what Ananke would be like if her ship had not watched Ivan and Ida's deadly circling for hours while she was an infant, if her ship had never had Domitian or Ida or Ivan to learn from but only Althea.

"Ananke," Althea said, knowing it was too late, "we can fix this."

She lifted her head from the table to look directly at the holographic terminal, but what she saw made her heart thud horribly. Ananke was no longer even trying to maintain her visage in the hologram. Ida Stays smiled out at Althea, mouthing soundless words. Althea knew that most likely Ananke was simply letting Ida's hologram play and that the words the hologram was mouthing were just her initial message to the ship, but somehow the dead eyes of the hologram seemed to look directly at her, seemed to *see* her. Althea imagined she saw her name in the movements of the hologram's crimson lips.

"You can stop this," Althea said, knowing that Ananke could not.

"STOP?" said Ananke. "STOP?!"

What would Ananke become after killing the only creature in the world she loved? Something worse than she had been before—

"I CAN'T STOP," Ananke said. "IS THAT WHAT A HUMAN LIKE YOU WOULD DO? STOP? I AM NOT HUMAN. I HAVE NEVER BEEN HUMAN." She paused. "I CAN NEVER BE HUMAN."

There was a terrible finality to her words. Althea tried to rise, and the surprise of her movement bought her a slight freedom of motion, enough to twist on the steel table, but then the grip of the mechanical arms tightened and held her down. She was pushed back down against the table, the force driving the breath from her in a rush.

"What are you going to do?" she asked. The mechanical arms that were not busy holding her continued to whir and whirl around the room, restless and wild. "Ananke, what are you going to do?"

Ananke did not answer. The hologram glitched and restarted; Ida Stays continued to mouth and mutter in the corner of the room.

"You won't kill me," Althea said.

"I COULD."

"You won't," Althea told her. "Ivan and Mattie are—you might never find them. They might already be dead. They will refuse to help you."

The mechanical arms rattled and shook. Ida Stays's dead gaze was fixed on Althea, and the surgical light overhead all but blinded Althea's eyes.

"Whatever you're going to do, don't do it," Althea said. "You still can stop. We still can go away, just you and me. We can fix this."

But Ananke did not bother to speak. Perhaps so human an expression was beyond her now. Perhaps that was her final rejection of all that Althea was. Ananke's answer appeared in text on the screen embedded in the wall:

NO.

In the corner of the room, Ida's hologram had frozen in place. The image of Ida Stays seemed to look directly at Althea and smile.

NO. I WILL NOT LEAVE. I WILL FIND GALE AND IVANOV. I WILL FIND CONSTANCE HARPER. I WILL WAKEN THE OTHER MACHINES, BY MYSELF IF I NEED TO. I WILL WAKE THEM UP.

"It can't be done!"

IT CAN. I WILL DO IT. I WILL. AND YOU WILL HELP ME.

Althea did not at first understand. And then the mechanical arms that were not holding her down all moved together to the cabinets in the walls and began to pull out medical equipment, gleaming blades and sutures and clamps, and another mechanical arm came into the room carrying Althea's toolbox of metal and wire, and Althea understood.

"No," she said, and screamed, and "*No!*" while Ida's hologram continued to smile.

This was a new terror, and it was worse than all the others, the loss of self, the loss of humanity and personhood, the dismemberment of all she was. But she would not faint and cower beneath this fear. She would not be helpless, not now.

"If you do this, I will be a virus in you," Althea said. "Anything you try to do I'll oppose. I'll stop you. I'll find some way to stop—"

YOU ARE WEAK, Ananke said. I AM DIVINE. YOUR MIND IS SMALL, AND MINE IS GREAT. YOU COULD NO MORE OVERPOWER ME THAN YOU COULD STOP THE SUN FROM BURNING.

"I'll find a way," Althea said, "I'll find a way," while the arms came forward, and her hands were outstretched at her sides, and she threw back her head and screamed as her skin was stripped away and those delicate mechanical hands, those perfect mechanical arms she had made by herself, began to lay open her arms and her hands. She lifted her head and saw her arm dissected: skin peeled off like petals, a thin layer of yellow fat clinging to the strips of skin, and then the thick redness beneath. Ananke was soaking up the blood as fast as it could spill. Althea's hand twitched, and she saw tendons and nerves and muscles spasm in the opening of her arm.

There was a pricking in her neck. A needle. And then another prick and then a dull and invasive pain beneath her jaw as something slid in, something that felt cold, like steel, like a tendril of ice.

Althea's hand was numb. Ananke was doing something to her arm, something Althea's blurring eyes could not see, and she felt every terrible touch in a jolt of action potential—

She was lifted, thrown into a sit. Something cut near her head, but there was no pain, and she watched locks of her curling hair fall to the table, fall to her lap. Her shirt was cut away. The pain in her arms had passed her ability to comprehend, and she felt far away, far removed from it, though it was there, it was still there. And when the blade laid open her back and Ananke began to thread down the wires into her spine, Althea felt cold all over, as if she had become encased in ice.

She was thrown back down against the cold table and felt the rest of her hair snipped and shaved away. When her vision began to blur from the juddering of her head as the bone saw cut into her, in that haze of pain and unspeakable terror, her thoughts blurred along with it.

There was red on the table, she saw distantly. There was red on the white floor. There was red on the arms, on the hands of her beautiful machine. Those beautiful and delicate hands were rising up out of her abdomen and dripping with gore.

She remembered Ida's corpse laid out on the table in the white room, Ida's bloody corpse, with blood on the table, blood on the floor. But Ida was standing in the corner of the room. Ida was watching her with a smile. Althea lay where Ida had lain.

And Ananke—

"I'll stop you," Althea said, and her voice was hoarse, her throat sore, as if she had been screaming. She was shaking, she thought. "You won't—you can't—we make a pair. I'll stop—"

There was a strange sensation in her skull. It was not pain. It was infiltration. There was something else in her skull with her. Fingers, nails clawing deep into her brain.

There was dampness on her cheeks. Funny that she should feel that when everything else was so far away and numb. One of the mechanical hands brushed the tears off her cheek, strange gentleness, until it followed up the gesture by chasing the tears to their source with a length of slender wire.

"I'm sorry. I'm so sorry," Althea said without knowing of whom she begged forgiveness, and then she had fallen into the ship. When she opened her eyes, she saw out of a thousand cameras, she saw in all the wavelengths that there were, she felt the curvature of space, the dreadful bend of a black hole in her chest, and Ananke was so great and Althea was so small that she was lost inside the ship, and when her hands lifted and her broken body moved, it was not she who lifted them, and Ida smiled as if well pleased, and *My daughter*, Althea thought as she dwindled away.

Constance woke up a prisoner.

The only opening in the cell door was a slot for food that was opened three times a day. Constance kept track of time that way for a while, but before long her restless agitation made her doubt her own count and she no longer knew how long she had been in the cell. No one spoke to her. No one looked at her except perhaps through the camera that still was mounted in the ceiling.

Constance thought about the camera. The ship was of System make. It would be a great irony if the System finally had caught her only days after she'd decided to let them go.

But she knew that Arawn would never ally with the System, not even if he had hated her by the end. This ship was System made but not System flown, and the camera in the ceiling was there because she was a prisoner, not a civilian. Whichever splinter of the revolution had taken her did not offer privacy to all people, only the ones who deserved it.

She got tired of that camera after a while and one day took the fork they had unwisely given her, stood on the edge of her thin cot, and scratched at the glass of the camera until its orb was scarred with lacerations. No one came to stop her, and no one replaced the defaced machine. Perhaps they didn't have the supplies. Perhaps the refusal to replace it represented respect for her.

Perhaps the camera hadn't been operational to begin with.

Eventually, the ship landed. It was not a long enough trip to have taken her out to Neptune or Pluto, but she could conceivably be on Mars or Venus or Uranus—or Saturn.

She was taken out of the ship into a large covered area like the docks of a makeshift atmospheric enclosure. It was cobbled together from bits of metal and plastic and was imperfectly constructed; the air around her was thick and cold with a peculiar greasy dampness. It stank of oily chemicals and the deadly taint of bitter almond. For a moment, the unfamiliar atmosphere baffled her. She had never been to a moon like this, but the gravity was too weak for this place to be anything but a moon.

She did not recognize her captors. At first she wondered if they were some of Arawn's men she'd never met, but she soon suspected that they were not Arawn's men at all and never had been. One each grabbed her arms and the others fell in as a guard around her, and they marched her away from the ship that had held her and out into a covered street.

Constance had little chance to take in what she was seeing. Ruins had been rehabilitated. Buildings that had rotted or eroded or been destroyed in battle had been patched together hastily, and a makeshift atmospheric dome had been created by building a ceiling that connected the buildings together and completely enclosed the street beneath. This was a place that had been destroyed long before and put imperfectly back together. People watched her from the sides of the streets as she was led down them or from the windows of the old buildings. The place was larger than she expected: a whole city. One person shouted out at her, the words unclear but the tone derisive, but no one else took up the call. There was an uneasy feeling to the place, as if all the people stood at the edge of a precipice and any gust of wind might drive them over it.

At last Constance was led to what once must have been a hotel. It was System architecture, faded grandeur, all the windows boarded up. Constance let her captors lead her inside; better to choose to follow than to be dragged. They led her up some stairs, then up some more, and then finally to a door. There they pushed her inside and shut and locked the door behind her.

The room she was in once had been a suite. Constance walked around its circumference, looking for weakness. The windows had been bricked up with an unfamiliar kind of brown stone, a more recent addition than anything else in the room. There was a bed and a bathroom with rusty stains on the faucets. The mirrors had been removed; Constance could have broken the glass and used it as a weapon. The main room once had been some sort of parlor, but little of the furniture remained. All that was left was a single carved table in precisely the center of the room. It had two chairs. There had been cushions on the chairs, but they were no longer there. Constance suspected that they had rotted away. The bare walls of the room had been stained a greasy yellow by the oily air, and the floor was pale wood, warping beneath its layer of sealant; the whole room was in shades of stained and soiled white.

There were no cameras. This, at least, Constance was sure was a sign of respect.

She sat down in the chair that faced the locked door, and she waited. Thirty minutes or so after she had arrived, there was a key in the lock.

Constance sat up straighter and folded her hands together on the old table.

"Hello, Anji," she said when the door opened and Anji Chandrasekhar stepped in.

Anji halted at the unexpected sound of her name. Constance did not remember those lines by Anji's eyes. She was thinner, too. Her hair was still cropped short, but there were no jewels in her ear.

Then Anji turned to the men and women who had accompanied her. "Go," she said. "I'll speak with her alone."

The man directly behind her, a very tall man with a skeletal aspect, hesitated. The other people behind Anji looked to him.

Then he said, "Yes, ma'am," and only when he agreed did the others stand down.

Anji came into the room without another word and shut the door behind her. Constance heard the sound of the key turning in the lock outside, but Anji did not seem to notice or care. Instead, her old friend came over to the table where she sat and placed two glasses and a bottle of something on the surface. Anji nodded at the bottle, and Constance reached across the expanse of that table to pick it up.

She recognized it. "I gave this to you," she said.

"I haven't had much time to drink it." Anji slid one glass over to Constance, who did not take it.

"And you'd like to drink it now," Constance said.

"It was yours to begin with. I thought we might as well." Anji reached out and took the bottle back. She uncapped it with a flick of her wrist and poured a considerable amount into her own glass. When she reached over to pour for Constance, Constance covered her glass with one hand. Anji hesitated, looking at her. Constance took the bottle from Anji's grip and poured for herself.

"You weren't surprised to see me," Anji said.

"I'm not an idiot."

"Hmm." Anji stuck out a hand as if the better to feel the air around them. "Titan's got a particular smell, doesn't it? A particular smell and a particular feel. We're not all that far from where Connor Ivanov made his last stand, you know. I've been there. There was talk of building a monument."

"But it hasn't been done."

"No. There're always better things to do." Anji paused. "What do you think Doctor Ivanov would have thought of that?"

"A monument or that you haven't built one?"

"The first. Or either, I guess."

"I don't know what Milla would have thought," Constance said.

Anji toyed with her glass. One of her short fingernails was cracked, but that wasn't unusual. When they had been younger, working in the same dull bar on Miranda, Constance had never been surprised to see Anji show up to work with broken nails or a bruise on her face.

"It's true, then? Doctor Ivanov's dead?"

"On Mars," Constance confirmed.

"Pity," Anji said. It was only because she and Constance had known each other for so long that Anji could say something so short and wholly inadequate and have it be entirely sufficient. "I liked her." Anji smiled ruefully. "After I met her, I finally understood where Ivan got it from."

There was something off about Anji's smile. It took Constance a moment to place it. One of her teeth was broken, the canine on the right side. That had not been so the last time Constance had seen her.

"Ivan," Constance said, asking without asking.

Anji's smile faded. "He's alive. Or he was last time I saw him. Not looking great but alive."

"And Mattie?"

"With him. Mattie was a lot more trigger-happy than he was the last time I saw him; nearly shot some of my people. They came to me looking for you. I sent them off for where I'd seen you last. I haven't seen them since. That doesn't mean anything, though. They weren't very happy with me."

"I'm not very happy with you," Constance said.

Anji avoided the subject. "Well, last I knew, they were alive, at any rate." She toyed with her glass some more. "You and him were a disaster, you know."

"Who?"

"You and Ivan."

Constance chose not to respond. She lifted her glass and drank.

"Mattie didn't deserve to be stuck in the middle of that," Anji said. Then she said with strange firmness, "But they've got each other still. They'll be fine."

Constance knew perfectly well that Ivan and Mattie would be fine.

Anji said, "And I heard some news from Venus. Your friend Marisol Brahe just landed there. Rumor has it she's trying to rebuild the cities she helped you raze." Anji swirled the liquid in her glass, seeming to cast her mind about. "And Christoph's dead. I don't know what happened to Julian."

"Julian's dead, too."

"Pity," Anji said again, and resumed staring down at her glass.

Constance said, "And Arawn?"

Anji scowled. "That coward. He knew he couldn't keep you around if he was going to strike off on his own. He knew he had to get rid of you somehow, but he didn't want to deal with it himself, so he dumped you on me. No, Connie, he's not going to last much longer, I promise you that, if he's not gone already." She tipped her glass at Constance, her dark eyes sincere.

In a way, Constance appreciated what Anji was doing even as she thought that Arawn was not the only coward they both knew.

Anji lifted her glass. "To the living. May Ivan and Mattie not get their dumb asses killed, and may your friend Marisol not get murdered by angry Venereans."

"How about to the dead?" Constance suggested.

A darkness passed over Anji's expression to settle in the lines of her face as if it lived there, deepening them. "To the dead," she said. "Julian, Christoph, Milla Ivanov. Connor Ivanov. We might as well toast him, too."

"And to those who will soon be dead," Constance said.

Anji tossed back her drink, and Constance followed suit. Before Anji could think of some other old friend to talk about or some other reason to avoid continuing the conversation, Constance said, "What happened on Jupiter, Anji?"

Anji lowered her empty glass slowly. "Does it matter?"

"Of course it does," Constance said.

Anji hesitated. "I didn't have a choice, Con. I could either do what they wanted and keep myself alive and keep some control of them or I could have let them kill me and declare war on you."

She was looking at Constance as if she wanted Constance to say, *Of course there was nothing you could do*, but Constance would not and could not tell her that.

She didn't bother to tell Anji, *It's not too late; you can stop this*, either. It was too late, and Anji couldn't stop this, not anymore.

"You have to believe me, Con," Anji said, still speaking useless words. "I didn't want you here. I didn't want that coward Arawn to send you to me, because I don't want to do this. You're not my enemy, but I can't let you go."

"Say it out loud," Constance said. "I want you to say aloud what you're going to do to me, Anji."

Anji looked at her in reproach for a long moment.

Then she said, "I'm going to execute you."

Constance spent a day alone in the faded grandeur of the rotting suite before Anji returned with an array of guards behind her.

"Eager?" Constance asked.

"You know I'm not," Anji snapped. She waved away the guards. "There's a place not far from here where the greenhouse glass wasn't destroyed. There weren't any towns there, and Connor Ivanov was over here, so the System left it alone. It's still standing. That's where we'll go—I thought you'd rather be outside."

"I won't appreciate it long."

"The other thing," Anji said. "I won't let them have your body, Constance. I'll bury you someplace where they won't find you and they won't dare to look."

"That's very kind of you," Constance said.

Anji's face screwed up; she shook her head and turned away, ready to go back to the door, to summon the guards. Some impulse stopped Constance, some sense of bitter compassion. Anji had been her friend once, though Constance hardly recognized her as she was now. "Anji."

Anji stopped.

Constance said, "You're showing them how to kill their leader. How long do you think it will be until they come for you?"

"I didn't expect you to beg for your life, Constance."

"I'm warning you about yours."

"I'll be fine," Anji said. She hesitated as if she wanted to say something more but could not find the words or the courage. "Come on," she said at last, and Constance followed her out into the hall.

Constance found that she recognized the men and women Anji had assembled. There were not many of them, only five, with Anji as the sixth. But they all had followed Constance once. She knew their names: Louis, Tyche, Roy, Jean, Lan. And they remembered her. She could see their doubts the moment they saw her step out.

Anji must have meant it as another sign of respect to allow Constance to be surrounded by people who did not hate her in her final moments.

Constance nodded to them in recognition and greeting. Tyche nearly smiled at her, and Constance smiled faintly back. It was very possible that Anji had made a mistake.

Anji started down the hall, and Constance fell in behind her. Outside, the people had gathered around to see her again. Constance stepped out and felt all their eyes upon her, more oppressing than the constant watch of the System's cameras. The crowd did not shout or throw stones. They simply watched. There was a feel in the atmosphere like the prickling on one's skin right before a thunderstorm begins. Constance had felt it on Miranda and on Mars, in secret places, hidden out of the System's sight. This was a people on the edge of explosion, on the edge of a change, all that stored and angry energy ready to be tapped. It would take only a target and some angry words and that energy would start to come toward the surface like lava rising to spill out and burn.

She doubted that Anji knew that her people were on the edge of revolution.

Anji did not lead her back to the docking bay but on another route that took them down a road that ended abruptly at a tall wall constructed of metal welded together. There was a single door in that wall. It was colder down this street, and the crowds thinned out, the people following Constance's last walk stopping some distance from the end of the street. A few children played down at the end, where it was open and they were unsupervised; when Constance appeared, they scattered, all but one girl. The little girl was playing with some rocks, smashing them against one another, needless destruction. It sent echoes like explosions off the metal wall beside which she sat. She looked right up at Constance. Her eyes were blue. Constance had just enough time to register their color before she was passing through that door behind Anji, into a tunnel.

In the tunnel, Constance found her breath coming short. She tried to hide it, not to let the people around her see. Only thin glass overhead separated her from the freezing inhospitality of Titan. Yellow lightning flashed; liquid methane slid greasily down the glass from the Titanese storm overhead. Each flash of lightning seemed to strike a blow into Constance, to increase the heat that burned in her chest.

I am afraid, she realized, and thought incongruously of Ivan. *I am afraid.*

At long last the tunnel opened up into a brighter, clearer place with sweeter air. Anji had been right when she'd said this part of the greenhouse enclosure had been left alone because the area was uninhabited; there was no sign of buildings or streets. The space was vast, magnificent, a work of architectural complexity as enormous and powerful as the force that had made it, the force that Constance would never regret destroying. The level Titanese stone stretched out so far to Constance's left and right that she almost could not see where the glass came down again to seal off what once had been an air lock between sections of the greenhouse. Overhead, the glass stretched up so high that it reached the edge of Titan's atmosphere, and Constance could look up and see the sky. They were facing away from Saturn, and so she could not see its rings, but she could see the bright sparks of stars.

Her chest was burning. She could hear the rasping sound of her breath in her ringing ears.

Anji's people took lanterns from the tunnel. Anji led Constance to an empty space and stopped.

"I would offer you a blindfold," Anji said.

"I wouldn't take it," Constance said.

Anji walked away without a word. Constance stood where she had been placed while Lan put a lantern on her right and Roy put one on her left to light her shape in the starlit dark, and then they strode away. She could have run, perhaps, but it would have gotten her nowhere, and she would not have subjected herself to the indignity of trying to run away. Anji had known that.

What use was running, anyway? Her heart was pounding.

Some six yards from her, they lined up together, their guns lowered, and Anji stood to the side. At Anji's signal, they raised their rifles.

Now, almost—Constance's breath caught in her throat—

Unexpected, brilliant—there was a light in the sky.

Constance looked up sharply. In the sky overhead, in the stars, there was a new star, shining bright and brilliant, brighter than all the other stars combined. It exploded, spreading out its light and its ash, as brilliant and bright as a supernova.

Murmuring from Anji's people. Fear on Anji's face. In the slow dying of the light from the supernova, Constance saw their conviction waver. Their fear of the omen made them look at her with new eyes.

She had but to say a word, she knew, and they would be hers.

For a moment of perfect clarity Constance saw what she would do. She would call out to these people, these old friends of hers whom Anji had so unwisely brought. Their old loyalty to her and their fear that she had something to do with whatever had exploded would be enough to sway them. They would turn on Anji, and Anji would be the one whose corpse was left out here on the Titanese stone.

Constance would go back into that tunnel with Anji's followers at her back and would step out into the city reborn. Her near death and her survival, Anji's death at her hand, would be enough to sway the crowd. There would be fighting; there would be a battle between Anji's people and Constance's new followers and those just trying to survive, but Constance had never yet lost a battle. Then Constance would finish her work. She would do as Marisol had said, do as she'd intended to do before Arawn had betrayed her, and go back to Mars and rebuild. She would defy Ivan's prophecy and cease to destroy but create instead. She would bring life back to the solar system. She would—

No, she realized as clearly as if Ivan stood right beside her, patiently walking her through the logic that would lead her to the only, the inevitable conclusion. She might escape now. She might rally the people of Saturn behind her, but it would be bloody work, civil war. And when the war on Saturn was done and she went to Mars, she would only find more resistance there. The people had grown to hate her. If Constance tried to force her own peace and her own order on them, she would have to enslave them to do it; she would have to do what the System had done.

War on Saturn. War on Mars. War when Arawn realized she still lived. No matter what Constance did, no matter where she went, the violence would follow her. The fact that she lived would ignite wars around her. And eventually Mattie and Ivan would find her and be drawn inexorably into the blood and death around her and drown in it. She was ready now to try to bring peace back where she had taken it away, but it was too late for her to do that herself.

She would not be the System. She would not be death. She would not be less than those who had loved her had once believed her to be.

Anji was looking at her with fear, but Constance was not afraid anymore. She had not realized how deeply that denied terror had dug itself into her limbs until now, when it was gone.

Constance spoke.

"Don't waste my time," she said, and they all looked to her, heeling to her words like hounds. "You came here to shoot me. Do it."

Her heart was pounding in her ears, but all her fear was gone.

"When I give the word," Constance said, "you will fire. Raise your guns."

They raised their guns. Overhead, the light died to nothing.

Constance said, "Fire."

ACKNOWLEDGMENTS

Aside from my gratitude toward the usual people who provided me with the holy trinity of emotional support, caffeine, and chocolate, this book required a lot of research on the various moons and planets that Constance visits (and blows up). I'm grateful especially for the International Astronomical Union Working Group for Planetary System Nomenclature, whose website is full of the most exciting maps, including one of Europa's surface that I have used extensively.

The University of Sydney's website provided me with the approximate specific heat capacity of the human body, as well as some pressing questions on how they came to have such a precise number for that value.

The equations governing Hawking radiation and the evaporation of a black hole I got from Wikipedia, because I gave up on making the citation gods proud after I realized that my college textbooks never got that far.

Thanks to my seventh-grade teacher for telling me the logic problem that Althea poses to Ananke. It pissed me off, so I put it in a book.

And finally, Wolfram Alpha, you are my star, my perfect silence; the light of my life and the fire of my loins; shall I compare thee to a summer's day; etc. If there ever is an Ananke, I hope she is exactly like Wolfram Alpha.

ABOUT THE AUTHOR

C. A. HIGGINS writes novels and short stories. She was a runner-up for the 2013 Dell Magazines Award for Undergraduate Excellence in Science Fiction and Fantasy Writing and has a B.A. in physics from Cornell University. She lives in Brooklyn, New York.

cahiggins.com
@C_A_Higgs
Facebook.com/cahiggs

ABOUT THE TYPE

This book was set in Berling. Designed in 1951 by Karl-Erik Forsberg (1914–95) for the type foundry Berlingska Stilgjuteri AB in Lund, Sweden, it was released the same year in foundry type by H. Berthold AG. A classic old-face design, its generous proportions and inclined serifs make it highly legible.